IMMORTAL
NIGHTS

LYNSAY SANDS

IMMORTAL NIGHTS

AN ARGENEAU NOVEL

AVONBOOKS

An Imprint of HarperCollinsPublishers

This is a work of fiction. Names, characters, places, and incidents are products of the author's imagination or are used fictitiously and are not to be construed as real. Any resemblance to actual events, locales, organizations, or persons, living or dead, is entirely coincidental.

IMMORTAL NIGHTS

ONE

"Abs!"

Abigail Forsythe had just stepped inside the country-and-western-themed bar when she heard that shout. Finding the owner of the deep baritone wasn't hard. Jet was six foot six when bare-foot. In his cowboy boots he stood more than a head taller than pretty much every other person in the bar. Hell, he was a head taller than most of the people everywhere, she thought.

Spotting her dark haired friend standing by two empty stools at the end of the bar, Abigail found a real honest-to-God smile tipping her lips. It was the first time that had happened in at least three months, and she immediately headed in Jet's direction, suddenly eager for the affectionate hug that she knew awaited her.

"Ahhhh, baby girl," Jet groaned, bending to wrap his arms around her the moment she reached him.

It was all he said, but a lump was suddenly lodged in her throat and Abigail couldn't speak, so she merely hugged him back silently. As usual, the hug went on longer than was perhaps normal between friends, but Abigail didn't mind. She simply rested her head on his chest and released a long drawn-out sigh.

"Let me look at you," Jet said after a moment, and grasped her upper arms to move her back a step.

Abigail tilted her head up to peer at him. Her eyes traced the fine lines of his familiar face with affection. He looked older. But then they both were. Although they'd written each other faithfully each week, she hadn't seen Jet in three years now. He'd been off in foreign lands, flying fighter jets for the navy, while she'd been here in Texas, nursing her mother to the grave.

"I was so sorry to hear about your mom, Abs," Jet said suddenly, as if his thoughts ran along the same lines as her own. "She was always good to me. I thought the world of her. You know that."

Abigail nodded.

"I'd have been right there at your side for her funeral if I hadn't been overseas, but I was only released from the navy and got home the week after," he said with regret.

"I know," she assured him, managing a smile.

"She was the best, Abs."

"Yeah, she was," Abigail agreed, her voice going husky and tears glazing her eyes. Afraid that if they didn't soon change the subject she'd be bawling like a baby, she glanced to the bar and forced another smile. "I need a drink."

She glanced back to find Jet watching her. There was concern in the depths of his eyes and she turned away with discomfort, knowing exactly what he saw. Her skin was pale and blotchy, her eyes bloodshot with dark circles under them, and she was carrying a lot of extra weight that hadn't been there the last time they'd seen each other. All were the result of spending the last year inside, doing little but watch over her mother as she faded away under the ravages of cancer. Abigail had always carried around an extra ten or twenty pounds. She'd been more round than society liked, but the three years since her mother had been diagnosed with breast cancer had done her few favors in that department. Others might have wasted away under the strain, but Abigail had gained a good thirty pounds, going from rounded to just plain round. She was terribly self-conscious about it at the best of times, but with Jethro Lassiter looking her over and taking it in, Abigail was painfully aware of just how bad she must look.

"A drink it is," he said suddenly. "Here, take a load off."

Abigail's eyes widened and she bit off a startled squeal as the man caught her under the arms and lifted her onto the bar stool. He'd picked her up as if she weighed little more than a feather, but she knew that wasn't the case and wrinkled her nose at him as he claimed the empty bar stool next to hers.

"Keep that up and you'll pull something," she said dryly, swinging to prop her elbows on the bar. "Then you'll have to take time off and lose that new job you just started."

Jet merely snorted at the claim and tugged at the backpack still strapped to her back. "Take this off. We'll set it on the floor between us."

Abigail shifted the straps off her shoulder and allowed him to pull the pack away. She watched him set it on the floor between the stools, and then glanced around as a cheerful voice asked, "What'll it be?"

A pretty young blonde in a tight T-shirt with the bar's logo on it now stood on the other side of the bar. She smiled at them engagingly, or smiled at Jet really, Abigail thought as she noted that the woman's bright blue eyes and generous breasts were pointed exclusively at him.

Jet smiled faintly at the woman, but then turned to Abigail. "Long Island Iced Tea?"

Abigail snorted. That had been their drink of choice three years ago for his send-off party when he'd left to become a navy pilot. They'd sucked back the drinks well into the early hours of dawn, long after everyone else had left the party. Abigail had paid for it the next day, waking with a killer hangover. That night was a fond memory. The following day—which she'd spent hanging over the toilet—was not.

"Come on," he urged. "I think you're in serious need of letting loose a little. One Long Island Iced Tea and then we'll switch to something less deadly."

Abigail smiled faintly at his wheedling tone, but then shrugged. "What the hell."

"What the hell," he agreed with a grin and turned back to the barmaid. "A Long Island Iced Tea for the lady, and a draft for me please, ma'am."

"Hey!" Abigail protested.

"I'm driving," Jet explained, then grinned and added, "Besides, iced teas are sissy drinks."

Abigail scowled at the claim. "As I recall, that sissy drink kicked your ass the last time we had them."

"Yeah," he laughed. "Boy, was I sorry the next day. The first day in boot camp is not a good day to be suffering a hangover."

Abigail smiled faintly. "I can imagine."

"No. I'm quite sure you can't," he assured her with a grimace.

"Well, your letters were pretty descriptive," she said with amusement. "Hard, huh?"

"Hard doesn't begin to describe it," Jet said, but didn't expand on it, and turned to smile at the barmaid and thank her for their drinks when she set them down.

Abigail looked Jet over curiously as he paid for their drinks. His tour in the navy had changed him. He'd been tall but too thin, and lacking in muscle when she last saw him. He'd been all arms and legs then as she recalled, but not any longer. He'd filled out and grown into his height. Her best bud was now a strong, handsome guy with confidence and even swagger. The navy had done wonders for him, and she actually envied him for it.

Her mother's illness and death had done the exact opposite for her, taking away what looks and confidence she'd had and leaving her feeling like a lump.

A depressed sigh slipping from her lips, Abigail drew her drink closer and sipped at it as she asked herself what the hell she was doing here. It had seemed like a good idea when Jet had written and said his time in the navy was done and he was taking a job offer in San Antonio and she should come visit. They'd written a lot of letters back and forth over the last three years since he'd finished college and joined the navy, but had never seemed to be able to actually get together for a face-to-face visit. Their schedules had just never allowed for it. Abigail's choosing a medical school on the other side of the country had hindered them at first. She might have got a chance to see him while he was home on furlough after dropping out of school to move home to nurse her mother, but by then, her mother had given up their home in their small town and moved to Austin to be closer to the hospital where she got her chemo treatments. Jet's furloughs hadn't been long enough for him to visit their small town and the city too. Not that there would have been room for him in the tiny, one-bedroom apartment her mother had settled on when she moved. Abigail had already been occupying the couch. Jet would have had to sleep on the floor.

Glancing up, she caught her reflection in the mirror behind the bar and grimaced. The truth is, Jet would have visited anyway. He would even have been fine with a sleeping bag on the floor. She was the one who had made excuses for why he shouldn't. She hadn't wanted to see him, or more to the point, she hadn't wanted *him* to see *her* and how much she'd changed. The only reason Abigail was seeing him now was . . . well, she had nowhere else to go really. Her mother, the only family she had, was dead and buried, and Abigail had spent the last month since then settling the estate. This translated to paying off the medical bills, which had eaten up all of her mother's life insurance, plus most of the college fund they had painstakingly built up for her over the years before she'd got ill.

Abigail had been left with an apartment full of mementos and furniture and very little money. She intended on spending this week figuring out what the hell to do with the rest of her life.

Finishing medical school was obviously out of the question. That took money. But she had no idea what kind of job a medical school dropout could get. Or where she would live. Her life, at the moment, was a complete and utter mess.

"So," Jet said purposefully as the barmaid slipped away to attend to other customers.

Abigail tore her eyes away from her less-than-attractive reflection and glanced warily to her friend.

"How bad is it?" he asked seriously.

Her mouth tightened and she turned back to her drink with a shrug. "I'll survive."

"You were worried about the medical expenses in the last letter. Did your mom's insurance cover them?" he asked.

"Mostly," she muttered.

"And the rest?" he asked. "How much is still owing?"

"Nothing," she assured him, sitting up a little straighter. That was something at least. She wasn't drowning under a sea of debt.

"Hmm," Jet murmured and she glanced his way to see that his eyes were narrowed. She wasn't surprised when he asked, "How?"

Abigail scowled and looked away, but after a moment admitted, "My college fund."

"Ah, hell, Abs," Jet muttered. "Your mother would be pissed to know that all that money she socked away for so many years was even touched by this."

"Yeah, good thing she's not alive to see it, huh?" she joked lamely, and wasn't terribly surprised when Jet didn't laugh. It really hadn't been much of a joke, and truth be told, she'd give anything to have her mother back whether she'd be pissed or not. She'd give everything she owned, including her body and soul. God, she missed that woman so much. It just wasn't fair.

"How much is left?" Jet asked grimly, interrupting her thoughts before she could begin sobbing there at the bar.

Abigail hesitated, then reached into her pocket and pulled out a wad of bills. There were eleven twenties, a ten, and some change. She knew. She'd counted them several times, hoping against hope that they'd somehow double like horny bunnies if left alone in her pocket.

"That's it?" Jet asked with real concern, scooping up the bills and quickly counting them.

"Hey, at least I'm not in debt up to my eyeballs and having to pay off the useless bastards who killed my mother," she pointed out with feigned good humor.

When his gaze shot to hers, Abigail shrugged and added bitterly, "It wasn't the cancer that killed her in the end so much as that stupid expensive chemo. Every time they gave it to her, the pleura around her lungs filled with liquid, compressing the lungs. In the end, she basically suffocated to death after a chemo treatment."

"Ah, honey." Jet pulled her into a hug that nearly dragged her off her stool and onto his lap. "I'm so sorry."

Abigail struggled with her emotions, fighting back the tears that wanted to escape. Once she thought she had control of them, she eased back and managed a crooked smile. "Like I said. At least I'm debt free."

"Yeah, there is that," he murmured, but sounded no happier than she did. They fell silent for a moment, each of them picking up their drinks and sipping at them. After a moment though, Jet set his beer back on the bar and asked, "How are you going to finish school? Sell your mom's apartment and—"

"Mom didn't buy the apartment. She just rented it after she sold the house," Abigail interrupted. "She used the money from the sale of the house to help pay expenses. That's the only reason I'm debt free."

Jet muttered a curse he must have learned in the navy. He'd never cursed that vilely before that she recalled. His mother would have washed his mouth out with soap. So would her mother. Marge Forsythe had always looked on Jet as the son she'd never had.

Abigail watched him tip the beer to his mouth and guzzle down a good quantity. He then set it carefully back on the bar and asked, "Okay, so what are you going to do about her apartment and all her things?"

"Already taken care of," she assured him. "I packed everything and moved it all into a storage unit. And I paid the rent for the storage unit for the next six months in advance."

"Was that smart?" he asked with concern. "You could have paid monthly and used the money yourself."

"It wasn't that much. Wouldn't even have covered more than a month's rent in a dive," she assured him, and then shrugged and added, "Besides, I didn't want to take the chance of losing everything if I missed a payment. I'm hoping that by the time six months have come and gone I can afford the added expense. Or that I'll have a place I can move her stuff to."

"Right," he said quietly and took another drink. This time when he set the mug down, he announced, "Well, you can stay with me until you're back on your feet."

Abigail stilled. It was such a generous offer, and so sweet, but she had no intention of sponging off her friend. She would visit for a week, but then she was leaving whether she'd sorted out what she was going to do next or not. Before Abigail could say as much, though, Jet added, "We have to figure a way for you to go back to school. You have to finish your degree and become the doctor you were meant to be."

Abigail scowled and admitted, "I'm not sure I want to be a doctor anymore."

"What?" he cried, askance. "You've wanted to be a doctor since we were in grade school. You talked about it nonstop."

"Yeah, well that was before I realized that doctors are pretty much useless," she said angrily.

"Abs," Jet said sadly.

"It's true," she snapped. "They couldn't do a damned thing for Mom. They couldn't even prevent her suffering. Their stupid drugs took the edge off, maybe, but she was still in agony all the time."

"That doesn't mean you couldn't still help people as a doctor," he protested. "Just don't go into oncology or whatever it's called." When she merely scowled down at her drink, he added, "Abs, you only have one year left of medical school—"

"Two," she corrected. "I dropped out not quite halfway through the third year. I'd have to do the whole year again . . . if they even let me back in. So it would be two years of medical school."

"Fine, two years left of school and you could be a doctor."

"Not quite," she said unhappily. "It would take two years of school and then at least a three-year residency before I could get my license and call myself a doctor."

"Abs," Jet said solemnly. "You can't throw away six years of schooling. You have to finish this and get your doctorate. It's what your mom would have wanted."

Abigail winced and took another drink. Setting the glass back she said, "Pulling the mom card? That's not fair."

"Life's not fair, babe," he said gravely. "If it was, your mom would be sitting here bitching you out for even considering not completing your degree."

Abigail lowered her head and stared blindly at her drink. He was right. Her mother had always been proud of her determination to be a doctor. She'd been terribly upset when Abigail had insisted on "taking time off" from school to nurse her. Only promising that she would finish later had eased her mind at all.

"Okay," Jet said suddenly. "Enough of that now. You've had a rough couple years and I shouldn't be making it tougher. Let's make a deal."

Abigail glanced at him in question.

"For the next week, you're going to just chill with me. We'll sort out how to get you back into medical school after that, but for now you need some downtime and fun. Deal?"

"Deal," she agreed with relief.

"Good." He held up his beer and she raised her own glass to clink his, then they both drank.

"So, what's the plan for the week?" she asked as they set their drinks down. "By the way, how did you convince them to give you time off work when you've just started?"

"I didn't," Jet admitted and when her expression turned alarmed, he laughed and said, "I thought you could come to work with me."

"You're a cargo pilot," she pointed out. "How can I come to work with you?"

"Cargo planes have seats in the front, you know. You can ride with me and we can day trip around the exciting and exotic places I fly to."

That didn't sound too bad, she thought, and asked, "And your boss would be all right with that?"

"I don't know if he'd care or not, but I wasn't planning on telling him," Jet said with a shrug, and then pointed out, "He's not in the plane with me so how would he know?"

"Hmm," Abigail murmured. She didn't want to get him in trouble. On the other hand, she didn't want to sit around in his apartment worrying about her future for the next week either.

"What exciting and exotic places do you fly to?" she asked with interest now.

"Well, I'm free tomorrow, but then I'm booked for a shipment to Quebec the day after that."

"Canada?" she asked with disgust. "You consider that exotic?"

"It's a foreign country," he pointed out defensively.

"Barely," she said, her voice dry.

"They speak French," he argued.

"Barely," she said again. "And it's wintertime. It will be cold as hell up there."

"Come on, it'll be fun," he assured her. "We've never been there and it must have something interesting to offer. Besides, we only have to kill a day there, then I load up again and fly to Chicago."

"Better and better," she said on a groan.

Jet laughed at her dismay and leaned sideways to nudge her with his shoulder. "We'll have fun, I promise. You and me in the cockpit, yapping and laughing . . . it'll be like old times."

"Yeah," she said with a slow smile. She'd missed yapping and laughing with Jet. He'd been a sort of stand-in girlfriend/adopted brother through high school and the first four years of college. Hard to believe when she looked at him now. No one would mistake him for a stand-in for a girlfriend. Jet was definitely all man. If he wasn't so much like a brother to her, she might even be at risk of falling for him herself. The thought made her smile faintly as she asked, "So what exotic locale follows Chicago?"

"After Chicago, it's—" He paused midsentence and dug in his pocket as the sound of a guitar strumming reached their ears.

Pulling out a phone, he peered at the display, his eyebrows rising. "My boss. Gotta take this."

Abigail nodded in understanding and watched as he hit the answer button, placed the phone to his ear and stood to move a few steps away, saying, "Hey, Bob, what's up?"

"Can I get you another?" the blonde barmaid asked, suddenly appearing on the other side of the bar again. Abigail turned to glance at the woman, noting that she was eyeballing Jet as she asked the question. That being the case, she wasn't terribly surprised when the woman didn't give her a chance to respond before asking what she really wanted to know. "So, is your friend available?"

Abigail supposed it was insulting that the woman didn't even imagine for a minute that she might be Jet's girlfriend, but let it slide and merely admitted, "As far as I know he's not dating anyone."

"Yeah?" The blonde beamed at her. "Do you think—?"

"Abs, we gotta go."

Abigail and the bartender both turned with surprise at that announcement when Jet suddenly returned.

"We do?" she asked with a frown as he bent to scoop up her backpack.

"Yeah." Straightening, he urged her off the stool, then began walking her quickly toward the exit.

"Why?" she asked with bewilderment, jogging to keep up with his long steps. She'd always had to jog to keep up with Jet. His legs were nearly twice the length of her stubby little ones and she had to take two steps for every one of his.

"Got a job," he announced with a grin.

"*Now?*" she asked with amazement. "But I just got here. I haven't even seen your apartment yet."

"I know, and I almost refused because of that, but then Bob said where the shipment was going and I decided we should go."

"Where?" she asked at once. He was beaming so brightly, she knew this had to be good, certainly better than cold Canada, or Chicago.

"How do you feel about a couple of days on a beach in Caracas?"

"Venezuela?" she squawked with dismay.

He paused at the exit to peer at her uncertainly. "What's wrong with Venezuela?"

"I read an article just last week that claims Venezuela is the kidnap capital of the world or something."

"Oh, pffft," he responded, tugging the door open and ushering her out of the bar. "You'll be with me. I'll keep you safe. And Bob was so desperate to find a pilot for this flight that he agreed to let me out of the Quebec flight. We can spend a couple days there. That gives us time to kick around, hit the beach, see the sights." Stopping suddenly, he turned her away from him and helped her get the backpack on again. "It's definitely more exotic than Quebec, right?"

"Right," she agreed wryly, and supposed kicking around and seeing the sights didn't sound bad. She wasn't too keen on the beach part though. Not in the shape she was in. Still, it could be fun.

"You have a passport, don't you?" he asked suddenly. "Please have a passport."

"Yeah. I even brought it with me," she assured him. Abigail hadn't thought she'd need it, but it had seemed smarter than leaving it in storage.

"Good, good, we're all set then," he said happily, finishing with her backpack. "Put this on."

Abigail turned and stared at the helmet he was holding out. Her gaze then slid to the motorcycle behind him and her eyes widened incredulously. "You expect me to ride on *that*?"

She'd expected a car, maybe even a pickup, but a motorcycle? Where had her old, slightly goofy, geek of a friend Jethro gone? Apparently, he'd grown up and morphed into Jet the adventurer.

"You'll love it," Jet assured her, settling the helmet on her head and strapping it on. Once done with that, he quickly donned his own helmet, then swung a leg over his bike and glanced over his shoulder at her. "Come on. This is an emergency flight. We have to get to the hangar ASAP."

"What kind of emergency?" Abigail asked, climbing gingerly onto the seat behind him. He flew a cargo plane, for heaven's sake. What kind of emergency flight could there be for a cargo plane?

"I don't know," Jet admitted, starting the motorcycle. Raising his voice to be heard over the engine, he then added, "I guess it's a time-sensitive shipment. The client has their own plane, but it broke down and they need to get their cargo to Caracas ASAP so called us. That's the only reason I'm getting the flight. Normally guys with more seniority get the exotic locales, but I was the only one available last-minute."

"Oh," Abigail murmured and then repeated it more loudly when she realized he'd never hear her over the roar of the motorcycle engine.

"Put your arms around me and hold on tight," Jet instructed, glancing around. Catching her worried expression, he grinned and added, "Relax, Abs. It'll be an adventure."

Two

"Relax, Abs, it'll be an adventure," Abigail muttered under her breath as she felt around in the dark, trying to find the jump seat Jet had told her to use. He hadn't warned her how dark it would be back here. But then perhaps he hadn't thought about that in his panic. If he had, he surely would have offered her a flashlight or *something*. Instead, she was feeling her way blindly down the side of the cargo hold of the airplane, trying to find a seat that apparently folded down from the wall and had straps she could belt herself in with for takeoff.

Abigail shook her head. This adventure was not going according to plan at all. They'd moved through the San Antonio traffic quickly on the motorcycle and arrived at the airport before the clients had arrived. While Jet dealt with flight plans and other paperwork, Abigail had mostly stayed out of the way, merely handing her passport over to some official type dude who'd asked for it. They'd then headed straight to the hangar where his cargo plane waited. She'd joined Jet in the cockpit while he went through what he called a preflight checklist and had settled comfortably in the big cushy front passenger seat, thinking this would be fun after all. But then the client had arrived.

Abigail had only caught a glimpse of the two men who had got out of the van before they'd moved out of sight, but they'd looked a bit shady to her—jeans, T-shirts, tattoos, and scruffy-faced, one bald and one with hair that needed cutting. They'd looked more like they belonged to a biker gang than like businessmen. Fortunately, they hadn't seen her when they arrived, because as it turned out, she definitely wasn't supposed to be there.

After going to talk to them, Jet had returned to the cockpit in a bit of a panic. It wasn't just going to be cargo. The "Clients" were flying with it and when he'd mentioned the possibility of a friend joining them, they'd nixed the idea at once. No one but them and the cargo would be passengers on this flight. Period.

Abigail had been alarmed at this news, thinking it meant she needed to get out and find her way to his apartment. But that had not been Jet's plan.

It was his plane, he'd have her along if he wished, he'd assured her firmly. It had all sounded very brave and manly until he'd added that she would just ride in cargo so they didn't know.

As Abigail had gaped at him over this plan, he'd explained that the door at the back of the cockpit opened into the cargo area. He'd watch the men load the cargo and once they'd closed the hold and started toward the cockpit, he'd bang on the side of the plane twice. She was to immediately slip into the cargo hold, find the jump seat and strap herself in. Once they landed, he'd wait until the men were heading around to the back of the plane to retrieve their cargo, then he'd tap on the door to let her know she was to get out of the cargo area and hide herself in the cockpit until the clients left with their shipment. Jet would come get her when the coast was clear and they could go through customs and start their "adventure."

Abigail took another step, banged her knee hard against something, cursed, then quickly covered her mouth and froze, expecting the door to the cockpit to burst open and angry, biker-looking dudes to come rushing out, shouting and brandishing firearms of some description. When that didn't happen, she let her breath out slowly, then felt around to see what she'd bumped into.

The cargo, Abigail decided, as she felt tarp under her fingers. They'd set it down closer to the front than expected. It was also pretty close to the side of the plane, she noted. If the jump seat Jet wanted her to use was behind it, there was no way she was going to be able to fold it down and sit on it.

Grimacing, Abigail placed her hands against the tarp to give it a tentative shove and see if she could actually move it. But instead of pressing flat against a solid surface, the fingers of her right hand curved around what felt like a bar under the tarp, while her left hand slid forward easily, pushing the tarp between two fixtures before hitting something that grunted in response.

Quickly retrieving her hands, Abigail squinted, trying to see what she had touched. It had felt to her like rather than a shipment of boxes, or even a crate, the tarp covered some kind of cage. A large cage too, she thought, recalling where her hands had been. The top of it was at chest level on her.

"You'll need a flashlight."

Abigail glanced toward the front of the plane at Jet's overloud announcement, then dropped to her knees as she heard the cockpit door being opened. She had no idea if she was hidden where she was, but there was no time to find a better hiding spot, so Abigail curled into as small a ball as she could manage and prayed her butt wasn't sticking out the end and her backpack wasn't showing at the top as the darkness in the hold lightened.

"Can't you turn the damned lights on here?" someone asked. It was a very unpleasant snarl, definitely not Jet's voice this time.

"It's a cargo hold. There are no lights," was Jet's response and Abigail knew him well enough to recognize from his tone that he was lying. "I'll get you a flashlight. Wait here so you don't bump into anything."

Abigail heard the shuffle of his feet as he moved around and then a flashlight beam suddenly switched on just inches from her face. The sudden shock of the bright light almost startled a gasp from her, but she managed to cut it off before it was born and merely blinked her eyes closed.

"There are two more flashlights here on the wall if you need them."

Abigail eased her eyes open to see that the flashlight beam had been turned away from her. She could just make out Jet's shape in the darkness behind the light he was now flashing toward his "clients" and Abigail was pretty sure he was looking at her. She was also pretty sure that the information about the extra flashlights had been for her as well. She wasn't surprised though when the clients assumed it was for them, and one of them said, "One'll do. Just give me the damned thing and get out of here so I can check my cargo."

Jet hesitated briefly, but then moved out of sight. As the light moved away with him, Abigail quickly analyzed her situation. She was crouching between the wall and the tarp-covered crate that the client wanted to check and there was nowhere to go that she knew of. Jet was obviously hoping she wouldn't be discovered, but she was pretty sure she would be.

"Go do your preflight check or something."

Abigail stilled at that order from the snarky client.

"Already done," Jet answered easily. "That's what I was doing when you got here."

"Well, then go sit on your thumbs or find something else to do, I don't care what. I want privacy while I check my cargo," the man said.

"I'd rather—"

"I'll keep you company," another voice said, and Abigail supposed it was the other client.

"Hey, watch it, buddy. I—" Whatever Jet was saying was cut off when the cabin door closed with a sharp click. Abigail could only guess from what she did hear of his comment that the second man had either pushed or dragged Jet out of the cargo hold. It was hard to imagine anyone being able to do either. Jet wasn't a gangly kid anymore. Still, she was quite sure that's what had happened and was straining her ears, trying to hear what was happening in the cockpit when something landed on her head.

Abigail reached up instinctively to feel what it was. She was both surprised and relieved when it turned out to be the edge of the tarp. The client had apparently flipped it up from the opposite side to where she knelt. She might go undiscovered after all, Abigail thought. Maybe.

A groan from the crate she knelt beside made her glance toward it, but she didn't have Superman's eyes and couldn't see through the tarp still covering the cage on her side.

"Just checking your IV, buddy," the client muttered. "Wouldn't want you waking in the middle of the flight and causing trouble, or tearing up the plane like you did the doc's. Especially don't want it to happen once we're in the air. We were lucky you got loose before we took off last time," he added.

Abigail frowned at these words, wondering just what the heck the cargo was. A monkey? She'd heard they could be pretty destructive. No, the cage was too big for that. Maybe it was a gorilla?

Abigail was distracted from her thoughts by a loud sound she instantly recognized as the noise duct tape made when it was being pulled off a roll.

"Just gonna wrap this around your IV. Make sure you aren't knocking this one out with your tossing and turning. This ain't our usual pilot. Can't have you squawking about being kidnapped or something. We'd have to kill the poor bastard . . . or maybe just deliver him onto the island with you. I'm sure Doc has some experiment or other he could use the guy for. Poor bastard. Frankly, I'd rather be dead," he added gravely. A brief silence followed, broken only by the rustling sounds, and then the man grunted. "That oughta do it."

There were sounds that must have been the man backing out of the cage and straightening then, because what followed was the clang of what she guessed was the cage door closing.

"Enjoy the flight," the client said mockingly. "It's the last one you'll ever take. Once we get you to the island, you'll never leave."

Abigail felt the tarp slide off the back of her head and went completely still. She waited for an exclamation of surprise as she was spotted, but there was nothing but the rustle of the tarp being dropped back into place and then the soft sound of the client walking away in the direction of the cockpit door. She heard it open and close and then darkness and silence returned once more.

A moment passed, and then another, and still Abigail didn't move. It wasn't until the idling plane engine revved up a bit and the plane began to taxi forward that she gave up her position and lifted her head to peer around. This time she was glad to see nothing but darkness. It meant the flashlight, and the man carrying it, were gone, even if his words were still spinning in her head.

Kidnapping? Her mind shrieked the word in alarm. And what had that been about killing the pilot or just giving him to some doctor to experiment on?

Jeez, she had to warn Jet. He had no idea who he had sitting in the cockpit with him right now. Shrugging her backpack off, Abigail pulled it in front of her on the floor and began blindly searching it for her phone. She'd send Jet a text. Tell him to use some excuse to shut down the plane and get out of the cockpit. He needed to call the police. They had a situation here.

Cursing when she couldn't find her phone by feeling around in the dark like that, Abigail left her pack on the floor and got quickly to her feet. The flashlights were in front of her, just past the crate. At least that's where Jet had been standing when he'd turned the one on. The client had taken the flashlight Jet had got for him, but Jet had said there were two others there.

Recalling that her backpack was on the floor in front of her, Abigail stayed where she was and quickly ran her hands over the expanse of wall she could reach. When that didn't turn up anything useful, she muttered under her breath and pushed her backpack forward with one foot. Stepping forward into the small space the action made, she tried again. This time her hand hit something on the wall.

Abigail ran her fingers cautiously over the item, feeling that it was a long metal tube held in place on the wall by a metal clamp. Grasping the bottom of the tube, she pulled, relieved when it slid easily out of its holder. It took another moment of fumbling about before she found the button to turn it on, but then light exploded in the darkness. It was blinding after so long in pitch-black and forced Abigail to close her eyes. She gave them a heartbeat to re-

cover from the shock, and then slowly opened them again, allowing her pupils time to adjust.

Relieved when she could see this time, Abigail started to turn
the beam of light down toward her bag, but paused when it landed
on the corner of the crate beside her. The tarp was a dark brown
color, nothing interesting there. But she couldn't resist grabbing a
bit of the heavy cloth and tugging it up. The bottom corner of what
was definitely a cage was immediately revealed, but it was the foot
lying in the corner of the cage that made her catch her breath.

Definitely not an ape, she thought, but then she had known
that when the client had talked about squawking about being kidnapped. Apes did not talk.

Unable to stop herself now, Abigail tossed the tarp up and
away so that it fell back on the top of the cage, leaving the side
nearest her exposed. Her flashlight beam then slid quickly from
the foot she'd first seen, to an attached leg, before bouncing over a
bare bottom to the back and arm of a completely naked man lying
on his side in the cage.

He was a big one, some part of her brain acknowledged as
Abigail let the flashlight beam slide back and forth over what she
could see of him from this angle. Wide shoulders tapered down to
narrow hips, and both the upper arm she could see, and his revealed
outer thigh were huge and muscular. She couldn't see any of his
face, though; his head was turned away, long dark hair falling over
it and hiding it from her view. But she'd seen enough. He was a
sleeping giant, lying drugged and helpless in a cage like an animal.

Cursing under her breath, Abigail dropped to her knees and
dragged her backpack closer to search it again, this time with the
flashlight to aid her. Even with the light, though, she couldn't
find her phone. What the hell had she done with it? she wondered
frantically, then gasped and tumbled forward as the plane suddenly
put on speed and surged forward.

Shit! They were taking off, she thought with alarm. Grabbing
at the bars beside her, she tried to brace herself to keep from sliding along the floor of the plane as they picked up speed, but her

mind was now screeching in panic. Once they were in the air, they were on their own with the two men who had kidnapped the fellow in the cage beside her . . . and there wasn't a damned thing she could do about it. This so wasn't good.

Abigail stayed where she was, holding on to the cage bars until long after the plane had left the ground. She waited until they'd reached the point when the plane leveled out and steadied before daring to move, and then she merely released the bar she'd been clutching with her left hand and eased carefully into a sitting position. She still grasped the flashlight in her right hand and rested it on her legs, her eyes absently following the beam of light to the naked man next to her.

His skin was a nice olive tone, the fine hairs on his behind a dark brown or black, she noted absently. Then, realizing how rude she was being letting the light remain there, she quickly shifted it away.

Sighing, Abigail dragged her backpack closer and opened it again for one more search. If she could get a text to Jet, there was still a chance he could turn the plane around, land it, and get help to them before it was too late. He could claim engine trouble or something, couldn't he?

When this third search didn't turn up her phone, Abigail decided she must have lost it somewhere between the bar and here, and pushed her backpack away with frustration. She then sat back to try to think what to do. She had no idea if the clients were carrying weapons, but suspected they probably were. The check-in to board the cargo plane hadn't seemed very strenuous to her. She hadn't been subjected to a search of any kind. Perhaps that was just because she was with the pilot, but there hadn't been metal detectors or anything that she'd seen.

That reminded her, when they'd got to the hangar before the clients, Jet had commented that they were probably held up by customs checking their cargo, so how the hell had these men got a caged, unconscious man through customs? The only answer seemed to her to be that they must have paid someone off, and she

supposed if they'd paid someone to let them bring a caged unconscious man through, guns would hardly be a concern. Both men
could be carrying machine guns for all she knew.

Her gaze shifted to the cage again, and Abigail moved the
flashlight beam over its inhabitant once more. The client had said
something about his waking up and causing a ruckus on "the doc's
plane." It seemed that was why this was an "emergency run."
Their plane hadn't broken down. This man had apparently woken
up and wreaked havoc in it before they'd managed to subdue him.
She wasn't quite sure what that could mean. What kind of damage
did you have to do to ground a plane?

Whatever it was, she didn't want him to do it now while they
were in the air. If he was as strong as he looked, though, he would
definitely come in handy when they landed.

Shifting to her feet before she could think about this too long
and hard, Abigail walked around to the front of the cage and dragged
the tarp off. She then shone the light on the cage door. She was a bit
surprised to see that it didn't have a lock on it, just a standard sliding
bolt that he could have unlocked himself were he awake. But then
he wasn't awake, and wouldn't be so long as the IV the client had
mentioned was in his arm. At least, she assumed it was in his arm.
Abigail shifted the flashlight beam to the man inside.

His front was now on display to her, but there still wasn't
much to see. An IV bag hung from the upper bars of the cage, a
tube running down and disappearing under the man's arm which
lay across his chest, blocking most of it from her view. That was
a shame, she decided. It looked like he probably had an amazing
chest and she would have liked to see it. She would have liked to
see his face too, but his hair covered it completely. Likewise, his
one leg was bent and lay forward, completely covering his genital
area and hiding that from view as well.

"Thank goodness for that," Abigail muttered, but even she
could hear the lack of sincerity in the words. It had been a long
time since she'd even said the word *date*, let alone been on one,
and she apparently wasn't above gawking at a helpless man's junk.

Clucking her tongue with disgust at herself, Abigail slid back the bolt and opened the cage door, then crouched to enter and approach the man. If he'd caused a ruckus the last time he'd woken up, he could do it again when they were safely on the ground. She just had to take the IV out . . . and hope he woke up before they landed. He obviously hadn't managed to gain his freedom the last time in "the doc's" plane, but he'd been alone then, she thought. This time he had her and Jet to help.

Abigail was short, but still had to move on her hands and knees inside the cage. It made carrying the flashlight hard, so she set it to the side, shining on the man she was approaching. She then crawled up to him and lifted the arm that lay across his chest to find the arm beneath it.

As she'd assumed, it was the one with the IV attached, although *attached* didn't quite describe it. Duct tape was definitely what she'd heard when the client was in here. The man's arm was wrapped in the gray stuff from just above his elbow, all the way down to his wrist.

Definitely overkill, she decided. And it was going to hurt like a bitch when it was taken off. Probably best to remove it all while he was unconscious, Abigail thought next. It might take a little time, but that would be the kindest route. Besides, they probably had the time. They couldn't risk doing anything while they were in the air anyway. The last thing she wanted was a crash landing because Jet got hurt or shot in their attempt to overcome the clients.

Settling to sit cross-legged beside the unconscious man, Abigail pulled his arm forward as much as she could and set to work. It took a lot longer than she'd expected. The client must have used an entire roll of duct tape on the man. She seemed to spend forever just unwinding tape round and round his arm. A knife would have come in handy, and Abigail even stopped at one point and did a quick search of the cargo hold for one, but while she found the third flashlight, what she thought might be a parachute, and even a first aid kit, there hadn't been a handy dandy knife anywhere.

She'd got excited when she'd found the first aid kit, thinking correctly that it might have a pair of those tiny scissors to cut gauze or something. But even as she'd found them she'd known they would be no help. The scissors were not only tiny, they were flimsy, fit only for cutting gauze. There was no way they would cut through the duct tape. Setting the first aid kit back, she'd returned to the cage to continue unraveling the duct tape from around the unconscious man's arm.

Abigail worked steadily until she got down to the last layer. That was the one that was going to hurt. It was going to snatch the man's arm bald and there wasn't a darned thing she could do about it.

Going slow might save some of the hair, she supposed, and grasped the piece of tape up past his elbow to begin slowly pulling it off. Abigail watched the skin and hair cling to the tape and winced, glad the man was unconscious when the skin released but the hair didn't and was torn out almost one strand at a time. The IV line stuck to the tape as well and pulled up a bit before she grasped it and pulled it free to lie against his arm again. Abigail had no desire to dislodge the IV before she finished this task. She doubted the man would wake right away once the IV was removed, but she wasn't taking any chances.

She only realized that the IV line had already been dislodged when liquid began to drip out between the tape strips. Either the line had separated from the needle apparatus, or the needle had been pulled from his arm. Whatever the case, he was no longer receiving the drug. Wondering how long he would stay under now, Abigail began to work more quickly, then gasped in shock when his body suddenly uncoiled like a snake and he half sat up, his free hand suddenly at her throat and squeezing.

Releasing the tape she'd been trying to remove, Abigail grabbed for his hands, trying to pull them away so she could breathe again, but even half-baked from the drugs the man was incredibly strong. And he was definitely feeling the effects of the drug. Even as she struggled to free herself and find air, some part of her noted the dazed look in his beautiful black eyes . . . eyes that were presently focused on her face as if she were the only woman in the world. Which she was in that moment, Abigail supposed. Or at least in that cargo hold.

Just when Abigail thought she would pass out from lack of air, and probably follow that up by dying, the hold on her throat eased. In the next moment his hand fell away altogether and the man slumped weakly back against the bars of his cage. His body appeared at rest, but his eyes were alive and now focused on her like lasers.

Gasping in great gulps of air, Abigail eyed him warily and began to shift backward toward the cage door.

"Who are you?"

She stopped at that question. His voice was husky and so deep and gravelly it was like hearing the earth move. Breathing under control now, Abigail swallowed and whispered, "Abs."

His eyebrows rose at that and he glanced down at his stomach and frowned. "What about them?"

Realizing he thought she was talking about *his* abs, she shook her head and smiled crookedly. "My name," she explained and then babbled, "It's really Abigail, but my friends call me Abs, or Abbey, but mostly Abs. At least Jethro does. I haven't seen much of my friends lately. He's the first one I've had the chance to meet up with since Mom died so I—"

"Who is this Jethro?"

Abigail blinked at the interruption. "He's my friend," she answered simply, glancing toward the door to the cockpit and suddenly worried that they might be heard. She couldn't hear voices from the front though, so hoped that meant they couldn't be heard from up there either.

"A boyfriend?" he asked, drawing her attention back again.

"Hell no," she said, surprise making her response more emphatic. Wrinkling her nose, she added, "Ewww. He's been my best friend since we were kids. He's like a brother to me. I could never think of him like that. It would be—"

"You are with the kidnappers?"

Abigail's eyebrows rose at the pained sound to the question.

His expression matched it. He was obviously upset that she might be with the men who had put him in this cage, but then she couldn't blame him. He must be furious to find himself in this situation. She supposed she was lucky he hadn't choked her to death.

"No," she assured him quickly. "I'm rescuing you."

When one eyebrow rose dubiously on his forehead at that, Abigail scowled at him. "Well, I took the IV out, didn't I? At least I was working on it," she added with a grimace. "I was hoping to get the duct tape off before you woke so you wouldn't have to suffer—"

The words died in her throat as he suddenly reached down and tore the rest of the duct tape off in one quick jerk. As she'd feared, it took most of the hair on his arm with it. It looked to her like it took a six-inch-wide layer of skin off all the way around his arm as well, and she winced as she noted the raw red flesh left behind. He, however, showed no sign that it caused him pain. He merely tossed the tape aside with distaste and then sat up a little straighter.

The action left him completely on display. Not just his wide, beautiful chest, but his groin was now on show too, she noted, and then realizing that she was gaping at his family jewels like a fish out of water, Abigail forced her eyes back to his face and distracted herself by looking at that. He was a handsome man. His nose was straight and sharp, his cheekbones high, his mouth full and almost too sensuous for a man, and his eyes were a deep, dark midnight black with little silver flecks that almost seemed to glow in the beam from the flashlight. He presently had a five-o'clock shadow and Abigail wasn't much for facial hair, but even that was attractive on this man.

In truth, Abigail didn't think she'd ever seen a man quite so beautiful as this one, not even in movies or magazines. The pretty blonde barmaid at the country bar where she'd met Jet earlier would have trampled her friend in an effort to get to this fellow, she was sure. It made her glad they weren't at the bar.

"Where are we?"

Abigail watched his lips move as he asked the question and had the craziest urge to lick them. Damn, he was powerful pretty, she thought on a sigh. And she had been shut in for too damned long looking after her mother if just being in his presence made her want to jump the guy.

"Somewhere over the ocean would be my guess," she said finally. "We've only been in the air about—" Abigail paused to glance down at her wristwatch and was surprised to see how much time had passed when she pressed the button to light it up and saw the time. They'd been in the air almost two hours. Had she been that slow at working on his arm? *Good Lord,* she thought, but said aloud, "Two hours. We have to be out of the States and over the ocean by now. Probably somewhere over or near Havana or Cancun depending on Jet's flight pattern," she added.

He didn't gasp in surprise and ask how she could possibly know that, but she explained anyway. "It takes something like five hours to fly from San Antonio to Caracas. The Cayman Islands are about halfway there, and I'm pretty sure both Havana and Cancun would be half an hour or so before that. I was always really good at geography," she added, simply because his staring was making her nervous again and Abigail babbled when she was nervous. That's also why she continued talking.

"Most kids hated geography in my class, but I always wanted to travel so I researched maps and atlases and stuff, memorizing where places were."

He hadn't moved, at all. Abigail began to worry that the drug had done him some harm, but babbled on. "My mom always wanted to travel too. She wanted to go to one of those resorts on St. Lucia or the Cayman Islands. I promised her we'd go once she recovered. To keep her spirits up while she was going through chemo, we used to research those places and look up stuff like how long the flights were to get there, what the wildlife was like, what there was to see and so on . . ."

Still nothing. Was he even breathing? she wondered with a little concern.

"What's your name?" she asked abruptly. It was a good way

to see if he was still alive and breathing and not just a corpse lounging in the corner staring at her with dead eyes. Besides, she simply couldn't keep thinking of him as the guy or fellow, and she wanted to know what his name was. She was guessing it would be something sexy like—

"Tomasso Notte."

Yeah, that was sexy, Abigail decided. At least it was the way he said it. It was also a relief that he was still alive, she thought, and considered him briefly. She'd noted that he had a bit of an accent before this, but now thought she had it pegged and asked, "Italian?"

Tomasso nodded, but didn't expand on the comment. He obviously wasn't the talkative type. And she wished he'd stop staring at her like that. She didn't think he'd taken his eyes off her face since they'd opened. Abigail supposed she shouldn't be surprised, there wasn't much else to look at, but it was the way he was looking at her that was making her a bit uncomfortable. He was focused on her like he was trying to cut through her head with his eyes or something.

Maybe he couldn't see her well in this light, she thought suddenly and glanced down to note that the flashlight beam was squarely on him where she'd left it. None of the light was really reaching her. It probably left her a slightly darker shadow in the darkness around them.

That thought was a bit reassuring and Abigail was just starting to relax when he suddenly announced, "I'm hungry."

It wasn't the words so much as his fixed stare on her that made her anxious when he said that. It gave her the distinct impression that he was considering her for his next meal. Telling herself she was being silly, Abigail forced a smile and scooted quickly backward out of the cage, saying, "I have a chocolate bar in my bag. I'll get it."

This time she was relieved when he didn't move or speak. Straightening outside the cage, Abigail scurried around it to where she'd left her bag. She hadn't thought to bring the flashlight, but since it was pointed in this direction, she had no trouble seeing and quickly knelt to scoop it up. She straightened with it in hand and, now out of the light, began rifling blindly through it in search of the promised chocolate bar. Her hand had just closed over the bar when she felt heat along her back and a warm breath stirring her hair.

Abigail didn't have to look to know the man was right behind her. She could feel it in the goose bumps that had suddenly risen from the back of her neck, all the way down to the backs of her ankles.

"It's an Oh Henry bar," she babbled nervously. "I like nuts." Her words died on a squeak as his arms slid around her from behind, crossed at her waist and urged her back against him. Now the heat from his body seemed to be pouring into hers and warming her wherever they touched, her back, her bottom, the backs of her legs.

"I—" It was as far as she got before his hand rose to catch her chin and turn her face up and back so that he could kiss her.

Abigail's eyes widened incredulously as his mouth covered hers. This kind of thing just did not happen to her. Big, hunky, naked men just did not kiss her out of the blue. And damnnnnn, he was a good kisser, she thought faintly and felt her eyelids begin to droop closed as her body responded to the caress.

Realizing what she was doing, Abigail forced her eyes back open and tried to fight the excitement he was stirring to life within her, but his hands were moving now, sliding to her breasts and covering them through her clothes.

Abigail moaned into his mouth as he cupped and squeezed her hungry flesh, and found herself kissing him back. She hadn't intended to. She'd intended to fight the sensations rising up in her, but it was like trying to hold back high tide, or keeping the sun from rising. The man was stirring things in her that had been too long denied. Only the fact that he was a complete stranger and that her mother was now up in heaven, maybe able to see what she was up to, made her tear her mouth away and gasp desperately, "I thought you were hungry?"

"Mmm hmm," he murmured, and brushed the hair away from the side of her neck to plant a kiss there and then lick the sensitive area. Abigail was so distracted by the sensation that she almost missed the fact that one hand had left her breast and was gliding downward. Almost. Once it registered, however, she dropped her bag and reached down with her free hand to catch his in an effort to try to stop it.

"Tomasso, I don't think we should be—" This time her words ended on a gasp as his hand continued down despite her best efforts to halt its progress, and slid between her legs to pour molten lava there. Dear God, she was on fire, she thought faintly as the combination of his hands on her body and his mouth at her throat stirred her into a frenzy.

"This is so crazy stupid," she moaned as his fingers massaged her through her tight jeans. "We're in the cargo of a plane . . . flying to Venezuela . . . with kidnappers in the cock . . . pet," she groaned and then muttered, "I meant cockpit."

"Cockpit," he agreed by her ear before nibbling his way back down her throat.

"Yes," Abigail breathed, but was quite sure he knew it wasn't in response to what he'd said. The hand she had covering his was now urging him on, and her body was moving of its own volition, pressing into the hand at her breast, and shifting under the hand between her legs, and Abigail knew without a doubt that she wasn't the only one affected by this action. She could feel the proof of his excitement pressing into her lower back and thought that she was so damned short that he'd have to lift her up to—

"Oh God," Abigail cried as her mind filled with an image of his stripping her jeans and panties away, and then turning and raising her up against the wall so that he could slide into her. The vision was so real and so damned exciting that it pushed her over the edge he'd been driving her toward. Barely noticing the pinch at her neck and the drawing sensation that followed, Abigail cried out and bucked in his arms as the flashlight went out and darkness consumed her.

THREE

The first thing Abigail became aware of was that there was a heavy weight pressing down on her back and that she could hardly breathe. Concerned by this realization, she shifted slightly, and then stilled as a warm breath stirred the hair by her ear. The heavy weight was Tomasso, she realized. The same Tomasso who was a complete stranger and whom she'd been grinding up against just moments ago. At least she hoped it was only moments ago. But for all she knew, she could have been unconscious for hours.

That thought made her still and listen for the hum of the plane engine. Much to her relief Abigail not only heard it, but was quite sure she could feel it vibrating through her body from the floor. They were still in the air then. Thank God! There was still time to prepare. She just had to get Hercules off her back and . . .

Actually, she didn't have a clue what they should do then. She had no idea how they were going to get out of this situation. Should they rush the cockpit before they landed and attack Jet's clients, counting on surprise to help them in their endeavor?

That seemed a bit risky. Jet could get hurt in the tussle and they could crash.

So, maybe they should wait until the plane was on the ground and tackle the men as they came to retrieve their "cargo." That too seemed risky. The men might have weapons.

Perhaps they should just wait until the plane landed, slip into the cabin when Jet knocked to announce that it was all clear, grab Jet and flee the plane for the airport. Surely they would find help there? She considered that plan and found all sorts of holes at once. What if Jet knocked as he left the cabin and they weren't able to catch him before he was outside? She didn't want to leave him to the mercies of his kidnapping clients. There was also the possibility that should they manage to catch Jet before he left the cockpit, they might all be shot in the back as they fled the plane for the airport.

"You smell good."

Abigail stilled and turned her head slightly, trying to see the man on top of her. She'd actually managed to forget he was there despite her problems breathing. Now she recalled him, though, and how they'd landed in this position, or at least what they'd been doing before she'd fainted like a sissy from the strength of the first orgasm she'd had in what seemed like forever. Damn, it had been good, and it never should have happened. She had more respect for herself than this, or she should anyway. That's what her mother would have said.

Grimacing at the thought, Abigail opened her mouth to ask Tomasso to let her up, but then closed it when she felt him shift and his weight was suddenly removed from her. Oddly enough, she immediately missed his warmth and was sorry that moving was necessary.

Abigail began to push herself to her hands and knees to get up as well, and then gasped when she was caught by the waist and lifted to her feet as if she weighed nothing. This time she didn't make a crack about his hurting himself if he kept doing things like that as she'd done with Jet. Tomasso obviously hadn't got a good look at her yet and had no idea how large she was, and she'd like to keep it that way. Of course, she knew he'd see her eventually, but she'd like to put that off as long as possible. Abigail had no desire to witness the disappointment that would no doubt come when he saw just how rounded she was.

"Are you all right?" he asked in a rumble.

"Yes," Abigail murmured primly and then bent to retrieve her backpack. It too had apparently been crushed, but by both of them. The chocolate bar, when she found it again, was a little the worse for wear because of it, but she offered it to him anyway.

"Thank you," he murmured, taking the chocolate bar. He then slid an arm around her waist, pulled her forward and bent to kiss her. Caught in the act of starting to say "you're welcome," Abigail found her mouth suddenly full of tongue before the words could leave her lips. And delicious tongue it was. Still, she was startled enough that it took a moment for her to respond to the kiss. But when his hands slid over her bottom, then cupped her cheeks to lift her so that there was full body contact as they kissed, Abigail began to respond.

Like the last time he'd touched her, things got heated pretty quickly, and Abigail was just thinking they were going to end up back on the floor in a heap again, when he suddenly broke the kiss and set her back down.

"Later," he promised, then turned away and disappeared into the darkness.

Abigail blinked after him, her mind slow to recover from the passionate if brief interlude. Damn, the man was like a match to her tinder. All he had to do was touch her and she went up in flames, burning all her good intentions to behave.

Shaking her head, she focused her gaze, trying to pinpoint where Tomasso was. He hadn't moved back to the cage where the flashlight was and was nowhere its light touched, which admittedly wasn't a large expanse of the cargo area.

Abigail almost went to fetch the flashlight from the cage to find him, but then recalled that there was still one on the wall nearby and felt around until her hand brushed against it. The next moment she'd pulled it free and turned it on and was swinging it around the cargo area in search of Tomasso.

She found him down by the parachute she'd discovered earlier. He was examining it with interest, she noted, and wondered
what he was thinking. She supposed he could escape using it, but
it would really leave her and Jet in a pickle. The men would find
him missing, find her there, know she'd released him and probably
kill both her and Jet. Or take them to the island the one fellow had
mentioned. Neither option sounded like a good one, so Abigail
was more than relieved when he left the parachute in place and
moved on.

A moment later he stopped again, this time to examine a set of
buttons on the wall by the back of the cargo area. Abigail had no
idea what they did. If he did, he didn't say anything, but instead
turned and started back towards her, asking, "How long have we
been flying now?"

Abigail glanced down at her watch, her eyebrows rising.
They'd been unconscious longer than she'd realized, or at least she
had and she assumed he had also since he'd been lying on top of
her when she'd woken. He, of course, had more of an excuse for
fainting since he was no doubt still suffering from the aftereffects
of the drug.

"A little over four hours," she admitted solemnly. By her esti-
mate, they had less than an hour before they set down in Caracas.

"Can you grab the first aid kit?" he asked.

"Of course," she murmured and turned to where it was affixed
to the wall, suddenly worried that his arm was bothering him after
all. It took her a bit of time to get the first aid kit from its holder.
The moment she did though, Abigail hurried to Tomasso's side.

"I saw some ointment and bandages in there earlier. I can bandage up your arm for you if you—" The words stopped abruptly
as she saw that he had paused beside the parachute and donned it
while her back was turned. "Tomasso, what are you—"

Her words ended on a grunt of surprise when he caught her
around the waist and dragged her to his side. Her surprise was
not eased when he then hitched her up onto his hip as if she was
nothing more than a child.

"Wrap your arms and legs around me," he ordered as he strode back toward the cargo door. "And hold on to that first aid kit."

"What—" she began with alarm, only to swallow her words as he hit one of the buttons he'd been examining earlier and the cargo door began to open, dropping slowly downward like a lower jaw would. She gaped at the growing opening with alarm and then turned to Tomasso, gasping, "But Jet—" It was too late, however. Even as she said her friend's name Tomasso was stepping out into thin air, and taking her with him. Panicking, Abigail pushed at his chest and twisted away from him, grunting in pain when her head slammed into something hard just before the lights went out.

TOMASSO CAUGHT THE first aid kit as it slipped from Abigail's hand and peered worriedly back up toward the plane he'd just jumped out of. He half expected it to turn and come back to look for them, but it didn't. That made him wonder. If his kidnappers were aware he'd escaped, he was quite sure they'd want to turn back, and he didn't doubt they'd force the pilot to do so. They had to know the cargo door was open, and the minute they knew, he was sure they'd go back and check to see what was happening. Tomasso was pretty sure that there must be some kind of light or warning that would come on in the cockpit so the pilot would know when the cargo door opened. If not, there should be.

On the other hand, maybe they wouldn't bother to turn back. What could they do? Fly under them and try to somehow force them back into the plane? That would take some fancy aeronautics, he was sure. He supposed it was more likely they would set down at the nearest airport that would give them permission to land, and then strike out in a boat to search for them.

That made sense, Tomasso decided, and turned his worried gaze to Abigail. She was lying limp in his hold, her head back so that all he could presently see was her chin and the two small puncture wounds on her throat from where he'd bit her earlier. It had been a necessity. Tomasso hadn't fed in several days by his

guess, and he'd needed to be strong if the escape was to be suc-
cessful. He raised his arm slightly, managing to tip her head up
a bit, and let his gaze shift from the small puncture marks to her
face, but he couldn't see much. Her head was still tilted back, so
that the wound was out of his view. He needed to see her head,
though. The crazy woman had thrown herself backward just as
they'd dropped out of the plane. If he hadn't been holding her so
tightly, he probably would have dropped her when she did it. As it
was, she'd tossed her head back enough that she'd banged it on the
cargo door as they'd dropped out of the plane and had knocked
herself out. That had definitely not been part of the plan.

Tomasso was desperate to check the wound and see that she
was all right, but at the moment there were more urgent issues to
contend with, like the fact that they were plummeting toward the
earth at probably two hundred miles an hour.

Shoving the handle of the first aid kit up his arm to leave at least
one hand free, Tomasso turned his attention downward, trying to
sort out where they were and when he should throw up the pilot
chute to get the main parachute to deploy. He'd never skydived
before, but had once read the mind of an enthusiastic skydiver.
That was the only reason Tomasso knew that rip cords had gone
out in the eighties and modern parachutes had a pilot chute tucked
into a pocket in the back over your butt that had to be thrown up
hard over your head. Once caught by the air, it would force the
main parachute to deploy . . . or so the theory went.

The problem was, Tomasso had no idea when he was supposed
to pull out and toss the pilot chute. The guy he'd read had apparently counted one one thousand, two one thousand, three one
thousand, but Tomasso wasn't sure what height that fellow had
jumped from compared to what height they'd just leapt from. He
had no idea what altitude the cargo plane had been flying at either.
He did know, however, that they were dropping fast.

They weren't in the right formation, Tomasso thought, the
spread-eagle, flat-out position that would slow their descent. Unfortunately, with his need to hold on to an unconscious Abigail,

Tomasso had no idea how to get them in that position. He certainly couldn't spread his arms out and hold on to her too. That being the case, he decided that throwing out the pilot chute sooner rather than later was probably a good idea.

His gaze shifted again over the darkness below. Tomasso was beginning to be able to see spots of light below. His guess was that they were either towns or resorts on the islands below, and his hope was that once the parachute was up he could somehow direct them toward one of them. He just wasn't sure how to do that.

"You live and learn," Tomasso muttered and retrieved the pilot chute from the pocket over his butt to toss it upward as hard as he could. Apparently he did it right, as he could actually feel the parachute being jerked from its packing. When the wind caught and filled it, there was a much larger jerk as they were immediately slowed and Tomasso instinctively tightened his arm around Abigail to keep her from slipping from his grasp. Their descent slowed considerably then. It seemed more like they were floating than dropping now.

With the concern about the parachute out of the way, Tomasso was finally able to turn his attention to Abigail's head wound. She had dropped a little lower in his hold, but her head was still tilted back, so he used his free hand to tilt it forward and frowned when he saw the blood flowing freely from the wound. The amount of blood itself didn't worry him so much, head wounds often bled freely, but it obscured his view of the wound and he really needed to see how bad it was. Tomasso didn't think she'd hit her head too hard, but it had all happened so quickly that he couldn't be sure. He needed to clean the blood away.

That thought uppermost in his mind, Tomasso started to reach for the first aid kit dangling from his arm, thinking there should be something in there to clean away the blood, but he then paused as he realized how ridiculous he was being. He couldn't open the damned thing while they were dropping through the air; everything would fly out. But the blood was obstructing the view of her wound and he wanted to know how bad it was. It was also now running down toward her eyes and he didn't even have a shirt-sleeve to wipe it away with.

After the briefest hesitation, he leaned forward and licked away the blood, then pressed his mouth to the wound itself. After sucking gently for a moment to clear away as much blood as he could, he quickly pulled back to see what he'd revealed. The blood was quick to bubble back to the surface, but Tomasso was still able to see that the wound was a small quickly coloring bump and a tiny split in the skin. In truth, as head wounds went, it wasn't bad at all. At least it didn't look that bad, but he wouldn't stop worrying until she woke up and he knew for sure that she was going to be fine.

Shifting his gaze from her wound to her face, Tomasso took a moment to just drink her in. Her face was rounded with high cheekbones, and her hair was a gorgeous chestnut shot through with reds and lighter browns that gave it a depth he found lovely. But it was her mouth he found his eyes constantly drawn to. She had full, pouty lips that made him want to kiss her. Even now, with her unconscious in his arms, just looking at her lips made him want to press his own to them.

Resisting the urge, Tomasso shifted his gaze to her eyes. They were closed now, but he recalled them as a beautiful bright green that sparkled as she talked. He'd noted earlier that they were also a little bloodshot. She obviously hadn't been getting enough sleep. But the red had actually seemed to make the green brighter. The shadows under her eyes, however, hadn't done the same.

Wondering what troubles had so exhausted and worn her down, Tomasso brushed a thumb across her soft cheek. It felt so nice that he did it again. Abigail's complexion was perfect, if quite pale—another sign that life had been hard of late for this woman, but it didn't detract from her beauty for him. Tomasso found her lovely.

Abigail, he thought and liked the name. His mind had still been foggy from the drugs they'd been giving him when he woke up. That was the only reason Tomasso had gone for her throat when he'd opened his eyes to find himself in the cage with her bending over him causing him pain. He'd immediately assumed she was with his kidnappers. But then good sense had returned and made him try to slip into her mind to be sure of who she was and that she was, indeed, one of the bad guys.

Instead of reading her mind and learning that she was, or even that she wasn't, Tomasso hadn't been able to read her at all, and that had been enough to make him stop choking her at once. He'd then fallen back in the cage, his mind awhirl. For immortals, not being able to read someone was a sign that they were a possible life mate, and Abigail was the first mortal female he'd encountered that he couldn't read. That realization had circled around in his mind, along with the thought that it was just his luck to meet his life mate and find she was one of the bad guys.

He'd been somewhat relieved when she'd assured him that she wasn't with his kidnappers. However, Tomasso hadn't dropped all of his suspicions right away. At least, not until she'd started babbling. Five minutes of the woman's nervous chatter had been enough to convince him that she simply did not have it in her to be running with bad guys. It might be foolish on his part to come to this conclusion so quickly, but he felt quite sure that Abigail was as sweet and innocent as modern society would allow. He suspected she was one of those kindhearted mortals others would take advantage of. He could be wrong of course, Tomasso hadn't known her long, and part of his judgment might be based as much on a desire to want her to be like that, as a belief that she was, but he was hoping he was right. And if he was, he intended to protect her from her own kindhearted ways as well as the rest of the world in future.

That decision made, Tomasso's next concern had been escape. He had been quite sure that if they were still on the plane when it landed, they would never get free, so his next step had been to get them both off that plane and away from the kidnappers.

Mission accomplished there, he thought wryly, peering down again to check their progress. They were off the plane. The problem was he suspected they were going to land in the ocean instead of one of those spots of light he could see below. Which meant one hell of a swim to reach shore . . . using one arm as he dragged Abigail behind him. Tomasso could do it. He had to. But it wasn't going to be easy, and he was worried about the blood from her head wound attracting unwanted attention from predators like sharks. Things could get hairy.

Mouth tightening, he watched the dark water below grow nearer and began planning in his mind. Once low enough he would shrug himself out of the parachute and drop into the water with Abigail. Without their weight, the parachute should continue on past them and set down a distance away where he and Abigail would not get tangled up in either the chute or its lines.

If he had a knife Tomasso would be cutting one of the lines off now to tie Abigail to his back so that he could swim with both hands. Unfortunately, he didn't have anything as useful as a knife in his pocket. Hell, he didn't even have clothes, let alone pockets, he thought and then noted how low they had dropped while he thought. At the speed they were descending it would only be seconds before they hit the water.

It seemed his planning was over. And with all of his woolgathering he hadn't managed to direct them anywhere. Not that he probably could have anyway, Tomasso acknowledged, and tried to figure out how far from land they were going to set down.

Moonlight was making things a little easier. The islands were darker masses against the water, often with lit-up sections of inhabitation. Tomasso surveyed the area below and did a quick calculation of the distance they were likely to land from the nearest land mass and almost winced. It was going to be a long night.

FOUR

Abigail woke up moaning. It was her head. The damned thing was pounding like a bass drum. Boom boom boom. Grimacing at the sunlight that struck her eyes when she opened them, she quickly closed them again and cursed herself for not closing the living room curtains before lying down to sleep on the couch. It was something she rarely forgot to do when she was up late nursing her mother through the occasional really bad night.

They were becoming more and more frequent of late, Abigail thought, and then frowned with confusion as her memory began to nudge her, gently reminding her that Mom no longer had bad nights, and she no longer had a home, let alone a living room. Though she still had a couch and curtains. They were packed away in storage back in Austin.

She, on the other hand, was visiting Jet in San Antonio. No, she had been flying with him to Venezuela, but had had to ride in the cargo section and—

"Oh, hell," Abigail muttered and sat up abruptly, forcing her eyes open despite the pain the bright sunshine sent shooting through her skull.

Her gaze slid over a long stretch of sandy beach and crystal-blue water and for one moment she simply sat, stunned by the beauty of the scenery, but then she shifted her gaze to herself and her position. She was sitting on sand in the shade of the palm trees that lined the beach . . . and Tomasso Notte was asleep beside her.

He was still as naked as he'd been when she first found him, Abigail noted, absently slapping her arm and squishing a feasting mosquito as her eyes slid over Tomasso's body with interest. She could see him much better now that she wasn't trying to look him over by flashlight and . . . the man was just perfect. Too perfect. He was obviously a health buff. He probably spent half of every day at the gym to build up the muscles that bulged on his body.

The realization was a disheartening one. Someone who put so much time and effort into his body would not be impressed by someone as dumpy and out of shape as she was. Abigail was quite sure about that and the knowledge nearly broke her heart. After what had happened on the plane . . .

Abigail bit her lip, and struggled briefly with her body as it immediately responded to the memories now flooding her mind. His hands on her, his mouth on her, her cry as she reached her release . . . God, her nipples were getting erect just at the memory, and there was a sudden dampness between her legs too. What was the matter with her? She'd never reacted like this to a man, yet this one didn't even have to touch her and she was a trembling mass of need.

Which might be a good thing, she thought suddenly. Certainly, she doubted he'd want to touch her again after getting a look at her in daylight and seeing what he hadn't been able to see in the dark. So maybe fantasy and memory would be all she'd have.

Depressed by the thought, Abigail pushed herself to her feet. She immediately had to wave away a cloud of hungry mosquitoes that suddenly seemed to be swarming around her head. When that had little effect at dispersing the hungry bloodsuckers, she moved out of the shade, headed for the water.

Abigail was itchy from at least a half dozen mosquito bites she'd apparently received while she was sleeping and didn't have any After Bite. She was hungry and thirsty and knew without question that they didn't have any food or water. All they'd taken with them was the first aid kit, and that wasn't likely to have much but gauze and antiseptic. This was the ocean. She couldn't drink it, but she could splash it on herself and hope that soothed her itchy spots and fooled her body into thinking it wasn't as dehydrated as it probably was.

She'd barely taken half a dozen steps on the unshaded sand before Abigail stopped abruptly and almost turned back. The sand had been heated by the beating sun and was unbearably hot underfoot. Her gaze slid to the sparkling blue water and rather than turn back, she burst into a run instead, rushing to the cool relief of the water.

A relieved moan slipped from her lips as the soothing water closed over her feet. Here the sand was much nicer, and the water felt good against her skin. Uncaring that her jeans were getting soaked, Abigail moved out into the water until it reached her knees, then bent to scoop up handfuls of the cool liquid and splashed it on her arms, her face, her throat, and even her chest above her neckline. It immediately dribbled down to soak her tank top, but Abigail didn't care. She was hot and the water was refreshing, and she was wearing too damned many clothes. Jeans, a tank top, and a light blouse over it might be fine for a bus ride on an air-conditioned bus, and a cool evening in San Antonio, but it was definitely not appropriate for this hot, sandy beach in the Caribbean. It must be a hundred degrees or better here, she thought and wondered what time it was.

Pausing suddenly, Abigail straightened and raised a hand to shelter her eyes as she glanced to the sky to find the sun. It wasn't quite directly overhead, but was a little to the side, either on its downward path, or still on its upward path. Abigail had no idea which it was. She didn't know where they were or which direction was east or west at the moment. So by her best guess, it was either an hour or so before noon, or an hour or so after. She supposed she'd find out soon enough. The one sure thing in her life right then was that the sun would continue to move and the direction it moved in would tell her if it was late morning or early afternoon.

Abigail started to lower her hand, but stilled as the sunlight glared off something on her wrist. Her watch, she realized with self-disgust. She'd forgotten she was wearing one . . . probably because she didn't usually wear it. It had been a graduation gift from her mother, meant to be used at medical school. Abigail had found wearing it depressing after dropping out of school. Besides, there simply hadn't been much need for one. She'd been stuck in her mother's apartment with clocks at every turn and nowhere to go but doctor's appointments.

Grimacing, she turned her wrist to see the face and noted that it was still working, and that, if it was right, it was a bit after one in the afternoon.

Sighing, Abigail let her hand drop and scanned the water briefly, only to stiffen as she spotted a boat coming around the point on her right. Excitement rising in her, she waved happily despite knowing they probably couldn't see her yet. Then she began to jump up and down excitedly as she waved, and added shouting to her repertoire to get their attention. She'd only let out one shout when she was suddenly grabbed from behind, dragged off her feet and carried quickly backward into the trees.

"Tomasso!" Abigail shrieked with dismay as he slowed once they were deep in the woods and out of sight of the beach. "What are you doing? We need help."

"That could be Jake and Sully," he answered grimly, setting her down on her feet. Keeping a hand on her so she couldn't run, he then tilted his head to peer around the palm tree and back the way they'd come.

"Jake and Sully?" she asked with confusion.

"My kidnappers," he explained. "I heard them say each other's names once or twice when I woke up."

"Oh," she murmured and frowned. It hadn't occurred to her that his kidnappers might come looking for them, but she supposed it made sense. They probably knew the coordinates of

where they'd jumped out of the plane. All they had to do was get
a boat and search in that area for them. Still . . .

"But what if it isn't your kidnappers?" she pointed out. "We
have no water, or food. Hell, you don't even have clothes. We
need help, Tomasso."

"*Sì,*" he agreed bleakly, but shook his head. "If the boat had
a lot of people then we could have flagged them down. But there
were only two men on the boat. It raises the possibility that it is
them."

"Two men? You could tell that?" Abigail asked dubiously.
She'd barely been able to see the boat let alone anyone on it, yet he
was claiming he could and had counted two men?

Something about her tone drew his gaze to her face and Tomasso frowned at what he saw. Drawing himself up, he said with
dignity, "I have very good eyesight."

Abigail bit her lip and glanced away, stifling a sudden urge
to laugh. It wasn't what he'd said that had roused her humor, it
was his demeanor. It was hard to manage dignity when you were
buck-ass naked, and his attitude just seemed ridiculous in her eyes.

"What?" Tomasso asked suspiciously.

"Nothing," Abigail said quickly, glanced to him and then just
as swiftly glanced away. She then cleared her throat, waved back
toward him, her hand at waist level and said, "Maybe you should
do something about that."

A moment of silence passed and then he shrugged and said,
"I apologize, but there is little I can do about my erection. Your
presence has that effect on me."

"*Erection?*" Abigail squawked and whirled to take a look at
what she'd been politely avoiding letting her eyes land on. Her
eyes found—yes, indeedy, it was an erection. "Holy cripes!" she
muttered, and then raised her gaze to his and gasped, "You've got
an erection!"

"I am aware of that," he said stiffly.

"Yeah, but—I mean, you're saying *I'm* the cause of it?" she
asked, sure she'd misunderstood.

"Is there anyone else here?" he asked, his tone just as dry.

"Noooo . . ." Abigail drew the word out as she glanced around to be sure there wasn't some young Bo Derek type sauntering around with her boobs hanging out. Not finding anyone, let alone a beautiful buxom blonde, she turned back to him with bewilderment and said, "But it's like daylight and everything. You can see what I really look like and stuff." Shaking her head, she added firmly, "That boner cannot be for me."

Tomasso didn't argue the point. He didn't soothe her insecurities and assure her that he found her attractive. He simply closed the small gap between them, caught her by the waist, lifted her into the air and kissed her. It was no hello-nice-to-see-you kiss. It was a full-on carnal ravaging that said, "This-erection-is-definitely-all-for-you-and-I-want-to-rip-your-clothes-off-and-use-it."

Abigail had to hand it to the guy; he was a hell of a kisser. Three seconds after his mouth claimed hers she was a trembling, panting, clinging mass, moaning into his mouth and ready to rip her own clothes off.

"Abigail," he muttered suddenly, tearing his mouth from hers and kissing a trail across her cheek.

"Yes?" she gasped, turning her head to give him better access.

"We cannot do this," he groaned by her ear, just before sucking her lobe into his mouth.

"No," she agreed on a moan as he nipped at the tender flesh.

"That boat could land. Our kidnappers could find us in flagrante delicto."

"Delicto," she mumbled. "You're delicto. That means delicious, right?" she added before biting lightly at his shoulder.

Tomasso chuckled helplessly against her ear, then suddenly turned with her in his arms. "We will move further from shore. There will be less chance we will be found after we pass out."

"Pass out?" She pulled back to peer down at him. "I know I fainted when you—I mean, when we . . ." Aware that she was blushing, she wrinkled her nose and waved away what she couldn't say. "That doesn't mean we're going to faint again. It was probably the altitude or something. And you were just coming off those drugs they had you on."

"It was not the altitude," he assured her, glancing over her shoulder to watch where he was carrying her. "We will faint again."

Abigail frowned. He wasn't giving any explanation for why they might faint, but he sounded very sure they would.

She glanced toward the passing woods, her mind working. She'd never fainted before when messing around with someone, but she'd definitely lost consciousness with him on the plane. But they were no longer on the plane. They were basically in the jungle, where there were snakes and icky bugs that could bite them while they slept. Passing out here did not seem a good idea to her.

In fact, now that Abigail was able to think again, messing around with Tomasso didn't seem that good an idea either. She still hardly knew the man, and yes, he said he was attracted to her, but heck, men were horny bastards, they could be turned on by a hot apple pie. It didn't mean they wanted a relationship with it any more than his desire to bang her meant that he wanted a relationship with her. And despite what had happened on the plane, Abigail just wasn't the sort to go around indiscriminately sleeping with gorgeous men just because they were naked in the woods and made her blood boil with just a kiss.

"Put me down," she said suddenly, kicking her feet.

"Why?" Tomasso asked, stopping.

"Because I don't want to do this," Abigail said simply, pushing at his chest. "Put me down."

Tomasso hesitated, but then eased her to the ground and stepped back. His expression was confused, though, and she couldn't blame him. Her nipples were still erect, she probably had a wet spot between the legs of her jeans from the excitement he'd inspired, and she had definitely been responding to him like a woman who wanted to get laid.

Turning her head away to avoid his gaze, she admitted, "I'm attracted to you."

"*Sì.*" It was a simple acknowledgment that he knew that, no ego or arrogance involved.

"But . . . I'm not the kind of girl who . . ." Abigail paused, feeling stupid. This was not the 1950s or something, and she didn't want to be the gal shrieking, "I'm not that kind of girl!" with virginal horror. She was not a virgin. What she was, was a woman who had just lost her mother, was emotionally vulnerable, and afraid of getting hurt by this big beefcake when a prettier gal came along and he lost interest in her.

Well, at least part of her felt that way. That was her brain. The other part, a much lower one that was situated between her legs, was shrieking at her to enjoy him while she had the chance. Telling her this would be a really good memory for her to enjoy later. Assuring her that it would be worth all the heartache that would probably follow. Just go on and bounce on his pogo stick now, it begged.

That part of her was a much less dignified communicator than her brain.

"Okay."

Abigail blinked and glanced up to see that Tomasso had turned and started back toward the beach.

"Okay?" she asked uncertainly, quickly following him.

"*Sì.*"

Abigail bit her lip, and then asked, "You're not angry with me?"

"*Sì* and no," he answered, continuing forward.

"What does that mean?" she asked with a frown. "*Sì*, you're angry, and no, you're not?"

Turning, he eyed her with mild amusement and said, "You women, you like to talk, *sì*?"

"I'm afraid so," she admitted wryly.

He nodded. "Then I will tell you. It is *sì* because what I want most in the world is to strip every bit of clothing from you, lay you in the sand and lick every inch of your skin before sliding my aching *pene* into your body."

"Jeez," Abigail mumbled, fanning her face with one hand. The guy may not talk much, but when he did . . . *Pene* was Italian for penis, right? she wondered suddenly, and was quite sure that was the case.

"However, it is also no," he continued. "Because I understand if things are moving quickly for you and you wish to take time. Fortunately, so long as we avoid my kidnappers we have that time, more than you can imagine. So I will be patient and wait until you are ready for me to pleasure you with my mouth and hands and body until you scream my name and the stars explode behind your eyes."

"Jeez," Abigail muttered again, using both hands now to fan her face. The guy was—walking away again. Clucking her tongue, she hurried after him to ask, "You're willing to wait for me?"

"*Sì.*"

Apparently the more verbal guy had gone back into hiding, Abigail thought with irritation. She had kind of been hoping for some sort of proclamation. Like, that she was gorgeous and brilliant and sexy and worth waiting for or something. It seemed he wasn't going to try to sweet talk his way into her pants though. Which was just a crying shame because really it wouldn't have taken much sweet talk at all, Abigail thought, and then rolled her eyes at herself. She was the one who had put the brakes on their having sex. He was just adhering to her wishes. Now she wanted to jump him?

Yes, she did, Abigail admitted if only to herself. She also found herself staring at his ass as he walked and wanting to grab and squeeze it like his cheeks were melons. What on earth was the matter with her?

"The boat is gone."

Abigail dragged her mind out of his pants, well, his metaphorical pants since he wasn't wearing any, and shifted her attention to the coastline. They were standing at the edge of the trees with a perfect view of the ocean, and he was right. No boat. She glanced to him again, her gaze shifting to his bare bottom as he bent to grab something off the ground.

"Now what do we do?" she asked, a little distracted.

"Now I check your wound," he announced, straightening and turning to catch her hand. He led her back the way they'd come, but this time taking her deeper into the trees.

Probably in case the boat came back around again, Abigail thought as she followed him docilely. She then frowned and raised her free hand to her head to search for the wound he spoke of. For one moment she had no idea what he was talking about, but when she felt the cloth around her head she recalled hitting it on the cargo door as they'd left the plane. In fact, that was the last thing Abigail remembered before waking up here.

"How did we get here?" she asked curiously as they walked. "Did the parachute bring us to this shore?"

"No. The parachute landed us in the ocean. We swam all night," he answered.

She translated that in her head to mean he had swum and dragged her with him since she hadn't been conscious to swim herself. She also gathered it meant they'd landed really far out, although he hadn't wasted the words to actually say that. Now she wondered how far out they'd landed and how far he'd had to drag her unconscious body to get here. It couldn't have been easy swimming while dragging her.

He'd saved her life, she realized. And bandaged her up, she added, feeling the cloth around her head again. It felt like gauze, which reminded her of the first aid kit she'd been holding when they'd left the plane. She doubted she'd managed to hold on to it after she'd lost consciousness, so supposed he must have taken it from her. It was a wonder he'd been able to swim at all while dragging everything with him, she thought guiltily. She hadn't really been much help in this escape. Although, to be fair, she hadn't wanted to escape this way, leaving Jet alone with the kidnappers.

"Here is good." Coming to an abrupt halt, Tomasso turned to face her and gestured to the ground.

Abigail translated that to a suggestion to sit and did so only to find herself staring at his junk now swinging in front of her face.

"Really, Tomasso, we need to find you something to wear," she muttered almost wearily, averting her eyes. His erection had wilted in the past few moments, but wasn't completely gone. It was still magnificent and distracting.

"Here," he said abruptly, and held out what he'd picked up earlier.

The first aid kit, Abigail realized as she took the red packet. He'd been picking it up when she'd asked "Now what do we do?" She just hadn't seen it because she was distracted by his bare bottom as he bent over. He really had a nice one, Abigail thought. And a nice chest, and nice arms, and legs and—

She gave her head a shake, which not only ended her inner recital of his pretty body parts, but dislodged her eyes from his bottom as he disappeared into the jungle again. He did seem to walk away a lot, Abigail thought now. The good news was that he always came back . . . so far.

Tomasso wasn't gone long this time; five, maybe ten minutes. Abigail stared at him blankly when he returned, her gaze caught by the splash of green over his groin. He'd fashioned a sort of loin-cloth out of leaves, weaving the stems together with some kind of vine that ran around his waist. But the man obviously had no clue just how big his junk was, the leaves didn't quite cover the tip.

"Better?" he asked as he approached.

"You need bigger leaves," she said dryly. Her words made him pause and frown down at himself. She doubted he could see the problem from above though, so she wasn't surprised when he said, "Is fine."

"Right," she muttered and simply resigned herself to continuing to avert her gaze . . . at least when he was looking. She took too much pleasure in looking at him to do it all the time. She wouldn't want him to notice her devouring him with her eyes though, so she'd just have to peek when he wasn't aware she was.

"How bad is it?" Abigail asked when Tomasso settled to sit cross-legged in the sand in front of her and began to unravel the bandage from around her head.

"Not so bad," he assured her. "Does it hurt?"

"Not at the moment," Abigail admitted with some surprise, only now becoming aware of the fact, and then she added, "But it did when I woke up."

His response was a grunt as he finished removing the bandages and dropped them to the sand. He then took her head in hand and tilted it down so he could better examine her wound.

Abigail waited patiently, her gaze dropping to the discarded bandages, but when she saw the blood on the cloth, her eyes widened with alarm. "It bled."

"*Sì*. Why else the bandage?" Tomasso asked patiently, poking at the wound.

"Yes, but . . ." she began, then let the words die away. He was absolutely right. Why else would there be a need for bandages? She just hadn't realized she'd actually bled and was a little startled to know she had. Sighing, she waited as he took the first aid kit from her and opened it. Abigail frowned though when she saw him retrieve an antiseptic ointment and open it.

"Is it bad?" she asked with concern as he smeared the cool gel on her forehead.

"No. This is the jungle."

That was all he said. Fortunately it was enough. This was the jungle. Infection could set in easily in this moist heat. The ointment was a precaution. She remained silent and merely watched as he retrieved a large bandage from the pack and quickly opened it. Abigail found it somewhat reassuring that it was just a bandage this time, and not gauze he felt needed to be wrapped around her head. Surely that meant the wound was healing. Right?

She hoped so. But she also wished she had a mirror to check it out herself.

"Wait here. Rest."

Pulled from her thoughts, Abigail glanced up with surprise at this latest order, but he was already disappearing into the woods again. Honestly, the man spent most of his time walking away from her, she thought and noted absently that his butt cheeks were the last part of him to disappear into the trees. He hadn't covered *them* with leaves, she noted and was glad.

Rolling her eyes, Abigail glanced around briefly, and then looked down to where she sat. It was a nice sandy bit in the crook of the roots of a tree. A perfect bed, really, she decided. And realized she was tired. They couldn't have been awake long, but she was already exhausted. It must be the heat, Abigail thought. Or perhaps just the emotional turmoil she'd been through since waking up. Whatever the case, the idea of lying down and resting for a minute was an attractive one despite her earlier worries about snakes and bugs. Abigail did perform a quick inspection of the area first though, just to be sure there wasn't anything around that might bite her, but then she stretched out, shifted onto her side and closed her eyes. She would just rest for a little bit. Just until Tomasso returned, she assured herself. Then they would no doubt have to start walking in search of civilization. They needed a phone so she could check on Jet and so Tomasso could call . . . whoever.

TOMASSO'S FOOTSTEPS SLOWED as he broke out of the trees and stepped into the small clearing where Abigail waited. She was curled on her side under the tree where he'd left her, sleeping soundly.

His gaze slid over her pale skin and the exhausted shadows under her eyes. She'd remained unconscious for quite a while after they'd left the plane. She hadn't woken through the swim to this island, or even as he'd carried her ashore and settled her next to him under the palm trees as dawn broke. But unconsciousness wasn't the same as sleeping and she obviously needed rest.

Tomasso shifted his feet, and then set down the coconuts he'd gathered and straightened to peer at her as he considered the situation. They needed to find civilization and a phone. He needed to call in and let his family know he was all right and that Caracas was where they needed to look for the other missing immortals. He also needed to find out whether his brother had managed his escape successfully or not. Dante hadn't wound up in a cage next to him again, which seemed to suggest he had, but Tomasso needed to know for sure.

However, all of that would apparently have to wait. Abigail had been wounded and was in dire need of rest. So rest she would have.

She also no doubt needed food and drink. He'd intended the coconuts to take care of that. She could drink the coconut water and eat the white fleshy fruit inside, but fish would probably be better. He just had to sort out a way to catch some. Maybe he could somehow fashion a spear, Tomasso thought as he turned to head toward the beach.

ABIGAIL WOKE UP with her nose twitching in interest. Something smelled delicious. Stifling a yawn, she sat up to glance around, but couldn't see anything but trees. Curious, she got to her feet and moved around the tree she'd been sleeping by, and blinked as she spotted Tomasso on the beach at the edge of the jungle, turning something over a fire in the shade of a large palm tree.

Stomach rumbling, Abigail started forward, her gaze shifting to the sky beyond the trees. The sun was setting on the horizon and it was growing dark. She must have slept quite a while, she thought with a frown.

"Why didn't you wake me?" she asked as she stepped out onto the beach.

Tomasso glanced to her with surprise, and then smiled crookedly as if at an adorable puppy. All he said, however, was, "You needed rest."

Abigail considered him briefly, noting that his five-o'clock shadow was more a seven-o'clock shadow now. But it was his smile that was making her suspicious, so she simply moved past him and walked down to the shore. The water was still. There wasn't even a hint of a breeze to stir it. It made the surface a serviceable mirror and Abigail stepped a few feet into the water, then peered down at her reflection and moaned. Her hair was standing up in every direction. That combined with her pale face made her look like a clown.

Muttering under her breath, Abigail shrugged out of her blouse, tugged off her jeans, and then pulled off her tank top. Leaving her clothes in a pile on the beach, she then strode determinedly into the water in just her underwear and bra. It was as good as a swimsuit, Abigail reassured herself as she went, and she was not returning to the fire looking like this.

The air had cooled while she slept, but the water was even cooler and Abigail shivered as she moved deeper into its embrace. That didn't slow her down though. She had always loved swimming. Her mother had insisted she take lessons as a kid and she was good at it. The moment she was up to her waist in the tide, she dove under and kicked, coming up several feet further out.

Finding her feet again, Abigail turned then to look back to shore, her eyes widening when she saw that Tomasso had followed and was now waist-deep in the water. As she watched, he dove as well. A moment later he popped up in front of her.

"Never swim alone," he admonished, but his gaze was not on her face. In fact his eyes seemed locked on her chest and she glanced down to see that her plain white bra was not much of a covering when wet, but had gone transparent. Her nipples were showing through, and they were growing erect, whether from the cold or his nearness, she didn't know, but it didn't matter. They were still erect and on show.

Groaning with embarrassment, Abigail turned away and struck out in a strong swim away from shore, aware that Tomasso followed and then caught up and swam beside her. Apparently he was serious about her not swimming alone.

She didn't swim far. Abigail was aware that she was out of shape and would tire easily, so stopped again after several feet to tread water. Tomasso immediately stopped as well and turned to face her just a little more than a foot away. Close enough she could have reached out and touched him, but not so close she felt un-comfortable.

"Hungry?" he asked.

Recalling the smell that had woken her, Abigail nodded and glanced back to shore. The smoke from the fire was barely visible from here. He'd kept it small, no doubt to prevent drawing atten-tion in case Jake and Sully were still looking for him.

Thoughts of his kidnappers were quickly followed by thoughts of Jet, and Abigail frowned. Tomasso had dragged her off that plane, leaving Jet behind in the company of a couple of nefarious dudes. That was why she'd tried to break away from him at the last minute and had managed to hurt herself. Frowning, she turned back to Tomasso.

"What will they do to Jet?" she asked with concern.

"The plane?" he asked, confusion obvious on his expression.

"No. My friend, Jet. Jethro," she added, using his proper name, and then explained, "He was the pilot of the plane we were on."

A scowl claimed his lips and he growled, "That is the Jet you kept mumbling about in your sleep?"

Abigail's eyebrows rose at this news. She'd been mumbling about Jet in her sleep? Actually, that was a bit reassuring. It meant she *had* been thinking about him, and didn't have to feel guilty for not bringing him up until now. Of course, he probably should have been her first concern on waking the first time, but Abigail decided to blame that on her head wound. No doubt her think-ing had been a little muddled. That excused her, right? Actually, it was probably even true, Abigail acknowledged. She wasn't the sort to just forget about a friend who might be in trouble like that. Instead, she was a worrywart. In college she used to make friends call when they got home from visiting her place, just to be sure they made it all right. Not thinking and worrying about Jet until now definitely hadn't been the norm for her.

"What is this Jet to you?"

Abigail blinked her thoughts away and glanced to Tomasso curiously. He was sounding kind of cranky. Like maybe he was jealous, which was just ridiculous of course. She wasn't the sort men got jealous over. Besides, they'd already had this conversation on the plane. He'd asked then if Jet was her boyfriend and she'd said no, he was a friend. Of course, Tomasso had probably been a little fuzzyheaded from the drug they'd been giving him in that IV and maybe didn't recall, so she excused him.

"He's a friend. We grew up together," she said patiently and explained, "He's been my best friend forever. He's like a brother or something. Jet is *not* my boyfriend."

"Hmm," he muttered, not sounding much happier, and then he asked, "What kind of name is Jet?"

"His name is Jethro," she explained, despite having said his proper name earlier. "But he always wanted to be a jet pilot, so I shortened his name to Jet when we were kids and it stuck."

Tomasso merely grunted at that, but the slight sneer that had claimed his lips eased now and he frowned and asked, "So this Jet, your friend, was the pilot of the plane?"

"Yes." Abigail glanced toward the sky as if he might fly over them right then, and sighed when she didn't see his plane.

"So he works with the kidnappers?" Tomasso asked darkly.

"No!" Abigail shifted her attention back to Tomasso. "He was a fighter pilot for the navy, but finished his tour a couple weeks ago. A buddy of his who got out a month before him had a job with a cargo company and arranged an interview for Jet when he heard he'd finished his tour. Jet got the job. He only started a week ago, and this company is legit. I'm pretty sure they wouldn't get involved with transporting a kidnap victim."

"Then why was I on his plane?" Tomasso asked simply.

Abigail frowned. "From what I overheard the guy saying when he was wrapping up your arm, you must have got loose and trashed their plane?"

Tomasso nodded slowly.

"Well, it seems they needed to find alternate transport and quickly. Jet was told it was an emergency trip. Had to be right away, that sort of thing."

"Probably they were running low on the drug they were using to keep me under," Tomasso said thoughtfully.

"That could be it. I don't know for sure. All I know is that I'd just got into San Antonio and met up with Jet at a bar as planned. He was supposed to have a couple days off, but then he got a call from his boss about this flight. Jet said he was going to refuse, but then decided it could be fun. I could fly down with him and we could kick around Caracas for a couple days and then fly back."

"Why were you in the cargo area and not the front of the plane?" he asked, his eyes narrowed.

Abigail stiffened in the water at the suspicion in his eyes. The moment she stopped moving, she started to sink and immediately started treading water again, but it was an effort. She was tiring, Abigail realized, and turned to head back toward shore. Once she'd reached water shallow enough that she could stand, Abigail walked out of the surf and dropped to sit next to her pile of clothes.

"I was in the cargo area because the clients didn't want me on the flight at all," she said quietly when Tomasso dropped onto the sand beside her. "Jet had me hide in the cargo area so they wouldn't know I was going despite their wishes."

"You *were* a stowaway," Tomasso murmured as if that was what he'd thought all along.

"Not really," she argued. "Jet was the pilot and knew I was there."

"But Jake and Sully did not," he pointed out.

Abigail shrugged. Stowaway, shmowaway. She didn't care. What she did care about was Jet and that he was okay. Picking up a shell half buried in the sand, she tossed it out into the water and asked, "What will they do to him?"

Tomasso was silent for a minute, and then shook his head. "He will probably be fine."

It didn't sound to her as if he really believed that and Abigail frowned and said, "He's one of the good guys, Tomasso. I'd feel awful if anything happened to him because I left the plane with you."

"I did not give you much choice," Tomasso muttered, his gaze on the horizon. Shaking his head, he added, "I should have found out all the particulars before donning that parachute and taking you off the plane. I just assumed you were a stowaway and . . ." He shrugged, not bothering to finish.

Abigail's mouth twisted unhappily. "You know what they say about assuming, right?"

"That it is foolish," he said soberly.

"Yeah, that too," she said wearily.

"Come," Tomasso said abruptly, gathering her clothes for her and getting to his feet. Catching her hand, he then helped her up as he said, "The fish will be done. We will eat, then start walking."

"At night?" she asked with alarm.

"It is better at night," he assured her, starting up the beach. "No sun."

Abigail considered that as they walked and supposed it was good to avoid the heat and sun of daylight. It would prevent their getting too dehydrated, which had to be good. *And* she had just woken up from sleeping, so should be good for walking. Still, Abigail didn't think Tomasso had slept at all while she was down for the count. The man had caught fish and cooked it instead.

They probably wouldn't walk far then, Abigail thought hopefully. An hour or two, and then they'd probably stop . . . Not that she didn't want to walk all the way to civilization tonight. She did. The sooner they found a phone, the sooner she could find out what had happened to Jet. It was just that she hadn't done anything physical in a long time and wasn't sure she could manage much more than a couple hours of slogging through the sand. She was pretty sure she wouldn't have to though. Tomasso would need sleep. An hour or so and he'd no doubt be ready to bed down.

FIVE

"Sure, sure, an hour or so and he'd be ready to stop," Abigail muttered to herself, glazed eyes fixed on her feet in the darkness. The coconut water had been surprisingly yummy, refreshing even despite being warm, and the fish had been delicious. Then they'd started walking, and by her guess, had been doing so for four or five hours now. Abigail was ready to drop. The only thing that kept her moving was her worry about Jet and the fact that Tomasso, who hadn't slept, was still going.

"What?"

That question made Abigail glance up to see that Tomasso had stopped again to wait for her. Like Jet, he had much longer legs than her and she couldn't possibly keep up. Every time he stopped to wait for her, they started out together again once she reached him, only for her to drop back a bit with every step. Raising her eyebrows at his questioning expression, she asked tiredly, "What what?"

"You spoke," he pointed out.

You spoke, she thought. Not *you said something*, just *you spoke*. The man always used the minimum amount of words to express himself, she thought wearily and waved away his comment. "I was just talking to myself."

Tomasso didn't turn away and continue walking then as she expected, but eyed her with concern. "You are exhausted."

"We've been walking for hours, Tomasso. Of course I'm exhausted."

She saw his eyebrows rise in the darkness. Thank goodness for moonlight, she thought, and then blinked at him when he shook his head and said, "One."

"One what?" she asked, hoping he meant they'd only walk for another hour, although even that seemed way too long for her at that point. She really was dead on her feet.

"We have been walking one hour," he explained.

"No way!" Abigail raised her watch to press the button to light the face. She'd thought it was still working when she'd checked it earlier, but when she saw that, according to it, he was right and only an hour and a couple of minutes had passed since they'd set out, she tapped it with irritation and muttered, "It must not be working. I'm sure we've been walking forever."

She glanced to Tomasso then, expecting to see impatience or irritation. Instead what she found was a combination of what she thought might be amusement, sympathy, and affection.

Rather than chastise her for slowing him down, he said, "You have been through a lot. You are exhausted. We will rest."

Abigail sagged with relief. She *was* exhausted, and was happy to blame it on everything they'd been through instead of being out of shape. She was less happy to rest, however. At least her conscience was. Her body was ecstatic at the thought, but her conscience was oozing guilt at the delay in finding civilization and getting help for Jet.

If he needed it, the exhausted part of her commented to ease her guilt. Maybe he didn't. Maybe Jet was fine and she was worrying for nothing.

Or, her conscience countered, maybe Jet was even now being transported to that island the client had mentioned. The island where "the doc" would perform experiments so horrid the client had claimed he'd rather be dead.

Abigail knew there was also a chance Jet might be dead. The client had mentioned that option, but she simply couldn't face that possibility. She couldn't lose Jet on the heels of the loss of her mother. She just couldn't.

"One hour," she said firmly, moving the last few steps to Tomasso. "We'll rest for an hour and then start walking again."

Tomasso grunted what might have been an agreement, and took her arm to urge her into the line of palm trees. He led her to one a good twelve feet into the jungle, brushed away the detritus on the sand beneath it to clear a spot for them, then urged her to sit. Settling next to her, Tomasso leaned back against the tree, and then slid an arm around her shoulders and drew her to rest against his chest.

Abigail didn't resist his actions, but she didn't relax either. It was impossible to relax in his arms. It just felt too good being there and she was too aware of the feel of his naked skin under her cheek and hand . . . and his scent. Tomasso smelled good. There was no cologne or perfumed shampoo to cover his natural aroma, but he still smelled lovely. Like wind and sea and sun. His skin was also a little cooler than her own where her hand and face rested . . . and as she'd suspected, his leafy loincloth hid everything from this angle, she noted with a little disappointment.

"You are not sleeping."

Abigail grimaced at the comment and then pulled back as much as his arm would allow to peer up at his face. "How did you end up in that cage?"

It was something she had wondered about as she'd worked on removing his duct tape, but with everything going on she'd never really got the chance to ask until now.

Tomasso tugged her back to his chest, holding her head against his shoulder with one hand, but then said, "My brother and I were shot with drugged darts as we left a bar in San Antonio, and woke up some time later naked in cages."

"They have your brother too?" Abigail jerked out of his arms to peer at him with dismay.

"They did," he said, and pressed her to his chest again. "He escaped."

"What?" Abigail asked with outrage, immediately upright again. "He escaped and just left you there? Your own brother?"

Tomasso didn't bother to force her back to his chest this time, but merely explained patiently, "He had to. Else he would have been recaptured and caged up again. One of us had to get free and contact . . . our people."

Abigail stared at him blankly. "Our people? Who are these people?"

"The reason we were in Texas," he responded and Abigail immediately scowled.

"Well, that tells me absolutely nothing," she said grimly. "Who—"

"An organization who were looking into the disappearance of several young . . . people who had gone missing from the bar scene in San Antonio," he explained carefully.

"Oh. So, like the Feds," Abigail said, relaxing back against him again. She was pretty sure it was the FBI who were called in on kidnappings and such. But . . . "You mean you guys weren't the first kidnap victims? Jet's clients took others?"

Tomasso nodded. "Several."

"That's awful," Abigail said with a frown as she considered it. Several young men like Tomasso locked up naked in cages and being shipped to Venezuela. It was probably some kind of sex ring, she thought as her fingers brushed over Tomasso's chest. Pretty, sexy young men like Tomasso with all his sex appeal and naked prettiness and sex.

Realizing she seemed to have sex on the mind any time she got close to Tomasso, Abigail gave her head a shake and sat up again. Once there was even that little distance from his body she was able to think more clearly and recalled the client saying something about someone called "the doc" and experiments. Maybe not a sex ring then, she realized.

"So you were working for the Feds, trying to catch these kidnappers, but got kidnapped yourself," Abigail reasoned out.

Tomasso hesitated and then said, "*Sì*. We volunteered."

She considered his words, wondering what they'd volunteered to do and suddenly thought she knew the answer. "You volunteered to be bait? To be kidnapped? Are you insane?"

"We did not expect to be kidnapped," Tomasso said calmly. "They had only taken individuals prior to this and we were two. We intended only to see what we could find out."

Abigail eyed him narrowly. She didn't think Tomasso was being wholly honest with her. She suspected he'd known there was a good possibility that they might be kidnapped, or at least that one of them might, and yet they'd volunteered for the job anyway. Letting it go, though, she said, "And it worked. You were both kidnapped."

"*Sì*."

"But your brother escaped," Abigail murmured.

"*Sì*, and according to you, I was being transported to Caracas. It must be where the others are," he added with a frown. "I must get that information to . . . the organization so that they can begin to search the city and—"

"Not Caracas," Abigail interrupted.

"What?" Tomasso asked.

"Your final destination wasn't Caracas," she explained.

"What?" he repeated with dismay. "But on the plane you said we were flying to Caracas."

"We were," Abigail assured him, and then explained, "But that guy who was duct taping your arm mentioned an island. He said . . . now what was it," she muttered, trying to recall. "I think he said, 'Enjoy the flight. It's the last one you'll take. Once you reach the island, you'll never leave.'" She paused briefly, trying to recall if she'd got it right and then shrugged helplessly and said, "Or something like that anyway. I know he mentioned an island and experiments and someone he called 'the doc' though, so Caracas wasn't your final destination. An island was. They probably had a boat waiting in Caracas or something."

"Or another plane," Tomasso muttered with a frown. "For all

we know, Caracas may only have been a halfway point and they were going to fly on to Brazil or Argentina."

"Maybe," Abigail allowed. "But I doubt it. The island is probably somewhere off the coast of Venezuela. Otherwise, why not just have Jet take them to Brazil or Argentina?"

"True," he murmured and looked a little relieved at this news. "So we need only look for an island they might take them to."

Abigail snorted at his words. "Only? Venezuela has something like 1,750 miles of coastline and maybe seventy-two islands." Noting the dismay on his face, she added quickly, "But the airport should help narrow it down."

"I do not understand," he began with a frown.

"Well, there are only two international airports in Venezuela— Simon Bolivar in Caracas and La Chinita in Maracaibo. As far as I know anyway," she added, because while she was good with geography and had researched some stuff with her mom to keep her spirits up, they hadn't focused terribly hard on Venezuela after reading about the whole kidnapping capital of the world bit. According to the information they had looked at, there were something like five kidnappings reported a day and most kidnappings weren't even reported. Apparently, they actually had an anti-kidnapping squad, for heaven's sake. What other country had that? Abigail and her mom had quickly lost interest in that country as her post-cancer-celebration trip destination so hadn't researched it as hard as some of the others.

"I do not understand what matter it is that there are two international airports," Tomasso said impatiently.

"Oh, right," Abigail said, recalled to their conversation. "Well, the island's likely closer to Caracas than Maracaibo, right? Otherwise they would have had Jet land at La Chinita."

"Ah, I see. Sì," Tomasso murmured. "So we should concentrate our search for the island on Venezuela's eastern coast."

"I would," she said with a shrug. "And the smaller islands too. I mean, this 'doc' could be on an inhabited island, but that bit about 'once on the island you'll never leave' kind of makes me think there can't be other people on the island that might aid in an escape."

"You're right." Tomasso smiled and gave her a quick crushing hug. "Thank you. You are brilliant."

Flushing, Abigail shook her head and barely restrained herself from saying, "Pshaw. It was nothing."

God, she was pathetic, Abigail thought suddenly. He gave her a compliment and she went all melted caramel inside. Boy, how low had her self-esteem dropped this last year? And why? She may have dropped out of medical school, but she'd done it to tend to her ailing mother, not because she hadn't been able to handle the classes. Abigail had loved medical school. She'd thrived there. She'd felt strong and smart and important. She was going to be a doctor.

Now, a year later she felt like a big fat lump of a loser. And she shouldn't, Abigail told herself firmly. She was just as smart as she'd been a year ago, and she *could* finish medical school. She might have to work her way through the last two years, but she could do that.

As for the fat lump part, so what if she'd added thirty pounds to her already generous weight? Her size didn't seem to bother Tomasso, why was she letting it bother her? She should be more concerned about her health. Not being able to manage more than an hour's walk before feeling like she was going to die probably wasn't good. It wasn't like they'd been walking fast.

Of course, it was harder to walk in sand than on a solid sur- face, Abigail acknowledged. And she was suffering a head trauma. She probably had a concussion too. And that would be hard on the body. Perhaps she should just cut herself some slack and stop being so critical of every little thing she did or didn't, and could or couldn't do. Tomasso may be Hercules with loads of strength and stamina, but she was not Wonder Woman, and that was okay.

"Come on," Abigail said suddenly, getting to her feet.

"Where are we going?" Tomasso asked with surprise, popping to his feet beside her.

"I've rested long enough. We can walk again," she announced, making her way out of the jungle and toward the beach.

"Are you sure?" Tomasso asked. "We did not rest long."

"I'm sure," Abigail answered without glancing back. "But this time I think we should walk along the shoreline. The firmer sand will make it less tiring. It feels good on bare feet too," she added, then paused and turned back to ask, "Which reminds me. What happened to my shoes?"

"Oh." Tomasso shrugged helplessly. "I am not sure. One was missing by the time we got to shore. You either lost the other in the air, or when that shark was nosing around us in the ocean."

"Shark!" she screeched with dismay.

"It was a small shark," he said soothingly. "But it did keep nipping at your feet so I had to punch it in the nose to make it go away. It probably pulled your shoe off."

When Abigail just stood gaping at him, Tomasso caught her hand in his and swung her toward the shoreline. "I will hold your hand this time so I know you are beside me and not dropping back. Every time I turned around you'd fallen behind earlier. I must remember you have shorter legs than mine, and therefore shorter steps, and adjust accordingly."

Abigail was quite sure that was babbling for Tomasso. He just didn't talk that much, but apparently felt the need now. She suspected it was an effort to soothe and distract her with words . . . from the fact that a shark had been *"nipping" at her feet.*

"Good Lord," she muttered, quite glad she'd been unconscious for that part of their adventure. Shaking her head, Abigail asked, "What did you do with my other shoe?"

"I took it off to examine your foot and make sure none of the punctures went through and had pierced your skin," he admitted with a grimace and then quickly added, "It hadn't. Both of your feet were unharmed by the shark."

"Jeez," Abigail muttered, peering down at her feet. She couldn't see them well in the dark, but hadn't noticed any injuries earlier when it was still light, so presumed her feet had escaped the shark's interest without injury as he said.

"Your shoe is probably still back lying by the palm tree where we rested," Tomasso announced, then paused to ask, "Shall I fetch it for you?"

Abigail goggled at the suggestion. Surely he wasn't offering to run all the way back to fetch one, now useless, shoe?

It seemed he was, she realized when Tomasso added, "It would not take me long. I can run very fast and you could rest here a little longer and wait for me."

"No," she said dryly, starting forward again. "I think I can do without the shoe."

Tomasso merely grunted and resumed walking too.

They continued in silence for several moments, and then Abigail decided conversation would help pass the time. Hoping it would also distract her from the tingles his holding her hand was sending up her arm, she asked, "What's your brother like?"

"Like me."

His short answer made her smile wryly, and she teased, "You mean, big, gorgeous, sexy and heroic?"

"You think me gorgeous and heroic?" Tomasso asked with interest.

"You left out the sexy part," Abigail pointed out with amusement.

He shrugged that away. "Of course you find me sexy. We are life mates. I am more interested in the gorgeous and heroic part."

Abigail stopped walking, forcing him to a halt. She stared at him with amazement for a minute, and then asked, "Life mates?"

Tomasso considered her briefly, his lips pursed, and then turned to continue walking, pulling her along with him as he said, "My question first."

She frowned, but supposed that was fair and took a moment to try to recall what his question had been. The life mates bit had pretty much knocked her for a loop. It was just so . . . Abigail didn't even know what to call it. It wasn't like calling her his girl-friend, which would have thrown her as well since they'd known each other for such a short period of time. But somehow the term *life mate* sounded more . . . important somehow. More official or something. She had no idea why.

"So?" Tomasso prompted.

Abigail made a face. "Right. Gorgeous and heroic."

"Si?"

"Well, you must know you are gorgeous," she said with exasperation. "You have an amazing body, and your face would be an artist's dream. It's almost too pretty for a man."

"Thank you," he said sincerely. "I find your body and face lovely too."

Abigail snorted at the claim. She didn't yet love her body so found it hard to believe he could.

"What does that snort mean?" Tomasso asked, pausing again to peer down at her. "You do not agree you are lovely?"

Abigail shrugged uncomfortably, but then decided what the hell, and admitted, "I'm too big. I wish I was slimmer for you. Like one of those swimsuit models. You know, perky breasts, a flat stomach, and slim hips."

"Boys have slim hips," he said firmly. "Women have curves. It is how it is meant to be."

"Yeah, but I have way too many curves," she argued at once.

"I like your curves," Tomasso assured her, moving closer. "And your breasts are perfect. Every time I look at them I want to peel your clothes off and hold and kiss them."

Abigail swallowed. His hands had moved to her waist and slid up her sides as he spoke. They now rested there, his thumbs lightly brushing the sides of her breasts. It was an innocent caress really, at least his thumbs were nowhere near her nipples or anything, but that light caress was still sending shivers down her spine. His words hadn't helped, of course. Now Abigail had that image in her mind, of his peeling her clothes away and—

"You are trembling," he said, his voice a husky growl. "And you are looking so . . ." Tomasso closed his eyes briefly and then opened them again and said, "You must stop looking at me like that, Abigail, or . . ."

"Or what?" she whispered, moving a little closer.

Tomasso hesitated and then shook his head slightly and frowned. "We should not do this. Not here. Not now."

He was probably right, Abigail acknowledged to herself. They should keep walking, should check on Jet and report in to Tomasso's people. But her body *was* trembling . . . with need for him. Still, she tried to fight it off, and eased back the step she'd taken forward with a little sigh. Trying to distract herself, she asked, "What is a life mate?"

Tomasso groaned as if she'd asked him to make love to her and growled, "A life mate is everything."

Abigail's eyes widened at that, and then his thumbs stopped sliding along the sides of her breasts as his hands shifted position. One slid around her back to urge her forward, while the other rose to cup the back of her head and tilt it as his mouth descended on hers.

Like every kiss she'd experienced from this man, this one was a powerhouse of passion and need. Honestly, Abigail didn't stand a chance of resisting him. Not that she wanted to really. Surely a few minutes' delay in their walk would not make so much difference, she told herself.

When his hands suddenly dropped to her waist to lift her up so he didn't have to bend so far, she didn't just wrap her arms around his shoulders, but her legs instinctively wrapped around his hips too to help him bear her weight. The action positioned her core right over his leafy loincloth, and Tomasso growled into her mouth as his hands shifted to cup her behind and press her more firmly against him.

Abigail gasped at the contact, and adjusted her legs so that she dropped a little lower, sliding along his shaft.

"*Dio!*" Tomasso gasped, breaking their kiss and dropping to his knees in the sand. "*Ti voglio.*"

Abigail didn't have a clue what that meant and didn't care. Grasping his head, she pulled his face back to kiss him again, this time thrusting her own tongue out to find his. Tomasso responded at once, kissing her back, his tongue dueling with hers.

She felt the cold wet sand on her back and then the cool breeze on her stomach as his hands pushed the material of her tank top up, and then that evening breeze was caressing her breasts and she broke their kiss to glance down and see that her blouse had fallen to the side, her tank top was now gathered under her chin, and To-masso had managed to tug her bra down to get at her breasts. They were now squeezed up and together by the neckline of the simple white cotton of her bra. Even as she noted that, Tomasso's head ducked and he closed his lips over one hard, rose-colored nipple.

"Ahhh!" Abigail cried, her head falling back onto the sand and her back arching upward as he drew gently on the already erect nub.

Tomasso's leg was between both of hers, his upper thigh press-ing firmly against her core, and Abigail twisted her head and moaned as he began to knead and squeeze her breasts while his mouth drifted from one to the other. Just when she didn't think she could stand it another moment, he abandoned her breasts and returned his mouth to hers, covering and devouring it in another passionate kiss that had her clinging to him with desperate need.

Shifting her hips to ride his leg, Abigail broke their kiss and turned her head to the side to gasp, "Please, Tomasso."

"Sì, bella," he muttered, kissing his way to her throat as his hands left her breasts to slide down across her stomach. She felt her jeans suddenly loosen, and then felt them being pushed down over her hips to just below her bottom, but that was as far as they went before his hand replaced them, dipping between her legs to explore what he'd revealed.

"Oh God!" Abigail cried, thrusting into his caress. She felt some-thing sharp scrape her throat, and then Tomasso's weight was gone.

Blinking her eyes open with confusion, she saw that he'd shifted up to kneel over her. His hand was still between her legs though, still dancing over her damp skin, but now he was watch-ing her through hooded eyes, his mouth tight as he pleasured her.

"Tomasso?" she gasped uncertainly, her hips still dancing to the tune he was strumming.

"Enjoy it, bella. You are so beautiful. I want to watch you find your pleasure."

They were pretty words, but Abigail was suddenly terribly aware that she was lying there with her tank top under her neck, her breasts poking out of the top of her bra and her pants around her ass. She was almost completely on display, every love handle, any cellulite, even her muffin top, which could better be described as a cake top. He could see all of it.

No, no, no, no! Her mind screamed and Abigail's hips immediately stopped moving, her hands started dancing around trying to hide everything he was looking at. She just didn't have enough hands for that task, or big enough ones, or—

"Abigail, stop. You are beautiful," Tomasso growled, and caught one of her hands with his free one. Dragging it down her body, he placed it around his erection under his leafy loincloth. "Feel how beautiful I find you."

Eyes wide, Abigail stared up at him as she felt just how beautiful he found her. Damn, if one was to judge by how hard and large he'd grown, she was Aphrodite in his eyes. The man must be blind, she decided and–grateful for that blindness—she tightened her hold on him and let her hand slide his length.

Tomasso cried out, his hips bucking under the caress, but strangely enough, so did Abigail as a new shaft of pleasure shot through her as well. Eyes wide, she tried the action again and got the same result. A sharp, keen shaft of pleasure pulsed through her as if he had caressed her, yet his hand had suddenly gone still.

"No. *Dio. Smettila, mi stai uccidendo*," he growled, catching her hand and trying to stop her.

Abigail had no idea what he'd just said, but had no intention of stopping now. Instead, she clasped him more firmly and began to move her hand in a continuous pumping action. Within seconds she was squirming in the sand under the assault of wave after building wave of excitement and pleasure.

God, this was—Her thoughts died on a startled cry and she arched so hard Abigail was surprised she didn't break her back as Tomasso didn't just begin to caress her again, but slid one finger inside of her, hard, filling the aching emptiness. Stars burst behind her closed eyes and her cry became a long drawn-out scream as pleasure exploded over her. Her voice only died when unconsciousness crept in to claim her.

Six

Abigail was the first to wake up. Hot morning sunlight was beating down on her face and blinding her when she first opened her eyes. She threw her arm sleepily over her eyes to protect them, and then just lay still for a minute as she became aware of the sensations she was experiencing.

Warm water was lapping at her right arm and hip. The sand under her was hard and cool, something prickly was tickling the skin of her upper leg, and something heavy was lying on her lower stomach and legs keeping her warm. Abigail was also thirsty as all get-out. Crazy thirsty. She had some serious cottonmouth and could have used a toothbrush followed by a large glass of water right then. She'd follow that up with a buttermilk biscuit, sweet cream waffles, and a side of applewood-smoked bacon, Abigail thought, her mouth watering at the imagined meal. But then memory returned and she knew she'd be making do with coconuts and coconut water. It wasn't like there was a handy restaurant anywhere nearby.

Dragging the arm from her eyes, Abigail opened them cautiously and looked up at the sky. The sun was high overhead. So much for their hour break. By her guess they'd slept more than eight hours. It looked like it was close to noon. Recalling her watch, she lifted her arm again and surveyed the time. Yep. Eleven thirty A.M. Not only had they slept through the rest of the night, they'd slept away the morning as well. She was a pathetic excuse for a friend. The only bright spot was that Tomasso apparently was too, she thought, and lifted her head to peer down her body at him.

The view afforded to her from this angle was not a pretty one. It wasn't Tomasso. He was always gorgeous, and even from this angle the top of his head and his wide shoulders looked sexy as hell to her. It was herself that was less than inspiring. She was as pale as the belly of a dead fish, and all of her lumps and bumps were depressing. Even her breasts, which she normally thought were okay, just did not win any prizes squeezed out of the top of her bra as they were. They looked like popping eyeballs in a cartoon.

Grimacing, Abigail quickly pushed her boobs back into the bra and straightened it the best she could. She then tugged her tank top down to just above Tomasso's head. There was nothing she could do about her jeans being around her ass, though, at least not as long as Tomasso was lying on her. The problem was, if she woke him up, he'd sit up and see her lying there with her va-jay-jay on display. *Can we say awkward?*

Really? some corner of Abigail's mind asked with derision. *Playing the modesty card now? After what had gone down last night?*

Deciding that corner of her mind was a bitch, Abigail considered her situation and how to get out of it. Maybe she could just slide out from under him. If she did it slowly, he might not wake up. Right?

Grimacing now, Abigail braced her hands in the sand on either side of her, one resting on wet sand, one sinking into dry, and then tried to worm herself to the side. All she did was kind of roll her hips a bit, and Tomasso immediately murmured sleepily, smacked his lips as if he was dreaming of pancakes, and then turned and lowered his head so that his mouth was practically kissing her between the legs. The only good thing was she now knew what had been so prickly against her upper leg, Tomasso's now ten-o'clock shadow. It was now prickly against her inner thigh.

Oh, yeah. This wasn't going to be awkward at all, Abigail thought sarcastically and wondered what the deal was with this passing out after sex business? Not that they'd actually had sex, she reminded herself. They'd mostly just fooled around a bit.

Abigail smiled wryly at the term. It didn't seem to cover the earth-shattering experience she'd had. Neither did groping, touching, fondling, or stroking. That may have been what went on, but . . . *wow*! A little fondling from Tomasso was like a full-on orgy with anyone else. Gawd! She was still wet this morning. Although, to be fair, she *was* lying half in the surf which might be part of it, Abigail thought. Certainly her jeans were soaking wet from absorbing the water.

But last night, when Abigail's orgasm had crashed over her, fireworks had exploded behind her eyes. The man had some powerful mojo, and if that's what some heavy petting with him was like, she couldn't wait to experience the full meal deal with him.

Just not right now, Abigail thought with a frown. Right now she was becoming aware of a rather urgent need to relieve herself, which meant she had to get out from under Tomasso, get up, and find a private spot to tend to the matter.

Her gaze slid with longing to the jungle at the top of the beach, and then back to the top of Tomasso's head. Her last move had made him shift his head off of her stomach and between her legs. That was something anyway, Abigail thought and sat up slowly. Once upright, she let out a little huff of relief. She hadn't disturbed him. Yet.

Grimacing, Abigail considered their positions, then slid one hand under his cheek and began to ease his face up and away from her groin. She'd lifted it perhaps an inch and had just started to try to shift it to the side and off of her when his eyes suddenly snapped open. Abigail froze at once and offered him a weak smile.

"I need to get up," she explained with embarrassment.

One eyebrow lifted on his forehead. Actually, both might have, but she could only see one at that point, and then Tomasso rolled away from her and launched himself to his feet.

Letting out the breath she'd been holding, Abigail immediately started to try to get to her own feet. It was surprisingly hard to do with your jeans around your upper thighs and she was struggling with it a bit when Tomasso bent and simply grasped her by the waist and lifted her to her feet.

"Thank you, I—" Abigail bit off her own words and grimaced with embarrassment. Not satisfied with helping her up, Tomasso had bent to pull first her panties and then her jeans up for her. He then even did up the fly and button of her jeans as if she were a child. When he finished with the task, he started to straighten, and then paused half upright to press a kiss to her forehead.

"You look *bella*," he complimented as he straightened.

Abigail smiled weakly at the comment, suspecting the man was just being kind, then moved past him toward the jungle. "I need to go."

Apparently Tomasso understood what that meant. At least he didn't ask questions, but simply let her slip away to find a private spot.

TOMASSO FOLLOWED ABIGAIL up the beach to the edge of the trees. He paused as soon as he reached the shade though. He didn't want to intrude on her privacy; he'd just needed to get out of the sun. Leaning against the trunk of a large palm tree, he stared out at the ocean, absently rubbing his stomach with one hand.

He felt horrible this morning, worse even than the day before. Unfortunately, he knew exactly why and there was little he could do about it. Tomasso needed blood. Yesterday he'd been suffering mild stomach cramps with the need. Today those cramps had multiplied in strength and spread out. Every organ in his body was being attacked as the nanos that gave him his strength and speed searched for blood to support themselves.

As idyllic as this little *aventura* with Abigail had been, and it had been delightful at times, Tomasso needed to get to civilization and a blood source. It was that or he might soon lose control and attack Abigail. He didn't want that. He'd already come too close to doing so last night while he'd made love to her. It was after she'd broken their kiss to cry his name with such need. Eager to fill that need, Tomasso had been kissing her neck as he undid and pushed her jeans down. With his nose against her throat, the scent of her blood had been easily detectable through her skin, and he'd felt its pulse against his lips and tongue. Tomasso's fangs had immediately slid out and scraped across her skin. Just as he was about to unthinkingly plunge them into her throat, he'd realized what he was doing and had abruptly sat up and shifted to his knees to get his fangs as far away from her throat as he could. After that, he'd allowed himself only to caress her. There had been no more kissing, no more licking and he'd refused to risk making love to her as he wished for fear he might inadvertently bite her in his excitement if he got near her throat again.

Fortunately, Abigail hadn't seemed to mind. At least not after the first moment or two of surprise. But once he'd placed her hand on the proof of how much her body pleased him, she'd seemed to be fine with this new turn.

Tomasso felt his cock harden at the memory of her firm, silky hand sliding over it and smiled wryly to himself. It was a state he knew he might as well get used to. As his life mate, Abigail would always have that effect on him. Touching her, tasting her, making love to her . . . hell, just thinking about her and looking at her would quickly produce this reaction in him. He'd definitely met his life mate.

Now he just had to hold on to her, Tomasso thought wryly, and suspected losing control and attacking her would not be likely to aid in that endeavor.

Sighing, he pushed away from the tree and headed for the water. It wasn't good for him to be out in the sun. That would just increase his need for blood, and raise the chances of his losing control, but he needed to cool off and think. He had to get them to civilization quickly, and this walking business was not proving to be much of a success so far.

It wasn't Abigail's fault. True, she'd tired quickly last night, but after a brief rest she'd been game to continue walking. It had been his inability to keep his hands off of her that had brought a halt to the walk in the end.

Perhaps he should tie a vine tightly around his penis, he thought. That way any kind of erection would cause him enough agony to kill his excitement. The idea had merit. At least, it was worth a try. Actually, just the threat of that kind of pain might be enough to make him avoid contact with Abigail, Tomasso decided as he dove into the water and began to swim.

"SO YOU DROPPED out of medical school to look after your mother."

Abigail glanced to Tomasso at that comment. It wasn't a question, more a murmured statement, but she nodded anyway.

"I imagine that was hard," he said solemnly.

"Which part?" she asked wryly. "Dropping out of school was pretty bad. But watching my mom fade away like that . . . ?" She shook her head wearily. "No one should suffer like that. And no child should have to witness it."

"I'm sorry," Tomasso murmured and caught her hand briefly in his to give it a squeeze.

Abigail glanced to him with surprise at the show of affection. She supposed she shouldn't be surprised. He'd held her hand as they'd walked the night before, and done a lot more than that in the sand afterward, but that had been yesterday. Today—

Tomasso released her hand as if her touch had scalded him, and Abigail had to bite back a sigh as she finished the thought— today, Tomasso had seemed to be going out of his way to avoid any contact with her at all. At least he had after she'd gone off to find her private spot. When she'd first woken up, he'd helped her up, pulled her pants up and even done them up for her, but that was the last time he'd touched her.

Abigail had returned from her brief excursion into the jungle to find him swimming and had decided it was a good idea. But the moment she'd stripped down to her bra and panties and started into the water, he'd got out and said he was going in search of a piece of wood he could use as a spear. This was the same man who had chastised her the day before about swimming alone. Suddenly, her swimming alone was apparently okay.

Abigail had finished her dip quickly and got out of the water, intending to let her bra and panties dry before pulling on her jeans and tank top again. Letting the heavier clothes dry from sleeping in the surf had seemed a good idea too, but Tomasso had insisted he thought she should dress right away. Her clothes would dry on her, he'd said, and it was better to be prepared for anything. So she'd pulled on the damp clothes.

Instead of a spear, Tomasso had returned from his sojourn into the jungle with half a dozen coconuts. She'd supposed he hadn't been able to find anything to use as a spear. They'd had to make do with the coconuts for breakfast. She hadn't minded. Fish would have been nice too, but she liked coconut. Besides, when you were hungry and thirsty enough, coconut water and coconut fruit were like manna. However, Tomasso had urged her to eat quickly so they could get on their way. Abigail had been a little surprised at that, since he'd thought traveling at night was better the day before, but she hadn't said anything, merely drank and ate quickly and stood up to join him when he said it was time to leave.

Now they were walking along the edge of the jungle, slogging through sand, but in the shade and they'd been talking the whole while. Well, truthfully, Tomasso had been asking short questions, and Abigail had been answering, telling him about her life. He hadn't done much talking at all. He'd listened, grim-faced and pale, and she was beginning to worry that he might be coming down with something serious.

"Your father?" Tomasso said suddenly.

Abigail glanced his way, noting anew that his skin was really, really pale, and that the strained look to his face had intensified. It looked almost as if he were in pain, she thought with a frown.

"You never mention him," Tomasso added, when she didn't respond right away.

"Oh. He wasn't a part of my life," Abigail muttered, then asked with concern, "Are you all right?"

"Fine," Tomasso said shortly. "Why was he not a part of your life?"

She hesitated, quite sure this new testiness was a sign that Tomasso wasn't fine at all, but finally explained, "He was Mom's high school sweetheart who got her pregnant, then wanted her to get an abortion. She refused. She wanted to have me so he dumped her, took off to college and followed that up with moving to California, never to be seen or heard from again."

"Never?" he asked, sounding shocked at the thought.

Abigail hesitated, but then admitted. "I got a card from him when Mom died. His family in our hometown had heard of her death and had given him the news. Apparently they also told him I was in medical school, which was erroneous since I wasn't in medical school anymore," she said bitterly, and then added, "He wanted to come to her funeral and meet me."

"And?" Tomasso asked.

"And I told him he wasn't welcome," she admitted. Pursing her lips, Abigail explained, "To me he's just a stranger who happened to donate sperm to my existence. He's never been a part of my life, and I have no interest in his being a part of it now. Besides," she added with a grimace, "Mom would have rolled in her grave at the thought of his attending her funeral after ignoring us all these years. She never said it, but I know raising me on her own without emotional or monetary help was hard."

Shrugging, Abigail added, "He just didn't deserve to be there, and her funeral was hard enough on me without adding him into the mix. I didn't want to have to deal with that on top of everything else."

"I can imagine," Tomasso said quietly.

Abigail fell silent, wondering why she'd told Tomasso about that when she hadn't told anyone else. Not even Jet knew that her father had contacted her, and she usually told him everything in her letters. But this she'd held back. Strange, she thought, and then decided they needed to change the subject and glanced to him to ask, "Your accent is thick, you were obviously raised in Italy. How old were you when you moved to America?"

"I do not."

Abigail blinked. "You do not what?"

"Live in America," he explained. "My home is still in Italy."

"It is?" she asked with amazement.

"Sì."

"Oh." Abigail turned her gaze down to her feet, wondering what that meant. He'd said he'd been taken from a bar in San Antonio and she'd just assumed that he lived there now, but if he still lived in Italy . . . Had he only been in San Antonio because of the kidnappers?

"I visit family in California, New York, and Toronto on occasion, though," Tomasso added now.

She couldn't help but notice that San Antonio wasn't mentioned as someplace he visited. He must have been in the city because of the kidnappers then, she thought. But—

"Wait a minute," she said suddenly. "If you live in Italy, how did you get involved in this kidnapping thing?"

"My brother and I volunteered to help," he said.

"Yeah, I know. You told me that," Abigail pointed out. "But how? Why fly all the way from Italy and—"

"We were in Canada," Tomasso interrupted.

"Okay," she drawled in dry tones. "Why fly all the way from Canada then? How did you even hear about kidnappings happening in Texas all the way up in Canada?"

Tomasso frowned briefly, and then muttered, "It is complicated."

"Yeah, I'll say. Feds don't usually involve outsiders in their cases," she said. "At least I don't think they do, and—oh!" Abigail gasped with surprise as she tripped over a large palm stem on the beach and nearly tumbled to the ground.

Fortunately, Tomasso immediately caught her arm and drew her against his chest to save her from falling. She went still as she came to rest against him, and so did he, but Abigail could hear his heart thumping under her ear and it was racing as if they'd been running.

Raising her head, she peered uncertainly up at him, saw his head lowering toward her and closed her eyes as his mouth descended on hers. It was like the sunlight after a long winter, or a cool breeze on a boiling day. He'd been so distant with her all day that Abigail hadn't known what to do or think. She'd worried she'd done something wrong, or that she'd unintentionally said something to offend him. Or perhaps she'd been too easy, turned him off with how quickly she'd given in to him, and how far she'd let him go so soon after meeting.

Abigail had racked her brain trying to figure out what had happened to change things, so this return to their earlier passion was more than a relief. He still wanted her. And she knew he did want her. She could feel the proof of it pressing against her stomach and couldn't resist brushing her hand lightly over the leafy loincloth barely covering that proof.

Her touch brought a growl from Tomasso's mouth that reverberated through her own, and then he suddenly picked her up and carried her to the nearest palm tree.

Abigail felt the trunk press against her back, and then blinked her eyes open when he suddenly pulled back slightly. Holding her in place with his lower body pressed to hers, he began to tug at her tank top, dragging it up her body and out of the way. She raised her arms then to allow him to remove it completely and it soon went flying to the sand. Her bra quickly followed. Tomasso immediately bent his head to claim what he'd revealed, running his mouth and tongue over the soft globes and suckling briefly at each nipple as he squeezed with his hands.

Continuing to knead the soft flesh, he then began to kiss a trail up to her neck and Abigail moaned and leaned her head back and to the side to give him better access. His mouth stopped, she felt something press against her skin and then he suddenly released her and jumped back like she was on fire. Without his weight to hold her up, Abigail immediately dropped to the jungle floor like a stone. It happened so fast she didn't even have the chance to get her feet beneath her, but landed on her butt in the sand.

"We should rest and eat."

Abigail blinked her eyes open in shock both from her fall and at that snarl. She was just in time to see Tomasso's bare ass disappearing into the trees. His hands were clenched, his back stiff. It looked to her like he was angry and she had no idea why. In fact, she had no idea what had just happened.

He'd kissed her. She'd responded. And then he'd jumped away from her like she was a leper. Had she been too responsive? Had she turned him off with her eagerness? Should she have played the maidenly virgin and given him a protest or two? What the hell was going on?

Yesterday he'd been all over her at every turn. Today he was Mr. Freeze, then he was all over her again, and then in the middle of it dropped her like a hot potato. *Really*, what was happening here?

Shaking her head, she got slowly to her feet and brushed the sand off her bottom. Fortunately, she hadn't been hurt when he'd dropped her, at least not physically. Emotionally, though, Abigail was confused and hurt and completely at sea. She didn't understand what had changed . . . except that they'd walked all day, so were a day closer to civilization.

Perhaps that was it, Abigail thought suddenly. They were a day closer to civilization. Another day or so and they should find people and habitation. At least she hoped they would. She certainly didn't want to be walking like this for days on end. One or two she could handle, but days or weeks? Man, she couldn't take that. Abigail needed clean clothes, real food, and a huge bubble bath to scrub all this sand and grit away. She also needed a good shampooing to wash this strawlike feel out of her hair. The outdoors were fine, but you could only eat coconut so many times before it began to get old.

Sighing, Abigail scowled into the trees. The truth was, she was lying her ass off. She'd loved the fish and coconut, and she would have continued to love them, and the beach, the sand, the water, the lack of amenities, and *everything*, if Tomasso weren't acting so distant. But it seemed the closer they got to civilization, the less interested he was in her.

That was exactly what she'd feared would happen from the beginning, Abigail thought unhappily. So much for all his hooey about her being his life mate, and life mate's meaning "everything."

Speaking of which, he'd never explained that nonsense, she thought with resentment. And nonsense was probably all it had been. A bunch of sweet words used to get into her pants. Not that he'd really got into them.

Well, okay, he had got into them, Abigail admitted, but they hadn't had sex. He'd probably been afraid she'd get pregnant or something. And she might have, Abigail realized with a grimace, so supposed she should be grateful that at least he had been thinking if she hadn't.

Turning to the water, she looked out over it through unhappy eyes. If Tomasso wanted to pretend what had happened between them hadn't happened . . . okay. She could do that. She'd give him the space he wanted and pretend she didn't want him to kiss her, touch her, and caress her. She'd pretend that she didn't care that he'd lost interest. And she'd pretend that it didn't hurt like crazy too.

"*IDIOTA. STUPIDO. IMBECILLE,*" Tomasso muttered, pounding his head against the trunk of a palm tree.

He couldn't believe he'd done that. He'd been so good all day, keeping his distance, resisting the desire to touch and kiss Abigail. Then she tripped over a stupid palm stem and the next thing he knew, he had her pressed up against a tree, his mouth at her throat and his fangs sliding out, aiming for her jugular. He'd damned near bit her. Again.

"*Animale,*" Tomasso muttered to himself with disgust. He had no control. He was no better than a wild beast right now. All he could think about, all the time, was sinking his aching cock into her warm, wet depths. But the moment he got near her throat, his fangs came out and he wanted to sink those into her too. He really needed blood. It was the only way he could make love to Abigail without feeding off of her too, and he was desperate to make love to Abigail.

Tomasso felt sure that if he spent a week or so just making love to her and sharing the life mate pleasure with her, he could tell her about himself and who and what he was and she wouldn't panic and rebuff him. At least that's what he was hoping. He was hoping to tie her to him with life mate sex so that she would accept the truth about him more easily. Or maybe overlook it to enjoy the incredible sex life mates had.

Abigail was a very sensual woman. He was sure she wouldn't be able to turn her back on him once she experienced the full breadth of pleasure they could have . . . no matter how horrified or disgusted she might be to learn what he was. Tomasso just needed to get them to civilization as quickly as possible to manage that. Of course, once he got them there he would have to make a few phone calls too, but that shouldn't take long. Then he could concentrate on her, on pleasuring her in every way imaginable and binding her to him with sex.

Breathing out slowly, Tomasso tugged his makeshift loincloth aside and examined himself. He hadn't tried the vine thing earlier when he'd thought of it. He'd decided to try just keeping his distance. Well . . . that hadn't worked out so well. It was time for more drastic measures. If his cock wouldn't behave, he'd tie it up. Although, to be frank, he wasn't sure that the added pain would really help. Certainly the agonizing cramps he was suffering with his need for blood didn't seem to be beating back his libido. But it was worth a try.

Letting the loincloth drop back into place, he turned to head further into the woods in search of vines that would serve the purpose.

SEVEN

Abigail reached into the shower to test the water and sighed with pleasure when she felt that it was warm enough. After these past several days of making do with dips in the ocean, it felt like forever since she'd been truly clean. She couldn't wait to soap up her body and shampoo her hair. She might even follow it with a lovely long bubble bath. Abigail loved bubble baths and would have started with that, but had worried that the water would be brown when she got out if she didn't shower away the past several days of grit and sand first.

Tugging her tank top off over her head, she tossed it aside, and then quickly removed her bra, jeans and panties before stepping under the hot spray and pulling the shower door closed behind her. At first, she just stood there, letting the warm water pound over her head and shoulders. Perhaps that's why she never heard the shower door open again, and wasn't aware of Tomasso until his chest pressed against her back.

Gasping in surprise, Abigail tried to turn, but his arms were already sliding around her waist from behind to hold her in place.

"I will wash your back," Tomasso growled by her ear, his hands gliding up toward her breasts, one of them dragging a bar of soap across her skin.

"That's not my back," Abigail gasped, squirming despite herself in his arms as he began to run the bar over first one breast and then the other.

"*Sì,*" he murmured.

"No," Abigail assured him on a moan, pressing back into him as the hand holding the bar dropped down across her stomach, leaving his other hand to massage the soap into the skin of her breasts.

"Tomasso," she gasped, rising up on her tiptoes as he dropped the bar and let his soapy fingers slide between her legs. "What are you—I don't understand. I thought you—"

"I know," he said apologetically, his deep voice soothing. "I promise I will explain. Later."

"Later," Abigail agreed on a groan, riding his hand. "Oh God."

"*Sì,*" Tomasso muttered, from between what sounded like clenched teeth and then he suddenly retrieved his hand and spun her under the water so that he could kiss her.

Abigail kissed him back eagerly, relieved that he was back to his old self again. She had no idea why he'd been acting so strangely the last days of their journey to find civilization, but he'd said he'd explain later, and she could wait. Especially when he was doing this to her, she thought vaguely as his hand slid between her legs again.

Eager to pleasure him as well, she reached down and closed her hand around the erection that had sprung up between them. But she'd barely managed to stroke him once, when he broke their kiss, caught her hand and growled, "*Dio,* Abigail, you make me so hungry for you."

In the next moment, he'd caught her by the back of the legs and lifted her up against the wall. He immediately moved forward then as he eased her back down, and she gasped as he filled her. It was the first time he'd actually been inside her, and Abigail moaned long and hard at the sensation as her body stretched to accept him.

"Tomasso," she cried, clinging to his shoulders as he began to raise and lower her.

"Oh God, Abigail," he ground out. "You are so tight."

"Yes," she panted, digging her nails into his back. "Please."

"You are killing me," he gasped in a strangled tone and then was suddenly gone.

Abigail woke with a start and stared with confusion at the crab sidling across the sand in front of her face. For a moment she was caught between sleep and waking and then her brain began to make sense of everything and she realized she'd been dreaming. She closed her eyes on a small moan. They had not yet reached civilization. There was no shower, no soap, no return of the passionate Tomasso. She was lying on the sand, under a palm tree in her filthy clothes, with the distant Tomasso sleeping somewhere behind her.

Sighing, she opened her eyes again and sat up to look around. By her guess it was mid-afternoon. Abigail didn't bother to check her watch this time, mostly because she didn't care what time it was. Time meant little until they did reach civilization, she thought, and glanced around for Tomasso. He was exactly where he'd been when she'd fallen asleep that morning, about twelve feet away with his back to her. This after passing out and sleeping on top of her twice or three times now. Apparently, he couldn't even bear to sleep close to her anymore. He'd chosen to bed down as far away as possible. That had hurt more than his distant behavior yesterday.

Mouth tightening, Abigail got to her feet and headed out of the trees to make her way down to the shore. They'd walked through the afternoon, evening, and night yesterday, not stopping until the sun had begun to crest the horizon. It had damned near killed Abigail to walk for so long, but she hadn't once complained, or asked to stop. The new, remote Tomasso made her so miserable, all she wanted in the world was to get to civilization and escape him.

Well, that and to find that Jet was safe and okay and not in the clutches of the kidnappers, she thought glumly. The truth was Abigail would give up her own peace of mind in a heartbeat in exchange for Jet's safety. But she'd rather have both.

Especially if she was going to start having sex dreams about Tomasso, she thought unhappily. Abigail didn't know what she would do if these dreams continued once he was out of her life. They were hot and awesome while they were occurring, but waking up to reality afterward . . .

Shaking her head, she glanced back toward the trees, wondering how long she would have to wait for Tomasso to wake up.

TOMASSO CONTINUED TO lie where he was long after Abigail slipped away. He had to wait until his erection fully deflated before even considering getting up, mostly because he didn't think he could do so without screaming. In truth, he was amazed he hadn't woken up screaming when the agony in his cock had dragged him from the dream. He had not been kidding when he'd said she was killing him. He'd simply been confusing the tightness of the vine around his cock in reality with her tightness in the dream.

Groaning, he closed his eyes and simply waited.

Wrapping a vine around his cock had seemed like a good idea when he'd had it. Unfortunately, Tomasso hadn't thought to remove it before lying down to sleep, which would have been good considering that another symptom of life mates was shared dreams.

To be fair, he hadn't experienced them with Abigail before last night, so hadn't thought of them as an issue. And that did make him wonder. Why hadn't they had the shared dreams before this? A couple of explanations came to mind. Perhaps he had, but because he hadn't woken up in the middle of them he simply hadn't recalled them when he did wake.

An alternate option was that since those other times they'd slept had been after passing out from the shared pleasure, perhaps they simply hadn't had them. Perhaps life mates didn't experience shared dreams when well pleasured.

He should ask someone about that, Tomasso decided. And he would, as soon as they reached civilization. But now he had to get up. His erection was gone, the tightness around his penis had eased, and the pain had receded a bit. Not completely. He suspected some damage had been done, which at this point meant that it would not heal until he'd fed and the nanos had blood to make repairs with.

However, since the rest of him was suffering agony due to a lack of blood, Tomasso supposed adding one more pain to the list was not a big deal. At least he thought that until he tried to move.

Oh yes, penis pain beat all the others hands down, he acknowledged miserably.

On the bright side, he could probably take the vine off now.

"TOMASSO, STOP!" ABIGAIL snapped, and caught his arm to force him to a halt when he continued his hobbling gait forward. "Stop. You need to rest or something."

"I am fine," he said through his teeth. "Really."

She snorted with disbelief. "Look at you. You can't even walk upright. And your legs are so far apart you could fit a bull in there. What the hell is—?"

"Abigail," he snapped, silencing her. "I will be fine as soon as we reach people."

She stared at him silently, her lips pursed. She'd thought he might be in pain yesterday. She'd even wondered once or twice if that might explain his distant behavior, but he'd assured her he was fine. He was still doing so, but now she wasn't buying it. The man was in obvious agony. He was sickly pale, sweating and walking with his legs as far apart as he could get them. The only thing she could think was that he had an infection of some sort, or maybe a boil in an embarrassing spot, like his upper thigh or maybe even on his balls.

Whatever it was, it was obviously causing him a great deal of discomfort that he was trying to muscle through and she wasn't having it. If it was an infection that had grown over the last couple days then it needed tending. Infections could get deadly in hot, humid jungle situations. He could develop jungle rot. If he didn't already have it.

"I want to see," Abigail said finally.

"No," Tomasso growled.

She narrowed her eyes. "I've had some medical training, Tomasso. Let me see. Maybe I can help."

"No. Is fine. I—" His words died on a curse as Abigail suddenly dropped to her knees and jerked his leafy loincloth aside.

"Dear God," she whispered, staring at his abused member. She'd thought a boil, or some other infection, but this . . . Abigail shook her head slowly. This was—"Was it a crab?"

"I do not have crabs," he growled indignantly.

Abigail glanced up to him with surprise. "I didn't mean *crabs*. I meant—" She glanced back to his penis and winced. "It looks like a big old crab crawled up while you were sleeping and clamped down on your penis with its claw a couple dozen times or more. I've never seen anything like it," she added with fascination, shifting her head from one side to the other to get a good look at the cuts and abrasions striping his skin.

Tomasso closed his eyes on a sigh. This was not the kind of fascination for his penis that he'd been hoping to elicit in Abigail.

"Well," she said now. "I'll have to put antiseptic on it."

Tomasso blinked his eyes open again and said wearily, "It is fine, Abigail."

"And antibacterial cream," she added ignoring him.

"Leave it," he almost begged.

"It should probably be bandaged as well to prevent further infection," she muttered, glancing around with a frown before asking, "What did we do with the first aid kit? Oh, there it is," Abigail answered herself as she noted it hanging from the strap of vines he'd fashioned and slung over his shoulder to save having to actually carry it.

Standing, she grabbed the vine strap and started to lift it off his shoulder, but he caught the strap before she could fully remove it. "Abigail, no."

"Stop being a baby," she scolded, tugging the vine free of his grip and kneeling to open the first aid kit. "This needs to be tended to. Do you want your penis to fall off?"

"I should be so lucky," Tomasso muttered. Right now he'd be happy for that to happen. At least the pain would ease then. He might actually be able to think again then too.

"Think of me as a doctor," Abigail suggested, selecting different tubes and swaths from the pack.

Tomasso stared down at the top of her head and raised an eyebrow. Doctor? Despite his throbbing penis, his thoughts ran more along the lines of *playing* doctor with this woman. It did not help that she was kneeling in front of him in the same position she would be in were she about to take his cock in her mouth.

Much to his amazement the thought was enough to stir interest in his poor penis and it began to swell, bringing on even more pain as the cuts and abrasions the vines had caused in his skin stretched and in some cases split open. Tomasso bit back a groan and closed his eyes.

"Wow, that's gotta hurt."

Abigail's mutter brought his eyes open again to see that she was visually examining his penis as it swelled. Fortunately, she was not touching him. Yet. The thought of her actually touching him made him swell further.

"Abigail, please," Tomasso groaned miserably. "Just leave it alone."

"No, I'm sorry," she said firmly, opening the antiseptic. "It has to be tended. You could develop a tropical ulcer, better known as jungle rot. It's called that for a reason, you know. Tropical ulcers can invade deep tissue, even bone. Your penis could literally fall off if this isn't—"

Abigail paused to give him an apologetic look as he gave a startled shriek of agony. She'd applied the antiseptic and to Tomasso, it felt like she'd poured liquid fire over his sore cock. He'd never experienced such pain. Nearly having his arm severed from his shoulder some years back did not compare to the agony her nursing caused.

"Yeah, that's really gotta hurt," she muttered and did it again.

SHE WAS PUNISHING HIM.

That thought drifted through Tomasso's mind and he opened his eyes to peer around the makeshift camp Abigail had created in the hours since she'd "tended" his injured penis. She'd scavenged several armfuls of palm fronds to make a sand free bed for him, and then insisted he lie on it, saying it would reduce the risk of sand getting into his wound. Tomasso had been too exhausted from the pain she'd caused in her "tending" his wound to argue and had dropped onto it. But it was the most uncomfortable damned bed he'd ever lain on. The leaves of the fronds weren't so bad, though the fronds tended to stick to his skin. It was the stems that made the "bed" unbearable. They were hard and at angles, poking into his skin.

Abigail had also wrapped a coconut in her jeans and blouse to make him a pillow, which was sweet, but even the jeans and top did not soften the hard shell of the coconut. She might as well have given him a rock.

Once she'd had him settled to her satisfaction, Abigail had scavenged up some coconuts that had fallen from the trees nearby and left them for him to drink and eat. Unfortunately, three of the four coconuts she'd found had cracked as they'd fallen from the trees and were infested with bugs. He'd had trouble opening the fourth coconut. It would have helped if he'd been allowed to get up and find a rock to bash the coconut on, but Abigail had shrieked at him twice when he'd tried to rise from the sickbed she'd made him.

The sweet angel who moaned and sighed in his arms was a harridan as a doctor, Tomasso decided. Giving up on the possibility of a rock, he'd made do with his own brute strength and made a mess of it, splashing the coconut water everywhere when he'd finally managed the task. More of the precious liquid had landed *on* him than he'd got *in* him and now he was uncomfortably sticky everywhere. He was also attracting ants.

While Tomasso had been busy with that, Abigail had actually fashioned a crude spear using the scissors from the first aid kit and a branch she'd scavenged while hunting up the coconut. She had also then caught a fish, and built a fire to cook it over. Tomasso had had to rub two pieces of wood together to make a fire when he'd built his. But Abigail had found waterproof matches in the first aid kit to help her with the task. She now sat on the sand at the edge of the jungle, in only her tank top and panties, burning that fish. He could smell that it was burning from way over here, but she was just sitting there letting it burn.

Definitely punishing him, Tomasso thought on a sigh and glanced down toward his penis, which was presently a white gauze-wrapped stump sticking out between his legs. This time it wasn't sticking out because it was erect. It was sticking out because Abigail had wrapped it in gauze, and then wrapped a metal roll-up splint around that, before finishing with another round of gauze. The splint was to protect it from being bumped, she said. What it did, however, was make it look like he had a whale penis. All right, it wasn't *that* bad. Whales' penises were eight feet long or something. So, horse penis was probably more correct. Whatever the case, it presently appeared to be twice the size it really was, and was extremely heavy.

Tomasso had no idea what he was supposed to do when he had to relieve himself. The idea of removing the gauze and splint, only to have her insist on replacing it, was not a happy one. And Tomasso was already a very unhappy camper. Not only was he in pain and uncomfortable, but her insistence that he lie here and recuperate was not getting him closer to relieving his discomfort and pain. All he needed was to feed and everything would be fine. The cramping in his body would stop, his penis would return to its normal, happy state, and Tomasso would be his usual, strong, pain-free self. But Abigail wouldn't even consider his suggestion that they keep walking. He was to rest today. Tomorrow they would continue on their journey if she judged him well enough to do so.

When he had given up suggesting and determinedly insisted that they forge ahead, Abigail had dropped on her ass in the sand and said *fine*. Then he should go on without her, because she was not moving. Tomasso could hardly leave her there in the middle of nowhere by herself, so he'd caved in to her demands. One day of rest and they would head out again. He just hoped that day of rest didn't leave him in an even worse state than he was presently in, although it was hard to imagine being any worse off than he was at the moment.

Grimacing, Tomasso glanced to Abigail again and couldn't help noting that while he was miserable, she appeared to be in her element. Tending to his wounds seemed to have boosted her spirits somehow. She had turned into this bossy little take-charge dynamo, bustling about and getting things done. She was born to be a doctor, he thought wryly, and decided once this was all over and everything was settled, he was going to make sure she finished medical school and became the doctor she was meant to be. He would see to that even if she didn't agree to be his life mate. She deserved it.

ABIGAIL'S CHIN FELL off the arm she'd rested on her upraised knees and she woke up with a start, frowning when she smelled the charred odor in the air. *Damn. The fish*, she thought and quickly removed it from the fire. She'd dozed off while cooking it and now it was a little overdone.

"Dammit," Abigail muttered, but then heaved a sigh and shrugged. It wasn't too bad, not black or anything, at least not everywhere. They'd just have to make do.

Heaving herself to her feet, she quickly kicked sand over her fire, dousing it. Abigail then carried the skewered fish to where Tomasso rested.

"Here we are. I'm afraid I nodded off and it got a little crispier than I would have liked. Just don't eat the black bits. The rest should be good," she said cheerfully, offering him the skewer.

Tomasso eyed the offering dubiously and then glanced to her to ask, "Are you not having any?"

"Actually, I'm not hungry. I am tired though, so I think I'm just going to nap," she said, stifling a yawn.

"You need to eat," he insisted as she settled on a clean bit of sand not far from him. "And you need liquid."

"Later," Abigail muttered, stifling another yawn as she dropped onto her side and curled sleepily into a ball. They hadn't been up that long but she was exhausted. Dead tired. She heard Tomasso saying something else, but it was just a "wah wah wah" in the background as she slipped into sleep.

TOMASSO STARED AT Abigail's back and frowned. He was quite sure she'd fallen asleep in the middle of his lecture that she needed food and sustenance to keep her strength up for their journey. It was probably that lack of food and liquid that was causing her exhaustion, he thought with irritation. She would feel better if she ate.

Tomasso glanced to the skewer he still held, and then held it aloft as he eased up to a sitting position. When he managed the task without terrible agony shooting from his groin, he released a sigh of relief and then proceeded to get to his feet. That wasn't as pain-free as just sitting up had been. The gauze and splint shifted with his next efforts and he sucked in a deep breath as pain shot through him. Truly, with the agony the rest of his body was in, he was surprised the pain in his groin was so troublesome. But the rest of the pains wracking his body were nothing compared to the penis pain. He even forgot about them when that pain struck.

It took some time, but Tomasso managed to get to his feet and make his way to Abigail in a sort of half duck walk that left his appendage unmolested. He was mightily relieved to be able to stop when he reached her side though.

"Abigail." Squatting beside her, he nudged her shoulder.

She mumbled sleepily, but didn't really stir.

Frowning, he nudged her again. "You need food."

Her response was an incomprehensible mumble, so Tomasso tried again, this time reaching to brush the hair off of her face. He paused though when he felt the heat radiating from her. Tomasso was no expert on mortals, but she seemed quite warm to him. Not dangerously so, but he suspected she had a low-grade fever.

"Abigail," he said with concern, trying to turn her over.

"Go away," she muttered, reaching out blindly to push him away, and smacking his mummy-wrapped penis.

Tomasso let out a stunned whimper, dropped the fish and fell back in the sand as agony shot through him. He lay there on his back for he didn't know how long, his legs bent and in the air and his hands on either side of—but not daring touch—his bandaged penis as stars exploded behind his tightly shut eyes. When the pain finally receded and he had the presence of mind to open his eyes and look around, Abigail hadn't stirred, the skewer of fish was half buried in the sand, and night had fallen.

Tomasso eased his feet carefully to the sand and when he completed the task without further pain, released a relieved sigh. He then closed his eyes again briefly, wondering when his life had gone so out of control? He'd thought his situation bad when he'd woken up to find himself naked in a cage and unable to escape. But waking up to find Abigail there, and realizing she was not only a good guy, trying to rescue him, but his life mate, had seemed to be a gift from God. How had it all gone so wrong?

The hum of an engine caught his ear as he was pondering this and Tomasso stiffened, and then turned his head to peer through the trees toward the ocean. His eyes narrowed as he saw a boat cruising slowly into view. Thoughts of Jake and Sully, the men who had put him in the cage, immediately came to mind, but there were four or five men on this boat, and most of them were carrying long thin sticks that he suspected were fishing rods.

The engine cut out suddenly as the boat paused almost directly in front of where Abigail had made their camp, and a burst of laughter floated across the water and sand to his ears.

A chartered fishing boat, Tomasso thought, his eyes scanning the occupants as they dropped their lines and settled in with beer and chatter. The long walk he'd subjected Abigail to through the afternoon and night before had definitely got them closer to civilization, and luck had brought civilization closer to them when these fishermen had chosen this spot to stop in. Things were looking up, he thought with relief, and rolled cautiously onto his side and then eased to his hands and knees to get up.

The white gauze wrapping at his groin was like a beacon when he made it to his feet. It stood out in the darkness. Tomasso tugged his makeshift loincloth around to cover it, and then moved cautiously out of the trees. Walking hurt like hell, but knowing it would soon be gone, Tomasso was able to ignore the pain as he crossed the sand and started into the water.

He expected the salt water to sting the abrasions on his damaged member, so was pleasantly surprised when the cool water was soothing rather than painful. Tomasso could only think the gauze was filtering out the salt and keeping it from getting to his wounds. Relieved by that, he struck out for the boat resting about a quarter mile out in the water.

They'd stopped over the reef to drop their lines, he guessed, and they were so busy laughing it up and drinking that no one even noticed his approach until he was pulling himself onboard.

"Whoa, hey! Look here, we got us Tarzan visiting," the first man to see him said on a laugh as he turned to notice Tomasso pushing himself to his feet after pulling himself over the side of the boat.

Tomasso didn't wait to see what the response of the others would be. He slipped into first one mind and then another, soothing and calming each in turn as he learned that they were Americans from Detroit on a fishing vacation in Punta Cana.

He now knew where they'd washed up after parachuting out of the plane, Tomasso thought with satisfaction. Near Punta Cana, on the tip of the Dominican Republic. A little more than an hour flight from Caracas. Although, as he continued to read minds, he began to suspect they'd actually come ashore just this side of a village called Boca de Yuma and that, had they walked the opposite way, they would have encountered civilization almost right away. Instead, they'd followed the shore away from the town and were now just an hour or so from another village called El Cabo. Punta Cana, where the fishermen were staying, was further north along the shore past it.

Tomasso grimaced at that, but continued to read minds and learned that, as he'd expected, this boat was a charter, and while the men had spent the last week deep-sea fishing, they'd decided to spend their last night "chilling with some near-shore tight-lining." He gathered that translated to dropping their lines in the water and getting drunk while they waited for fish to take the bait.

Having gained all the information he needed, Tomasso moved on to the other items on his list of necessities, which included clothing, food, transportation, and blood. Not in that order.

EIGHT

Abigail rolled onto her back and winced as she became aware of the mild headache throbbing behind her closed eyes. She raised a hand thinking to rub her forehead and hopefully ease the pain, only to blink her eyes open with surprise when something soft brushed her skin before her fingers could reach it.

It was a sheet covering her hand, she saw with amazement. Tugging her hand free of the silky cloth, Abigail sat up and looked around in confusion. She was in a bamboo canopy bed draped with netting in a room that was more windows than walls. What walls there were, were the same white as the ceiling where a bamboo fan turned lazily, moving the cool conditioned air around the room.

Letting her breath out on a little murmur of pleasure, Abigail tossed the soft sheets aside and slipped her feet to the floor. Cold tile met her warm skin, making her smile as she stood and moved to peer out the sliding glass doors. Her eyes moved with awe over tables, chairs, lounge chairs, and a large pool in a private courtyard surrounded by palm trees and flowering bushes.

"Yes, yes, yes," Abigail sang as she turned away from the terrace, eager to explore the rest of the place.

The next door she opened led into a large bathroom with a

big soaker tub, a huge shower, double sinks, and a toilet. It was the bathroom of her dreams, Abigail thought as she entered the room, and then she paused as that thought registered.

The bathroom of her dreams . . .

She was dreaming again, Abigail realized with disappointment. Of course she was. She'd fallen asleep on a beach. What were the chances of waking up here in a magnificent . . . whatever this was?

Zilch, she answered herself. She was as poor as a church mouse, for heaven's sake, and Tomasso had left the plane naked. Unless he'd had it up his butt, he hadn't been carrying money or credit cards or even ID. Even if he had, this place looked like a five-star resort. Abigail didn't think he could afford this kind of luxury any more than she could. No. Staying in a place like this was something she could only dream of.

Abigail looked from the bathtub to the shower and suddenly smiled widely. If this was a dream, she was going to make the most of it, she decided. She was going to enjoy herself before she really woke up back on the beach, hungry, thirsty, and wearing filthy clothes. That thought goading her on, she moved quickly to the tub, dropped the plug, and turned on both taps.

Leaving the water to fill up, Abigail then moved to examine the bottles lined up on the long sink counter. Finding the bubble bath, she snatched it up and dumped the entire small bottle into the slowly filling tub. She paused then to judge how quickly the water was filling. Deciding after a moment that she had the time, Abigail left the taps running and moved back to the counter to grab the bottles labeled shampoo and conditioner, then carried them to the shower with her.

If this were reality, Abigail would have been concerned that turning on the shower would affect the water running into the tub, but since it was a dream, she didn't worry about it. Besides, in a luxury hotel like this one, that probably wouldn't be an issue, right?

Within seconds of turning on the shower taps, the water pouring down to the tile floor was warm and tempting. Abigail reached for the hem of her tank top, intending to pull it off, only to find she wasn't wearing her tank top . . . or her jeans, her panties or her bra. She was completely naked already, and raised her eyebrows at the realization.

She'd been dressed in her last dream and had had to strip, Abigail recalled, but then shrugged. Being naked now in this dream saved her that effort. She stepped under the warm spray and pulled the door closed.

Abigail half expected Tomasso to appear again in her dream at that point as he had the last time. In fact, she'd kind of looked forward to having him there, his body pressing up against her and his hands on her eager skin. But when she'd finished washing her hair and a quick cleanup of her body a couple minutes later, there was still no Tomasso. It seemed this dream was more about being clean than sexual gratification.

Clean was good, Abigail supposed, turning off the taps and stepping out of the shower to cross to the tub. It probably meant she was getting self-conscious about going so long without a proper bath. Swimming in the ocean was nice, but she suspected the lack of drinking water plus the salt from the ocean were combining to dry out her skin. She'd been itchy the last day or so and had noted the beginnings of a rash as she was cooking the fish.

Her stomach rumbled as she stepped carefully into the tub and Abigail recalled that she'd been too tired to eat before lying down to have this dream. It was something she'd no doubt regret when she woke up with an empty, aching tummy. But maybe she could dream up a smorgasbord of all her favorite foods along with her longed-for bubble bath, she thought now. She didn't know how to do that. Maybe it would just happen naturally when she got out of the tub. Although, in a really good dream it would appear all around her now, she thought. Her favorite foods and a bubble bath sounded even better than a wet dream to her at that moment.

Of course, the best dream would have food, the bath, *and* Tomasso, Abigail thought wryly as she eased down to sit in the steaming water. God, the temperature was perfect, she decided on a small moan as the bubbles rose up to surround her until only her head from the nose up was above the white foam.

Smiling, Abigail reached out to turn off the taps, then leaned back in the tub. The bubbles immediately made way behind her and closed over her chest and shoulders in front. She'd just closed her eyes when she heard her name called in Tomasso's deep rumble.

Abigail blinked her eyes open again, but didn't sit up, even when the door opened and Tomasso glanced in. He paused at once on spotting her, his eyes widening, the silver flecks in his irises almost seeming to glow as he noted her position in the bubble bath.

"I was worried when you were not in bed," he said, his voice a soft growl.

Abigail looked him over slowly. He was still shirtless, but his long hair looked like it had benefited from a good shampoo and cream rinse. He was also clean-shaven now, the advancing stubble gone, which she didn't mind at all. He'd looked surprisingly good with it, but it had been prickly against her skin.

Sadly, his leafy loincloth was gone too, Abigail noted. It had been replaced with a pair of tight shorts he never could have worn in reality, at least not with the shape his penis had been in the last time she'd seen it. The real Tomasso would have been in agony in these shorts.

"I brought fruit," he said suddenly, opening the door wider to reveal the large plate he held in one hand. Strawberries, grapes, melon, and pineapple slices filled one side of the plate, while various cheeses and crackers filled the other side and Abigail sat up with interest as her stomach growled again.

Tomasso grinned at her eager expression and entered the room to bring the plate to her. "I ordered room service. But it will be a while. The fruit plate is to tide us over."

"Brilliant," Abigail murmured, reaching out to pluck a piece of cheese off the plate, only to pause before touching it when she saw the bubbles covering her hand.

"Allow me," Tomasso murmured. He picked up the cheese for her and delivered it to her lips.

Blushing, Abigail opened her mouth and he set it on her tongue. He watched her mouth as she chewed and the moment she swallowed, plucked a slice of strawberry off the plate to offer next. This time he didn't wait for her to open her mouth, but ran the juicy fruit across her bottom lip. He then leaned in to lick off the juice he'd just applied before straightening and placing the strawberry in her now gaping mouth.

When Abigail didn't close her mouth but simply stared at him wide-eyed, her mouth still hanging open, he pressed a finger to the bottom of her lower jaw, easing it shut for her.

"Chew," he instructed in a sexy growl, setting the plate on the marble tub surround at the foot of the tub and standing. "I will get the champagne."

"Champagne," Abigail breathed as she watched him slip from the room. She'd never had champagne. How was that going to work in her dream? Would she just dream it was the best thing she'd ever tasted? She supposed she was going to find out.

At least she was if she didn't suddenly wake from her dream again as she had last time, Abigail thought with a small frown and sincerely hoped that wouldn't happen. She was enjoying this. Food, a bubble bath, and Tomasso? Gad, she wouldn't be sorry to never wake up from this dream, she thought, and then glanced to Tomasso as he returned to the room carrying two champagne flutes of sparkling liquid.

After handing her one, he sat on the side of the tub with the other and smiled faintly when she wrinkled her nose as the champagne bubbles tickled it when she raised the flute to her lips. Once she'd taken a curious sip and smiled though, he plucked a grape from the plate and held it in front of her lips until she opened her mouth. He then placed it on her tongue. A slice of pineapple followed, but this he ran along her lips as he had the strawberry.

Abigail remained still as he did, and then closed her eyes and tilted her head eagerly up when he bent to lick the juice away again.

"Nice," Tomasso murmured against her lips. "But the strawberry was sweeter."

"You naked and in the tub with me would be sweeter still," she whispered brazenly back, and then opened her eyes to find he was gone. For one moment she thought it was like the first dream and she would suddenly wake up and open her eyes to the beach where she knew she was presently sleeping. But then Abigail realized Tomasso had just stood up and apparently stripped off his shorts superfast. Like Superman fast, she thought, because he was already naked and raising a foot to step into the tub at the other end.

Abigail had one hell of a view at this angle and her gaze slid over his already semierect penis with interest. Not only was he not bearing the slightly infected wounds he had in real life, but also there were no scabs or scars to suggest they'd ever been there. Dream Tomasso was perfect.

"It is a big tub," Tomasso commented as he settled across from her, his legs sliding along the sides outside of her own so that they rested on either side of her hips.

"Yes," Abigail agreed, suddenly shy. Apparently, even in dreams she was only so brazen.

"But you are too far away," he complained. "Come sit in front of me. I will feed you."

Abigail felt her face flush and knew it had nothing to do with the hot water. Neither did the sudden heat between her legs, she was sure, or her sudden shortness of breath.

"Come," Tomasso coaxed, taking the champagne glass from her with one hand. Catching her now free fingers with the other, he then tugged gently.

Abigail swallowed, but allowed him to pull her closer between his legs, then turned in the water so her back was to him. Before she could ease back closer herself though, he'd released her fingers and slid his hand around her waist to pull her back firmly against

his body. Her bottom slid up against his erection, trapping it between her bottom and his stomach, and her back pressed against
his chest. He then kept that hand at her waist, his fingers gliding
up and down over her stomach, dropping a little lower with each
pass. Just a little lower each time, not a lot.

"Your champagne," Tomasso murmured, distracting her from
what his other hand was doing as he reached around her shoulder
to offer her the champagne flute he'd held while she moved.

"Thank you," Abigail whispered. She accepted the glass, but
didn't drink from it. It tasted good, but the first sip had seemed
to irritate her throat. It had also increased the slight pounding in
her head that she'd noticed at the start of the dream and had been
trying to ignore. However, when his fingers appeared before her
lips with another offering, this time a grape, she did open her
mouth to accept that.

Tomasso didn't just drop it on her tongue this time as he had
the last time he'd fed her a grape. He placed it on her tongue. He
was also slow about removing his fingers so that when Abigail automatically started to close her mouth, her lips closed around the
lingering digits.

Eyes popping open with surprise, Abigail found herself staring
at their reflection in a mirror on the wall opposite. To say she was
shocked was something of an understatement. She hadn't even noticed the wall was mirrored before this, and seeing herself reflected
with Tomasso at her back, their naked bodies bathed in bubbles,
was just not a sight she'd expected to see . . . ever.

His entering the tub and her shifting to sit in front of him
had disturbed the bubbles, she noted. They were no longer all
the way up to her nose. Some had foamed over onto the marble
surround that ran around three sides of the tub, while still more
had slipped over the outer edge of the tub and were sliding toward
the tile floor. It left fewer bubbles actually in the bath and her bare
white shoulders down to just above her breasts were left on view
with the duskier olive skin of Tomasso's chest and wide shoulders
behind her. It held Abigail fascinated for a moment and then she

shifted her gaze to meet Tomasso's in the mirror, and found her attention caught by the way the silver flecks in his irises seemed to be growing to overwhelm the dark main color.

Once her eyes locked with his, Tomasso began to slowly retrieve his fingers from her mouth. Abigail had no idea what instinct made her suck on his withdrawing digits, but she did, and was shocked when the action sent a shaft of excitement tingling through her body. Her eyes widened incredulously, while Tomasso's closed briefly, and then he groaned and lowered his head so that his mouth was by her ear.

"Ah, *Dio*, Abigail, you ruin me." His voice was a deep rumble, his breath teasing the sensitive skin under her ear, and then he nipped at the lobe dangling there and lamented, "I had such plans."

"Plans?" she asked weakly. Her head automatically tilted as he nibbled his way down her throat, but her eyes remained open, watching their reflection. When the hand at her stomach suddenly glided up to cover one breast, she saw as well as felt it, and her body's response seemed to be twofold.

His own eyes were suddenly on the mirror, watching his fingers pluck and knead her flesh, and then he murmured, "The things I was going to do to you."

"What things?" Abigail asked breathlessly, her bottom pressing back against him and her back arching as his other hand claimed her untouched breast. Abigail groaned as she watched his hands toy with her body. He squeezed and kneaded, then plucked at the nipples, pinching gently, before covering and squeezing them again. It was so damned erotic to actually see what he was doing. Although the bubbles probably helped with that. They hid some of the features she was less pleased with, leaving only the better bits on view.

Rather than answer her question, Tomasso gave up playing with one breast to move that hand to her chin. He caught it between thumb and forefinger and turned her head gently, tilting it both up and back so that his mouth could descend on hers. The hand still on her breast tightened almost painfully then, and Abigail groaned into his mouth, her body half turning toward him in the water as she kissed him eagerly back.

When Abigail felt the cold splash of liquid down her shoulder and chest, she gasped in surprise. She wasn't sure what it was until Tomasso broke their kiss and she was able to glance around. Much to her surprise, she was still holding her champagne glass. She'd forgotten all about it until now, and apparently had let it tip, spilling its contents down over herself.

"Perfetto," Tomasso muttered and Abigail suddenly found herself lifted and turned in the water so that he could lap up the spilled liquid. He caught a droplet just as it slipped off her nipple, paused to suck the rosy bud briefly between his lips, then released it to follow the trail of champagne up the slope of her breast to her clavicle. When he reached the shoulder, Tomasso lifted his head to claim her lips as he set her down straddling him in the water.

Abigail groaned into his mouth as she slid along his erection. She was vaguely aware of his taking the champagne glass from her trembling fingers. Once free of the need to hold it, she immediately slid her fingers into Tomasso's hair, clutching at the silky strands as she kissed him back.

Her hips were now moving of their own accord, sliding her back and forth over the hard shaft trapped under her as they kissed. The action was ratcheting up her excitement by leaps and bounds instead of just the leaps she'd expected, but before Abigail could make herself too crazy with the action, Tomasso plucked her up out of the water. Just as Abigail blinked her eyes open, Tomasso stopped raising her. He'd lifted her until her breasts were directly in front of his face and now closed his mouth over one nipple and began to suckle earnestly.

It brought on an almost pleasure/pain and Abigail cried out, clutched at his shoulders and squeezed her eyes closed in response. She felt him move in the water, but was still startled when she was set down on something cold.

Opening her eyes she saw that he'd set her on the marble surround along the back of the tub. She couldn't see their reflection from there, and was glad of that now that she no longer had bubbles to hide her. But she had no idea why she was sitting there. Abigail glanced to Tomasso with confusion just as he finished situating himself in front of where he'd set her. Even as she looked to him, he slid his hands along the inside of her upper legs to grasp her thighs, pushed her legs wide open on the edge of the tub and buried his face between them.

A scream slipped from Abigail's throat as his tongue lashed her heated flesh. That first one was partially surprise, but the cries and broken screams that followed were wholly a response to what Tomasso was doing as his lips, teeth and tongue suckled, grazed, and laved her eager flesh. Abigail plunged her hands into his hair and held on for dear life as he drove her mad, taking her to the brink and then backing down only to push her to the edge again. Her hands pulled at his hair, and then tried to push his head away in turn and her back was pressing so hard into the wall behind her, she almost feared pushing through it. She tried several times to close her legs to end the torment, but Tomasso held her firmly in place.

Just when Abigail was afraid she'd have a heart attack or something if he didn't stop, Tomasso lifted his head and dragged her off the side of the tub to straddle his lap again. This time he was on his knees, his erection half out of the water, and this time he didn't set her down so that his erection was trapped between them. Tomasso lowered her directly over the tip, held her there briefly, and then eased her down until her bottom slapped the top of his legs. He held her there too for a moment, then lifted and lowered her again.

That was all it took. Abigail heard Tomasso's shout before her own could make its way out of her throat. She opened her eyes to look at him just as her own voice pierced the air, and then felt the darkness claim her.

TOMASSO WOKE UP crumpled in the bottom of the tub, with Abigail's foot in his face. He stared at her cute little toes briefly, thinking it was good he'd thought to push the button to let the water out of the tub near the end of their passionate encounter, and then lifted his head to try to get an idea of just what position they were in.

The last thing Tomasso recalled was kneeling with Abigail on his lap in the receding water. Apparently he'd fallen back and then slid to the side, unfolding his legs as he went so that he lay on his back in the bottom of the tub. Abigail had seemingly done the same. She was still on his lap, sort of, but her upper body had fallen so that her back was on his legs and her own limbs were stretched out, her feet on either side of his head.

It was like a case of that Twister game gone bad, Tomasso thought, recalling the time his cousin Zanipolo had once convinced them to play. He'd thought it a stupid game at the time, but then who wanted to be twisted around his brother and three other male relatives while Zanipolo called out colors and body parts? Now, playing with Abigail might be more interesting, he thought with a sudden smile.

Storing that possibility away in his mind for later, Tomasso turned his attention to disentangling himself from Abigail and getting them both out of the tub. It wasn't as difficult as he'd feared in the end, and he even managed it without waking her, which he thought was an amazing feat. Until he stood up next to the tub, bent down to scoop her up and felt the heat radiating off of her.

Straightening, Tomasso tightened his arms around her and peered down at her pale face with concern. He'd thought she'd felt a bit warm that last evening on the beach, and her not waking when he'd gone to collect her to take her to the boat for the trip here had worried him. But when he'd returned from using the office phone to call the Rogue Hunter house, she'd been up, in the tub and apparently fine.

Frowning, he turned to carry her out to the bedroom and lay her in the canopy bed. Tomasso then placed the back of his hand against her forehead.

Abigail definitely felt feverish. He was beginning to think it hadn't been his efforts to be careful that had prevented her waking as he'd shifted her off him and then carried her in here. She was sick. He needed to get her a doctor.

Bending, Tomasso tugged up the sheets and duvet to cover her, and then moved around the bed to the phone on the bedside table. After a quick glance at the labels to the left of the number buttons, he punched in the one for the main desk and waited . . . and waited. Scowling, he hung up, and then tried again. When he got the same results, Tomasso set the phone back with a curse and ran a frustrated hand through his hair as he took in Abigail's pale face. Then he turned to rush out of the room.

He'd go to the reception area and talk to someone himself. He'd probably get a doctor here faster that way anyway.

ABIGAIL WOKE UP in the canopied bed again. And again, she was alone. She was just starting to think she was going to get to enjoy an instant replay of her last dream, when her stomach lurched rebelliously and tried to crawl up her throat. Slapping her hand over her mouth, Abigail stumbled out of bed and hurried for the bathroom. The floor wobbled alarmingly as she went, but didn't prevent her making it to the toilet in time.

What followed was a most unpleasant several hours or so. At least it felt like that much time passed, but it probably only took a couple of minutes for her to toss up the meager contents of her stomach. That was followed by another ten minutes or so of dry heaves.

Once her stomach muscles stopped their violent contractions, Abigail sagged against the toilet with a moan, and rested the side of her face on her arm on the toilet seat.

She felt like hell. She was burning up, but shivering with chills. She was nauseous, her head was pounding, there was a terrible pain behind her eyes, and every joint in her body ached. Abigail hadn't felt this bad since . . . Actually, she couldn't recall the last time she'd felt this bad.

Abigail considered it briefly, but then shook her head. Nope, she'd had the flu several times, suffered colds, even appendicitis, but Abigail was pretty sure she'd never felt this sick in her life. And she was also sure that this time she wasn't dreaming. The pain was too intense, the taste of vomit in her mouth too realistic, and her teeth were beginning to chatter. She was awake and sick as a dog.

Oddly enough that didn't really bother her as much as the fact that she was now quite sure that her first waking in this room hadn't been a dream either. It couldn't have been. She'd recognized the bits of food her stomach had tossed out. The grape skin had still been intact, the strawberry recognizable if a little masticated and the cheese had been in smaller chunks but also identifiable.

She really needed to chew better, Abigail thought on a sigh. Grimacing, she raised her head and started to try to get up, but stopped immediately when her stomach shifted threateningly. Apparently, it wished to stay right where it was. Who was she to argue?

Abigail rested her face back on her arm, then wrinkled her nose and straightened enough to sag back against the wall rather than return to her previous position. Closing her eyes, she recalled the interlude with Tomasso that she'd thought was a dream and tried to decide why she was bothered by the fact that it had most likely really happened. It wasn't the first time she and Tomasso had been intimate . . . or even the second.

It *was* the first time they'd had full-on sex, though, Abigail acknowledged.

As she'd expected, it had been incredible. Mind-blowing. The best sex she'd ever had.

And almost embarrassingly short, Abigail realized suddenly, her lips twisting wryly. The foreplay hadn't been, she thought now, but the man had barely got inside her before they were both screaming their heads off and passing out.

Did it matter if it was short if they enjoyed it? She wondered. And they *had* enjoyed it. At least she had. Last night, when her orgasm had crashed over her, Abigail had seen stars and—

"Fangs?" she muttered with confusion as that memory returned to her. Abigail had been opening her mouth on a cry of passion as her body began to convulse, heard Tomasso cry out with his own release and opened her eyes to look at him. His whole body had been as stiff as a rod, his back arched, his head thrown back, his mouth open on a shout . . . and there had definitely been fangs poking out of his mouth. Tomasso had looked like a big, sexy, mostly naked vampire about to chomp down on some neck.

Abigail gave her head a shake. That couldn't have been real. It must have been part of a dream. In fact, she decided now, the *whole thing* had to have been a dream. Because Tomasso's penis during their interlude had been just fine, and the real one was a ruin. Abigail had seen it. She'd poured antiseptic on it. She'd even rubbed antibiotic on it, and the penis she'd done all of that to was not the one in her dreams last night. Dream Tomasso's penis had been perfect.

"Definitely a dream," she muttered with a short laugh, and then shook her head at herself for imagining otherwise.

Abigail caught a glimpse of the contents of the toilet as she shook her head and froze again. The food she'd thrown up was the food Dream Tomasso had fed her.

Everything in Abigail seemed to go quiet for a moment as her brain wrestled with what the contradictory evidence was telling her.

The food she'd thrown up was the food from the dream, therefore if this was real, that had been real too. However, Tomasso's penis had been fine in the dream, while his real penis was damaged. Therefore the sexual interlude had been a dream.

Abigail was scowling over the two contradictory truths when a little voice piped up inside her head with, *But vampires are supposed to heal quickly, aren't they?*

Her eyes closed on a sigh. Of course they did. At least they did in the movies and shows she'd seen with vampires in them. Give them a little blood and they could heal almost anything.

Abigail had barely acknowledged that to herself when the little voice spoke up again, pointing out, *Besides, he has fangs. You saw them.*

She was beginning to dislike that little voice, Abigail decided.

Do you think he bit you while you were sleeping and that's why he's all better now while you're sick as a dog? the little voice asked next.

Abigail frowned, trying to understand what her subconscious was suggesting. "What?" she muttered finally with confusion. "Like I'm sick because I'm turning into a vampire?"

Oooh, hadn't thought of that, the voice replied. *I was just thinking we were weak from blood loss, but becoming Vampirella makes more sense with the puking and such.*

Abigail's eyes widened incredulously. It did make more sense. Blood loss would make her dizzy, maybe short of breath and tired, definitely pale. It would not, however, cause fever and vomiting.

At least it would make more sense if Tomasso had bitten her, she thought suddenly and was immediately moving. Her stomach protested at once, turning unhappily, but Abigail ignored it and managed to get to her feet to stumble to the counter. Leaning forward she raised her chin and examined her neck in the mirror behind the double sinks.

The air left her lungs on a slow hiss as she spotted two puncture marks next to each other on her throat. Abigail raised one shaky hand to touch them. They were about the right size and distance apart to be from the fangs she'd seen protruding from Tomasso's upper jaw.

Dammit! He'd bit her! Abigail thought with dismay.

Was that why she'd passed out on the cargo plane? Probably, she decided grimly. And he'd probably bit her again last night too. Loss of blood was probably why she'd fainted again. The man was feeding off of her like a leech. A big, sexy leech instead of a slimy, slug-like leech, but a leech just the same. That probably explained his finding her attractive, she thought. Nice rich chubby-chick blood was probably loads tastier than weak, stringy skinny-chick blood.

Scowling, Abigail leaned closer to get a better look and frowned as she noted the marks weren't fresh. They had already healed quite a bit. She'd guess they were at least three days old. Maybe four . . . which was about how long it had been since she'd met Tomasso on Jet's cargo plane. At least she thought it was. The days had sort of begun to blur a bit, and she wasn't sure of anything at the moment.

Abigail ran a finger over the healing wounds again, recalling Tomasso standing behind her in the cargo section, his arms around her, hands caressing as he nibbled at her neck . . . and the sharp pinching pain followed by the drawing sensation she'd experienced just before she'd blacked out.

This certainly did explain that blacking out business. He must have been feeding on her every time they—

Her thoughts dying, Abigail twisted her head around, trying to see more of her neck and find other puncture wounds. There weren't any. At least not on her neck or shoulders or chest where she could see them in the mirror. Abigail felt around the back of her neck where she couldn't see, but didn't feel anything there either.

Letting her hands drop, she frowned slightly. If he'd only bit her the once, why had she fainted each time they'd been intimate? This last time in the tub she'd passed out like a light being switched off, but she didn't recall him spending a lot of time around her neck. He'd spent more time—

Abigail glanced down at the apex of her thighs and narrowed her eyes. She needed a flashlight and a handheld mirror. Or a lamp and a mirror, she thought, suspecting she wouldn't find a flashlight in the hotel suite. She probably wouldn't find a handheld mirror either, but it was worth a look.

Turning away from the counter, Abigail started for the door, but slowed when the room began to spin. She stopped and reached for the counter to balance herself, but it was too late, the floor was coming up to meet her.

NINE

"Feverish, you say?"

"*Sì*," Tomasso muttered as he unlocked the door to the villa he'd arranged for him and Abigail when the fishermen had let them off at the resort dock here. It was a luxury resort and where the men had been staying, and since Tomasso didn't know the first thing about Punta Cana or what was available here, he'd decided their resort would do. Besides, they were leaving early in the morning, practically at sunrise, so he only had to make sure he avoided them until then to ensure the memories he'd tampered with about their encounter with him stayed buried.

"Any other symptoms?" the doctor asked, following him inside when he opened the door.

"No," Tomasso said, but frowned. He hadn't really examined Abigail before rushing off to find the doctor, and while he felt he probably should have thought to do so, he was glad he hadn't. Doctor Cortez did not live at the resort and had been getting ready to head home after having dinner and drinks here when Tomasso had found the man. It had taken his special brand of persuasion— aka mind control—for him to get the man back here to the villa.

Leaving the doctor to follow, Tomasso led him through the villa to the master suite, opened the door, and then paused briefly when he saw the empty bed. Frowning, he rushed to the bathroom door, calling, "Abigail?"

There was no answer. He understood why when he reached the open door and saw Abigail sprawled naked on the tile floor. She lay on her side with her back to him, her arms and legs askew. She looked like a doll who had been tossed away. Cursing, he hurried forward, calling her name again, aware that Doctor Cortez was following.

Tomasso knelt at Abigail's side and turned her over, only to sit back with dismay when he got a good look at her face. She was as pale as death, the circles under her eyes almost black against her paper-white skin.

"She's vomited."

Tomasso glanced around at that calm comment to see that Cortez had set his medical bag on the sink counter and was now peering into the toilet. After flushing the toilet, the doctor walked over to squat on the other side of Abigail. He felt her forehead briefly, lifted her eyelids to check her eyes, and then pulled her lips back to look at her gums, before turning his attention to her arms. After lifting each one to examine all sides of them, he then returned Abigail onto her side to look at her back.

"She has a lot of insect bites," the doctor commented. "And she appears to be developing a rash."

Tomasso frowned as he noted that the doctor was right.

"Has she been complaining of a headache?" Doctor Cortez asked, straightening to move to the tub.

"No," Tomasso growled, his concerned gaze sliding over Abigail's face as he eased her onto her back again.

"Achy joints?" the doctor asked, bending to press the button that would set the stopper. "A pain behind her eyes?"

"No," Tomasso snapped impatiently, his eyes now moving over the mosquito bites he could see. Had Abigail had them and the rash when they were in the tub earlier? He hadn't noticed.

Turning the cold tap on full force, the doctor asked, "How long has she been in the Dominican?"

"Four days," Tomasso answered.

"Hmm." The doctor straightened. "Sounds about right."

"What does?" Tomasso asked with a frown. "You know what it is?"

"I will take some blood and have it tested," Doctor Cortez said cautiously as he moved to his medical bag to retrieve several items. Returning then to kneel beside Abigail, he finished, "But my guess would be dengue fever."

"What's that?" Tomasso asked with concern. He was sure he'd heard the name before, but hadn't a clue what it was.

"This is just a band. I wrap it around her arm to make the vein—"

"No. What is dengue fever?" Tomasso ground out with irritation, interrupting the unwanted explanation of what the doctor was doing in preparation for taking blood.

"Oh." Doctor Cortez finished tying the band around Abigail's arm, then slipped a needle into her vein and watched blood begin to pour into the attached test tube, before explaining, "A virus that's quite common here. It's transmitted by mosquitoes."

"Is it bad?" Tomasso asked with concern.

"Unpleasant," the doctor said with a grimace. "But she should be fine."

"Thank God." Tomasso sagged with relief, then stiffened and glanced to Abigail's face when she moaned and began to stir.

Her eyes fluttered open, and Tomasso tried for a reassuring smile when her confused gaze found his. But it dropped away into dismay when she accused in a raspy voice, "You bit me!"

"She's delirious," Cortez said soothingly when Tomasso merely stared at her, his expression blank.

Abigail's eyes rolled to the man, her head slow to follow, and she frowned with confusion. "Who are you?"

"I'm Doctor Cortez, child. Now just rest. You're ill."

"Nooooo." She moaned the word, her head flopping in the other direction as she muttered, "I'm turning. He bit me."

"Is that so?" Dr. Cortez asked mildly, switching out the now full test tube for an empty one.

"Yes." Her head swung back sharply, her beautiful green eyes now wide and panicked. "You shouldn't be here. I could bite you." Raising her head she added plaintively, "I don't want to bite anyone."

"That's good," Doctor Cortez murmured, his attention on the quickly filling second vial.

Tomasso glanced from the man to Abigail, his mind in an uproar as he tried to decide what to do. She obviously knew what he was, or knew something anyway. And she was blabbing to the doctor who shouldn't be hearing any of this. The man seemed to be assuming this was all fever-induced delirium, but what if he got thinking about it later and—

"I taste blood," Abigail muttered fretfully, her head twisting again. "Why do I—oh!" her expression filled with horror. "I already bit someone. Didn't I? I did," she decided and moaned, "I don't want to be a bloodsucking fiend!"

"She's quite delirious," Doctor Cortez diagnosed, finished with drawing the blood and straightening with his apparatus and the test tubes in hand. Returning to his medical bag once more, he ordered, "Put her in the tub. You need to get her temperature down."

Tomasso hesitated, still torn over what he should do about the doctor.

"Whose blood is this?" Abigail moaned, peering at her hands as if they were covered with the substance. They weren't, but her believing they were made Tomasso's decision for him. Scooping Abigail off the floor, he carried her to the tub. He'd leave the man alone for now. He could always wipe his memory later if it became necessary.

The water was halfway up the side of the tub. Tomasso lowered Abigail into it, noting that it was extremely cold as it closed over his arms and her body. Still, he wasn't prepared for Abigail's reaction. Her eyes flew open, she began to shriek as if in pain, and immediately tried to get out of the tub. She did so by trying to climb Tomasso's chest and head, her nails digging ruthlessly into his flesh to manage the task.

"*Calma*. Abigail, *calmati*," Tomasso said soothingly as he caught her wrists and pulled her claws out of his skin. Forcing her back into the water, he held her there, just repeating those same words over and over again. Much to his relief, after barely a minute, she suddenly collapsed, the fight going out of her and her eyes closing again.

"I'll call you as soon as I get the test results."

Tomasso glanced around sharply to see that the doctor had packed up his bag and was heading for the door.

"Wait!" he barked with dismay. When the man paused and glanced back, he asked, "What about medicine?"

"I'll have the front desk find some acetaminophen for her to help with the pain. Stay away from aspirin though, it will encourage bleeding," he instructed. "And keep bathing her in cold water when her fever gets too high."

"That's it?" Tomasso asked with disbelief. "What about real medicine? Antibiotics or something?"

"Dengue fever is a virus. Antibiotics aren't effective with viruses," the doctor explained patiently. "Just give her the acetaminophen and cold baths and keep an eye on her. She should recover on her own in a few days. If she doesn't, or she starts bleeding, call for me. It could mean complications."

"What kind of complications?" Tomasso growled, not liking the sounds of that.

"In some rare cases the patient can develop dengue hemorrhagic fever, and even dengue shock syndrome, which can be deadly," Cortez admitted, but then quickly added, "However, that is rare. It usually only happens to people with weakened immune systems. So just keep an eye on her and call if there are problems."

Tomasso's head turned slowly back to Abigail, his concern leaping as he recalled that she'd been pale and exhausted when he'd met her. Run-down from tending her dying mother. And they hadn't eaten or drunk much these last few days. No doubt she was dehydrated. Would that combination of things be enough to weaken her immune system? Maybe he should take control of the doctor and make him stay until they knew if Abigail was going to be able to recover on her own or—

The sound of the bedroom door shutting made him glance around and Tomasso cursed when he realized that Dr. Cortez had slipped away. He considered chasing the man down and bringing him back, but couldn't leave Abigail alone in the tub while she was unconscious. He also didn't want to take her out of the water until her temperature had gone down though, so he let the doctor go and concentrated on keeping Abigail's head above water with one hand while turning off the tap with the other.

Sighing then, Tomasso settled more comfortably beside the tub and simply peered at Abigail with concern. Not only was she sick, but she seemed to have some idea of . . . Well, she knew he'd bit her. He didn't know how since he hadn't bit her since the plane four days ago, and she hadn't said anything about it before this. Unless she'd known, but hadn't cared until she'd started to get sick.

Abigail *had* said something about her turning and not wanting to be a bloodsucking fiend, he recalled with a wince. No one had ever called Tomasso a bloodsucking fiend before, and he didn't like it. More importantly though, it didn't suggest that she was taking the idea of what he was very well at all.

But she was delirious, Tomasso reminded himself encouragingly. Perhaps she didn't know what she was saying. Maybe she was just spouting stuff from a dream she'd been having before waking up.

"Yeah, right," Tomasso muttered to himself unhappily and acknowledged that he really should have sat her down and explained everything to her while they were still in the jungle. He suspected he'd made things much harder for himself by not doing so.

TOMASSO GAVE A snuffling snore that made his chin bob where it rested on his chest and Abigail smiled faintly. She'd been awake and watching him sleep in the chair next to her bed for perhaps ten minutes, and she'd spent that time sorting out where she was, what was happening and just who or what Tomasso was. Abigail had come to several conclusions.

They had reached civilization and, from her guess and what she'd seen of the room she was in, had to be at a luxury resort. She didn't recall actually finding civilization or checking in here, so supposed she'd been too sick at the time to remember it now. Which actually was part of her second conclusion. Abigail had been seriously sick. Like deadly ill. From what she could recall since waking up in this room the first time, Abigail knew without a doubt that she had never in her life been as sick as this. Ever.

She was aware that she'd been out of her head with fever for a while, although she wasn't quite sure how long that while might have been. She'd also had a few lucid moments, though, too, and during one of those she'd woken to see Tomasso talking quietly to a man he'd addressed as Dr. Cortez. They'd been by the door, the doctor obviously leaving, and she hadn't been able to hear much of what was said, but she had caught the mention of dengue fever before dropping back into her restless sleep.

Abigail frowned. She had read about dengue fever while researching vacation destinations with her mother and knew exactly what that was. Or, she'd thought she knew exactly what that was. It had sounded like an unpleasant flu-like illness to her. However, having now suffered it, she could honestly say that in the competition for Worst Illness to Have, dengue fever could kick every flu's ass up and down the block ten times. Honestly, she'd never felt so awful in her life. She hadn't been able to keep down any of the broths or even the water Tomasso had tried to give her to keep her hydrated. Every joint in her body had ached so that she felt like she'd been run over by a semi. Her head had been pounding like a tribal drum, and the pain behind her eyes had been unbearable. Abigail had been sure she was going to die.

And then she'd woken up this time feeling a lot better. Well, comparatively speaking at least. Her head still ached, as did her joints, but the fever appeared to be gone. That was a good sign, right?

Abigail sighed and moved her tongue around inside her mouth, trying to work up some saliva to ease the dryness she was suffering. The effort didn't seem to do a thing. She needed a glass of water or something.

Her gaze slid over Tomasso again, but she didn't say his name or do anything else that might wake him. Abigail was pretty sure he'd not slept since her illness had started. Every time she'd woken up, he'd been right there taking care of her. Crushing up pills he then stirred into water and made her drink, assuring her it would help with the pain. Spoon-feeding her broth, murmuring to her the whole time that she had to eat and keep up her strength to fight this off. Supporting her head and holding her hair back as she vomited up both the water and broth. Helping her to the bathroom and back when she needed it. Lowering her into icy baths, his voice full of apology and regret as he tried to soothe her and told her it was necessary.

She'd also woken a couple times to find him simply holding her hand and mumbling away to her in Italian. Abigail wasn't sure what he'd been saying to her those times, but there had been a lot of *caras*, *bellas*, and life mates mentioned so she thought he probably wasn't telling her tales of his childhood.

Tomasso stirred restlessly in his chair, mumbled something in Italian, and then settled back into deep breathing, and Abigail let out the breath she'd held as she'd waited to see if he'd wake up or not. She wasn't disappointed that he hadn't woken up. While she was thirsty and restless, she also wasn't looking forward to offering him the apology she knew she owed him. And she did owe him an apology, because another conclusion Abigail had come to was that she'd briefly lost her mind to imagine even for a minute that he was some kind of vampire and had even bit her. That had obviously been some fever-induced madness, because now that she was lucid again, she could see how ridiculous that idea was.

First, there was no such thing as vampires. That went without saying.

Second, the man had been running around in daylight, swimming, spearing fish, climbing trees to get coconuts and so on, and everyone knew that vampires couldn't go out in daylight. They burst into flames and turned to ash if they dared it . . . which of course they wouldn't, because vampires didn't exist.

And third, she hadn't been suffering from blood loss and the turn as she'd feared, she'd had dengue fever, so . . . well, she'd obviously just lost it. Those fangs she'd thought she'd seen before she passed out? Probably just a fever-induced hallucination. And the passing out itself? Probably her body weakened from trying to fight off the illness.

Of course, that didn't explain why *he'd* passed out each time too. Or the marks on her neck for that matter, but there was just no way that Abigail could accept that the sweet man who had shown her such pleasure, and cared for her so tenderly while she was ill, was a vampire. No way. No how. No sir.

"You're awake."

Realizing that her gaze had somehow dropped and fastened on Tomasso's bare chest as she'd run through her thoughts, Abigail shifted her gaze back up to his face and managed a smile as he lunged out of the chair to perch on the edge of the bed next to her.

"The fever is gone," Tomasso said with relief as he felt her forehead, and then he frowned and noted, "But you are—how you say? Not like the clam, but something like that."

Clammy, Abigail translated in her mind and grimaced. She *was* clammy. No doubt the aftereffects of the fever or something. Before she could speak the correct word aloud, though, he asked with concern, "How do you feel?"

"Thirsty," she replied, surprised when her voice came out a barely audible dry rasp.

"Of course. You must be parched," Tomasso muttered, turning to a table next to the bed where a pitcher of water sat next to an empty glass.

"Yes. Very," Abigail whispered as she watched him pour the lovely clear liquid into the glass. Setting the drink on the table, he then quickly swung back to slip an arm under her shoulders and lift her upper body. Tomasso then piled some pillows behind her back before easing her back against them and turning to reach for the glass of water.

Abigail sipped eagerly at the water when he urged it to her lips. She then closed her eyes on a relieved sigh as the sweet liquid dampened her tongue and filled her mouth. It felt so wonderful that she held it there for a moment, letting it fill and wet every crevice, before allowing it to slide down her equally parched throat.

"More," she mumbled, trying to hold onto the glass when Tomasso started to pull it away.

"Slowly," he cautioned, giving in and raising the glass to her lips again.

Abigail tried to go slowly, but it was just so nice after feeling parched for so long, she swallowed more than she probably should have. Tomasso was trying to ease the glass away from her lips again when she noted the drop of red liquid that landed in the water and quickly spread, then dissolved even as a second drop followed.

"Tomasso?" she mumbled uncertainly, raising a hand instinctively to her face just as the blood began to course from her nose in earnest. She could taste it in her mouth too, and what was that on her arm? Abigail wondered with concern. She noted what looked like blood blisters under the skin even as droplets began to form on top of the skin—like sweat, but bloodred. Before she could become too alarmed at that, a sudden shaft of agony ripped through Abigail's stomach. A cry of pain slipping from her lips, she immediately hunched forward on the bed, her arms instinctively wrapping around her stomach, and then she felt the liquid she'd just swallowed trying to climb its way out of her throat and muttered, "I think I'm gonna—"

Cursing, Tomasso set the glass aside and scooped her from the bed. They were in the bathroom a heartbeat later, so fast that Abigail thought she must have missed some time somehow. He carried her to the toilet and started to lower her, but Abigail didn't make it. Her stomach tossed out the water all over the back of the toilet and the seat. It was mixed with blood, she noted hazily.

Some part of her brain acknowledged that probably wasn't a good thing, but Abigail had little time or energy to consider it; her heaves hadn't stopped despite the fact that she was pretty sure there was nothing left to throw up. The pain hadn't stopped either, but had intensified. It felt like someone had stabbed her with a knife and was now dragging the weapon up and down and left and right inside her gut.

The moment Tomasso finished setting her on the cold tile floor next to the toilet, Abigail instinctively curled into a protective ball around her stomach. She was vaguely aware of Tomasso leaning over her, calling her name and asking questions, but simply lay there releasing little gasps of agony and misery until a blessed darkness dropped over her, taking away the pain, or at least her awareness of it.

"DENGUE HEMORRHAGIC FEVER," Doctor Cortez diagnosed grimly, straightening from examining Abigail. She was back in bed, under the sheet and sleeping, or unconscious really, Tomasso thought. She'd passed out in the bathroom and hadn't stirred once since he'd carried her back in here and called the doctor and then waited for him to arrive.

"Yes, you said dengue before, but she—"

"It's not simply dengue fever anymore," the doctor interrupted sternly. "It is dengue *hemorrhagic* fever now."

Tomasso stared at him blankly, not sure what the difference was.

"You let her get dehydrated," Doctor Cortez accused, moving to the phone and beginning to punch in numbers.

"I gave her broth and water. She could not keep anything down," Tomasso said, moving closer to the bed to peer down at Abigail.

"Then you should have called me," Cortez snapped.

"I did. Repeatedly," Tomasso growled. He'd called the main

desk at least twelve times a day for the past two days since the man
had left him here alone with Abigail. Each time he'd been promised the doctor would be sent to him, but the man had never shown
up. Tomasso had almost gone out himself to hunt down the doctor,
but hadn't been willing to leave Abigail alone here while he did it.
He was actually surprised the man was here now. Perhaps it was his
telling the front desk that she was bleeding from everywhere and
he would go down there and beat the person on the other end of
the phone to death if Abigail died that had worked. If he'd known
that would do it, he would have made the threat sooner.

"They just installed a new message system. I never got the
messages," Dr. Cortez muttered, and then began to speak into the
phone in rapid-fire Spanish. He paused to listen to whoever was
on the other end of the line for a moment, spat out another round
of Spanish and then slammed the phone down violently.

"What?" Tomasso asked, knowing the news wasn't good.

"She needs a hospital. Immediately," the doctor snapped, sounding frustrated. "She needs to be put on an IV to raise her fluids and
she no doubt needs a blood transfusion too." He paced over to peer
at Abigail again and shook his head. "But apparently the road has
been washed out just outside the resort and with this tropical storm
there is no way to get a chopper or boat here to transport her."

Tomasso frowned and glanced to the glass doors. He'd been
vaguely aware of the storm raging outside for the past several
hours or so, and had noticed that the doctor was soaked through
and out of breath when he got here. However, Tomasso had been
so concerned about Abigail, he'd paid little heed to anything but
her since she fell ill. Now he saw at a glance that this was more
than just your average tropical storm. Mother Nature was pissed,
and she was taking her fury out on anything in her path, which
apparently included this resort, Tomasso thought as one of the
lounge chairs went sailing past the window.

Frowning, he turned to Cortez to see that he was taking Abigail's blood pressure again. "What do we do?"

Doctor Cortez was silent for a moment as he removed the pressure cuff and wound it up. "If we can't get her to a hospital, she doesn't stand a chance, and right now, we can't get her to a hospital." He put the cuff away in his bag only to pull it back out again. Returning to Abigail he started to put the cuff on her again as if intending to take her readings in case they'd changed in the last moment and said, "I suggest you pray . . . and say your good-byes."

Tomasso stilled at those words, his mind suddenly screaming. Good-byes? No! He couldn't lose her. Not now. Life mates were rare and precious finds. Some waited millennia to find one. He'd been lucky to have her placed in his path while so young. He could not lose Abigail.

"Get out," he growled.

When Dr. Cortez glanced to him in surprise, but when he didn't immediately get up and leave as requested, Tomasso slid into the man's mind and took control. Within moments all of the man's medical gear was back in his bag and the doctor was walking out the door. Tomasso watched him leave, and then sat down on the side of the bed.

"Abigail?" he said, grasping and shaking her shoulders gently. When that got no response, he tried again, but as he'd suspected, she was unconscious, not sleeping. Tomasso eased her back onto the bed, leaving his arm under her neck so that her head fell back slightly over it, and her mouth opened.

He remained like that, simply peering at her for a moment, and his mind raced, and then he opened his own mouth and let his fangs slide out. Tomasso hadn't got to tell Abigail that he was immortal, or explain what that was to her. He didn't have her permission to turn her, and had no idea if she would be willing to be turned. But there was no way in hell he was risking losing her at this juncture.

Raising his wrist, Tomasso tore into it with his fangs, and raised Abigail up slightly to press the gushing wound to her mouth. He remained like that until the bleeding slowed and stopped, then removed his wrist. He was easing Abigail back onto the bed when a muffled knocking reached his ears.

Frowning, Tomasso glanced from Abigail to the door and back, then stood and hurried out of the room to make his way to the villa entrance. The window in the front door was frosted glass. Tomasso could see shadows through it as he approached, but that was all. Mouth tightening, he unlocked and opened the door, then froze; shock rippled through his body as he stared at the people on the doorstep.

TEN

"Well? Are you going to let us in, or what? We're getting soaked out here."

That comment drew Tomasso out of his shock, but he didn't respond to Justin Bricker, who had asked the question. He didn't even step back to allow the foursome on the doorstep inside. Instead, he stepped out into the wind and rain and threw his arms around his brother with relief, saying loudly, "Dante. You are safe."

"Yeah." Dante returned the hug, his own voice a near shout to be heard over the storm. "I was worried about you, brother."

"I was worried about you too," Tomasso assured him as they broke off the hug and stepped back to look each other over. Dante looked exactly as he had the last time Tomasso had seen him. Except for the fact that he was dressed, of course. The last time he'd seen his brother, Dante had been as bare-assed as Tomasso had been on the cargo plane.

"Why were you worried about me?" Dante asked with surprise. "You knew I had escaped. It was you who got left behind, stuck in that cage."

"You ran from there naked with no money and no phone," Tomasso pointed out. "I was not sure how far you would get like that. I feared they had recaptured you and transported us separately."

"No." Dante smiled. "Fortunately, I ran into the arms of an angel who helped save me." His smile turning wry, he added, "Actually, I ran into her RV, but she *is* an angel and she did help save me. Tomasso, this is my life mate—" His voice broke off as he turned to glance beside him and saw only empty space. "Where did she—Oh! There she is. Come."

Catching Tomasso's arm, Dante pulled him into the house and toward the threesome now standing in the entry.

Tomasso pulled the door closed behind them, shutting out the storm, then turned to survey the trio who had left them outside and moved in out of the inclement weather without them, Lucian Argeneau, Justin Bricker and a petite little blonde with a wide smile.

"This is my life mate Mary, *fratello*," Dante said proudly, using the Italian term for brother. Slipping his arm around the woman, he added, "Mary, this is my brother, Tomasso."

"One look was all it took to know that," Mary said with a laugh. Slipping from under Dante's arm, she stepped forward to hug Tomasso in greeting as she pointed out, "You two are identical."

"*Sì*, but I am the better-looking brother," Dante assured her, pulling Mary away from Tomasso and tucking her back under his arm again.

Tomasso's eyebrows rose slightly at this sign of jealousy from his twin. Dante had never had a jealous bone in his body before now. They'd even shared women in their younger years. Life mates were a different matter, however. And, Tomasso thought suddenly, Dante didn't yet know about his Abigail so might be worried that as twins, Mary might be a possible life mate to him too.

Tomasso didn't try reading her to find out. For one thing, as pretty as Mary was, he wasn't the least attracted to her. The other reason Tomasso didn't read her was because he didn't want images of his naked brother dancing through his head. And judging by the way Mary was looking at Dante right now that was what he'd find there.

"You are quite right. That is exactly what is dancing through Mary's head right now," Lucian said, obviously reading Tomasso's thoughts. "And since Dante and Mary are newly mated, you should be picking up on that whether you want to or not, unless—" He paused and narrowed his gaze on Tomasso, and then his eyes widened the slightest bit and the hint of a smile curved the corner of his mouth as he murmured, "I believe you have something to tell your brother?"

Tomasso noted the way Dante stiffened and knew at once that he'd misconstrued Lucian's words. He thought Tomasso hadn't been *able* to read Mary, not that he'd refused to try. Smiling wryly, Tomasso opened his mouth to explain, but just as quickly snapped it closed again and ran for the master bedroom as Abigail began to shriek.

When he burst into the bedroom, Tomasso found Abigail with her eyes squeezed tightly closed, her body stiff and arched on the bed, and vibrating like a tuning fork as she screamed her head off.

"Cara!" he shouted, rushing to the bed to pull her into his arms. It was like hugging a board. Her body seemed locked in the position and her screaming didn't even falter when he gathered her against his chest. Glancing around wildly, he saw with relief that the others had followed. Focusing on Lucian he barked, "What is happening?"

The man moved up next to him to peer at Abigail, and then reached down to lift one eyelid.

"You turned her?" Lucian asked in a near roar to be heard over her screaming.

Tomasso met his gaze and nodded. Much to his relief Abigail went silent then. She was still stiff and vibrating, but at least she was no longer emitting that terrible shriek. Swallowing, he looked over her pale face, unsure what was happening. He would think this was just part of the turn except that it could not possibly happen this quickly. Could it? He wasn't sure. He'd not witnessed a lot of turns, but he would have thought it would take at least a little bit of time to cause a reaction like this.

"How long ago?" Lucian asked, releasing her eyelid and straightening.

"I had just finished when you knocked," Tomasso muttered, pressing her tighter to his chest.

"Wait." Dante moved up beside them. "You turned her? When you had no blood here to—"

"I had to," he growled. "She was dying."

"Dying?" Mary asked with concern. "What—?"

"Dengue hemorrhagic fever," Tomasso said wearily before she could finish the question.

"Dengue?" Mary asked with surprise. "But that's not usually fatal."

"She was dehydrated and losing blood. She needed fluids and transfusions but the road was washed out and—" Pausing suddenly, he glanced to the others with confusion. "How did you get through?"

"A borrowed military jeep and Justin's driving," Lucian said dryly, and then turned to the younger man. "Get the cooler of blood out of the jeep."

As soon as Justin left, Lucian turned to Tomasso. "I am guessing you did not think to gather chains or rope before turning her?"

Tomasso shook his head. He hadn't really thought this through, he supposed. It was very fortunate that the others had shown up. He didn't know what he would have done. Tied her down with sheets and led a parade of maids and resort clientele through the room for her to feed on maybe?

"Jesus," Lucian muttered and Tomasso was quite sure the man had read that thought from his mind.

"Dante, you and Mary go find some rope or chain or something to tie her down," Lucian ordered. "And rent rooms for us."

"No need. This villa has four rooms," Tomasso said quickly, glad he at least had something useful to offer. Dante nodded and offered him a reassuring smile as he ushered Mary out of the room.

"I thought you would head to Caracas once Mortimer passed on my information," Tomasso commented once he and Lucian were alone. Tomasso had made two calls after carrying Abigail off the fishermen's boat at this resort. He'd made the calls from the registration desk. The first had been to his brother's cell phone, but it had gone directly to voice mail. He'd hung up and made his second call then, to Mortimer, the head of the Rogue Hunters. That too had gone to voice mail. Deciding he would try again after getting Abigail settled, Tomasso had turned his attention to getting a room here at the resort. This villa, apparently kept for the exclusive use of the owners when they were here, had been all that was available. Tomasso had used mind control to convince the registration manager to give him the villa, as well as to bypass the problems caused by his lack of identification or credit cards. He'd also made sure that the villa wasn't listed as occupied on the registration. Basically, they didn't exist.

Tomasso frowned as it suddenly occurred to him to wonder if that was why his messages had never reached the doctor. Why send one to an unoccupied villa? With the new system the doctor had mentioned they'd probably thought it a glitch.

Shaking his head, he glanced to Lucian, wondering how they had got here so quickly. With Abigail so sick, Tomasso had quite forgotten about making those calls again until just hours ago. They shouldn't have got here this fast.

"We were on a plane on the way to Venezuela when Mortimer called us with the news that you had escaped and were safe here in Punta Cana," Lucian announced. "I had the plane stop here instead. We were going to collect you and take you on to Venezuela with us."

Tomasso raised his eyebrows in surprise. "You already knew about Venezuela?"

Lucian nodded. "Decker and Nicholas found the connection."

Tomasso nodded briefly, recognizing the names of two of Lucian's nephews who also happened to be Rogue Hunters.

"They did some snooping around in San Antonio after Dante

escaped your kidnappers. They found a warehouse the kidnappers were using and paperwork for shipments to Caracas. Mary then recalled the men who held her mentioning a Doctor Dressler. But we did not know about the island," he added.

"Abigail heard one of the men mention the island," Tomasso admitted, peering down at her face. "She rescued me. Took out the IV they had in my arm and—"

"I have already read all of that from your memories, Tomasso," Lucian said, ending any need for him to regale him with what had been happening. "I also read that Abigail has no idea what you are and what you have turned her into, or even that you have. You turned her without gaining permission first."

The accusation was made softly, but Tomasso stiffened defensively anyway. "It was an emergency. She was dying."

Lucian nodded. "And that is the only reason you will not be hauled up in front of the council for judgment."

Before Tomasso could point out that since he lived in Italy and had turned Abigail in Punta Cana none of this really fell under the purview of the North American council that Lucian was the head of, Justin came hurrying in, carrying a huge cooler.

"Got the blood," the man announced unnecessarily, setting it down and opening the lid. "I saw Mary and Dante on their way back here too. They must have found some chain or rope."

Justin retrieved several bags of blood from the cooler, tossed them on the bed, slammed the lid closed then straightened and raised an eyebrow at Lucian. "Can I go call Holly now? She'll be worried."

"Yes, fine," Lucian snapped impatiently. "If you must."

"I must," Justin assured him, and then headed for the door, adding, "And if I were you I'd call Leigh and let her know we landed safely or the next ringtone she puts on your phone could be 'Fuck it, I don't want you back' by Eamon."

Lucian scowled after Bricker, shifted his feet, then sighed and retrieved his phone from his own pocket. Heading for the door, he muttered, "I need to make a call."

"Say hi to Leigh for me," Tomasso said with an amusement that only grew when Lucian muttered what he was sure was a curse and slammed the door on the way out. Smiling, Tomasso turned his eyes down to Abigail and gently brushed her hair back from her face. "You will like Leigh. She is small and kind and seems so sweet, but she has steel in her spine and an evil streak. Which is a good thing," he assured her. "She needed it to tame the likes of Lucian Argeneau."

"I can hear you!" Lucian barked through the door.

Tomasso chuckled softly, but his amusement died when Abigail suddenly began to scream again.

ABIGAIL REGAINED CONSCIOUSNESS slowly, first becoming aware of birdsong and the scent of flowers on a breeze. She then felt soft sheets under her fingers and knew she was in a bed, not the beach. When she finally opened her eyes, she did so cautiously, positive she would be assaulted by terrible pain again as she had been every other time she'd woken up lately. But much to her relief there was no pain waiting to drop on her like a hammer. No fever either. Though she did still have dry mouth, she noted with a frown.

"Tomasso is going to be so annoyed with me."

Abigail stiffened at that soft feminine voice and turned her head toward it, eyes searching. She blinked in surprise when she spotted the lovely blonde sitting in a chair by the bed.

Sitting forward, the blonde smiled at her and said, "Hi, Abigail. I'm Mary. And I'm afraid I'm the one who talked Tomasso into leaving your bedside to get some rest. I assured him that you would be out for hours and that I would wake him if you showed signs of stirring. But I didn't notice any signs, you just suddenly opened your eyes, and now he'll be upset that after sitting at your bedside throughout your entire turn, he missed being here when you woke up."

Abigail smiled crookedly, mostly because it was hard not to

return this woman's smile, and then frowned as something that she'd said struck a chord in her. "My turn?"

She'd meant to speak the words; however, they came out a whisper. Mary heard them though and sat back in her seat, worry briefly flashing across her face. "I'm sorry, of course, you don't know."

"Know what?" Abigail asked with confusion. This time her voice was a little louder, but it was also broken and raspy, and her throat was sore, as if she'd been screaming a lot or something.

"Here." Mary was suddenly on her feet, collecting a glass of what appeared to be water from the bedside table and helping her to sit up to drink it.

Concerned about a repeat of the last time she'd done this, Abigail hesitated, but then sighed and took a sip. Her stomach didn't hurt right now. Nothing did, so perhaps it was safe. At least she was hoping so. Still, she only took one sip before gesturing that it was enough and leaning back against the pillows. She didn't swallow right away, but swished the water around inside her mouth before letting it slide down her throat.

"Better?" Mary asked, settling on the side of the bed, still holding the water.

Abigail nodded, but then asked, "What did you mean when you said that he sat by me through the entire *turn*?"

"Tomasso didn't leave your side once," Mary said quietly. "He was very concerned about you. It's pretty obvious he's crazy about you."

Abigail felt her heart give a little flutter at those words. A man like Tomasso crazy about her? The thought was a bit heady, or would have been if she hadn't been distracted by the word *turn* that kept playing through her head. Shifting restlessly, she repeated, "Turn?"

Mary hesitated, then sighed and set the water on the bedside table. Turning back to her then, she asked, "How much do you know?"

"About what?" Abigail asked at once.

"About Tomasso and what he is?" Mary asked gently.

Abigail stared at her, finding those words ominous. *What he is?* That suggested he wasn't just a man as she'd kind of been hoping, and that, put together with the word *turn*, was bringing back her earlier worries that he was a vampire, which was ridiculous, of course. There was no such thing as vampires, so she kept those mad thoughts to herself and merely asked, "What is he?"

Mary's eyes narrowed and then she suddenly stood. "I think I should get Tomasso."

"No. Wait." Abigail caught her hand before she could move away and was surprised to find that she was stronger than she'd been the last couple of times she'd woken.

Mary paused, but said gently, "He should probably be the one to explain things to you."

Abigail made a face. "Communication doesn't seem to be his strong suit. Tomasso is more a grunter than a talker."

"Most men are," Mary said with amusement.

Abigail smiled faintly, but pled softly, "Please. Tell me."

Mary hesitated, and then her eyes narrowed on her expression and she frowned. "You're afraid."

Abigail released her hand and looked away.

"Oh, Abigail, you have nothing to fear, I promise you," Mary said earnestly, catching her hand before she could move it away. Squeezing gently, she said, "I'm new to all of this myself, but I already know that life mates are everything to these men."

Abigail glanced back to her with a start. "Tomasso said something about my being his life mate."

"Yes. You are," Mary assured her. "And as such, you are more important to him than you can imagine."

While Abigail tried to wrap her mind around that, Mary patted her hand and set it back on the bed. "I'm going to go get him. I really think he needs to explain all of this. Please let him," she added solemnly. "Don't allow your fears to keep you from hearing what you need to know. Once he's explained it all, then you can make your decision. But let him explain everything first. Okay?" she asked at the end.

Abigail met her gaze and then nodded slowly.

"Good. If you do that, I promise it will all work out," Mary assured her and slipped from the room.

Abigail blew her breath out between her lips and tried to relax back in the bed as she waited for Tomasso to arrive, but that seemed to be an impossibility. He was about to come in here and explain "what he was" to her, and as ridiculous as it was, she was beginning to suspect he was going to tell her he was a vampire. It was those fangs she'd spotted in the bathroom when he made love to her. That with the bite marks on her neck. Those two things were combining in her mind to convince her of what he was and that somehow vampires did exist and he was one.

Oddly enough, the thought didn't terrify her now as it had the first time she'd had it. Abigail took a moment to consider why that was and the answer was simple. The man had taken care of her when she was sick. He'd nursed her as attentively as she'd nursed her own mother. From the few recollections she had, he'd been gentle, kind, sweet, and just amazing really. How could she fear him when he'd done that? Even if he was a vampire?

So, maybe vampires did exist and he was one, but a good vampire. If there was such a thing, she thought wryly. They were supposed to be soulless, after all. Still, why couldn't there be good vampires, soul or no soul? Having a soul didn't guarantee against someone being evil, so why did not having one mean they couldn't be good? Maybe they were like pit bulls. That dog breed all got a bad rap, but she'd had a friend growing up who'd had a pit bull named Otis who had been an absolute doll. Otis had been gentle, obedient, and incredibly patient with Abigail and all the other kids in the neighborhood. He had stood patiently, suffering them to dress him up in princess dresses and whatnot, had chased stray balls when they were playing baseball, and had let the littler kids hang off his ears and hold onto his nose to get up without ever growling or otherwise complaining even though it must have hurt at times.

So, maybe Tomasso was a vampire, but a good one, like Otis was a pit bull, but a good one.

Abigail shifted in bed and glanced toward the sliding glass doors. They were open, she noted, letting a warm breeze and lots of sunlight in. It was nice, she thought, but in the next second she began to worry about Tomasso. If he *was* a vampire, then sunlight surely wasn't good for him.

Sitting up in bed, Abigail slid her feet to the floor. She paused then, the sheet still wrapped around her. She stopped partially out of surprise because the room didn't spin and she wasn't feeling ridiculously weak or anything. But she also paused because she was afraid the pain would return any moment now that she was moving around. When that didn't happen, she tried standing up and was able to do it without a problem. The dengue had definitely passed then, she decided with relief. The only thing she seemed still to be suffering with was thirst. She was terribly thirsty, which was probably her own fault since she'd only taken a sip of the water Mary had offered her.

Glancing to the bedside table, Abigail picked up the glass to take a drink. She paused after the first swallow to see if it would stay down. When her stomach didn't rebel or otherwise protest the presence of the water, she took another drink and then another, and then downed the rest of the glass.

Water had never tasted so good. Truly, it was lovely. But it wasn't enough. She was still thirsty. Unfortunately, this time there was just the glass and no pitcher to refill it with. Setting the empty glass back on the nightstand, Abigail glanced toward the door she knew led to the bathroom and considered getting a refill from the tap. But in the next moment she shook her head and wrinkled her nose at the thought. One thing she'd read over and over again while researching these kinds of places was to never drink the water. She really didn't want to be sick again.

Sighing, she started to turn her gaze back toward the sliding doors, but paused as it fell on the large cooler by the bed. Abigail peered at it, her eyebrows rising. A cooler. It might have soda, or juice or something else lovely in it, she thought and was immediately on her feet, making her way toward it. She'd nearly reached the cooler when the bedroom door opened again.

Abigail paused and glanced to it just as Tomasso froze halfway into the room. The way his eyes widened and began to glow as they ran over her made her glance down to see that she'd been so caught up with her worries about the pain returning and then at the thought of something to drink that she hadn't noticed that she was completely naked. Releasing a high-pitched squeal, Abigail whirled and rushed back to the bed. The sheet had slid off the mattress when she'd stood, so rather than jump back into bed, she snatched up the soft linen sheet and quickly pulled it around her shoulders to gather in front.

Abigail froze briefly then, blinking as she recalled what she'd seen when she glanced down. She then turned her back to Tomasso, opened the sheet and looked down at herself, before snapping it closed again with disbelief.

"Abigail?" Tomasso said gently.

Rather than respond, she reopened the sheet, took another look down, and then snapped it closed once more.

"Abigail?"

This time she turned to face Tomasso, but she was sidling around the room as she did, making her way toward the bathroom door. "Sorry. I need to—I'll just be a minute. I have to—"

Abigail had reached the door by then and left her explanation unfinished as she slipped inside and slammed the door. A heartbeat later she was standing in front of the sinks, staring at the mirror behind them and her reflection in the voluminous sheet. She looked ridiculous. Her head was the only thing sticking out of the sheet and she had the worst bed head ever. Honestly, it looked like she'd stuck her finger in a light socket and been electrocuted or something.

Grimacing, Abigail ignored that, took a deep breath and opened the sheet for a third time.

"Holy Mother of God," Abigail whispered as she stared at her body in the mirror. Honest to God, she had a figure, and a knock-out one too. She'd kill for a figure like that. Or she would if it wasn't hers already. Dengue fever was like the best diet *ever*.

She closed the sheet, just to have the pleasure of opening it again with a "Pow-pow!" And then she bounced on her feet to see what happened and was gratified to see that everything bounced with her, but her flesh didn't move around like a bowl full of jelly or anything.

Abigail closed the sheet just to have the pleasure of opening it again with another "Pow-pow!"

"Abigail?"

She snapped the sheet closed and whirled toward the door, relieved to see it was still shut. "Yes?"

"Are you all right?"

"Oh, yeah, I'm great," Abigail assured him cheerfully, moving to the shower to turn the taps on. "I'll just be a minute."

"Okay," Tomasso murmured and she could hear the uncertainty in his voice.

He'd probably heard her pow-powing and thought the fever had damaged her poor brain or something, she thought wryly. Abigail wasn't sure she'd mind if it had. It seemed a fair trade-off, this body for some of her brains.

Or maybe not, Abigail thought with the next breath. She kind of liked being smart. She didn't feel any different mentally though, so hopefully that wasn't an issue.

Letting the sheet drop to the floor, she whirled quickly to the mirror, her hands imitating guns, and said, "Pow-pow," again as she pretended to shoot her reflection. She then raised one hand to her lips, blew on her index finger that was the "gun barrel," and said, "Smokin' hot."

"Er . . . Abigail? Do you need help?" Tomasso asked through the door.

"No," she said, her hands quickly dropping. "I'm good. I promise. I'll be right out."

When silence followed, she bit her lip, and then slipped into the shower for a quick rinse. Mostly it was to tame her wild hair, but when she realized the fever had left a faint, greasy film on her skin, Abigail grabbed the hotel soap and performed a fast cleanup. Even so, she didn't take long and presented herself in the bedroom a couple minutes later, but with a fluffy white towel wrapped around her damp body rather than the sheet.

"Hi," she said brightly, trying to act nonchalant about her state of dress as she stepped into the bedroom and stopped.

Tomasso's eyes widened slightly as he looked at her in the towel, and his voice was deep and raspy when he responded with, "Hi."

They were then both silent for a moment, but when it became obvious that Abigail wasn't going to move back to the bed, Tomasso cleared his throat, hesitated, and then with worry filling his expression, said, "We need to talk. There are some things I need to explain and—"

"It's okay," Abigail interrupted. She just couldn't take his worry. He looked like a puppy dog knowing it was about to get kicked, so she took a deep breath and said, "You don't have to tell me. I know. You're a vampire, right?"

She waited briefly then, half sure he would laugh and say she was crazy, and that there was no such thing as vampires. But instead his eyes widened incredulously and he gasped, "You know!"

Well, at least she wasn't crazy, Abigail thought with a grimace, and then noting the worry on Tomasso's face, shook the thought away and tried to take that worry away by saying, "It's okay. Really. The way I figure it, you're like Otis."

"Otis?" he asked uncertainly.

"My friend Amy's pit bull when I was growing up," she explained.

"You think I am like a pit bull?" he asked, his voice choked.

"Not like just any pit bull, like Otis," she corrected.

"Dear God," Tomasso muttered, running a hand through his hair.

Beginning to think Otis hadn't been the best opener for this conversation, Abigail frowned and said, "Never mind, forget Otis."

"No. Please," Tomasso said stiffly. "Continue telling me how you see me as a vicious dog."

"That's just it!" Abigail said at once. "Pit bulls get a bad rap but Otis wasn't vicious at all. He was sweet, and affectionate and so very patient. He let us dress him up in tutus and tiaras and let the little kids hang off his ears and lead him around by the tongue . . . He was an awesome dog," she assured him, and then added, "And I think that just because you're a vampire it doesn't mean that you're this evil fiend and stuff. I think, like Otis, you're awesome too."

A long silence followed as Tomasso stared at her and then he said simply, "No."

Abigail blinked uncertainly. "No, you're not awesome?"

"Not a vampire," he corrected.

"Oh." Abigail shifted, feeling suddenly foolish. Wow. She'd really blown that. He probably thought she *was* crazy-town now. She should have kept her mouth shut and let him talk.

"We are immortal," Tomasso announced.

Abigail stilled and then pursed her lips as her mind did a complete flip. So . . . he was the crazy one, she thought and said, "Okaaaay."

"And so are you now."

"Me?" she squeaked out with surprise.

Tomasso nodded, and admitted apologetically, "I turned you."

"You turned me?" she asked, sure she'd misheard him.

But he nodded and said, *"Sì."*

Abigail heard the word through a kind of fog. Much to her alarm, it felt like a filmy curtain had closed over part of her brain or something. And the room was now spinning as she'd feared it would since she'd woken up.

Eleven

"Breathe," Tomasso said soothingly, immediately at her side and urging her over to the bed.

Abigail sat, laid her head on her knees and breathed as instructed, but it didn't really seem to help. The room was still spinning and now her mind was racing too. In all her worry about Tomasso being a vampire and her eagerness to convince herself that was okay, and then with the added excitement of seeing her new figure, she'd forgotten all about that part. The bit about the turn.

Tomasso had turned her. Just as she'd feared when she'd first got sick. She was now a vampire, and—well, so much for the dengue fever diet, she thought with a grimace. Her new body must be a result of the vampire diet.

Oh, sorry, the immortal diet, Abigail thought a little hysterically and lifted her head to snap, "What the hell is an immortal if not a vampire? Because I saw your fangs, buddy. And I know you bit me, I—"

Her words died with surprise as her fingers went to her throat, but didn't find the marks that had been there. Frowning, she stood and hurried into the bathroom to peer in the mirror at the spot where the marks had been, but they were completely gone, without even the tiniest scar to prove their previous existence.

"They healed when I turned you," Tomasso announced, appearing in the mirror behind her.

Abigail glanced to his face in the reflection and straightened, her eyes narrowing. "You have a reflection."

"I can eat garlic too," he said, his deep voice a dry growl. "And enter churches without bursting into flames."

"But I saw your fangs," she insisted, and then turned from his reflection to glare directly at him, demanding, "Show them to me. I know they're there. Show me."

Tomasso glared back briefly, and then sighed and opened his mouth. A heartbeat later she watched two of his teeth shift and drop down forming two perfect, pearly white fangs.

Gasping, Abigail raised a hand to her own teeth and turned to peer into the mirror.

"They are there," he assured her. "And you too will be able to bring them on after some training."

Abigail's gaze shot to his in the mirror and she asked with disbelief, "Is that supposed to be a good thing? Are you kidding? I don't want to be able to do that. I don't want to be a vampire."

"An immortal," Tomasso corrected, and then assured her, "And you do want to be one."

"Why the hell would I want to—"

"Because otherwise you would be dead," he snapped.

Abigail blinked and stared at him. "What?"

"You were dying," Tomasso said somberly. "The dengue fever had become dengue hemorrhagic fever and was heading for dengue shock syndrome. Liquids and a transfusion might have saved you, but there was a tropical storm on, the road was washed out, and we could not get you to a hospital. The doctor could not do anything for you. He suggested I pray and say my good-byes. Instead I did the only thing I could to save you. I turned you."

Running a hand through his long hair, Tomasso looked away, then back and admitted, "I wanted to. I was happy to. But if you had not been so sick I never would have turned you without your permission. I would have explained and asked—begged if necessary, but I would not have done it without your permission had you not been dying and beyond accepting or refusing the gift."

Abigail sagged back weakly against the counter. She believed him. She believed he'd done it to save her. Because she believed that she'd nearly died. Abigail distinctly recalled several times that she'd woken up sure this dengue was going to kill her. Between the fever, the pain, and the blood—

"My nose was bleeding," she murmured. "And my mouth, and—" Pausing, she lifted her head to peer at him uncertainly. "That was the dengue?"

Tomasso nodded. "You do not bleed with the turn. In fact, your body holds on to every drop it can and will continue to do so from now on."

"Why?" she asked at once.

"Because the blood is needed," he said simply.

"Why?" she repeated.

"Because the human body cannot produce enough blood to support the nanos now inhabiting your body."

That one kind of caught her by surprise and Abigail shook her head. "Nanos?"

"Bio-engineered nanos," he rumbled. "Programmed to repair damage, fight disease, keep us at our peak condition."

Her eyebrows rose. "How did I get them?"

"Blood," Tomasso said. "Mine."

"Like a transfusion?" she asked with a frown, because if they'd had the workings for that—

"No. I bit into my wrist and pressed the wound to your mouth until it stopped bleeding."

"Oh." Abigail's eyes widened, and then she made a disgusted face at the thought of his blood in her mouth and sliding down her throat. "Oh . . . Ewwww."

Tomasso raised his eyebrows as if to say, *"And you wanted to be a doctor?"* But Abigail barely noticed, her mind was now racing. She'd read some research in nano technology while at med school. What he was talking about was much more advanced than the experiments she'd found, but judging by what she'd read, what he was claiming could be possible. But why the need for blood? She considered the matter and then nodded slowly.

"Of course. The nanos use blood somehow," she murmured thoughtfully. "Either to complete their work or power themselves."

"*Sì*. Both," Tomasso said and smiled crookedly. "I love how quick your mind is, *cara*. You are brilliant."

Abigail blinked in surprise at the compliment and felt a blush claim her cheeks. But she said, "So, I'm guessing the nanos are somehow the source of the fangs?"

He nodded. "They are programmed to keep their host at their peak. To do so they need blood."

"So they force the changes on the host to be able to get it," she murmured, and considered some of the other mythological abilities of vampires. Not that she was really thinking of Tomasso as a vampire anymore, but myths often had a basis in reality, and her guess was that vampires were based on these immortals as Tomasso called them.

Although, she realized suddenly, that did seem a stretch, since vampires had been around a hell of a long time. Long before the word *nano* had even appeared on the human time line.

"*Sì*," Tomasso murmured. "The nanos bring on the fangs and cause other changes in their host, increased strength, speed, night vision. All our senses are improved really, not just sight. Hearing, touch, taste. We even smell better."

Abigail smiled faintly. She certainly thought he smelled better, and almost said as much, but thought that kind of flirty comment might sidetrack them. There was a bed just feet away, after all.

"So the immortal part?" Abigail asked slowly, and then her eyebrows rose and she answered herself, "Oh, of course. Peak condition. That's what? Twenty-four to twenty-eight?" she muttered. "The nanos would see aging as damage to be repaired too." Her eyes shot to him. "You don't age?"

"Oh, *mia bella*, the way you think. *Tu sei brillante*," Tomasso said, wonder on his face.

"Thank you," she said flushing. "But you don't age, right?"

"*Sì*. I mean, no, we do not age."

Abigail nodded and continued to think aloud. "And if the nanos repair wounds and illness, then very little would kill you. You'd pretty much have to be incinerated or something."

"Pretty much," he agreed. "Although if you remove the head completely so that the nanos cannot reattach it we die as well."

"And probably the heart too," she commented, her eyebrows rising when he shook his head. "No. You can survive without a heart?"

"It is just valves and chambers. The nanos would build a new one."

"But after five minutes or so, the blood cells would cease functioning and—"

"After about ten minutes they would cease functioning," he corrected.

"Ten?" she asked, her eyes narrowing on his face.

"*Sì*." He sounded pretty certain, she noted with interest, but then he continued, "And the nanos can work quickly when necessary. They replicate their number as needed to perform tasks."

"But to rebuild a whole heart out of just blood cells and   "

"A fertilized egg starts as but one cell, yet within three days has grown into sixteen, and in nine months becomes a human with trillions of cells," he pointed out. "The nanos work much more quickly."

"Hmm," she muttered, her eyes narrowing on him thoughtfully again. But then she shook her head and asked, "Using that logic, why does removing the head kill you? Why can't the nanos just rebuild it?"

He shrugged. "Our scientists are not sure, but I believe just as every army needs a leader—"

"There would be a lead nano too," she finished for him. "One that tells the others what to do."

He nodded.

"And you think this lead nano is housed permanently in the brain somewhere, giving orders?"

He nodded again and Abigail tilted her head slightly as she considered what he'd said over the last few moments. How many people knew how long blood in the human body would remain effective without the heart pumping? How many people knew the speed at which a fertilized egg developed and could tell you it was made up of sixteen cells in three days? The man was a big beefcake, he was built like a big old football player with arms as big around as her thighs, but *damn*, he was smart.

"Tomasso?"

"*Sì?*" he asked warily.

"You are a closet geek."

"What?" His eyes widened and then he quickly shook his head. "No."

"*Sì*," she said with certainty. "You look like a beefcake pinup model, and you grunt more than you speak, but I bet you have a huge fricking library at home and read *Popular Science* on the toilet."

Tomasso continued to shake his head briefly and then sighed and muttered, *"Le Scienze."*

Guessing that was the Italian version of *Scientific American* or something, she raised her eyebrows in question and merely waited.

"*Sì*, I like science," he admitted and then frowned. "How did you know?"

Abigail rolled her eyes. "Oh, I don't know, maybe because you knew that blood cells survive about ten minutes before effectively dying," she suggested. "Or because you know that the human egg divides into sixteen cells during the first seventy-two hours. I mean, really? Who knows that but scientists and closet science geeks?"

"This is why I prefer not to speak," Tomasso muttered.

"What?" Abigail asked with surprise. "Why?"

"Well, look at how you see me now. I am a geek to you."

"No!" she protested at once, and then grimaced and said, "Well, yes."

Tomasso sighed, his shoulders slumping.

Frowning, Abigail quickly stood and caught his hands in hers, saying, "But you're a sexy geek with a rockin' bod and very pretty."

Tomasso stilled and eyed her suspiciously. "You think I have a rocking body?"

"Sì," she assured him solemnly.

A smile curved his lips and he pulled her gently forward, his head descending just as someone knocked at the door.

"Yo! We're ordering room service for dinner. You guys want anything?"

Abigail placed her hand over Tomasso's mouth just before it reached hers and said apologetically, "Can we hold that thought? I'm *really* hungry. It feels like I haven't eaten in years."

A puff of air blew over her fingers on a short laugh from Tomasso and he straightened with a nod. "It has been a week since you ate. And I am hungry too."

"Wow, no wonder I'm hungry then," Abigail muttered as she slipped from his arms.

Shaking his head, Tomasso glanced to the door and called, "We will be out directly."

"Out?" Abigail squawked. "I can't go out there, I have no clothes."

"You do," Tomasso assured her. Moving to the closet, he opened it to reveal half a dozen sundresses hanging next to several men's shirts.

"Mary bought them," Tomasso explained. "She realized you were without and knew you would need clothes when you woke."

"And the men's clothes?" Abigail asked with amusement.

"She said she was tired of looking at my bare chest," he said, blushing slightly.

"That's odd," Abigail said with amusement as she grabbed a white dress with large red tropical flowers on it. Heading for the bathroom, she threw a flirty smile over her shoulder and added, "Because I love looking at your bare chest."

"Later," Tomasso promised with a smile.

Abigail returned the smile and started to close the door.

"Abigail?" he said suddenly.

Pausing with the door half-closed, she glanced to him and noted that concern had returned to his face. "Yes?"

"We did not really finish our talk," he pointed out. "There is much to explain."

Abigail smiled crookedly. "Later. I think I have the gist of it, and really it's kind of overwhelming," she admitted. "So maybe we could do it in increments, a little here and a little there? Yes?"

"*Sì*," he said, relaxing. "A little here and a little there."

Nodding, Abigail finished pushing the door shut and then leaned back against it and closed her eyes on a little sigh as her brain sorted through what she'd learned. Tomasso was an immortal, not a vampire. He had turned her, so apparently she was one now too. Which didn't seem so bad to her now that she knew it was due to nanos and not some curse that had left her soulless. Besides, the benefits were kind of awesome, Abigail thought. She had a rocking body, would never age and stuff . . . She wrinkled her nose and acknowledged that she wasn't completely sure what the "stuff" entailed, but supposed she would find out soon enough.

The thought made her smile crookedly and then she shook her head as she moved on to what else she'd learned . . . Tomasso wasn't just a hunk, he was secretly smart too. Wow! How hot was that? She could actually talk to the man about things that interested her. Something she hadn't even really considered before this. Until now, Abigail had mostly been lusting after his big beautiful body. And he did have a beautiful body worth lusting after, but as long as there was just lust between them . . . well, sexual attraction waned eventually, right? But now she was beginning to find his mind almost as interesting.

Almost, she acknowledged wryly. There was still an awful lot of lust in the way, but she found his smarts exciting too, and promising as well . . . especially if they were to be life mates.

That made her grimace. She still had no idea what that was. They hadn't got around to that bit, but she was sure they would eventually, and she could wait. They had time.

Her eyes popped open on that thought and she moved to the mirror to peer at herself. While there had been a lot of changes wrought by her being turned, she didn't look any younger to herself. But then, she was only twenty-six, already in that peak condition area the nanos kept their hosts in. Her skin did look smoother though, fresh and smooth as a baby's butt. It even seemed to glow a little and had a natural healthy blush. She definitely didn't need makeup.

Abigail smiled at her reflection, and then glanced down at her towel-wrapped tummy when it rumbled hungrily. Right. Food.

Letting the towel drop to the floor, she took the dress off the hanger and quickly donned it, and then examined herself in the mirror. Usually she wouldn't have gone without a bra even in a strapless dress like this, but she didn't need it with her new body. Her breasts, larger though they were, appeared to defy gravity.

"Sweet," she said and snatched up the brush lying on the counter to run it quickly through her hair. The brush was obviously Tomasso's which made her grateful he had long hair. Finished with it, she set it back on the counter and then swung around to hurry out to the bedroom.

Her steps slowed when she saw that the room was empty. Tomasso had left, she realized, but after a hesitation, she simply headed for the door he'd entered through. She'd never seen the rest of the suite, or villa, or whatever this was. Now she glanced around curiously as she stepped out into a large living room/dining room combo done in white and teak. The dining room table was white-painted wood, its chairs also mostly painted white but with unpainted bamboo backing. The large comfortable couches and chairs in the sitting area were white with colorful throw pillows, and the coffee and end tables were all teak. She thought the ceiling was too, though it was vaulted, pretty high up and she couldn't be sure.

Smiling, she lowered her gaze from the ceiling, only to freeze as she spotted Tomasso on the terrace just outside the glass doors . . . kissing Mary! And pretty damned passionately too, she noted with dismay. Abigail had thought she and Tomasso had something hot and special, the kind of passion that didn't come along every day. But apparently it did with Tomasso, because it looked to her like he and Mary were about to rip each other's clothes off right there on the terrace for all to see.

"Oh, you are out already. Here. I went to fetch the menu for you."

Abigail whirled and gasped as she found herself staring at . . . Tomasso? Frowning, she whirled back to the terrace, blinking when she saw that he was still out there, Mary in his arms.

But his clothes were different, she realized suddenly.

"Abigail?" Tomasso was suddenly by her side, his expression concerned. "Are you all right?"

"Who?" she gasped, pointing to the other him.

Tomasso followed her finger to the couple on the terrace and smiled faintly, then glanced to her with confusion. "I thought you met Mary? This morning? She is the one who was there when you woke up and fetched me to—"

"Not her! You!" Abigail snapped. "And how can you be in two places at once?"

Tomasso's eyes widened and then understanding filled his expression and he slid his arms around her and began patting her back. "That is my brother Dante. Did I not mention we were twins?"

"No," Abigail whispered. Closing her eyes she sagged against him with a shudder of relief. Once she'd seen that there were two of them, she'd thought perhaps nanos were not the only advanced technology she needed to worry about. Perhaps cloning would be in there too and there were dozens of Tomassos running around and—

"I am sorry. Did you think that was me kissing Mary?"

"Yes," she admitted, nodding her head against his chest.

"And you were jealous?"

Hearing the hope in his voice, Abigail laughed softly and shook her head. Pulling back, she looked up at him and said solemnly, "I wanted to tear Mary away from you, rip her hair out and then pull down your pants and cut off your—"

Tomasso saved his manhood from abuse by kissing her then and bringing an end to the description of what she'd wanted to do. Abigail went still at first, and then slid her arms around his neck, pressed forward against him and kissed him back.

"Hey! Romeos one and two! Do you guys think you can get your tongues out of your girlfriends' mouths long enough to decide what you want to eat? Am I the only one around here with a stomach? Honestly!" There was a pause and then the voice muttered, "I'm going to go call Holly."

"Who was that?" Abigail asked on a sigh when Tomasso slowly broke their kiss. She thought it was the same voice that had called through the door about ordering room service, but had no idea who it belonged to. Or even how many people were presently in this place, which she was quite sure was a villa.

"Justin Bricker," Tomasso growled, pressing a kiss to her nose before releasing her completely. "He is cranky because Lucian would not let him bring his life mate, Holly."

"What is—" Abigail began, only to cut herself off. She suspected the discussion about life mates would not be a quick one and she really was hungry. It was better left for later.

"You're up and dressed."

Abigail turned to Mary as the blonde led Dante inside, and offered the woman a smile. Gesturing to the dress she wore, she said, "Tomasso said you bought the clothes for me. Thank you."

"Oh." Mary waved her gratitude away. "I just picked them out. The council picked up the tab." She smiled as she looked Abigail over in the dress. "Glad to see I was right about the size."

Abigail smiled and nodded. "You were. Thank you."

"You must be Abigail," Dante said next, moving around Mary to hug Abigail in greeting. "Tomasso has told us a great deal about you."

Wishing he'd done the same with her about them, Abigail automatically hugged the man back. He not only had the exact same face as Tomasso, his body was identical too and hugging him should have been like hugging Tomasso, but it wasn't. Her head was at the exact same level as it would be on Tomasso, his arms were strong and enveloping like Tomasso's, and yet there was something missing. Abigail felt nothing in his arms. Weird, she thought. But in a good way. It would be extremely discomfiting to find herself attracted to both brothers. It made her wonder, though, what caused the difference. Was it chemistry? Or, since they kept mentioning this life mate business, which she'd never heard of before so assumed only happened with their kind, perhaps it had something to do with the nanos. Did they send out signals to the nanos in her body?

That made no sense, Abigail realized now. She hadn't had the nanos until recently. There had been none in her for his nanos to communicate with on the beach and there had been some serious attraction from the start.

Interesting, Abigail thought as Dante released her and stepped back. It was something she'd have to ponder later and even discuss with Tomasso. It would be a fun puzzle for them to work on together, she thought as Tomasso slid an arm around her waist to steer her through the dining area and into the kitchen beyond it.

Two more men waited for them there and Abigail looked from one to the other curiously. One had dark hair while the other's was ice-blond. Both were well built and handsome, and both looked to be about the same age as the rest of them physically, but Abigail found herself examining the fairer man's face, her eyes focusing on his and staying there. She was sure the icy silver-blue gaze she met belonged to someone much older than the twenty-five or so years he appeared to be.

"Finally," the dark-haired man said with relief, covering the phone he'd been talking into. "Look at the menu, pick what you want and I'll order it. But try to be quick. I'm hungry and it'll probably take an hour for room service to deliver as it is."

"Room service isn't likely to deliver here since this villa is listed as empty," Tomasso pointed out.

"Oh, right," Justin said with a frown.

"It doesn't matter. I'm too starved to wait an hour anyway," Mary said with a grimace.

"So am I," Dante announced.

"Then why don't we just go down to the restaurant? It would be faster," Mary pointed out, then frowned and glanced to Abigail with concern, adding, "If you're feeling up to it, I mean. If not, I'm sure we can—"

"It's okay," Abigail interrupted with a smile. "I feel fine. We can go down to the restaurant."

"Are you sure?" Tomasso asked, and she was surprised to see the concern on his face too.

"Yes. Really. I'm good," she said on a laugh. "Crazy hungry and thirsty, but good."

The fair-haired man with icy silver-blue eyes turned suddenly to Tomasso. "Did Justin bring you the fresh cooler?"

"Sì," Tomasso said.

"Three bags then to be sure there are no unfortunate incidents at the restaurant. I'll call for a van to collect us. You have five, perhaps ten minutes. Be quick."

Tomasso nodded, looking suddenly grim, and turned Abigail to lead her from the room.

"Do you want some help?" Dante offered and Abigail saw Tomasso nod though he didn't stop to look around or even slow.

"Help with what?" she asked curiously as he hurried her through the dining/living area. "Where are we going?"

"All will be well," Tomasso assured her, and despite the sexy bass of his voice, Abigail was suddenly worried where she'd only been curious before.

"What's going on?" she asked, digging in her feet.

Tomasso merely scooped her up and carried her the rest of the way to the bedroom door. He moved so quickly, they were inside the room before she could protest.

"Tomasso!" she said with confusion. "Put me down. What's—?"

Her question died on a gasp as he pressed a quick kiss to her lips.

When he ended it just as abruptly, Abigail blinked her eyes open to find herself sitting on the end of the bed. Tomasso was already six feet away, with his brother, opening the cooler she'd noted earlier. The one she'd thought might have pop or juice in it, she recalled as she watched them both bend to examine the contents.

"I know Lucian said three, but I'm thinking four might be better," she heard Dante murmur. "If she's anything like Mary, she'll be pretty thirsty the first little while."

Tomasso grunted in agreement and they both began to reach into the cooler.

"What on earth are you two . . ." Abigail's question trailed off as both men straightened, each holding two IV bags of what could only be blood. Gasping, she stood abruptly. "I've changed my mind. I think I'd like to eat in."

"Abigail," Tomasso chided, moving slowly toward her. "You have to learn sometime."

"Learn what?" she asked at once. "What do you plan to do with those?" Even though she asked the question, Abigail had already surmised the answer. There was no way they could get those four bags of blood into her in ten minutes using an IV. They meant to make her drink the blood, and she *so* wasn't doing that. She knew she'd have to eventually, her body would need the extra blood now that she'd been turned, but the idea of it was still new, and rather disgusting in her mind. She just couldn't chug blood down like it was a soda or something. Just the thought made her queasy.

"We are not going to make you chug it down like a soda," Dante reassured her.

"You aren't?" she asked warily, and then frowned. "Wait, how did you know I was thinking that?"

Dante glanced to Tomasso in surprise. "I thought you explained things to her? It is why Mary fetched you."

"I did," Tomasso muttered. "But we have not covered everything yet. Justin interrupted us before I could get to mind reading and control and such."

"Mind reading?" Abigail said with disbelief, and then scowled at Tomasso. "You can read my mind?" The thought was a horrifying one. Dear God, her thoughts had been pretty salty since meeting him. If he knew some of the fantasies she'd toyed with every time she'd looked at him . . .

"As your life mate Tomasso cannot read you," Dante said with amusement.

"Oh," Abigail exhaled with relief, then her eyes widened and she speared the man with a look as she squeaked, "But you can?"

He nodded with a grin and Abigail groaned. They were twins. He would surely tell Tomasso what he read in her mind. All the dirty little things she wanted to do to him. How much she already cared for him. The new fantasy she'd started having about him since learning he was a closet geek.

"Clark Kent?" Dante asked suddenly, confusion plain on his face, and Abigail groaned. That was the one. Tomasso in a suit and thick glasses, his hair back in a ponytail so that he looked like a geeky Clark Kent. Then he whipped off the glasses and ripped open his suit and shirt to reveal his big beautiful chest . . . Minus the Superman bodysuit and cape, of course. Fortunately, that particular fantasy hadn't got much farther than that so far. She'd only discovered Tomasso's smart side quite recently after all, which was a good thing, she decided, scowling at the wide grin on Dante's face.

Shaking his head, he turned to Tomasso and piled the two bags of blood he held on top of the two Tomasso already carried.

"You do not need me for this, brother," he assured him, patting his shoulder. "In fact, I think you will do better without me. Use the method we tried with Jackie."

"Vincent's Jackie?" Tomasso asked with a frown, managing to hold on to all four bags.

"*Sì.*" Dante headed for the door. "You remember. It failed with Christian, but succeeded with Vincent."

"Oh," Tomasso murmured thoughtfully. "*Sì.*"

Abigail's eyes narrowed suspiciously as she watched Dante

leave, and then she turned her gaze to Tomasso. "What method is he talking about?"

Rather than answer, he started determinedly forward.

Abigail backed up a nervous step, but paused when she felt the bed behind her and teetered briefly before dropping to sit on the edge of the bed. When Tomasso continued forward, however, resolve on his face, she began to crawl backward across the bed, but was too slow. Tomasso immediately tossed the blood bags on the duvet next to her, and then crawled onto the bed after her, moving forward until his body was over hers. He then dropped, his weight pinning her to the mattress.

"Er . . ." Abigail muttered uncertainly. "I thought I was supposed to—oh," she gasped with surprise when he bent his head to nip lightly at her ear even as he shifted his hips, to grind against her. "That's . . . er . . . oh," she said again as his hand covered her breast through the sundress.

Abigail's body immediately responded to the caress, her back arching to press her breast more fully into his palm and her hands creeping out to slide around his neck. The moment she did that, Tomasso kissed her, his mouth slanting over hers in demand.

Groaning, Abigail kissed him back, dinner quite forgotten as a new hunger claimed her attention. She was so caught up in the mounting excitement he was stirring to life in her, that Abigail hardly noticed the shifting sensation in her mouth. When she tasted blood on her tongue a moment later, rather than be repulsed, she found her excitement heightened and began to suck on Tomasso's tongue, the source of the blood.

She'd barely begun to do that though, when Tomasso broke their kiss, held her down with a hand on her chest and suddenly popped one of the blood bags to her mouth.

Abigail blinked at him over the bag, then lowered her gaze to peer at the bag itself, her eyes widening as she saw that it appeared to be shrinking. She didn't taste blood anymore though, she thought with confusion.

"Your fangs draw the blood up and straight into your system,"

Tomasso explained. If it weren't for the fact that she could feel his erection pressing against her leg, she would have worried that their kiss hadn't affected him at all.

Abigail stared at him as they waited for the bag to empty. A million questions were running through her mind, but she couldn't ask a single one, and didn't get the chance when he removed the bag either. Even as he tore the now empty first bag away, he was popping a second, full one onto her apparently extended fangs.

Sighing, Abigail relaxed back into the bed to wait. Much to her regret, Tomasso then eased off to lie on his side next to her. She immediately missed his warmth and weight, but couldn't protest with her mouth full of bag. They remained like that through the four bags Dante had recommended and then Tomasso tore the last one off, caught her hand and stood, pulling her with him.

"Waith, I wanth thoo—Ow!" Abigail gasped as her still extended fangs cut into her own tongue.

"Let me see," Tomasso murmured, clasping her face between his hands and tilting her face to examine her mouth when she opened it. "A small cut. It is already healing," he assured her. Then he met her gaze and advised, "Never talk with your fangs out."

Abigail nodded that she understood.

"They will shift back into place in a moment," he reassured her. "Now, we must go. Dinner, remember?"

Right. Dinner, Abigail thought. The others were waiting. Her questions would have to wait until later.

TWELVE

There were several restaurants at the resort, each with its own flavor. They had a choice between Mediterranean, Italian, French, seafood, haute cuisine, or a pub-style restaurant serving more pedestrian food. While they all sounded interesting, the group consensus turned out to be Italian.

Abigail had no idea what time it was. Her watch seemed to be missing; at least, it wasn't on her wrist when she went to check it, but apparently it was still early for dinner, and that was why they got a table without having to wait. They were seated at a round table near the back of the dimly lit restaurant, and offered water, red or white house wine, and a basket of bread to snack on as they perused the menu. Abigail was grateful for the bread as she looked over the restaurant's offerings. Everything on the menu sounded delicious and she was absolutely starved. Although the blood did appear to have curbed her thirst quite a bit, she noted.

"Everything looks so good," Mary said with a sigh.

"I know," Abigail moaned. "And I haven't eaten in a week. Do you think it would be rude of me to order one of everything?"

"I don't know about rude, but I'd like to see the waiter's face if you did," Justin said on a laugh.

"*Sì*," Dante said with a grin. "He would no doubt swallow his tongue if a skinny little thing like you ordered so much."

Abigail blinked at the comment. Skinny little thing? She hadn't been called a skinny little thing since . . . well . . . ever. Her gaze slid from the menu to what she could see of her body and she gave her head a little shake. Even with the turn she was not really skinny. She had curves and even a slightly rounded stomach, although it wasn't a muffin top, just a . . . Abigail couldn't think of a word to describe it, but it wasn't completely flat.

She supposed she shouldn't be surprised that she wasn't now model thin as she'd longed for her whole life. Models were not a healthy weight. If a person had to starve themselves or throw up to get to the desired weight, it probably wasn't a healthy weight to be. Actually, now that Abigail thought about it, models were a terrible role model for young girls, and they just made healthy women feel fat. Who picked those models? she wondered.

The waiter appeared at the table and Abigail let her thoughts drift away to concentrate on more pleasant matters. Food. Much to Justin's disappointment, she didn't order everything on the menu. She did order three dishes though, Fettuccini Alfredo, Bistecca Florentina, and Cappon Magro. Pasta, steak, and shrimp seemed like a good mix to her. Although to be fair to herself the Cappon Magro was actually a salad with vegetables and shrimp, so she didn't feel like she was being too, too bad by ordering the trio.

The moment they finished giving their orders, the waiter whisked away their menus and left them to chat desultorily around the table as they waited for their food to be prepared. Abigail sat back and listened as the group talked, but couldn't help noticing that Dante was almost as much of a grunter as Tomasso was and Lucian Argeneau surpassed them, hardly saying anything at all. It was Justin Bricker and Mary who carried most of the conversation, Mary asking gentle questions that soon had Justin Bricker spilling his guts all over the table about his family in California, his life mate Holly and their life together, until the meal arrived.

The conversation fell away then as they turned their attention to eating. Despite not having eaten for a week, Abigail could not possibly eat the three dishes they brought out to her. Each was a full meal on its own. Fortunately, Dante and Tomasso were happy to help and her plates were quickly picked clean.

Smiling over that, Abigail leaned back to get out of the way as their plates were quickly cleared away, and then glanced from Tomasso on her right, to Dante on the other side of Mary who was on her left. She was thinking back to when Justin had been talking about his family in California. Curious, she glanced to Tomasso and asked, "Do you have family?"

When he raised his eyebrows at the question, she rolled her own eyes and said, "I mean I know you have Dante." She smiled at the twin, before continuing, "But you've never mentioned parents or other siblings."

"Ah." Tomasso smiled faintly and nodded. "*Sì*. Three brothers. One sister."

"All older," Dante added. "But I am sure we will have younger siblings soon enough."

"Your parents are still alive and young enough to have children?" Abigail asked with amazement. She then slapped herself in the forehead before anyone could respond, and muttered, "Of course. Peak condition."

"*Sì*," Tomasso said gently.

"It makes for big families," Dante said wryly. "We have many, many aunts and uncles, and even more cousins. And our grandparents still live."

Abigail was gaping at this news when Mary asked, "What about you, Abigail? Do you have family? Siblings, parents, children of your own?"

"No," Abigail admitted, and then forcing herself to let go of the sudden trepidation she'd felt on learning the size of Tomasso's family, she managed a smile and explained, "I was an only child and my mother just passed."

"Oh." Mary's smile dimmed slightly and then she forced it wider, picked up her wineglass and held it up expectantly as she

said, "Then it is good that you have met Tomasso. He and Dante
have a large family to share with us."

"I'll drink to that," Abigail said brightly, and raised her own
glass to clink it against Mary's. She smiled as she sipped the wine,
but it was not a true smile. The fact was, Abigail found the idea
of Tomasso's family a bit alarming. It meant she would eventually
have to go through the whole "meet the parents" thing. Something he didn't have to go through with her. Lucky bastard, she
thought.

Shaking that worry away, she asked Mary, "So you don't have
family either?"

Abigail knew at once that she'd stepped in it with that ques-
tion. The silence around the table was immediate and complete.
No one even moved. Much to Abigail's surprise it was Lucian
Argeneau who broke the silence.

"Mary has family, including adult children and young grand-
children," he announced.

"Really?" Abigail asked with amazement, then noted the way
Dante was scowling at Lucian and followed his gaze in time to see
the blond man raise one supercilious eyebrow.

"Stop glaring at me, Dante," Lucian said mildly. "Not talking
about them will not make it easier on Mary."

"She cries when we talk about her children," Dante said stiffly.

"And she cries when you do not," Lucian said sharply. "But it
is better for her to get it out, than to hide her grief and let it fester
because she thinks it a burden on your conscience."

Dante glanced to Mary with dismay, and she immediately
patted his arm where it rested next to hers on the table. "It is all
right. I am fine."

"Are you hiding your tears from me, Mary?" he asked with a
frown.

Rather than answer, she turned to Abigail and explained, "I
am older than I now look. Until a week or so ago I was a sixty-
two-year-old grandma with, as Lucian said, kids and grandkids."

Abigail hesitated, but then ignored Dante's brooding expression and raised her glass as she complimented, "You look damned fine for sixty-two, Mary."

Mary smiled for real this time and clinked her glass against Abigail's. They drank, both of them actually downing what was left in their glasses, which was almost a full glass for Abigail, and half a glass for Mary.

"I don't suppose either of you Romeos mentioned to the ladies that alcohol has no effect on us, did you?" Justin asked with amusement as Mary and Abigail set their glasses down. "At least not the fun kind of effect."

Abigail glanced at him worriedly. "What kind of effect does it have then?"

"The alcohol will be cleaned from your system, but not by your liver," he said, phrasing it carefully enough that Abigail realized they probably shouldn't have been talking about Mary's advanced years as openly as they had.

Leaving that worry for now, she concentrated on what Justin had said, quickly working out that the nanos would flush the alcohol from their system, probably before it could affect them. But that it would mean having to take in more blood to make up for it.

Just as Abigail's eyes widened with dismay at that realization, Mary raised her hand to wave the waiter over.

"More wine, miss?" the waiter asked as he paused just behind Mary and Abigail.

"No, thank you," Mary said wryly. "In fact, can you take my glass away and bring me a glass of water instead? And perhaps a cappuccino?"

"The same for me, please," Abigail announced, passing her empty glass to the man so he didn't have to reach around her.

She wasn't terribly surprised when the men all followed suit, each requesting a coffee or cappuccino and water.

"Well," Mary said as the waiter moved away. "You learn something new every day."

"I am sorry, Mary," Dante murmured. "I should have mentioned . . ."

"Don't be," Mary interrupted, waving his apology away and smiling at him. "There is no doubt a lot you haven't got the chance to tell me. We'll get there eventually."

Abigail watched the couple smile at each other, waiting until they turned back to the group before asking, "So you and Dante haven't been together long either?" And then realizing how presumptuous that was she added, "Or have you had a long courtship?"

Mary chuckled softly and shook her head. "Not long at all. I think it's been . . ." She paused, peering upward as she tried to work it out. Finally she shook her head. "Maybe a week and a half."

Abigail's eyebrows rose. "Really? But that's how long it's been since I met Tomasso."

"Eight days," Tomasso corrected.

She glanced to him in question, then said, "Four days on the beach."

"Sì."

"And then I was sick."

"Two days," he announced.

"Really?" she asked with surprise. "It felt like forever to me."

"Me too," he acknowledged. "A very bad two days, but still two days."

"Oh," Abigail sighed. Then asked, "And how long was I under when you . . . er . . . did the . . . er . . ." Glancing around nervously, she whispered, "Turning thing?"

"Two days," he said again.

"Hmmm. Eight days then."

"You must have met on that plane the day after I escaped," Dante commented.

"Good," Mary said cheerfully, leaning sideways to bump her arm against Abigail's. "We can be newbies at this together then."

"Sounds good," Abigail responded with a smile. At least she wasn't alone in this. She and Mary could commiserate as they tried to adjust to their new lives.

"So," Tomasso murmured then, and glanced from his brother

to the other two men. "Have any more immortals been taken since Dante and I?"

Abigail stilled and glanced around the table at this question as some of what Tomasso had told her began to make more sense for her. She'd wondered why an Italian visiting Canada would be involved in helping to sort out kidnappings in Texas. Now she knew why. The victims had obviously all been immortals.

"No," Lucian answered. "The pair of you appear to have thrown a wrench in the works with your escapes."

"How?" Tomasso asked with a frown.

Lucian said simply, "The men pursuing Dante when he fled, later took Mary and died in a crash for their efforts."

Dismayed at the thought of Mary being taken, Abigail glanced to the other woman and caught guilt flashing across her face.

"I caused the accident," Mary admitted with a sigh when she caught Abigail's curious expression.

"Oh," Abigail said softly, and then added in her defense, "If they kidnapped you, they deserved it."

"They did," Lucian agreed and turned to Tomasso to continue. "And as far as Mortimer has been able to learn, the men who took you set down in Puerto Rico, raised a search to try to find you, then flew to Puerto Plata to start another search effort."

Abigail froze at this news, and then turned from Mary to grab Tomasso's arm, gasping, "Jet!"

"Tomasso asked Mortimer to look into your friend when he called," Lucian announced. "As near as he has been able to find out, the pilot Jethro Lassiter parted ways with his clients in Puerto Rico. He set down at the Puerto Plata airport two days after you two left the plane and has been searching all the coastal areas as well, on his own."

"Oh," Abigail said with relief. Jet had got away from his clients okay. And he was looking for her, she realized . . . while she had forgotten all about him. Jet should have been her first, or at least one of her first concerns on waking today, she thought unhappily. Instead it had taken someone else prodding her memory with news of others to even make her think of the man who was like a brother to her and the only thing even close to real family that she had left. Abigail couldn't believe she'd been so uncaring and such a horrible friend. Here Jet was searching the area all by himself and she hadn't even thought to ask if there was news of him.

"Mortimer was sending someone to find and handle Jethro Lassiter."

Abigail glanced around sharply at that comment from Lucian and narrowed her eyes. "What does that mean? Handle him?"

"He will be reassured that you are fine and sent back to his life unconcerned," Lucian announced.

"Unconcerned?" she asked with bewilderment. "What do you mean unconcerned? If he's gone to the trouble of mounting a search here, he'll want to speak to me to be sure I'm fine."

"No. He will not," Lucian said with finality.

Abigail stiffened in her seat, her eyes narrowing on the man with suspicion. "Why?"

Rather than answer, Lucian Argeneau glanced down as some-one began to sing, "I'm so Tacky." He pulled a phone out of his pocket, read the display and answered, saying, "One moment, Marguerite." Pressing the phone to his chest then, he glanced to Tomasso and said, "Take your woman back to the villa and ex-plain things before she becomes hysterical."

Much to Abigail's amazement, Tomasso stood and urged her to her feet to leave the table. She was so stunned by it, that they were out of the restaurant before she turned on him. "Are you kidding me? You just obeyed that man like a dog."

"No," Tomasso said patiently.

"Yes, you did," she insisted. "His telling you to take me to the villa is—Well, hell, he sounded like a father sending his kids to their room. And you just—"

"I did not urge you from the table because he said to," To-masso interrupted quietly, taking her arm to get her moving along the pathway as another couple approached.

"Right. So why did you?" Abigail asked with disbelief.

"Because he was upsetting you," he said simply. "And I want to protect you as much as I can from upset and pain."

Abigail actually stumbled over her own feet at those words. Pausing, she turned to peer up at him on the dark path.

"And we are not going to the villa," Tomasso added, and then frowned and added, "Well, unless you wish to."

"No, I don't wish to," she assured him. Lucian *had* been upsetting her. Actually, she didn't think she liked him much. So avoiding him was fine with her. She did like Mary and Dante though, and even Justin. Still, she was content to not return just now, and asked, "So where are we going?"

Tomasso hesitated and then admitted, "I thought a nice walk on the beach would be pleasurable."

"Really?" Abigail asked with amusement. "It seems to me we spent four days trying to get off the beach. Now you want to walk it?"

"As I recall, we did not try very hard," he pointed out, and knelt suddenly to slip her borrowed sandals off her feet as he added, "I fear the delights tempted me to dawdle more than I should have."

"The delights?" she asked softly as he quickly removed his shoes too and straightened with both in hand. Rather than respond, he clasped her hand in his and led her off the path and onto the sand.

It was much darker on the beach than around the resort. There were no lights to help, but Abigail could actually see very well. Those nanos were giving her better night vision, she thought as they stopped at the edge of the shore and Tomasso let their shoes drop and turned to her.

Clasping her face between his hands, he tilted her face up and murmured, "You were the delight tempting me to dawdle."

"I find you delightful too," Abigail whispered, her hands rising to clasp his hips.

Tomasso closed his eyes briefly and murmured. "I want nothing more right now than to drag you down to the sand, remove your dress, and make love to you."

"Okay," Abigail breathed, a tingling starting between her legs just at the thought of it.

Chuckling softly, Tomasso leaned his forehead against hers, and then turned it slightly from side to side as if shaking his head no and muttered, "Stop that. You tempt me again."

"Hey!" she said defensively. "You're the one who brought it up. I was just being amenable and agreeing."

"You are right, of course," he agreed. Smiling, Tomasso bent to collect their shoes, and then took her hand to start walking again as he commented, "I like that about you."

"What? That I'm easy?" Abigail asked dryly, and then tacked on, "At least for you anyway."

"Sì," he said simply.

"Hmmm," Abigail murmured. They fell silent briefly, but after walking several minutes, Tomasso stopped again, this time to urge her away from the water and up to a row of lounge chairs set in the sand.

She thought they'd each take one, but Tomasso had other ideas. Pulling her to a chair, he dropped the shoes again, and then settled himself on the lounger and tugged her down to sit in his lap. He took a moment to arrange her to his satisfaction, but once he had her seated between his legs and leaning back against his chest so they could both look up at the sky, he released a satisfied little sigh.

"This is nice. No?"

"Yes," she murmured, thinking it reminded her of their bath together. Only they were dressed and dry.

Tomasso was silent again for a moment, and then said, "Dante mentioned that we can read minds."

Abigail stilled. "Yes. But you can't read mine, right?" she asked suspiciously.

"No. I cannot," he assured her, and then continued, "But I think there was mention made of mind control too?"

Abigail tried to twist around to look at him, but he held her in place with his hands and legs and calmed her by simply saying, "I cannot control you either, Abigail. It is why we are life mates."

"Oh," she said, relaxing.

Tomasso grunted at her capitulation and cleared his throat. "That is how they will calm your friend Jet and send him back to his life. They will read his mind, control him if necessary, and alter his memories so that he is content to stop searching for you and return to his life untroubled by worries for your well-being."

"Oh," Abigail said quietly and tried to decide how she felt about that. She supposed it depended on—"How will they alter his memories?"

"They will most likely make him believe he successfully completed his flight to Caracas, and spent these past several days there on the beach with you, where you met a handsome Italian and parted ways with him to follow me back to Italy."

Abigail snorted at the suggestion. "He wouldn't buy that nonsense."

"What?" Tomasso asked indignantly.

"I would never willingly abandon a friend to go traipsing off after some random guy I met on a beach," she assured him.

"You did leave him and land on a beach with me," he pointed out quickly.

"Not *willingly*," she countered. "Hell, I brained myself trying to get away, as you'll recall."

"Hmmm," he muttered, sounding a bit annoyed at the reminder. "You did."

"Yeah." Abigail sighed. "They'll have to come up with something better than that."

"*Sì*," Tomasso murmured, and then began to toy with her hair and asked, "You do not mind?"

Abigail stilled again, sure she'd heard a frown in his voice. Wary now, she asked, "Mind what?"

"Having to give up your friendship with Jet for me?" he explained.

Abigail moved so abruptly, Tomasso didn't get to stop her before she leapt off the lounger. He followed quickly, but stopped when she whipped around and put up her hand.

"Why," she asked coldly, "would I have to give up my friend-ship with Jet to be with you? He is a friend, nothing more. Family really." Scowling, Abigail added, "If you think you can dictate who I can and can't be friends with, then we're going to have a real problem, buddy."

"I do not wish to dictate who your friends are," Tomasso as-sured her.

"Then what is this nonsense about Jet?" she demanded at once.

He hesitated and then said, "Mary has children and grandchil-dren."

Abigail blinked at the seeming change in subject, and then said, "Yes. I heard that part of the conversation."

"They think she died in an RV accident last week," Tomasso announced.

"No," Abigail gasped in horror. "Does she know that? We have to tell her so that she can—Why are you shaking your head? Of course we do."

"She knows," he said. "It is how it must be."

"What?" She stared at him askance, and then her brain began to work through the issues. Mary was sixty-two, but she had been turned immortal. Mary now looked about twenty-five. How did one explain a change like that without blabbing about immortals? Abigail was quite sure blabbing wasn't allowed, otherwise news of them would be all over the media.

Letting her breath out on a sigh, she nodded. "Okay, I under-stand why Mary has to let her family think she's dead," she con-ceded and then bit her lip and added, "No wonder she cries then. And no wonder Dante feels guilty. She gave them up for him."

"Dante turned Mary to save her life as I did to save you," Tomasso said. "He has nothing to feel guilty for, but loves her so feels that if he had not entered her life, she would not have lost so much. That is where his guilt lies."

"I see," she murmured, and thought that was tough for both Dante and Mary, but they would no doubt work it out. Raising her chin now, she said, "I understand why Mary can't maintain a relationship with her family. But I'm not sixty-two. I don't look much different than I did before you turned me. Well, other than being smaller," she added wryly, glancing down at herself. "But we can blame that on the dengue fever. I thought that was the source of the weight loss when I first woke up anyway."

"Yes, we could do that," he agreed. "But what happens in ten years?"

"What do you mean?" she asked uncertainly.

"Your friend will start aging and you will not," Tomasso pointed out.

"Right," she said with a frown.

"It is up to you," he said mildly. "But eventually you will have to break ties with him."

Abigail nodded in understanding and dropped to sit on the end of the nearest lounge chair. In truth, she supposed it wasn't so bad if she had to break ties with Jet. They could go back to writing as they'd been doing for the last couple of years. Still . . . "Wow. Complications, huh?"

"Less for you than for most," he said, settling on the lounge chair behind her and wrapping his arms around her waist.

"Yeah," Abigail murmured, thinking of Mary. Leaning back against his chest, she smiled wryly and said, "This is the first time that not having family doesn't seem like such a bad thing."

"You do have family," Tomasso assured her. "Me. Dante and Mary, and the rest of my family. You will be a Notte."

Abigail sat up and twisted to look at him seriously. "Isn't it kind of early to talk like that?"

"Not for life mates," he assured her.

"Right. Life mates." Abigail faced forward again, snatched up her shoes and stood up. "Maybe we should keep walking."

"Why?" Tomasso asked, but collected his shoes and stood up as well.

"Because you still have some things to explain to me, and I suspect we won't get much explaining done on that lounger."

"Ah, yes," he murmured. Lacing the fingers of his free hand

with hers, he started to lead her down to the water. "You wish to know about life mates?"

"Among other things," she admitted. "First I'd like to know who Lucian is. I gather he has some kind of position of authority among your kind?"

"Our kind," Tomasso corrected gently and then allowed, "He has some power here. He even has a little in Europe if only because the European Council members respect him."

"Council?" Abigail queried.

"A sort of government, I suppose," he explained. "It was formed ages ago when one of our kind, a madman, started building an army of his own progeny."

"Whoa, wait a minute," she said, drawing him to a halt. "What do you mean ages ago? There is no way this technology has been around for more than a decade or so."

"It was in Atlantis," he assured her.

"Atlantis?" Abigail asked, her voice barely more than a squeak. Tomasso nodded. *"Sì."*

"Oh jeez, all right, so you're saying Atlantis existed and had this kind of technology?" she asked carefully.

"Sì."

Abigail eyed him with exasperation. "Stop saying *sì*. Explain. Honestly, it's times like this your communication skills—"

A kiss ended her irritated rant quite effectively. Abigail was just softening into the embrace, when Tomasso lifted his head.

"Atlantis was an isolated state surrounded on three sides by water, and the last side by a mountain range between it and the rest of the world," he lectured, sliding his hands down her sides.

"Oh," she said, her fingers tightening around the straps of her borrowed sandals as she leaned into him.

"They quickly progressed beyond the technology of the rest of the world, and because of their isolation, or perhaps just because they were greedy, did not share it."

"Bad Atlantis," Abigail sighed as he pressed a kiss to the side of her neck.

"They eventually surpassed even the technology we have today."

"Smart Atlantis," she praised, tilting her neck and dropping the sandals to slide her arms around his neck.

"They developed the bio-engineered nanos now coursing through your body."

"Oh my," Abigail moaned as he nipped lightly at her neck where the blood was coursing full of those nanos.

"They had begun to test them on subjects when Atlantis fell."

"Fall down go boom," she muttered, tugging the top few buttons of his shirt open so that she could touch his chest.

"The test subjects with the nanos were the only ones to survive."

Blinking with surprise, Abigail pulled back slightly. "That's it? No one else?"

"No one," Tomasso assured her. "Lucian Argeneau and his parents, as well as my grandparents, were among the few who crawled out of the wreckage to join the rest of the world."

"That's it?" she asked again.

"No. There were others," he said, but didn't elaborate.

"Hmm," Abigail murmured. "When was this?"

"I do not know the exact date. Suffice to say a very long time ago. Before Christ anyway."

"Oh wow," Abigail muttered, "I suspected Lucian was old, but . . . just wow."

"*Sì*," Tomasso said with amusement, and then continued, "That is when the fangs evolved. In Atlantis, blood transfusions were used to deal with the subjects' problematic need for extra blood. However, after the fall, there were no more transfusions. The rest of the world did not have the technology."

"No, of course not," she said thoughtfully, thinking of a pre-Jesus world which was before the iron age, before . . . well, hell, basically before most everything. "So the nanos fixed the problem with fangs?"

"And speed, strength, night vision," Tomasso added.

"Predator skills," Abigail said dryly.

"If you like, yes."

"To make it easier to run around biting us guys," she said dourly.

"You are immortal now," Tomasso reminded her solemnly. "And yes, at one time immortals had to feed directly from mortals. But they had no choice. However, once society advanced to blood banks, most immortals switched to bagged blood and shunned hunting and feeding off their neighbors and friends."

Abigail didn't point out that he'd bitten her, but simply arched an eyebrow and asked, "Most?"

"The North American council forbids feeding off mortals. They consider it too risky and fear discovery of our kind so have banned it."

"And the European council?" she asked. That was where Tomasso lived after all.

Tomasso glanced away and muttered, "They are traditionalists. Slower to change."

"In other words, sucking neck is still okay over there," Abigail said with disgust.

He shrugged helplessly. "Most shun it."

"But not all," she pressed.

"No, not all," he admitted.

"Hmm," Abigail muttered, thinking she might not want to live in Italy then. Not that she would probably need to fear getting bitten, but she would hate to make friends with someone and then learn they hunted and fed off humans like cattle. Pushing that aside for now, she said, "So you guys joined the rest of the world and . . . one of your guys started an army?"

"An army of his own offspring," Tomasso agreed. "He was a little different than the rest. He had not developed fangs and had to cut his victims."

Abigail's eyebrows rose slightly. She suspected he was leaving stuff out, but let it go for now as he continued.

"He was also insane. He had begun to kidnap and rape immortal women, but he had also begun kidnapping mortals, turning them into immortals like him and then forcing them to bear his seed. His army was quite large before the others got wind of it, but once they did they got together to put an end to it. That was the first time they cooperated. It was also when they started making laws for all immortals to abide by."

"We have laws?" she asked with interest.

"*Sì,*" he said as if that should be obvious.

"Tell me."

"Each immortal female can only give birth once every hundred years."

"So no one could make an army," she guessed.

"If they are doing that, they are insane, or rogue and probably do not care about anyone's laws," Tomasso pointed out, and then said, "No, that law was to help keep our population under control."

"Oh," Abigail said with surprise, then commented, "I suppose lower numbers are better when you are trying to stay under the radar."

"It is also helps ensure you do not outgrow your food source," Tomasso pointed out.

"Oh, right," she sighed. Abigail really disliked thinking like that though. She was mortal, or had been until very recently. She didn't like to think that she had been as good as cattle to immortals before her own turn. Meeting his gaze, she raised her eyebrows. "Any other laws?"

"Each immortal can only turn one mortal in their lifetime."

"Once again, keeping the population down," she suggested.

Tomasso nodded.

"And you used your one turn on me?" she asked with a faint smile.

"Of course, you are my life mate. Most save their turn for their life mate."

Right, there was that term again, Abigail thought, but said, "Okay, so other laws?"

Tomasso shrugged. "That's about it."

Abigail gaped at him. "That's it? Like that's all you guys could come up with? There's no *don't murder your neighbor, or steal from people, or*—"

"We do have other laws, but those are the biggies that you can be executed for disobeying," he explained quickly. "Oh, and in North America you must stick to bagged blood, feeding off mortals is another one that can get you staked and baked. Unless it's an emergency," he added.

Abigail narrowed her eyes at that, and then pursed her lips. "So you could be executed for biting me on the plane?"

"Technically we were in Central America, not North America," he said with a grimace. "But it was an emergency anyway, and so, allowed."

"Yeah, an emergency like a midnight run to the nearest fast food place," she said sarcastically.

"No," Tomasso assured her. "I was very weak when I woke up in that cage. I needed strength to escape."

"Hmm," Abigail murmured and then sighed and said, "So you have other laws, but they don't carry the death penalty?"

"Basically, yes," he muttered.

"Like what?"

"Abigail?"

They both paused and turned to glance around at that uncertain voice.

A man was approaching them along the beach, tall, muscular, with short dark hair and a beard and mustache. The old Abigail wouldn't have been able to make him out well enough to recognize him. But the new Abigail did. Slipping from Tomasso's arms, she rushed toward him, crying, "Jet!"

Thirteen

"You saw everything?" Abigail asked with dismay.

"Yeah," Jet assured her. "There's a camera in the back and a small screen on my panel so I can keep an eye on the cargo. You know, in case ties break and something slides or whatever," Jet explained. "Fortunately, it's positioned so the two goons riding in front couldn't see it. But when I saw you throw back the tarp and reveal that guy in the cage . . . man," he said, shaking his head. "I thought we were all dead."

"So did I when I saw him," Abigail admitted with a grimace, glancing down at the glass of Coke in her hand. They were seated outside on the patio of the open bar, and Jet was explaining what had happened since they'd boarded the plane.

"Yeah, I figured," Jet said wryly, slinging an arm around her and hugging her briefly.

A low growl came from Tomasso's direction and Abigail eased back from Jet with a crooked smile. "So what happened then?"

"Well, I watched you help the guy in the cage. Then you went behind the cage and he followed and I couldn't see you anymore. The light didn't reach where you two went. I guessed you were sitting in the dark so the kidnappers wouldn't see you if they came to check on him again. I figured the two of you were trying to work out what to do to get us all out of the situation."

"Oh," Abigail murmured and refused to look at Tomasso. They hadn't been talking. First they'd been . . . well . . . and then they'd passed out.

"Then a couple hours later you both appeared again and started looking at stuff," Jet continued. "The next thing I knew Tarzan had the parachute on, the cargo door was opening and he was pulling you off the plane!"

"Yeah, I didn't know he planned to do that, Jet. Really," Abigail assured him. "I never would have just left you on the plane alone with those guys. Neither would he," she added quickly. "I found out later that he thought I was a stowaway and that you were working with the bad guys."

"Ah." Jet nodded. "I figured it was something like that. I did see you try to throw yourself back as he pulled you out." Jet frowned, his gaze rising to her head. "It looked like you might have hit your head."

"I did," she admitted.

"Yeah, I thought so." He shook his head. "After that, I didn't know what the hell to do. I was thinking should I wait until we landed and pretend to be shocked that the cargo was empty? Or should I say something about the cargo door being open right then and just not mention you?" Grimacing, he added, "I didn't want them knowing I knew what the cargo was though, so I was still trying to work it out when one of them noticed the red cargo light blinking on the panel and spazzed. He went to check his cargo and was back in like a heartbeat freaking out. 'Land the plane! Land the plane!' he's hollering." Jet waved his hands around in the air as if imitating the client.

"So, I land the plane. I wanted to anyway. I mean you were out there somewhere with Tarzan and I didn't know who the hell he was or what was happening," he pointed out.

Abigail winced and nodded.

"So, by this time we're almost to Puerto Rico," Jet continued. "With a little chatter, I get permission to land there. The whole time I'm lining up to land, I'm *freaking*, thinking these guys are gonna kill me as soon as we're on the ground. Or I'm gonna wind up in that cage, right?"

Abigail nodded, her eyes wide with concern.

"But no," Jet said on a laugh. "Hell, they just bailed. Couldn't get off the plane fast enough. Didn't even bother to take their cage, just took off, squawking about needing a boat and starting a search and stuff."

"Ahhhh," Abigail exhaled, glad they'd reacted like that and left Jet alone and safe.

"So then I'm trying to figure out what to do next. I knew you were out there somewhere with Tarzan. Didn't know if you were safe or what, or even if you were alive, but I couldn't just leave you out there. And those guys were looking for you too. Well, looking for Tarzan, and if you were with him . . ." He shrugged, took a drink from his rum-and-Coke, then continued, "So I rented a boat and searched around the area. I knew you guys had left the plane further back, but with currents and everything I thought it was better to be safe than sorry, especially with those other two looking, so I did check. But after two days I got back on the plane and flew to Puerto Plata to start a search here, but on land. I figured by now, you'd either have made it to shore, or . . ." He trailed off apologetically.

Made it to shore or died, Abigail finished the thought silently and nodded in understanding. What else could he think?

"So, I've been traveling along the coast, asking questions, seeing if anyone got picked up by a local fisherman, or came out of the water whether alive or dead. Then that storm hit, slowing me down. Couldn't travel that day at all, didn't even dare move around outside. Rented a room and waited for it to pass, then had trouble moving further along the road when it did pass. There were roads out and trees down and—" He shook his head, peered down into his glass, then glanced up to offer her a wry smile. "But then I get here, and I'm getting nowhere as usual. No one's seen anything or knows anything, and I think I'll just take a walk on the beach and figure out where to try next and I hear your voice and . . ." He held his arms out. "Here I am."

"Yes," she nodded. He was here indeed, and now she was in a bit of a quandary about what to do.

"Better yet, here you are," Jet said, his exuberance sounding a little forced as he leaned over to give her another hug. Holding her tight, he muttered, "Man, Abs, I was beginning to think I'd lost you. I kept remembering your head bouncing off the cargo door and thinking, that's it. She's a goner."

"No," Abigail said faintly, easing back from his hug again when another low growl came from Tomasso. It was coming from deep in his throat, so low she didn't think Jet could hear it, but she could. Smiling nervously, she said, "No, not a goner. Woke up the next day on a deserted beach with Tar—I mean Tomasso," she corrected herself quickly.

Jet stiffened and frowned. "Tomasso?" His gaze slid to Tomasso now. He'd been kind of ignoring him since she'd introduced them. But then Abigail had been babbling nervously at the time, and asking questions as she hurried him toward the restaurants and bars. She'd insisted they find somewhere to sit and "talk properly," mostly in the hopes of giving herself time to think. Abigail had known Jet would want answers and explanations and she'd been trying to work out a sanitized version of the tale of her time since leaving the plane that didn't include immortals or the fact that she was now one.

Not that Jet could have seen Tomasso well enough to recognize him on the beach. It had been extremely dark there. She suspected he'd only recognized her voice when he found them. He certainly couldn't have been able to see her well enough to recognize her, or notice the changes in her even. He probably still couldn't see her well enough to notice. Abigail had deliberately picked a table on the fringe of the patio, as far from the lights of the open bar as possible.

"You're the guy who was on the plane?" Jet asked, his expression tight as he squinted at Tomasso, trying to better see him.

"Looks different dressed, huh?" Abigail said with forced good cheer despite knowing he couldn't possibly see him well at all. She looked at Tomasso, able to see him quite clearly thanks to the nanos improving her night vision. With his long dark hair back in a ponytail and wearing the black dress pants and white dress shirt he'd donned for dinner at the restaurant, Tomasso didn't look anything like the naked wild man she'd first encountered on the cargo plane. She suspected that Jet wouldn't have recognized him even if he could see him better.

The two men stared at each other long and hard, and then Jet turned to peer at her and simply raised one eyebrow. There was a wealth of meaning in that eyebrow. It basically read, *What the hell? Who's this chump? What are you doing with him? Do I need to pop the bastard? Should the authorities be called? And you look fine so why the* hell *didn't you find some way to contact me and let me know you were okay?*

Grimacing, Abigail offered another weak smile and patted his arm. "Maybe I should explain what happened after we left the plane."

"Yeah," Jet agreed shortly. "Maybe you should."

Abigail nodded. "Well . . ." She paused and cleared her throat. "First off, I *did* knock myself out when he pulled me off the plane. Which meant poor Tomasso had to swim to shore pulling me behind him. He even had to scare off a nosy shark that came along. It stole my shoe, but he apparently punched it and scared it off," she added.

Jet didn't look impressed. In fact, there was now a skeptical gleam in his eye, like he was thinking Tomasso had made that up or something.

Grimacing, she continued, "Then we started trying to walk, hoping to find civilization."

"Trying?" Jet interrupted.

"Well, I wasn't much good the first day," Abigail admitted. "Too out of shape I guess, or maybe it was the head injury. Tomasso had bandaged it up by the way. We had the first aid kit from the plane."

"Uh-huh," Jet said.

"So, we didn't get far at first," she muttered. "I was lots better the second day though, or maybe it was the third," she added with a frown. It was so hard to keep things straight when she was leaving out whole chunks of time, like their bumping and grinding in the sand and passing out for hours, or bumping and grinding against a tree, or—Abigail rolled her eyes and shook her head. "Then Tomasso was injured and we had to stop walking."

"What kind of injury?" Jet asked at once.

Abigail opened her mouth, closed it, then glanced to Tomasso, panic the overriding emotion she was experiencing. She so wasn't telling Jet about Tomasso's junk. Abigail wasn't even sure what had happened to it anyway, but she wasn't admitting to cleaning and spreading antibiotic cream on his penis and then bandaging it up.

Apparently, Tomasso didn't have the same reservations. Actually, he seemed to get pleasure in announcing, "I woke up to find my cock looking like a crab had played patty cake with it."

Jet choked on the drink he'd just taken of his rum-and-Coke, and Abigail dropped her head into her hands on a groan.

Tomasso wasn't done though. While Jet gaped at him, Tomasso smiled and said, "Abigail got the first aid kit. She cleaned it up, smeared cream *all* over it, and then bandaged it."

Abigail was quite sure she didn't imagine the way he drawled out the word *all* as if to suggest—

"Abs?" Jet growled.

Sighing, she shrugged helplessly. "It was the jungle. What else could I do? Infections are dangerous in the jungle." Not waiting for a response to that, she added, "Anyway, I started getting sick after that and don't remember much. Tomasso apparently encountered some fishermen and they brought us here. He rented a villa and took care of me while I was sick."

"Yeah? And what were *you* sick with? Must have been something pretty bad if you couldn't even pick up a phone and call my cell to let me know you were okay so I could stop worrying. Right?" he asked bitterly, and then added, "Let me guess, the Italian version of jungle fever?"

Abigail stiffened at the slam, her chin lifting as she told him, "Actually, it was dengue hemorrhagic fever, Jet." She let that sink in and then rushed on, "I nearly died, and would have if not for Tomasso. He took care of me through the whole thing, held my hair while I vomited. Put me in cold baths to bring down my crazy high fever. Tried to get me to eat broth and drink water so I didn't get dehydrated. He really took care of me," she said stiffly, and then added, "This is the first time I've been out of bed, let alone out of the villa since we got here. We came down to have dinner with Tomasso's family, then went for a walk on the beach where we encountered you."

She swallowed, and then added, "And Tomasso contacted his family about you when he was able to get ahold of them. I'd explained that you weren't with the kidnappers and he knew I was worried about you, so he had them try to find out what happened and where you were. I already knew that you'd landed in Puerto Rico and searched there before flying to Puerto Plata to search along the coast here. They've been trying to track you down to let you know I was okay . . . Because Tomasso asked them to. Because he knew I would be worried when I woke up from *nearly dying*."

Abigail almost felt bad for throwing that last part in. She *had* almost died, but had already said as much and repeating it had merely been a slap at Jet for his Italian jungle fever bit. Which probably only hurt because there was a grain of truth in the insult. She *had* worried about Jet, but not as much as she felt she should have. She'd also been easily distracted by Tomasso's leafy loincloth . . . among other things. And Jet hadn't been the first thing on her mind when she'd woken up from being turned either. Or even the second or third. Abigail still felt guilty about that, but thought perhaps she'd gone too far, because Jet squinted at her briefly, frowning, and then he stood and walked away.

Mouth dropping open, Abigail gaped after him, but he only walked as far as the nearest of the tiki torches stuck in the sand along the sides of the patio. The nearest one was a good fifteen feet away. Jet pulled it out of the sand, carried it back and stabbed it into the sand next to their table and then turned to survey the two of them. His gaze slid over Tomasso first, taking in his tied-back hair and dress clothes and no doubt comparing that to the naked wild man he'd spotted in the display screen on his plane. After a moment though, his gaze then slid on to her and he froze, shock crossing his face.

"Jesus, Abs. You're so pale. And you're half your size," he exclaimed with dismay.

"Not quite half," Abigail muttered with embarrassment and then shrugged. "I was pretty sick."

"You must have been deathly ill," Jet muttered, and then all of the anger slid out of him and he sank back in his seat. "Ah, hell, I'm sorry, Abs. I've just been worried sick. I've been looking everywhere for you, scared the whole time that you were dead and it was all my fault for taking you on that flight." Running a hand through his hair, he added, "And then I had to tell Bob what happened to explain why I wasn't returning his damned plane, and he fired me. Threatened to have me charged with theft if I didn't return the plane at once. But I couldn't just leave without finding you."

Peering down into his drink, he muttered, "And then here I was tonight, facing being jobless and arrested and probably never getting another job because I'd have a record . . ." Grimacing, he let his gaze slide over her in the pretty sundress and finished, "And then I hear your voice and find you enjoying a romantic little walk on the beach with some guy seemingly without a care in the world."

Abigail wasn't sure if he was done or had just run out of breath, but she stood up and hugged him where he sat. The chairs around the tables were bar stool height, so even with her standing and Jet sitting, he was still a head taller than her. It was automatic for her head to nestle right into his neck.

Jet hugged her back fiercely. "You know I love you, Abs. You've been like a sister and my best friend since we were kids. I'm sorry I said those things."

"I know," Abigail murmured, finding herself inhaling his scent. How had she never noticed that Jet smelled so nice? she wondered. Really. He smelled good, Abigail thought and nearly nuzzled his neck, but then caught herself and stepped back with a confused frown. She'd never wanted to nuzzle Jet before. What the hell was going on?

Abigail glanced guiltily to Tomasso as she reclaimed her seat and noted that while he hadn't growled, he was watching her closely, his body tense as if prepared to spring into action.

"Man," Jet muttered, rubbing a hand down his face and shaking his head. "Screw my boss. You're alive. You survived head trauma while jumping out of a plane, and then dengue fever and being stranded on a deserted beach. *And* I found you. It's all good."

"Better than you think."

Abigail glanced around at that comment to see Lucian, Justin, Dante and Mary seated at the table behind them. She blinked in surprise. "When did you get here?"

"Shortly after you," Mary explained apologetically. "We saw the three of you coming in here as we left the restaurant. We didn't want to intrude, but with the kidnappers still out there somewhere, and your friend, Jet—" she smiled and nodded to him "—not yet tracked down, Lucian thought it would be best if we followed. We didn't want to intrude though, so we sat here."

"Oh," Abigail murmured, then glanced to Jet and smiled reassuringly, although she wasn't at all sure she shouldn't be telling him to run. "This is Tomasso's brother Dante, and his partner Mary," she said, introducing the couple closest, then gestured to the two men on the opposite side of the table. "And that is Lucian Argeneau and Justin Bricker."

"A pleasure," Jet said with a small nod and then glanced to Abigail uncertainly, before turning back to the others and suggesting,

"Why don't y'all come sit with us? Or we could push the tables together. There's no sense sitting apart if y'all are together."

Mary, Dante, and Justin all looked to Lucian, Abigail noted with irritation. She wasn't surprised when he was the one who answered, but he didn't address Jet. Instead, his eyes shifted to Tomasso.

"Take Abigail back to the villa. She's still recovering and needs her . . . medicine," he said cryptically, and then added, "Dante, Mary, and Justin will accompany you in case your kidnappers have also tracked the two of you down."

When Abigail frowned and glanced to Jet, Lucian added, "Mr. Lassiter will stay with me. We have business to discuss."

Abigail scowled at the high-handed man, then turned back to Jet. "You don't have to stay with him if you don't want. Come back to the villa with us."

Jet hesitated, his eyes suddenly caught on her mouth with confusion, and then his expression went blank and he stood. He then turned and moved to settle in the seat across from Lucian as Dante left it.

Abigail eyed him with concern, and then turned on Lucian. "What did you—?"

"He is safer with me than you just now," Lucian said.

"What?" she asked with disbelief.

"Abigail?" Mary said gently, and when she glanced at her, the blonde opened her mouth and tapped a fingernail on her upper front teeth.

For a moment, Abigail stared at her blankly, not understanding, and then she ran her tongue around her teeth and felt the sharp tip of first one point, and then another. They weren't fully out, just poking down a bit past her other teeth. They weren't even down far enough to impair her speech. But they shouldn't be out at all. She pressed her lips closed with dismay.

"They have been out since you hugged Jet," Mary said gently.

"Oh, God," Abigail muttered and turned to rush out of the bar.

She'd barely taken half a dozen steps outside when Tomasso scooped her up from behind and continued on without slowing.

"It is all right. He did not see. No one did," Tomasso murmured as he carried her along the path. "And you did not bite him. You pulled away."

"But I didn't even realize I was . . ."

"Hungry?" he suggested gently.

Groaning, Abigail buried her face in his neck, then quickly shifted her head lower when she noted that he smelled yummy too.

"This is new for you, Abigail." His voice was a soft rumble. "Of course you did not know. In time you will recognize the signs that you need to feed."

"But I had four bags before we left," she complained. "And we weren't even gone that long."

"You were very ill when I turned you," he said gently. "I am amazed that you are even conscious already. But the turn is not done. It is continuing as we speak. You will need a great deal of blood over the next little while. This is normal. I promise."

Abigail just shook her head, and then glanced around with surprise when he stopped and set her on her feet. They'd reached the villa. He'd walked all the way back. Or run, she thought with a frown. Good Lord, he moved fast when he wanted to. The villa was one of four on the very outskirts of the resort, separated from the rest of the buildings by pools and boutiques and then a stretch of mini jungle for privacy. The car that had collected them and brought them to the main area had taken longer than Tomasso had needed to bring her back.

Finished unlocking the door, he turned back to her, but Abigail shook her head, and slipped past him into the villa. She didn't need to be carried. She wasn't sick, just mortified and scared of what she could have done to her friend.

And apparently hungry, Abigail tacked on with disgust as she led the way through the villa to the room where she'd spent the better part of four days. Reaching the cooler, she flipped the lid open, a bit startled to feel how cold it was.

"It is a hybrid," Tomasso commented gently, apparently having noticed her surprise. "It functions as a normal cooler, but also plugs into electrical sockets starting a refrigerating unit inside. When plugged in it stays cooler than a fridge even. It is better for the blood."

Abigail let her breath out slowly and plucked out one of the bags of blood. Straightening, she opened her mouth and thrust the bag at her teeth as Tomasso had done earlier, but the bag just bounced and slid away. Frowning, she started to try again, but Tomasso caught her hand gently to stop her.

"Your fangs have retracted," he explained gently.

Frowning, Abigail ran her tongue along her teeth and, sure enough, they'd slid back to where they'd come from. There was nothing to pop the bag to.

"Figures," she muttered wearily.

"My poor Abigail. You have had a very tough time of late," Tomasso murmured. Bending to scoop her up, he carried her to the bed and settled himself to sit on it so that he could lean against the headboard with her in his lap. He then simply held her, and rubbed her back gently.

"Jet cares for you a great deal," he murmured when she finally relaxed and rested her head on his chest.

Abigail immediately tensed and sat up with a scowl. "I suppose Lucian is down there right now wiping me from his memory."

"I do not think so," Tomasso said thoughtfully.

"No?" Abigail asked with surprise.

"No," he murmured, and then met her gaze and smiled crookedly. "Shall we bring your fangs on and get you fed?" Running one finger down her cheek, he added, "Then we can make love. I have ached for you since the night we shared the bath."

Abigail's eyes widened and she started to nod, and then just as quickly shook her head as she recalled her screams as he'd pleasured her. "I make too much noise," she pointed out with embarrassment. "The others would hear."

"I could tie you to the bed and gag you," Tomasso offered with a wicked smile.

Abigail raised her eyebrows, and pointed out, "The gag I get, but the tying me up part wouldn't help me be quiet."

"It would keep you from tearing away the gag," he explained.

"Oh, right. Of course," she said with amusement, but the idea of being tied up and at his mercy had kind of turned her on. Actually, it had *really* turned her on, so she wasn't surprised when Tomasso took the bag of blood she was still clutching, popped it to her mouth and it stuck. Her fangs were out.

Apparently deciding to take advantage of that gag, Tomasso caught the edge of her sundress and started to tug it down.

Suddenly shy, Abigail grabbed at the cloth, trying to stop him.

Tomasso stopped at once, and bent to press a gentle kiss to her forehead, then drew his head down to claim one soft earlobe. Abigail moaned around the bag in her mouth, and tilted her head to give him better access as he released the lobe and nibbled a path down her throat. He didn't try to tug her dress down this time, but simply claimed one quickly budding nipple through the cloth, his mouth dampening the material around the erect bud as he nipped and flicked his tongue.

That brought a groan from her and now it was Abigail who pulled the material down for him, freeing her eager flesh. She felt more than heard the soft laugh that slipped from his lips and feathered across her sensitive skin.

Catching her by the waist, Tomasso lifted and turned her to straddle him. She started to sit on his lap that way, but he urged her to remain upright with her knees on either side of his hips. It put her breasts right in front of his face and he took advantage, cupping each breast in a hand and holding her in place as he leaned forward to flick his tongue over first one, and then the other nipple.

The bag was empty now. Relieved as she noted this, Abigail tore it away and caught Tomasso by his ponytail to tug him away from her breasts. When he lifted his head, she lowered her own head to kiss him, her mouth eager and demanding. Tomasso kissed her back briefly, his hands slipping away from her breasts to clasp her by the waist, and then he broke the kiss and lifted her off his lap. Abigail found herself set on her knees on the bed beside him and then he was off the bed and at the cooler. He was back before she could even sit down on her feet, three more bags in hand. Tomasso set them on the bedside table, then reclaimed his spot and lifted her to kneel over his lap once more.

"Perfect," he decided, his gaze roving over her breasts.

Tomasso then glanced to her face and smiled. His voice was a deep rumble as he murmured, "Let us see if we remain conscious for all three bags."

Abigail's eyebrows flew up and she opened her mouth to respond, only to have him pop a fresh bag of blood to her teeth.

Grinning at her startled gaze, he then leaned his head forward to begin laving and then suckling at one breast as his hands dropped to slip under the hem of her sundress and slide around to brush up the back of her legs.

Abigail watched wide-eyed, very aware that she'd had no panties to wear when she'd donned the dress. Mary had told her on the way to the restaurant that she had indeed bought her some. Apparently they were in a drawer in this bedroom, but Abigail hadn't known that at the time and had gone without. Actually, she hadn't even thought of them, Abigail acknowledged on a sigh as Tomasso's fingers reached her bottom and began to massage and squeeze.

"I love your body, *cara*," Tomasso growled against her breast as he let one hand drift around to the front of her leg. Leaning back then, he watched her face as he added, "I loved it on the beach, and I love it here. It is so perfect, so responsive to me and gives me such pleasure."

His hand had been drifting up her inner thigh as he spoke and now brushed between her legs. Abigail gasped, and jerked slightly at the teasing, featherlight caress. Tomasso smiled, but she felt his hand drift away, gliding down her leg and out from under her skirt. Confusion clouded her gaze, and then he tore away the now empty bag hanging from her teeth and popped a fresh one to them.

"Just two more bags left," he murmured, lifting the front of her skirt to tuck it into the neckline of her sundress where it had gathered around her waist. He then spent a moment just staring at what he had revealed, a smile playing on his lips until Abigail suddenly dropped to sit on his thighs, and reached for the button of his dress pants.

"Greedy," Tomasso teased lightly, but did not prevent her from undoing the button and zipper. However, once she'd managed to free him from the cloth and his erection sprang up, he caught her by the waist and lifted her back onto her knees again before she could touch him.

"Not yet," he cautioned, and when Abigail started to try to sit back down so she could reach him, Tomasso slid his hand between her legs to prevent her being able to. At least, she suspected that was his intention, but the moment his fingers pressed against her, Abigail gasped and shifted her hips, sliding across them.

Tomasso stiffened and groaned as pleasure slid through them both, and then began to move his fingers himself. Circling, rubbing, plucking. Abigail braced her hands on his shoulders as her legs began to tremble, afraid they would give out any moment, but her hips never stopped moving. Seeming to realize the problem, Tomasso grabbed her upper leg with his free hand, bracing her as he continued to drive them both crazy. Then his mouth found one breast again, but now he was suckling almost frantically, drawing almost painfully on the sensitive nipple as his fingers moved more swiftly.

"Tomasso," she gasped, tearing the now empty bag away. "Please."

He let her nipple slip from his mouth and glanced toward the side table. Suddenly the hand between her legs was gone. Even as Abigail moaned in protest at the loss, another bag was popped to her mouth, and Tomasso was urging her down until she felt his erection bump against her opening.

"Last bag," he gasped, his face strained as he met her gaze, but he was clasping her hips, his hands no longer caressing, but also keeping her from lowering further.

He was going to wait for the bag to empty. Abigail just knew it, but she couldn't wait. Eyes narrowing on his, she reached down to touch herself tentatively, then began to caress, a triumphant smile claiming her lips around the bag as she saw her reaction to the touch in his face.

"Oh, *cara*," Tomasso groaned, and let her slide his length until her bottom slapped his upper thighs. Abigail continued to touch herself, her caress becoming more urgent and her hips shifting on him. Then she clasped his shoulder with her free hand to help lever herself up and down, adding that friction to the caress.

"*Sì*. Do not stop, *cara*. Keep touching yourself," Tomasso ground out between his teeth, his hips bucking under her. And then his hands claimed her breasts, his thumbs and forefingers finding and pinching her nipples, and Abigail threw her head back on a cry as the night exploded around them.

FOURTEEN

Abigail woke up to find herself still in Tomasso's lap, slumped against his chest, her back complaining at the position. Grimacing, she eased carefully away from him to sit up, then froze, her eyes widening with horror.

There was blood everywhere. At least she, Tomasso, and the bed were covered with it. Recalling the still half-full bag of blood that had been at her mouth when they'd . . . finished what they were doing last night, Abigail glanced around for it and found the torn bag on the bed next to them. It had either exploded from the pressure of her clamping her mouth around it when they'd found their release, or it had got torn and splashed everywhere.

At least it was only on them and the bed and hadn't splashed on the walls or something, Abigail told herself with a grimace as she eased off of Tomasso's lap to stand beside the bed.

"No more sex while feeding," she muttered to herself as she tried to decide what to do. The blood was dry and sticky and Tomasso was still sleeping. She couldn't possibly clean it up without waking him. Grimacing, she shifted from one foot to the other, then sighed and turned to head into the bathroom.

She'd take a shower and clean herself up, and then see if Tomasso was awake, Abigail decided, crossing the bathroom without daring to look in the mirror. She didn't want to see the horror she no doubt was. She probably looked like a slasher victim with the dried blood everywhere. It was even in her hair, she noted as she brushed a stiff strand behind her ear.

Shaking her head, Abigail opened the shower door and turned on the taps, thinking that she'd never in her life imagined starting a day like this. Certainly as a child, she'd never daydreamed about growing up, becoming a vampire, and waking up encrusted in dry blood.

The moment the water was warm enough, Abigail stepped under the spray to let it start doing its work. Cleaning off dry blood turned out to be much harder than you would think. Some of it washed away quickly enough, but some seemed to cling determinedly and it took some serious scrubbing and three shampoos to get it all off her skin and out of her hair. Abigail managed eventually, though, and stepped out to quickly dry off, then wrapped the towel around herself to return to the bedroom.

Tomasso was still sleeping, although she wasn't sure how he could be in that position. He was slumped upright, with his back against the headboard and his head bent and resting on his chest.

Someone was going to have a crick in his neck when he woke up, she decided, and then wondered if the nanos would allow for that kind of thing, or prevent it. Her back had hurt when she'd first woken up, but that pain had been gone by the time she reached the bathroom door.

Yay nanos! Abigail thought wryly and moved to the closet to pick another sundress. Today she chose a baby-blue one with white polka dots. She also found the panties in the drawer where Mary had said they would be. There was no bra though, but then with her amazing new gravity-defying boobs, she could get away without one, Abigail thought as she carried everything into the bathroom to dress.

With no need for makeup, she was finished getting ready in maybe a minute and a half, two minutes tops, then she returned to the bedroom to find Tomasso still sleeping. Abigail paused and shifted her feet briefly, wondering if she shouldn't wake him. She was sure it would be less alarming than him waking up alone in a bloody bed later. But then she sighed and headed for the door instead. Abigail didn't know about him, but she could get pretty cranky when someone woke her from a deep sleep. It was better to just let him rest.

"And that decision has absolutely nothing to do with your suddenly feeling shy about the way you were bouncing around on his pogo stick last night," Abigail muttered as she left the room.

The living/dining area was empty when she crossed through it and Abigail was just beginning to think everyone else was up and had gone down to the restaurant for breakfast when she stepped into the kitchen and spotted Justin by a coffeepot that was giving off the most delicious scents. There was another man seated at the kitchen island, with his back to her. It wasn't Dante or Lucian though. Abigail followed the scent of coffee around the island, glancing curiously to the newcomer as she went, and then came to a stumbling halt.

"Jet?" she said with surprise . . . and not a little guilt. She'd left him down at the bar with Lucian, who she was quite sure could not be trusted, and hadn't given him a thought since. She so sucked as a friend.

"Morning, Abs." He grinned at her easily, looking completely relaxed and happy.

Abigail was less so. Her gaze shifted to Justin to give him a look of reprimand as she wondered why he hadn't come to let her know her friend was here. Then she glanced back to Jet and said, "I'm sorry. I didn't know you were here. When did you arrive?"

"Last night," he said on a laugh.

"What?" she asked with confusion.

"I slept here, Abs," Jet said with amusement, and then explained, "When Lucian learned I couldn't get a room in the area, he suggested I stay here too. I bunked with Justin."

"Oh," Abigail said weakly, her eyes now returning to Justin with concern as she worried that Jet might have been a midnight snack.

"There are twin beds in my room," Justin said with a shrug and then added dryly, "And he's fine. Completely unmolested."

When Abigail flushed guiltily, Jet frowned and glanced from one to the other. "What? You were concerned for my virtue?" he asked on a disbelieving laugh. "Abs, I can take care of myself. Besides, Justin's as straight as I am. He has a girlfriend named Holly. Apparently, she's a goddess," he added with a teasing glance at Justin.

"She is," Justin assured him, and then set down the coffee he'd just made and headed for the door. "I'm going to call her. Be back in a minute."

They watched him leave and then Jet glanced back to her in question. "Is there something I should know?"

"What?" she asked with alarm, and then turned quickly away, busying herself with fetching a cup and pouring coffee to avoid his gaze. "No. Don't be silly."

"Are you sure? 'Cause you seemed a little freaked out that I'd shared a room with Justin."

"No," Abigail muttered, adding cream and sugar to her cup and stirring. When she finally turned to see Jet eyeing her closely, she grimaced and moved around the island to sit on the stool next to his and shrugged. "I don't really know these people. I mean, I know Tomasso, obviously, and Dante and Mary seem nice, but I'm not sure about Lucian and Justin is all."

"Hmm." Jet took a sip of coffee, set his cup back and then said, "Well, I only met them last night, but they both seem okay to me. Justin is . . ." He paused, considering his words, and then said, "Well, he seems a bit of a smart-ass, but I think he has a good heart, and he definitely loves his girl. The guy couldn't stop talking about her. He's really missing her."

"That's sweet," Abigail murmured, her lips curving into a small smile.

"As for Lucian . . ."

She stiffened and glanced to him worriedly.

"He rocks."

"What?" she gasped with amazement.

"Yeah," Jet said excitedly. "He's arranging to have the plane returned to my boss, Bob, and he's going to take care of the criminal charges too. He guaranteed there wouldn't be any. And," he added, positively beaming now, "he hired me."

"Hired you?" Abigail asked with bewilderment. "What for?"

"To be a pilot, what else?" he said on a laugh.

"Really?" she asked with surprise.

"Yeah, Lucian is one of the Argeneau Enterprises Argeneaus," Jet announced as if that should mean something to her. When it obviously didn't, he clucked his tongue and explained, "Every pilot on the planet knows the name and would kill to work for them. Hell, some guys send resumes monthly just in the hopes that there will be an opening."

"Why?" Abigail asked with curiosity.

"It's a cushy, cushy job, Abs," he said seriously. "The pay is killer, and the benefits top-notch."

"Oh," Abigail murmured, but then frowned with confusion. She'd never heard of Argeneau Enterprises. "So he owns some kind of airline?"

"No, no." Jet waved the suggestion away. "Argeneau Enterprises is the mother company of a bunch of businesses situated in Canada, the US, and Europe. They have some techno companies, financial businesses, a blood bank even. Mostly the planes are to fly executives and other VIP type people around." Expression serious, he said, "This is more than a cushy job, Abs. It's an awesome opportunity, and I owe it all to you."

"Me?" she squawked with surprise.

"Well, I never would have met them if not for you," he pointed out. "And Mr. Argeneau doesn't know me from Adam, so he must have hired me because of my connection to you."

"Right," Abigail murmured, wondering what the hell Lucian's game was. Tomasso had said they'd probably control Jet's mind, change his memories and send him back to his life. Yet Lucian had hired him instead? And not only that, but invited him to actually stay here? In the villa? With six vampires—or immortals as they preferred to be called—and who knew how many coolers of blood lying around? The one in the room she shared with Tomasso could not be the only one.

What was Lucian thinking? What if Jet saw something?

"Life's weird, huh?" Jet said suddenly.

Abigail glanced at him in question.

"Yesterday about this time my life was hell," he explained, shaking his head with bemusement. "I'd been fired, was under the threat of being thrown in jail when I returned to America, and was worried sick about you. Hell, my life was in the shitter," he said on a wry laugh, and then continued, "But now, less than twenty-four hours later, everything's coming up roses. I found you, you're safe, the criminal charges are going away *and* I got a sweet ass job that is every pilot's dream."

Abigail let her breath out on a little sigh. When he put it like that, things did seem good. She just hoped they continued to seem that way. Managing a smile, she slid her arm through his and leaned her head on his shoulder in a sort of arm hug thing and said sincerely, "I'm glad for you, Jet. I hope it works out."

"Yeah." Jet slid his arm from hers and wrapped it around her shoulder instead to hug her more properly against his side, then complained, "You lost way too much weight. There's hardly anything to hug."

Abigail straightened with a grimace. "Dengue will do that to you," she said wryly, despite knowing it was only part of the reason behind her weight loss.

"Yeah, but you look different too," Jet said with a frown, his eyes narrowing on hers.

Abigail blinked and then turned forward so he couldn't see her eyes. They used to be green, and still were, but with little flecks of silver in them. She was guessing that had something to do with the nanos since she'd noticed the same flecks in the eyes of the others.

"I think I'm kind of insulted that it took you so long to notice the weight loss last night," she said to distract him.

"I noticed right away," Jet protested and then made a face and admitted, "Well, not right away, but I did notice before I got the tiki torch. I just didn't want to hurt your feelings by pointing out that you looked sickly."

"Oh, piss off," Abigail muttered, knowing he was just being his usual PITA self. PITA meaning a Pain In The Ass.

Jet chuckled softly and took a sip of coffee, and then asked, "So? What about you?"

Abigail glanced at him in question. "What about me?"

"Well, I wasn't the only one bunking with someone last night," he said heavily. "And I'm betting that room you shared with Tomasso *doesn't* have twin beds. What's going on there? Do I need to pop him?"

"No, of course not," Abigail said flushing. She turned her face away and picked up her coffee. "He's . . . We're . . ."

"Hooking up?" Jet suggested when she fell silent.

Abigail clucked her tongue with irritation, and asked, "How do you know where I slept?"

"Because Justin gave me a tour of the place last night when Lucian brought me back and he showed me the guest bathroom near the entry, then the living/dining room and pointed to the door off of it and said—and I'm quoting here—" Jet added dryly, "'That's the door to the master bedroom, Tomasso and Abigail sleep there.'"

Abigail closed her eyes. The master bedroom and a powder room were the only rooms on the main floor besides the kitchen and the living/dining room combo. The rest of the bedrooms were on the second floor.

"So?" Jet asked, nudging her with his arm. "What gives? Are you two shacking up? Is it serious? You're using protection, right?"

Abigail stilled, the cup slipping from her fingers and dropping the two inches to the counter with a thump that sent coffee sloshing over the rim. Jet jumped up and ran around the island to grab paper towels.

"I'll take that as a no you aren't using protection," Jet said grimly as he returned and began to mop up her mess.

Abigail met his gaze, her eyes wide with dismay. She hadn't

thought of it. Not once. She hadn't thought of protection at all. STDs weren't a concern now that she knew about the nanos, but what about babies? She and Tomasso had had sex . . . well, fortunately only twice. The rest of the times they'd been together they hadn't actually copulated. But it only took one time to get pregnant and Tomasso was so damn big and sexy and virile and . . .

"Oh damn," Abigail breathed.

"Okay, breathe," Jet muttered, finishing with her mess and throwing away the paper towel. He came around the island and rubbed her back, his gaze full of concern. "It's not the end of the world. It's probably okay. I mean you've been super sick, so it's not like you two could have been going at it like bunnies this last week, so you've messed around—what? Last night? So once?"

"Twice," she muttered, rubbing her forehead with agitation. "Last night and before I got sick."

"Seriously?" he asked with dismay. "What did you do? Wake up on the beach and jump him?"

"Oh, jeez," Abigail muttered, dropping her face into her hands.

"I'm not judging," Jet continued. "But it just doesn't seem like you to bang some guy you just met. Hell, you punched Jimmy Coldsten for trying to grope you on your second date."

"I was twelve years old," Abigail pointed out with exasperation. "And we hadn't even kissed or anything. He just reached out and started squeezing like it was a bike horn that was going to honk."

"Yeah." Jet shook his head with a wince at the memory. "I'm betting the Italian Stallion has smoother moves than that, huh?"

"His name is Tomasso," Abigail growled and stood up.

"Where are we going?" Jet asked, keeping step with her as she moved out of the kitchen and headed for the front door.

"I need some fresh air to clear my head," she muttered, and then frowned and added, "And something to eat. I'm hungry."

"Good thinking," Jet said, opening the front door for her. "I'm hungry too."

Abigail merely grunted, and led the way outside.

"Do you think we should call for a car?" Jet asked with concern after pulling the villa door closed. "You've been pretty sick. The walk might be a bit much for you."

"I'm fine," she said firmly. "I can manage the walk."

Jet didn't comment, just fell into step with her as she started along the road.

Neither of them said anything at first. Abigail's mind was racing with the realization that she might that very moment be carrying Tomasso's child. The possibility was an alarming one. While Tomasso kept mentioning this life mate business, she still had no idea what it meant, and while immortals might do things differently, Abigail thought like a mortal, and this was only the start of their relationship. Way too soon to be bringing babies into the equation. Hell, call her old-fashioned, but she would have liked to be married before even having to worry about babies.

How the hell could she have had sex with Tomasso without protection? She! Who had always been all about protection before this?

The answer was simple enough. Abigail lost her head when Tomasso was around. All it took was a touch or a kiss and she melted like ice cream dropped on a hot sidewalk. Hell, even a look or a few words from him could make her wet. The man was a menace to her poor brain.

"It'll be all right, Abs," Jet said, rubbing one hand up and down her back reassuringly. "I'm sure you're not pregnant. But if you are, and Tom-boy refuses to step up, you've got me. I'll help. We'll deal with it together. Heck, I've always wanted to be uncle Jet and since I don't have any actual brothers or sisters, that means you have to produce my nieces and nephews for me."

Abigail smiled faintly and let her shoulders relax. She then slipped an arm around Jet's waist to hug him briefly with appreciation as she admitted, "I really missed you after you went off to join the navy."

"Yeah, trust me, I missed you too," he said wryly. "The navy was definite culture shock after spending my days running around with you."

Abigail chuckled and then wrinkled her nose as his beard

prickled her forehead. Straightening, she eyed the short beard and mustache covering his handsome features and asked, "What's up with the facial hair? Going for a new look?"

"Oh." Jet rubbed his bewhiskered chin with a grimace and shook his head. "No. Can't wait to shave this off, really." Then glancing to her, he added, "I wasn't planning on the Caracas flight so didn't have my bag with me when we flew out of San Antonio. I figured at the time it would be fine. I'd buy some shorts, a swim-suit, and shaving kit once we hit the ground. But after you went missing I didn't want to waste the time on shopping, shaving and shit, so . . ." He shrugged, and then let his hand drop away from the new growth on his face and said, "I have to hit the store and buy a razor. I can't wait to get this scruff off my face."

"We can do it after breakfast," Abigail promised.

"Or we could do it first since they're on the way," he suggested, catching her hand and tugging her toward the buildings on their right. The mini jungle had only given way to the buildings just moments ago. The stores lined both sides of the laneway and were comprised of everything from expensive jewelry boutiques to a corner-store type affair with snacks, drinks, and travelers' essentials like mini sewing kits, shaving kits, and sunscreen. Leading her to the corner store, Jet opened the door saying, "That way we don't forget."

"If we must," Abigail muttered, stepping inside when he held the door. "But be quick. I'm so hungry even you're starting to look tasty."

Jet chuckled at the words and moved off to find himself a shav-ing kit. Abigail hung behind near the register, her gaze shifting curiously over the items available. She had picked up some sun-screen when someone tapped her shoulder. Turning, she glanced around, her eyes widening when she saw Mary behind her.

"Hey, hi," Abigail greeted the other woman with a smile. Then she held up the sunscreen and asked, "Do I need this now?"

"It can't hurt," Mary said wryly. "But apparently we do better just to stay out of direct sunlight. The more sun you get the more damage your skin takes."

"Right," Abigail murmured and decided she'd buy the sunscreen. Turning her full attention to Mary then, she smiled and said, "I thought you guys were still sleeping when we left."

"Oh, is Tomasso with you?" Mary asked, glancing around.

"No. He was still sleeping. Jet and I came down alone." She hesitated, considering confiding her concerns about pregnancy to Mary, but then let it go and simply said, "We were going to grab some breakfast, but Jet wanted to buy a shaving kit first."

Mary smiled. "Dante said Lucian offered him a job and invited him to stay at the villa. I'll have to remember to congratulate him."

"Yeah, he's pretty pumped," Abigail murmured.

"But you're worried?" Mary suggested.

"A little I guess," Abigail admitted, and then scowled and said, "I don't know Lucian very well, but he seems . . ."

"Bossy? Arrogant? A hard-ass?" Mary suggested and Abigail gave a laugh.

"Yes, yes and yes," she said, her lips twisting.

"You were an only child raised by just your mother, right?" Mary asked.

Abigail raised her eyebrows. "Yeah. Are you reading my mind or just psychic?"

"I can't read minds yet," Mary said with amusement, and then said gently, "But Tomasso talked about you nonstop through your turn. He told me that about you, and I was just thinking that maybe, having been raised without a male role model, you find Lucian's authoritarianism hard to handle."

"Maybe," Abigail allowed, and then smiled wryly and said, "I don't like it when Tomasso gets all bossy either. Fortunately, he doesn't do that much. Or hasn't so far."

Mary nodded. "Well, if it helps, I'm usually a pretty good judge of character and I think Lucian tries to do what's right for the people he sees as in his care. And I suspect you and Jet have joined those ranks along with the rest of us."

"Mary?"

They both turned to see Dante approaching. He had eyes only

for the petite blonde beside Abigail and was nearly to them before he noticed she was there too.

"Abigail." He smiled in greeting and glanced around what he could see of the store as he slipped an arm around Mary. "Where is Tomasso?"

"Still sleeping when I left," she said.

When his eyebrows rose at that, Mary added, "Abigail and Jet walked down by themselves. Jet needed a shaving kit, and then they're going for breakfast too. We should go together."

Dante kissed the top of her head. "Sounds good."

Abigail nodded, and then stopped when she realized she hadn't thought to leave a note telling Tomasso where she'd gone. Of course she'd been a little upset at the time, still, she should have thought . . . Good Lord, he was going to wake up covered in blood to find her gone, she thought with dismay.

"What is it?" Mary asked.

"She did not leave a note," Dante said, apparently reading her mind.

"Oh." Mary frowned. "He'll worry when he wakes up to find her gone."

"Yes, and I have not replaced my cell phone yet," Dante murmured, and then shrugged and said, "I will have to go back."

"Oh," Mary said with disappointment, and Abigail was thinking the disappointment was because he was going to leave, but Dante's next words cleared up that matter.

"You do not have to wait on us. I know you are hungry," Dante said, pressing a kiss to Mary's cheek. "Go to the restaurant and start. We will be along shortly." He turned to start away, and then paused to glance back and add, "Make sure you get a table big enough for all of us."

Dante waited for Mary and Abigail to nod, before turning away again.

He'd barely slipped out of the store when Jet appeared beside Abigail, as excited as a puppy.

"Abs! Look at these. They're just like the sunglasses you had in high school."

"Oh, man," Abigail said with a laugh, taking the neon-pink sunglasses he was holding out. "They are," she agreed, "but it was grade seven, not high school."

"Whatever," Jet said with a grin. "Put them on. I bought them for you."

Abigail laughed, but slid the glasses on and raised her eyebrows up and down. "What do you think? Am I stylin'?"

"They look—Oh, hey, Mary, right?" Jet interrupted himself to say as he noticed the blonde. Glancing around, he asked, "Where's . . ."

"Dante," Mary supplied gently when he hesitated.

"Yeah. Dante. Sorry," Jet apologized sincerely. "Last night was a bit surreal what with finding Abs and all and then meeting everyone."

"I understand," Mary said with a smile and then added, "I hear congratulations are in order. Lucian hired you?"

"Yeah." He grinned. "I'm pretty chuffed. Can't wait to start."

"Well, you're gonna have to, 'cause I'm hungry and want to go get something to eat," Abigail said a bit impatiently. "Did you get what you needed?"

"Bought and paid for," he assured her, holding up a small plastic bag. "We can go hunt up some grub now."

"Good. Mary's coming with us," Abigail announced and then answered his earlier question, saying, "Dante was with her but went back to let the others know where we are and bring them along to join us for breakfast. But we can go over now and at least get our orders started."

"Awesome," Jet said, placing a hand on each of their backs and urging them toward the door.

"You won't have to order," Mary commented as they slipped out of the store. "Breakfast here is buffet style. Just grab a plate and go."

"Oh," Abigail murmured, a little disappointed.

"No, it's a good buffet," Mary assured her. "We came down yesterday and the day before and I swear they have a twelve-foot table full of just pastries alone. There's another just for bacon and sausages and stuff, and an egg station, and—"

"A twelve-foot table of bacon and sausage?" Jet asked with interest.

Mary nodded. "There were a good six or eight varieties of sausage too."

"Oh my gawd, I love this place," Jet groaned. "I'm going to fill four plates with sausage alone."

Both women chuckled, but Abigail said, "I might do that myself. I'm absolutely starving this morning."

"Abigail?" Mary said suddenly, and when she glanced her way, Mary made a slight grimace and asked, "Have you had your . . . medicine this morning?"

Noting where Mary's gaze was focused, Abigail glanced down and saw that she was rubbing her tummy, unconsciously trying to massage away the cramps that were eating away at her stomach. The sight immediately brought an image to mind of Tomasso doing the same thing. She knew now it was because he'd needed blood.

Biting her lip, Abigail glanced back to Mary and shook her head. "Not this morning. But I had four bags last night," she added quickly, and then recalling the blood all over her and Tomasso and the bed this morning, Abigail grimaced and muttered, "Or three and a half."

"Four bags of medicine?" Jet asked with bewilderment. "What kind of medicine comes in bags?"

"They put the pills in sealed bags here to keep the moisture from them," Abigail lied, quite impressed that she'd thought so quickly.

"Oh," Jet muttered, seeming to accept the explanation.

"Maybe we should go back to the villa so you can take your medicine," Mary suggested. "It will only take a minute, and it's better than taking the risk."

"Mary's right," Jet agreed. "You wouldn't want a relapse of dengue."

Abigail frowned. It wasn't dengue Mary was worried about. She was afraid she'd suddenly sprout her fangs and might bite someone. Probably Jet, Abigail acknowledged. He smelled oddly good to her again, and he hadn't when she'd first found him in the kitchen.

Throwing her hands up in defeat, Abigail turned and started back the way they'd come. She was pretty irritated by the need to do so though. This immortal business was turning out to be a bit of a pain in the butt without much in the way of benefits so far, she thought crankily and then almost smiled at the stupidity of that thought. One of the benefits was being alive, and that was one hell of a benefit.

"Come on, cheer up," Jet said coaxingly after a moment. "It's just a little delay."

"Yeah, yeah," Abigail said and managed a smile. She was only cranky because she was hungry and the blood would probably help ease that a bit anyway.

"Miss Forsythe?"

Pausing at the end of the commercial area, Abigail glanced around with confusion and stiffened as she was nearly run down by two men who had been walking behind them. However, the men quickly stepped to the sides to move around their group, saving them all an awkward moment.

"It *is* you!"

Abigail shifted her gaze to the rotund little man bustling across the lane toward them. She had no idea who he was, but he did look vaguely familiar, she thought, as she watched him hurry their way.

"You cannot know how happy I was that your friend was able to get you to a hospital during the storm." Reaching her, the mustachioed man caught one of her hands in both of his and squeezed enthusiastically. "When I left that night, I felt sure my next call back would be to pronounce you dead. But no! He found a jeep and got you to help despite the storm! And they were able to treat you! Now look at you!" he added with a wide smile. "Out and about and enjoying the sunshine."

"Dr. Cortez!" Abigail blurted suddenly as his name came to her. It was the doctor Tomasso had called in. The one who had told him to pray and say his good-byes. Obviously he'd seen the man since then and convinced him that he'd been able to save her. But then, what else could he do? Tell him he'd turned her into a vampire?

"*Sì! Sì!* You remember me!" Cortez said happily, regaining her attention. Clucking his tongue he confided, "I was not sure you would. The fever had you in its grip each time I saw you, though you did have a lucid moment or two." He shook his head. "Dengue fever is nothing to trifle with, but few have it turn into dengue hemorrhagic fever and suffer as you did. I am really most pleased to see you well and able to enjoy the end of your vacation."

"Oh, yes." Abigail smiled. "Thank you. That's very kind of you to say."

"Not at all," he assured her, then squeezed her hand. "Now you have fun. But stay away from mosquitoes," he added firmly, giving her hand a shake with both of his on each word. "You are now immune to one of the dengue viruses, but there are three more that you will not be immune to, and it is always worse the second time around."

"Oh dear," Abigail said weakly, wondering how it could possibly be worse than what she'd suffered. It made her glad Tomasso had turned her and she needn't fear things like that anymore.

"I shall let you go now," Cortez said abruptly, releasing her hand. "I am on my way to see a patient. Have a lovely day!"

"Yes. Thank you. You too," Abigail called as he bustled off as quickly as he'd appeared.

"What a nice man," Mary said as they turned to start into the mini jungle between the commercial area and the villa.

"He seems to be. I don't remember much about when I was sick, but I do remember his worried face bending over me. I thought that expression might be a really bad sign," Abigail said wryly.

"Yeah, it's always a bad sign when the doc looks worried," Jet agreed, his voice solemn.

"Hmm," Abigail murmured, and then glanced to Jet with surprise when he stumbled beside her and started to fall. She managed to catch his arm, but he still would have hit the ground if Mary hadn't caught his other arm. "Jet? Are you—?"

"He's fine. Or will be."

Abigail glanced over Jet's shoulders to see two men standing close behind Jet, one with a gun in his hand.

FIFTEEN

Tomasso woke to the sound of his brother's laughter. Opening his eyes, he spotted Dante standing next to the bed staring down at him and laughing his ass off. Tomasso glanced down at himself to see what was so funny. He was slumped up against the headboard, fully clothed, but with his pants undone and his penis lying exhausted in his lap. It and a six-or eight-inch-wide swath of material across his lap where Abigail had straddled him were the only things on the bed not covered in dried blood.

"What the hell happened?" he muttered, sitting up.

"That should be obvious," Dante said with amusement. "You tried to make love to Abigail as she was feeding and . . ." He gestured to Tomasso's bloodless groin with a grin. "The bag must have burst at the end."

Peering at the mess, Tomasso nodded. That made sense.

"You need a shower," Dante pointed out. "And clean clothes. I will fetch them."

Sighing, Tomasso sat up and got to his feet, just managing to catch his pants as they tried to slide off. Ignoring Dante's renewed laughter from where he stood in front of the closet, he made his way to the bathroom with as much dignity as he could muster under those circumstances.

"Are you not going to ask why I am here?" Dante queried with amusement, carrying clean clothes into the bathroom just as Tomasso turned the shower on.

"Why are you here?" Tomasso asked dutifully, and then added what he really wanted to know. "And where is Abigail?"

"She, Mary, and Jet are down at the restaurant waiting for us," Dante answered as he set the clothes on the counter by the sinks. "I came back to get you, Justin, and Lucian for breakfast. The girls are hungry."

Tomasso grunted at that, and then let his pants drop and quickly stripped off his shirt. "I will be quick."

"No you will not," Dante predicted, heading for the door. "But we will wait."

Tomasso merely grunted and stepped into the shower. He heard the bathroom door close a heartbeat later.

ABIGAIL PEERED OVER the two men slowly. She thought they were the same men who had nearly run into them when they'd stopped at Dr. Cortez's call. She couldn't be positive, though. She hadn't really paid attention to their faces, but they appeared to be wearing the same color clothes those two men had been wearing. She remembered a white T-shirt on one side and a red jacket or something passing on the other as a sort of distracted blur.

"Bring your friend and follow Sully here, ladies. I'll bring up the rear," the man in the white T-shirt added, waggling his gun.

Abigail stiffened. Sully was one of the names of Tomasso's kidnappers. Sadly she hadn't seen either man up close that day in San Antonio when they'd arrived with their cargo of a caged Tomasso. Actually, she hadn't caught more than a glimpse of them at a distance, and she'd been too busy hunching down behind the cage, praying she wouldn't be found, to take a look.

"Hurry up," the gun holder, who had to be Jake, snapped.

Abigail glanced to Mary, and almost sighed when she saw her grim expression. Immortals might be able to read minds and control people, but Mary hadn't been immortal more than a couple days longer than she herself had been. Mary hadn't learned that stuff either.

"Come on, turn him around and start marching. And don't try anything funny, I'll be right behind you with the gun. If you make Sully do anything weird, I'll shoot the three of you."

"Why don't we leave the guy here?" Sully muttered as Mary and Abigail struggled to turn Jet around. "I saw his eyes. He's not a vamp and he'll just slow us down . . . And the dark-haired girl too. You heard the doc, she had dengue. These vamps don't get sick. She can't be one either."

"Because if we leave them behind they'll call for help and de-scribe us, and if we kill 'em so they can't call for help and describe us, it'll cause a firestorm. Two Americans murdered in the middle of the day at a luxury resort? Shit, they'd shut everything down and start a manhunt."

"How do you know they're Americans?" Sully muttered.

"'Cause they speak English without a British accent," Jake said patiently.

"Could be Canadian or something. Maybe German. I've met a lot of Germans who speak English."

"Shut up, Sully. We're not killing them. Yet," Jake growled.

Abigail had taken the opportunity the men's brief distraction had caused, and glanced quickly around. They were only a dozen feet up the lane lined with trees that she referred to as the mini jungle. They could be seen from the commercial area if anyone was bothering to look. Unfortunately, no one was. People were all rushing to the breakfast restaurant, eager to get a table.

"Listen, Blondie," Jake snapped suddenly, and Abigail glanced over her shoulder to see that Sully had the gun pressed against Mary's side. "I know you're immortal and stronger than that. You could hump this guy over your shoulder and carry him alone without breaking a sweat. So stop pissing around and take most of his weight so your cute little human friend there isn't struggling so much."

Abigail opened her mouth to snap at the man to leave Mary

alone, but paused when the other woman caught her eye and gave an infinitesimal shake of the head. Biting the inside of her mouth, Abigail turned her face forward and simply hefted Jet a little higher and began to move.

The truth was, Jet wasn't heavy to her, and probably not to Mary either. It was that "increased strength of an immortal" business, she supposed. However, Jet was limp, and trying to move him was like trying to make a sock full of marbles stand straight.

Mouth tightening, Abigail paused and drew Jet's arm over her shoulder, waited for Mary to do the same, and then started forward again. Sully immediately turned to lead the way, but other than following him as he led them into the trees, Abigail gave Sully little thought. Her concern was Jake and his gun. She was very aware of that man following close behind them.

Abigail was also aware that while they couldn't do anything just then, they might actually have an advantage that could soon come in handy. These men didn't think she was an immortal. Overhearing the talk with Doctor Cortez had convinced them she wasn't. That might be useful. At least, she hoped it would. Although, she'd have to make sure they didn't see her eyes without the sunglasses on. *Thank you, Jet, for the sunglasses,* she thought, recalling Sully saying he'd seen Jet's eyes and he wasn't an immortal.

These men obviously knew about the silver flecks and recognized immortals by it. She definitely had to keep the sunglasses on.

"Get in."

Abigail shifted her attention to the van Sully had stopped beside. They were on a dirt laneway on the other side of the trees. She glanced around, but there was no help here. Sighing inwardly, she glanced to Mary and the two of them dragged Jet to the van. Mary stepped up into the van before Abigail could and met her gaze briefly before she caught Jet under the arms and dragged him in. The message had been clear: *don't do anything to give away that you're an immortal. Act weak and defenseless.*

"You too," Jake said, nudging her with the gun. He didn't nudge very hard though, and his voice wasn't as mean as it was when he addressed Mary. Abigail was beginning to think the man didn't like immortals, and wondered how she could use that—combined with his belief that she wasn't one—to her advantage.

For now, though, she just stepped up into the van. Mary was sitting in the back with Jet lying in front of her. Abigail settled beside her and then glanced to the van's open side door. She was just in time to see Jake fill the opening, raise his gun, and shoot. Gasping, she closed her eyes, expecting pain to rip through her. When that didn't happen and she heard a grunt next to her and felt Mary sag against her arm, Abigail blinked her eyes open and turned to her with alarm. Her worry eased a bit when she saw the dart sticking out of her chest, but she still reached for it.

"Leave it," Jake said quietly as he stepped up into the back of the truck with them. He settled himself on the floor just inside the door, and then nodded. Sully immediately slid the door closed. It shut out a lot of the light, but not all of it. Still it was enough that Abigail worried that the silver flecks in her eyes might glow through the sunglass lenses, so she closed her eyes but kept her head up, hoping Jake would think they were still open. She heard a door open at the front, the van dipped a bit, then the engine started. The floor vibrated with the engine's hum for a minute and then they were moving.

As DANTE HAD predicted, Tomasso spent longer in the shower than he'd hoped to remove the dry, crusted blood. While last night had been amazing, and it always was with Abigail, cleaning off the aftereffects of last night was not.

Deciding he would never mix feeding and sex again, Tomasso stepped out of the shower and grabbed a towel to dry off. However, memories of the night before assailed him as he rubbed the towel over his body, and by the time he was tossing the damp cloth aside, Tomasso was thinking perhaps they would only do it once in a while. The challenge of trying to hold off and remain conscious until the bags had emptied had been part of the fun.

Smiling to himself, Tomasso dressed quickly in the jeans and

T-shirt Dante had set out for him. He then cleaned his teeth, and ran a brush through his hair, briefly debating whether to put it back in a ponytail or not. It was cooler with his hair off his neck, but it left that sensitive skin exposed to the sun. In the end, he decided to leave it down for the same reason that he was wearing jeans rather than shorts. The less skin that was exposed to the sun's rays the better. It meant he needed to consume less blood.

Tossing the hairbrush on the counter, he headed out to join the others.

"Hurry, man. The car is here," Justin chivvied the minute Tomasso appeared in the living/dining area, and then explained, "I called as soon as I heard the shower turn off. They were a little quicker than I expected."

Tomasso merely grunted at that and grabbed his shoes on the way out the door. He wasn't surprised that Justin had called the car. All of them could have easily managed the walk, although the women might have had a little difficulty were they here. The road was uneven with pebbles everywhere and made walking in their strappy sandals a bit difficult. Still, the car was mostly a way to avoid as much sunlight as possible. A way to reduce the amount of blood they would need to consume.

The ride to the main section of the resort was quick. Tomasso followed Dante quickly out of the vehicle and straight into the restaurant, moving abreast of him when he paused to look over the room in search of their women and Jet.

"I do not see them," Dante muttered after a moment.

"Neither do I," Tomasso admitted, concern beginning to churn in his belly.

"They are probably still shopping," Lucian said with a shrug.

"No doubt," Justin said with amusement. "You know women and shopping. They probably spotted a pretty dress in a window on the way here and . . ." He shrugged as if the result should be obvious.

"I'll go check," Dante said, turning away. "You guys grab a table before they are all taken."

Tomasso hesitated. He'd really rather go with Dante to find

the women as well. He hadn't seen Abigail yet this morning and wanted to. And it wasn't just because he knew the kidnappers could still be around somewhere looking for him and any other immortals they could get their hands on. He missed Abigail when she wasn't there. Tomasso knew that would probably ease in time, but he didn't think it ever would completely. He enjoyed spending time with her, and quite simply missed her when she wasn't there.

"Dante will bring them back," Lucian said.

Tomasso glanced to him. He wasn't surprised to find that—rather than wait for a response—Lucian had already moved off through the crowded tables toward one that was unoccupied and large enough for them all.

Rather than follow, Tomasso made his way to a table where coffee, tea, water, and various juices were set up. He made coffee for himself and one for Abigail, and then—not sure which kind of juice Abigail would prefer—he selected a handful of different ones and then glanced around for a tray.

Justin was seated alone at the table when Tomasso got there. Setting down his tray, he glanced toward the door as he claimed a chair, wondering what was taking Dante and the women so long.

"Now that you're here I'm going to go get some food," Justin announced, getting up. "Lucian should be right back."

Tomasso nodded, but continued to watch the entrance.

"Still no sign?" Lucian asked a moment later as he returned with a plate piled high with food.

Tomasso shook his head and tried to relax in his seat. But his gaze kept moving back to the door.

"We are leaving today."

That announcement from Lucian did manage to tear his gaze from the door. Glancing to the man, he asked, "Caracas?"

Lucian took a bite of bacon and nodded as he chewed.

"What time are we leaving?" Tomasso asked.

Lucian took a sip of coffee and swallowed before saying, "The plane should get here sometime this afternoon. That gives you and Dante several hours to decide if you wish to accompany us."

Tomasso's eyebrows rose. "You do not want us there?"

"Yes, I do," he assured him. "We might need your assistance. But your women would no doubt have to accompany you. They cannot be left on their own without training," he pointed out. "But I understand if you and your brother are reluctant to bring Abigail and Mary along and expose them to the danger in Caracas. So, the choice is yours." He turned his attention to scooping up more food on his fork as he added, "Fortunately, the delay caused by our stopping here has allowed several of our teams to get to Caracas ahead of me. Hopefully, we have enough men to manage the task of finding and stopping this Doctor Dressler without you."

Tomasso frowned. He was quite tempted by the thought of skipping out on the rest of this investigation and simply taking Abigail back to Canada to indulge in training laced with a lot of sex. However, he was quite concerned about this Doctor Dressler and what he was up to. Having been captured and stuck, naked, in a cage, he knew what the missing immortals were going through. At least, he knew part of it. He didn't even want to think what might be happening to those who had not escaped before reaching the island Jake and Sully had mentioned. And his conscience was balking at dropping out of the investigation before the other immortals were free. Still, he had Abigail's well-being to worry about too. Lucian was right. He didn't like the idea of exposing her to the danger lurking in Caracas. He doubted Dante would be any more happy at the idea of taking Mary there either.

"What about Jet?" Tomasso asked suddenly, the man's name popping into his head.

"If you choose to return to Canada, Jet will be flying with you. I hired him as a pilot," he added.

Tomasso's eyebrows flew up. "That was . . . kind."

Lucian snorted. "Kind my ass, Marguerite would have made my life miserable if I refused."

"Marguerite?" Tomasso stilled, and then sat back, recalling that Lucian had taken a call from Marguerite just as he had led Abigail away from the table in the Italian restaurant.

"Yes." Lucian nodded. "Jet will be staying with Marguerite while he goes through his training."

"Training for what?" Tomasso asked slowly.

"To fly for us."

"He is already a pilot," Tomasso pointed out.

"Not for us. We have to decide what sorts of flights he can be used for, what knowledge he can be trusted with, and so on."

Tomasso nodded in understanding. There were some mortals who worked for them in capacities that made it necessary to let them in on their secret, some pilots among them. But they were thoroughly vetted first, their minds read and reread until it was quite certain they would never divulge the secret. Tomasso just didn't understand what Marguerite had to do with all of this. The woman was his aunt through marriage to his uncle Julius. She was also known to have a knack for matching immortals with their life mates. If she was showing an interest in Jet . . . But she hadn't met him. Had she?

"Why is he staying with Marguerite?" Tomasso asked now. "And why did she want him hired?"

"I do not know," Lucian said with irritation.

Tomasso frowned, and then asked, "Has she met him?"

"Apparently."

That made his eyebrows rise again. "How? When?"

"She and Julius are in a resort further up the coast having their third makeup honeymoon."

Tomasso nodded. Their adult son and his cousins had invaded Marguerite and Julius's original honeymoon in St. Lucia. It had been at Marguerite's behest. She'd met a woman at their resort who she'd been sure would prove to be Christian's life mate. She'd been right. But Julius had decided that as pleased as he was for his son, he and Marguerite should have another honeymoon, one where they were alone. As Lucian said, this was the third such honeymoon. Not because the second one had been interrupted, but because Julius just liked being alone with his wife.

"Apparently they encountered Jet when he stopped at their resort in his search for Abigail. They had a meal with him before he continued on his way and—knowing we were here—put it into his mind to skip the rest of the places along the coast and come here. Marguerite then called me to let me know he was coming this way." Grimacing, he added, "And to tell me that I should hire him. And that he would be staying with her during his training," he added shortly.

Tomasso smiled slowly. "Marguerite thinks he is a match for someone."

Lucian grunted around a mouthful of egg, not sounding at all pleased.

"It is a small world."

"Getting smaller all the time," Lucian growled.

Tomasso smiled again, and then glanced around as Dante came rushing up to the table.

"Are they here?" Dante asked sharply, glancing around the buffet as if expecting to see Abigail, Mary, and Jet filling plates with food.

"No." Tomasso was on his feet at once. "You did not find them?"

"No," Dante muttered, looking worried.

"Did you check the other stores, or just the one where you left them?" Lucian asked, pushing his plate away.

"I checked them all," Dante assured him. "When I did not find them at the store where I left them, I checked them all."

"Perhaps they returned to the villa," Tomasso suggested, trying not to panic.

"I looked there too. After the stores I went back to the villa, thinking they might have returned," Dante growled. "Nothing."

"Hey, Dante," Justin greeted, returning to the table then with a plate piled high with food. Settling in a chair, he set his plate down and began to cut eagerly into an omelet he'd apparently had prepared at the egg station. "Are the girls up getting their food? Why are you two just standing around? Go get some grub before it's all gone."

"Jet and the girls are missing," Lucian announced, getting to his feet.

Tomasso was already turning away, heading for the entrance, but he heard Justin's groan of disappointment and the scrape of his chair as he stood to follow.

WHEN THE VAN began to slow, Abigail cracked her eyes open to peer toward the window. All she could see at first were trees, but then the white stucco of a building came into view a little distance away just before the van stopped. She heard the front door open, felt the van move slightly, and then the door slammed. A moment later, the side door slid open across from her.

"Don't move," Jake warned, and shifted his legs to the door to slide out. Once standing, he turned back and gestured to her with one hand. "Come on. Get out. Don't worry about them," he added when Abigail glanced to Mary and Jet. "They'll be along soon enough, right now it's you though."

Mouth tightening, Abigail stood up in a hunched position, bent at the waist to cross to the door. She'd nearly reached it when she was struck with the mad idea of grabbing the door as if to get out, but slamming it shut instead and then jumping in the driver's seat and driving away in a mad rush.

There were two problems with that idea. One, she wasn't sure the keys were in the vehicle and she might be left sitting in the seat with no escape. The second problem was that she might get shot as she closed the door, which would not only blow this escape attempt, but any future ones. If she were shot, Jake and Sully would surely realize she was an immortal. Once that happened, they'd no doubt shoot her with one of those darts they'd hit Mary with. Right now she was awake, and even untied. She suspected they'd tie her up or even hit her over the head once inside as they'd done to Jet, but she'd heal quickly from a head wound. At least she hoped she would. And she could probably get free of ropes if they tied her up, but that depended on just how much stronger immortals were than humans.

No. Her best chance right now . . . *their* best chance right now, Abigail corrected herself, was the fact that these men thought her mortal. It meant they might let their guard down and there might be a better, less risky chance of escape later. One that wasn't likely to get Jet hurt.

"Come on. Out," Jake ordered impatiently.

Abigail got out of the van and winced as Jake caught her arm and jerked her around so she faced him with her back to Sully. She glanced to his face, expecting him to say something, and then glanced around with a start when her hands were tugged behind her back. She saw the rope Sully had, and then felt the gun Jake carried press into her belly, and simply stood still as her wrists were bound behind her back.

The moment Sully finished, Jake started to drag her up the slight incline toward the nearest building.

"Keep an eye on them. I'll be right back," Jake said over his shoulder.

Abigail glanced around as he led her up the short path to the building, and nearly bit her tongue off when she saw that it was one of the four private villas separated from the rest of the resort. It was the last one in the area, on the very edge of the property, but that still meant they weren't more than two hundred feet from the villa she and the others were staying in.

"Inside," Jake ordered, opening the door and waving her in with his gun.

Abigail stepped inside, her gaze sliding around as she took several steps into a replica of the living/dining area of the villa she'd woken up in just the day before. The only difference was the color scheme. The walls were still white, but the table was wood, the chairs wood with white backing, and the living room was filled with beige-colored furniture. She preferred their villa, Abigail decided as Jake caught her arm again and turned her toward the door that belonged to the master bedroom in their villa.

Her mouth tightened, but Abigail didn't panic. It wasn't like he was going to try to rape her while Sully waited out by the van with two unconscious people who could wake up at any moment. Right?

Abigail glanced around as he led her into the room. It was an exact replica of the master bedroom she and Tomasso shared at their villa. It had the same bed, the same night tables, the same everything. When Jake continued to just stand there, Abigail glanced his way to see that he was looking around the room with a frown as if trying to decide what to do with her. That made her relax a little. He obviously didn't have rape on his mind, she thought, and then her gaze slid past him to the open bathroom. Abigail stilled as she stared at the two bodies inside, lying on the cold tile. They looked dead to her, and any small bit of relaxation she'd enjoyed ended quickly.

"The bed," Jake muttered and began to urge her that way.

Abigail went without fighting, her mind still full of the image of the couple in the bathroom.

"Sit," Jake ordered.

Abigail hesitated, and then turned her back to the bed and sat on the side of it.

"Up against the headboard," Jake instructed.

She glanced at the bed, not sure how she was supposed to do that with her hands tied behind her back, but then turned to swing her legs up on the bed and tried to scooch back. It was a bit of a struggle, though, without her hands to help, and after a moment, Jake lost his patience. Muttering under his breath, he caught her by the upper arms, and moved her himself. He then quickly tied her bound wrists to the bedpost. Once the task was accomplished, Jake left the room without giving her a second glance.

He left the door open, though, Abigail noted. That seemed to her to indicate that she was right and he was just returning outside to help Sully bring in Jet and Mary.

Abigail hesitated, debating what to do. Her instinct was to immediately start trying to break her bindings, but she didn't know if she had the time to do it, or even if she could manage it. Tomasso had said the nanos gave them more strength, but she didn't know how much. He was as strong as a bull, or looked to be, but he was also a big guy. Abigail hadn't come out of the turn with a body-builder's bulk. So . . . was she superman strong? Or just stronger than she had been, which really hadn't been that strong at all.

Not that Abigail had been a complete weakling before the turn. She might have been out of shape from sitting around so much, but her arms had maintained their strength. Mostly because at the end her mother had barely been able to lift her head, let alone walk, and Abigail had needed to lift her out of bed and into her wheelchair in the morning, and then lift her out of the wheelchair and back into bed at night. But by that point, her mother had withered away to probably seventy-five pounds.

Sighing, Abigail ignored her instincts and didn't try to get herself untied just yet. She had no idea how much strength or speed she had, and it seemed safer to wait until Mary and Jet had been moved in here to join her and the men went away before she tried anything like that.

Shuffling sounds from outside the room caught her ear and Abigail turned her gaze to the door. A moment later, Sully backed through the doorway holding Mary under the arms. He was followed by Jake who had Mary by the feet as they half carried and half dragged the blonde along the floor to basically drop her against the wall opposite the bed. They then left the room, returning a couple minutes later transporting Jet the same way.

"Get the chain," Jake ordered as they straightened from dropping Jet. "And some rope."

Sully left at once to perform the assigned task and Jake turned to walk to the bed.

Abigail stiffened warily, but he only checked that she was still tied to the bed, and then returned to stand over Mary and Jet, hands on his hips and his gun tucked in the back of his pants.

This would have been a perfect time for her to snap her ties and speed across the room to snatch the dart gun from his jeans and shoot the ugly bastard, Abigail thought grimly. She didn't try it, though. Fear held her back once more. Not knowing how strong or fast she was meant she had no idea how good her chance of success was. She was afraid of getting Jet killed.

It was better to wait, some part of her cautioned.

But if she waited too long, they might all die, another voice pointed out. *Or be drugged and stuck in a cage to be shipped off to "the island."*

Abigail hesitated, not sure what to do, and then Sully returned to the room carrying chains in one hand and rope in the other.

SIXTEEN

"So?" Justin asked.

Tomasso turned from frowning out the window at that question. They'd returned to the villa to come up with a plan to find Jet and the women. But while Lucian had pulled out a map of the resort and appeared to be examining it, he'd said nothing yet.

"What are we going to do?" Justin asked when all three men glanced his way without comment.

Silence filled the room. The others were obviously at as much of a loss as he was, Tomasso realized. They'd searched the stores on the way back to the villa, Dante ducking into each store on one side and Tomasso doing the same on the other as Justin and Lucian stood outside, keeping watch to be sure they didn't miss the trio coming from an unchecked store on one side of the boutiques and entering an already checked store on the other.

When that had turned up nothing, they'd returned here to consider their next plan of attack.

A small sigh slid from Lucian's lips and he straightened from the map to peer from Tomasso to Dante. "I suspect your kidnappers have caught up with us and captured them."

That was Tomasso's fear too. Crossing his arms over his chest,

he ground his teeth and lifted his chin, growling, "If so they will
try to use them as bait."

"*Sì,*" Dante said with a nod. "That is what they did in Texas
when they took Mary. They were luring us into a trap."

Lucian nodded. "I expect they will try something of that ilk
again. Set up a ransom to lure us all to a controlled area where
they can take us out with their damned darts," he said shortly, and
then added, "Which means we will hear from them eventually."

Tomasso shifted impatiently and growled. "Well, I am not
waiting."

"Neither am I," Dante agreed.

Moving to the map Lucian had been scanning, Tomasso held
out his hand. Lucian raised his eyebrows, but handed him the pen
he'd been using to mark certain areas of the map. Tomasso suspected the spots Lucian had marked were ones he thought would
be the most likely places the kidnappers would select for their trap.
He ignored all of them and simply drew a line across the middle of
the map and tossed the pen aside as he said, "I'll take the area on
top of the line, Dante, you take the area under the line."

"Just a minute," Lucian snapped when Dante nodded and they
started to head for the door.

Turning back, Tomasso saw Lucian draw another line on the
map dividing it into four parts. Raising his head, he looked at
Tomasso, Dante and Justin and announced, "Each of us will take a
quadrant. Cover every inch of your area. Read the mind of every
person you encounter. We will meet back here in three hours."

"Okay," Justin said and when Tomasso and Dante headed for
the door again, cried, "But wait!" When they paused once more
and turned back, he asked, "Who gets which quadrant?"

Clucking his tongue impatiently, Tomasso moved back to
the map and surveyed it briefly before stabbing his finger at one
square. "I will be searching there. The three of you can decide
who searches the other areas."

This time he managed to leave the villa without being stopped
again. His quadrant included the beach, the open-air restaurant,

and the pool. Tomasso suspected he'd picked it because the beach made him think of Abigail. They'd spent most of their time since meeting on a beach, at least the time they'd spent together when she was conscious. It was where he'd got to know her. It was where he wished they were now, on a beach, alone and safe.

ABIGAIL WATCHED THE men tie up Jet, noting that they put a lot more rope and effort into it than they'd used on her. They bound his feet and his wrists separately and then tied them together so that he was lying on his side on the floor, arched backward with his hands and feet behind his back. Poor Jet was going to be in agony when he woke up, Abigail thought bleakly. The only bright side was that they didn't gag him.

Shaking her head, Abigail watched them turn their attention to Mary next. She sat still and silent, but utterly amazed as they didn't just chain Mary hand and foot as they had Jet, but then wrapped the chain around the petite blonde's body over and over again, turning her into a mummy of chains. When they finished, Mary was almost completely hidden by the chains from her shoulders to her ankles with just her feet, neck, and head sticking out.

"Don't you think that's a little overkill?" Abigail couldn't resist asking with dismay as they straightened from their task. Good Lord, if she managed to get free, there was no way Abigail could unwrap all that chain without them hearing.

Sully ignored the comment. He didn't even look her way, but turned and left the room. Jake, however, glanced at her, hesitated as if debating just leaving as well, and then crossed the room to peer down at her.

"You'll be grateful for it when she wakes up," he assured her. "She may look sweet and innocent, but she's a vampire."

Abigail raised her eyebrows and pursed her lips dubiously, hoping he'd buy the act. She'd never been any good at lying, and acting to her felt like the same thing, but she was trying to react as someone who didn't know anything about immortals.

"Yeah, I know it sounds crazy," Jake said, apparently buying her reaction. "But it's true. And another truth is that you got lucky we stopped you all when we did. She used some excuse to lure you two back to her villa, right?"

Abigail nodded slowly, thinking that the men obviously hadn't heard them discussing her need for "medicine" and didn't realize she and Jet were staying at the same villa as Mary. They obviously also hadn't recognized Jet as their pilot. She supposed it was the beard and mustache he'd grown since last seeing them. That was a lucky break. They seemed to think she and Jet had just encountered Mary.

"Well, if we hadn't prevented it and you'd got to that villa, you would have been breakfast for her—" Jake jerked his thumb back toward Mary as he added "—and her friends."

"You're saying she's a vampire and that she's staying at a villa here with other vampires?" Abigail asked, trying to sound shocked at the possibility.

Apparently, her attempt to appear shocked came across as disbelief too, because he frowned and shook his head. "I know. I'm not surprised you don't believe me. But you will. The fact is there are a bunch of 'em. I think their home base is Texas. We've found a lot of them there. In fact, the only reason we're here now is because we were transporting one of them and he got free and jumped out of the plane we were on somewhere over this area."

"Jumped out of a plane?" Abigail gasped. "He had a parachute?"

"No." Jake shook his head firmly and she was pretty sure he was being honest. He had no idea there had been a parachute in the back of the cargo hold. "He jumped without one, and he *survived*," he stressed. "These damned vampires are hard to kill," Jake added with disgust. "We've been looking for him this last week. Got here last night, but didn't really expect him to be here. Truth is we were starting to think the search was a waste of time, but we thought we'd poke around a bit and move on to the next place. But then we saw *her*." He jerked his thumb toward Mary again.

"She and her sire and another vampire were coming out of the open-air restaurant last night."

"Sire?" Abigail murmured, realizing that Jake and Sully must have arrived just after she herself had left the bar with Tomasso on her heels. It couldn't have been long after, though, she thought. Abigail was pretty sure Dante, Mary, and Justin had probably left close behind them. She would have guessed right behind them, but Lucian may have held them up giving further instructions. Either way, it was amazing that Jake and Sully hadn't seen her and Tomasso . . . seriously lucky. Now if she could just figure out a way to use that luck to her advantage—

"Yes, sire. The one who turned her," Jake explained and glanced back to peer at Mary. Shaking his head, he added, "Apparently she used to be as human as me and you, but the twin of the fellow who escaped us, escaped some buddies of ours and turned the poor old bitch."

Abigail had to bite her tongue to keep from snapping at him for calling Mary a bitch.

"When we saw them, we knew our boy must be here," Jake continued, turning to face her again. "So we followed them to their villa, then searched the others nearby and settled on this one so we could keep an eye on them while we came up with a plan."

Mouth tightening, Jake turned to glance toward the bathroom and the middle-aged couple visible through the open door. "Unfortunately, the people here weren't too cooperative. If they'd just done what they were told and stayed put, we might have let them live. But no, they had to try to escape." He eyed them with disgust as if the couple's trying to escape two madmen ranting about vampires was completely unreasonable.

"Anyway," Jake said, giving his head a shake as if that was all it took to remove the couple and any responsibility for their death from his mind. "This morning Blondie there and her sire headed down to the shops. We followed, hoping for an opportunity to grab them. Then she started talking to you in the store. The next thing we knew her sire was leaving, saying something about get a table big enough for everyone and he'd get the others. Then you three were headed to the restaurant.

"At that point, we weren't sure you and your boyfriend weren't vampires too. We weren't close enough to get a look at your eyes then. So we figured we'd follow, have breakfast too, and keep an eye on the group and sort out whether you two were vampires or not and who else was with them."

Abigail swallowed at this news as she recalled Sully saying he'd seen Jet's eyes and they were human. If they'd seen her eyes before they'd left the store, these men would have known she wasn't, but Jet had bought her the ridiculous sunglasses she still wore. She had no idea when Sully had seen Jet's eyes though. Perhaps when they'd stopped and turned on the sidewalk at Dr. Cortez's shout. Yes, that seemed likely. The pair had been close behind them and had parted to avoid crashing into them. Sully could have seen Jet's eyes then.

"Only you guys never went to the restaurant," Jake continued, grabbing her attention again. "All of a sudden, the three of you stopped. When we realized you were heading for the path back up here, we figured she'd somehow convinced you and your boyfriend to come up to their villa. It seemed the perfect opportunity. So Sully moved the van to the back road, and we waited for our chance."

Smiling wryly, he added, "Luckily for you that little fat doctor came running up to see how you were. Started yapping about you having dengue fever, so we knew you weren't a vampire either. Figured out then she'd been luring you back to the villa to be their breakfast." He shrugged and added, "Like I said, the fact is you're lucky we stopped you when we did, or by now you'd either be dead or a vampire yourself."

"Yes, lucky," Abigail agreed and almost winced as she heard the words. Even she could hear the lack of sincerity in them.

"I know you don't believe me, girl," Jake said harshly. "Can't say I'm surprised. I had trouble swallowing the fact that vampires really exist myself. But they do," he assured her. "And you'll believe soon enough when that one wakes up and gets hungry. You'll be glad then that we stopped you going to their villa, and you'll be glad we chained her up like we did too so she can't suck you dry."

Abigail stared at him silently, thinking he should probably worry more about himself just now. While she'd mistaken her hunger earlier this morning as a hunger for food, it was becoming more and more apparent to her that food wasn't what her body was craving. The man before her was starting to smell like a pork chop smothered in mushroom sauce, and she was quite sure it wasn't the cologne he was wearing. Grimacing at these thoughts, Abigail cleared her throat and asked, "What are you going to do with her?"

"Use her for bait to get the others," Jake said quickly, and then glanced to Mary again and frowned. "We just have to figure out how to do that."

"And once you have them all?" Abigail asked.

"Take them to the island," he answered absently, his gaze still on Mary. Abigail was pretty sure he was trying to come up with that plan to catch the others.

"What's the island?" she asked, hoping that in his distraction he might just mention its name and where it was. Instead, her question made him turn to look at her blankly.

"It's an *island*," he said slowly as if she might be slow in the head.

Abigail managed a nervous laugh. "Yes, but I meant, what happens there? Why not just stake them all here? That's what you do to vampires, right?"

"Oh." Jake smiled faintly. "Well, Dr. Dressler wants them. He's studying them. The man's got a bunch of freaks on his island," he added in a tone of disgust. "You wouldn't believe the shit he has caged up there—fishmen, snakemen, birdmen. Hell, he even has a kid who's half horse and half little boy."

"A centaur?" Abigail asked with disbelief.

"If that's what they're called," he said with a shrug. "I just call him freak. Makes the little shit cry and trot off, but man can he move."

Abigail sank back against the headboard, her mind spinning. This couldn't be true. There was no such thing as centaurs. They were mythological creatures.

Like vampires? the snarky voice in her head asked.

"Jesus," Abigail breathed.

"Yeah, shocking, huh?" Jake said, his voice wry. "I hear tell he's made female freaks too, but he keeps them and the female vamps separate from the male specimens and I've never been in their building."

Jake sighed and added, "But I'd like to. I'd really like to see if the female fishman looks like a mermaid or what. The male doesn't. Just has gills and stuff, but I wouldn't mind me a pretty little mermaid with perky titties. I'd make a real special big old glass fishbowl for her right in my living room so she could swim around naked all day and I could just watch and maybe squeeze her titties once in a while. If she has a hole for it, I might even get to make her my girlfriend good and proper. If not, she'd surely have a mouth to—"

Jake stopped abruptly when he caught the flash of disgust on Abigail's face. She hadn't been able to hold it back. But she was sorry she hadn't at least tried when he shut down like a clam, scowled at her, then turned and left the room, slamming the door behind him.

Abigail let her breath out slowly. Fishmen, snakemen, bird-men, and a centaur? Impossible, she thought, and then Jake's words slid through her mind again.

I hear tell he's made female freaks too.

"Made?" she murmured to herself.

From Tomasso's history lesson, Abigail knew this Doctor Dressler hadn't created immortals. But then Jake hadn't said he had, she realized, replaying his words again.

I hear tell he's made female freaks too, but he keeps them and the female vamps separate from the male specimens.

That suggested he'd created the female creatures Jake had mentioned, and kept them plus the female vamps who he hadn't created but had kidnapped, separate from the males of both groups. But . . . could this Dressler have really made hybrid humans?

No, Abigail assured herself. Jake was high or something, or maybe trying to impress her with nonsense tales. Still, she kept hearing Jake's words in her head. *Fishmen, snakemen, birdmen.*

Those three words played over and over in her head until a groan from Jet distracted her.

"NO ONE SAW or learned anything?" Tomasso asked with disbelief. He had been the last to return from scouring his quadrant, but supposed he shouldn't be surprised. This was a beach resort. Where else would most of the clientele be except on the beach? It hadn't been too busy when he'd first arrived to begin reading minds and searching, but had begun to fill up quickly soon after.

It seemed people had their breakfast and then headed directly to the beach to ensure they got a lounge chair in a good spot. From what Tomasso had seen today, the most desirable chairs appeared to be ones with shade. At least those were the seats that had been filled first.

"You need to feed," Justin said and Tomasso glanced to the man standing beside the fridge just as he retrieved a bag of blood and tossed it to him.

Tomasso caught it and popped it to his teeth at once. He had tried to stay in the shade as much as possible while he and Abigail had been on the beach. But that had been impossible today. He'd spent most of the last three hours under the burning sun as he read mind after mind after mind, searching for any little thought or memory of Abigail, Mary, and Jet and what might have happened to them. He had actually picked up on a couple of memories of the trio, mostly by men who had noticed the women and thought them attractive, or women who had felt the same way about Jet. But none of those memories had done more than make him want to punch a man or two. They certainly hadn't revealed where the trio had gone or what had happened to them.

"There has been no word from the kidnappers either," Dante said as Tomasso slumped onto a stool to wait for the bag at his mouth to empty.

"I am afraid we are back to waiting," Lucian added.

Tomasso stiffened and glared at the man over the bag at his mouth. He couldn't say so then, but there was no way in hell that he was going to just sit there and wait to hear from the kidnappers. He just couldn't. Tomasso needed to be doing something to find her. Anything.

"What if they do not do what you expect?" Dante asked. "What if they just take the women to this island Abigail heard one of the men mention?"

"Then we will find the island and get them and the other kidnapped immortals back," Lucian growled.

Ripping the now empty bag of blood from his mouth, Tomasso moved around the island in the middle of the kitchen to grab another from the refrigerator. He had no intention of sitting around waiting. But he needed more blood before he went back out under that tropical sun.

"It is a waste of time and blood to go back out there on a fruitless search," Lucian snapped.

"You should read my mind more carefully if you are going to read it at all," Tomasso said bitingly before slapping another bag to his fangs.

Lucian stared at him silently, eyes narrowed, and then his eyes widened and his head suddenly went back the slightest bit as if he'd been hit by the thoughts in Tomasso's head.

"The security tapes at the front desk?" Justin said, apparently reading his mind too.

"They may have caught the kidnappers on camera if they went to the desk to inquire after Tomasso," Dante murmured.

"How does that help us?" Justin asked.

"It will tell us if they took a room here, or tried to, and what direction they went in when they left," Lucian said.

"There are other cameras around the resort," Dante said suddenly. "One of them might have filmed what happened to Mary, Abigail, and Jet."

Tomasso glanced at him sharply, and could have kicked himself for not thinking of it. The sun must have got to him, he thought.

"Call a car, Justin," Lucian ordered and then opened the map again to look it over, no doubt to see where the security offices for the resort were.

ABIGAIL LET HER breath out on a small sigh and slumped back against the headboard again. She'd been watching Jet hopefully for several minutes, ever since she'd heard his second moan, but—like the first time he'd moaned—he hadn't followed it up by opening his eyes or even moving.

Abigail briefly considered calling his name softly or making some other sound that might wake him if he was just sleeping, but the truth was, he was probably better off asleep. At least he was until she figured out what to do. Escape seemed the obvious answer, but every time she tried to think of the best way to escape, Abigail found her eye being drawn to the open bathroom door. The couple in there had tried to escape and died for their efforts. That made her cautious. Now that she was immortal she would be hard to kill. And as an immortal Jake and Sully would have no desire to kill her once they figured it out. But Jet was mortal. He *could* die and Abigail couldn't risk that. She would not be able to live with herself for a moment, let alone centuries, if she had to carry the guilt that her actions had contributed to, or directly caused, his death.

Not even wishing to think about Jet dying, Abigail turned to the sliding glass doors and peered out at the beautiful sunny day on display. She could have been looking out from their own villa master bedroom, she thought as her gaze slid over the terrace, pool and lounge chairs surrounded by palm trees and flowered bushes for privacy. The thought made her swallow a sudden lump in her throat. She wished she was looking out from there, that she was safe in Tomasso's arms somewhere . . . anywhere.

Abigail scowled at having such thoughts. Her mother had been a single parent, a strong independent woman who had carried the burden of feeding, clothing, and rearing her child alone. And she'd raised Abigail to be strong and independent too, to take care of herself, and never depend on anyone. Yet now, all Abigail wanted in the world was for Tomasso to come charging in, rescue her, and then carry her off somewhere where they could make love until they passed out.

How lame was that? Her mother would be rolling in her grave at such a wimpy fantasy.

But Abigail couldn't help it. Just the thought of Tomasso made her close her eyes and hope. He was so strong and smart and sexy. Abigail had never met a man like him. Most of the guys she'd dated at college had either been pretty and stupid, smart and wimpy, or handsome and cruel. Tomasso was the first man that was not only beautiful, but brilliant as well. Honestly, she'd hit the jackpot with him. He was the first man she'd met that she not only liked and lusted after, but respected too.

Even Jet, her best friend for years, didn't meet all three criteria for Abigail. He was smart enough, and obviously she liked and loved him, and she even respected him, but that chemistry she had with Tomasso was missing with Jet. She'd known him too long, been friends for too many years maybe, Abigail thought as her gaze sought him out again.

Her friend hadn't moved a muscle as far as she could tell. Neither had Mary, she noted before turning her gaze back to the window and her thoughts back to Tomasso. Rather than thinking about a way to get out of there, Abigail found her mind replaying scenes of things that had happened since she'd pulled that tarp off Tomasso's cage more than a week ago. The memory of his naked wild man appearance when she'd first seen him made her smile. As did the thought of the leafy loincloth he'd fashioned and donned on the beach to please her. There were a whole host of memories that made her smile: his tending her head wound, cooking fish for her that he'd speared, bringing her coconuts so that she could drink the coconut water. Taking care of her while she was sick. Turning her when she was dying. The passion he showed her whenever they were together.

The man was special, both strong and brave, yet tender and caring, Abigail thought, and acknowledged that she might actually be falling in love with the big Italian stud who was also a closet geek. In truth, Abigail suspected she already was in love with him, but knew it was way too soon for such things so was trying to slow her ponies on that. "Falling for" sounded far more sensible than "already in love" at this stage of the game, even in her own head.

Grimacing, Abigail opened her eyes and froze as she saw that Mary's eyes were also open. She was awake.

"THERE," TOMASSO BARKED, pointing at the digital screen. "That's Dante leaving the store."

Dante nodded. "The girls and Jet were inside the store at that point."

They all watched silently as Dante walked away from the shopping area and back up the lane in the direction of the villas, moving out of the camera's view. Two, perhaps three minutes passed and then Tomasso and Dante barked together, "There!" as Abigail led Mary and Jet out of the store. The trio started walking toward the restaurant, Jet in the middle. They were all chattering and laughing happily, Tomasso noted. None of them even suspecting anything was amiss.

"They're stopping," Justin pointed out with a frown.

Tomasso leaned closer, trying to get a better look at Abigail's face. It looked to him like she was grimacing. Mary appeared concerned, and Jet did too.

"They're turning back," Dante murmured.

"Maybe they forgot something at the store," Justin suggested as the trio started back the way they'd come.

"No. They are heading back to the villa," Tomasso murmured with certainty just before the threesome walked past the convenience store.

"How did you know?" Justin asked with surprise when the trio continued past the last of the stores.

"Because unless one of you gave her blood, Abigail did not feed before leaving the villa," Tomasso said. "She had the last four bags last night. The cooler in our room is empty."

"Mary and I left before she got up," Dante said apologetically, indicating that he hadn't been there to suggest she feed.

"She and Jet were gone when I came downstairs," Lucian said and then glanced to Justin in question.

"Jet and I were in the kitchen," Bricker said slowly, his expression thoughtful. "I was sticking close to the fridge because it had the blood in it and Jet was there. I didn't want him finding it and asking questions. But when Abigail got up, I went to make a phone call," he added with a grimace and then shook his head and said, "When I came back, both of them were gone. So unless she grabbed a bag before leaving . . ."

"She would have hardly fed in front of Jet," Dante pointed out.

"No," Tomasso agreed, and didn't mention that she wasn't yet able to bring her fangs on by herself anyway, so couldn't have.

"Then you're probably right in your suspicion that they were returning to the villa so that she could feed," Lucian said, obviously having read that thought from Tomasso's mind when he'd first asked if Abigail had fed before leaving.

Tomasso merely nodded.

"Who's that?" Justin asked suddenly.

Tomasso glanced back to the screen to see that Abigail, Jet, and Mary had paused on the edge of the lane through the trees that led to the villas. They were turning back as a man rushed up to them.

Their abrupt stop made two men walking behind them split to move around each side of the group.

"Dr. Cortez. He was the doctor who tended Abigail while she was ill," Tomasso murmured, recognizing the little man hurrying up to the trio. His attention, though, was on the men who had just walked around Abigail, Jet, and Mary. Tomasso leaned down to get closer to the screen again, and as he watched, the pair moved up the lane a bit, but then scurried off the path and into the trees.

"Did you see that?" Dante asked, leaning in now too.

Tomasso nodded.

"Those two guys?" Justin asked, leaning in as well now. "Where'd they go? Who are they?"

"My kidnappers, Jake and Sully," Tomasso said darkly. "And I believe they are hiding in the bushes."

"One is hiding in the bush, the other is leaving. Look." Dante pointed to the screen, his finger first over Jake, just visible crouching by a flowering bush on the edge of the trees, and then his finger moved, pinpointing Sully's distinctive red jacket moving back toward the camera under cover of the trees.

"Where's he going?" Lucian muttered, leaning closer now as well.

They all fell silent as the man disappeared from the screen. Tomasso shifted his gaze back to Jake then, before returning his attention to the doctor as he clasped Abigail's hands in both of his. He was beaming and chattering away, and then he was shaking her hands as if to emphasize a point.

"What's that? A van?" Justin asked suddenly and Tomasso quickly scanned the shot, spotting the white through the trees. It was only showing a bit here and a bit there, but could be a van, Tomasso thought.

"And the guy in red is back," Dante muttered.

"Sully," Tomasso said quietly as he spotted the red jacket through the trees between what might be a white van and Jake. A moment later the two men were crouching together again, watching as the doctor finished talking and turned to rush away as quickly as he'd approached.

Abigail, Mary, and Jet turned back to continue their walk then, passing right by the pair kneeling in the bushes. They were nearly out of the screen shot when Jake and Sully stepped out of the trees and moved up behind them. Tomasso had a terrible urge to shout a warning to Abigail, but this was a tape. What was happening had occurred hours ago. So he watched helplessly, just able to see Jake pull what appeared to be a gun from his jacket and slam Jet in the back of the head with it.

"Damn, that's gonna hurt when he wakes up," Justin predicted as the startled women turned to catch Jet as he fell.

No one commented as they watched the men force the women to drag Jet into the trees toward what they thought was a van. A moment later the splashes of white moved forward, away from the camera and in the direction of the villas, apparently on a road on the other side of the trees.

"We need to see where that road goes," Tomasso said, straightening as the film continued with nothing of interest to them. He headed for the door, aware that the others were following.

"Oh! Hey, wait," Justin said just as Tomasso opened the door.

Pausing, he glanced back in question and Justin pointed to the resort's head of security and the security guard, both sitting blank-faced in chairs at the panel they'd all just been hanging over.

"Go ahead," Lucian muttered, waving them on. "I will take care of this and catch up."

Tomasso didn't have to be told twice; he was turning away before Lucian finished speaking.

SEVENTEEN

"Are you all right?" Abigail asked in a whisper that she was hoping the men couldn't hear from wherever they were in the house.

Mary nodded silently, but then peered down at the chains surrounding her from top to bottom. When her gaze returned to Abigail it held the question, *What the hell?*

Abigail offered her a sympathetic expression. Their kidnappers had really overdone it with the chains and—

On the other hand, she thought suddenly, if these men were the ones behind the disappearances of all those immortals that Tomasso had mentioned, they should know better than most how strong immortals were. Right?

Abigail glanced from Mary to Jet, her mind working. Just how strong was she now that she'd been turned? Was she strong enough to break the ropes binding her? Strong enough to throw Mary over her shoulder and carry her out of here? If Jet woke up and was able to move, and if she carried Mary, they might be able to—

"Where is Jet?"

Abigail glanced back to Mary at that question and then nodded to the left. Mary immediately twisted her head around until she could see him behind her.

"Poor kid," Mary muttered. "He's gonna have a headache too. Hopefully that's all though," she added with a frown and began to try to turn to get a better look at his head wound. The movement immediately made her chains jangle and Mary froze, her eyes shooting to Abigail's in panic.

In the silence that followed, the sound of the doorknob turning was like thunder. Mary's eyes widened, and then she closed them and let her head drop back to the floor as if she'd never woken up.

Following her lead, Abigail lowered her own head to her chest, feigning sleep. She heard the door open and footsteps as someone crossed the room toward her, but still gave a start when something brushed against her arm.

"I'm just checking your ties," Jake growled resentfully as she lifted her head.

"Sorry, you just startled me," she said.

"Hmm." He hesitated, obviously still stinging from her disgusted expression earlier. Irritation crossing his face, he reached for her sunglasses, muttering, "Why are you wearing those ugly things? I can't see you properly when you look at me."

Abigail leaned her head back sharply, hitting it against the wall as she tried to avoid his reaching hands. She had nowhere to go, however, and in desperation, closed her eyes as he lifted the glasses away.

"What are you doing? Open your eyes. I wanna see them," Jake snapped.

"I can't. I've been sick. My eyes were damaged by the dehydration and the doctor at the hospital said I shouldn't go without sunglasses for at least a week if I want to see properly again." Abigail had no idea where that lie came from. She was usually an awful liar, but boy, this was the second doozy to slip off her tongue since encountering these men.

"Oh right, the dengue," Jake muttered and she felt the glasses slide back into place on her nose.

Letting her breath ease out, Abigail raised her head, but kept her eyes closed to prevent his seeing the silver specks through the dark lens.

"Thank you," she murmured.

Jake grunted. "I had a friend go down with that dengue hemorrhagic virus. Nasty business. The doc wasn't on the island when he came down with it. We were sure he was gonna die. Bleeding everywhere, nose, mouth, eyes. He was even sweating blood . . . in buckets. I think he was close to taking his last breath when the doc got back. Put him on a liquid intravenous, gave him blood transfusions and a couple days later he was fine. But before the doc got there I thought he was a goner," he muttered. Abigail was sure she could actually feel his searching eyes on her face as he asked, "Was it like that for you?"

Abigail hesitated. Her instincts were telling her that he was testing her somehow. That perhaps the sunglasses made him suspect she might be a vampire after all. Finally, she said truthfully, "I don't remember most of it. Just waking up feverish and in terrible pain. And I remember my nose started bleeding as they were trying to get me to drink water and then I looked at my arm and it was like you said, like I was sweating blood, but only little pinpricks of it, not big droplets or buckets, or anything."

"Yeah, like that," Jake said and she could almost feel him relax. Apparently she'd passed the test if it had been one. "Little pinpricks of blood all over his skin . . . Yeah . . . You had it bad."

"Yes," she agreed.

They were both silent for a minute and then Jake announced, "Sully thinks we should kill you and your boyfriend."

Abigail stiffened and just barely kept from opening her eyes. Forcing herself to stay calm, she said softly, "He's not my boyfriend."

"No?" The word faded a bit as he said it and she suspected he'd turned to look at Jet. "Is he with them then?"

Abigail cautiously opened her eyes to see that he was looking at Jet. Afraid that if he looked at him too long he might recognize that under all that hair was the pilot who had flown them out here, she tried to think of something to say to draw his attention back her way, but before she could come up with something, he started to turn back. Abigail immediately closed her eyes again.

"Well?" Jake asked impatiently. "Is he with them or not?"

Abigail had read somewhere that in kidnap and hostage situations, establishing a rapport and appealing to their family feelings raised your chance of survival. So she lied. "He's my brother. We're here with our mom and dad, a family trip to celebrate his graduation."

"Yeah?" Jake asked with interest.

"Yeah," Abigail murmured, and then hoping to get Jet out of there so she could risk an escape attempt, she pointed out, "My brother didn't see anything. You guys knocked him out right away from behind. You don't have to kill him. Maybe you could just let him go? Dump him on the beach or something before he wakes up? That way my parents wouldn't have to lose both of us."

A long silence followed and Abigail almost opened her eyes to see what was happening, and then Jake said, "That's real brave of you. Selfless too."

"He's my brother. I love him," Abigail murmured, and all of that was mostly true. While Jet wasn't related by blood, he *was* like a brother to her, and she definitely loved the big idiot.

"How much?" Jake asked.

Abigail frowned with confusion. Did he want money? She wondered and asked, "How much what?"

"How much do you love him?" Jake asked.

She stilled as she sensed him moving closer, suspecting where he was going with this now.

"Enough to play nice with me to convince me to let him go?" he asked.

Abigail felt the gun barrel slide along her leg and had to press her teeth tightly together to avoid saying something she would regret. But she was thinking that she probably should have expected this from the man. After all, he was the sleazeball who wanted a "pretty little mermaid with perky titties" that he could keep in a fish bowl and use at will. Why wouldn't he think it was okay to force a gal he planned to kill to have sex with him in exchange for her brother's life?

Jake was scum, and Abigail was beginning to cramp with her need for blood, which was making her crankier than her time of the month ever had and even she would admit she was a complete bitch at that time.

"THERE'S THE VAN," Justin said.

Spotting the white vehicle up ahead as they came around a slight bend in the lane, Tomasso nodded. They'd followed the short road from the point the kidnappers had made the girls drag Jet into the trees. There had been no turnoffs or offshoots, the road was a straight shot up to here, and the van was parked where the lane ended . . . right behind the villas.

"It must be a service lane for the housekeeping staff to use," Dante commented as they approached the van.

"Are we sure it's the same van?" Justin asked suddenly, sounding uncertain. "It has the resort logo on it. I don't imagine they let clients drive them."

"Maybe they stole it," Tomasso suggested as he stopped to peer in through one of the windows.

"I'd definitely say they stole it," Lucian said, his voice grim, and Tomasso glanced around to see him standing in the vegetation at the side of the road. It reached almost to the top of his hips, hiding whatever Lucian now bent to examine.

Curious, Tomasso walked over. The man was brushing a strand of dark hair away from a woman's face. Obviously a local, she wore a white housekeeping uniform with the resort logo on its pocket. A man in white slacks and a white shirt also with the resort logo on the pocket lay next to her. Both were young, attractive, and dead, their throats slit.

"These kidnappers are rabid dogs and need putting down," Lucian growled as he straightened.

Tomasso nodded and turned to peer at the nearest villa to where they were standing. It was right next to their own villa, he saw, and was no doubt where Abigail, Mary, and Jet were being held.

"WELL? WHAT'S IT gonna be, girlie?" Jake barked, his voice raspy as the gun barrel slid up past her knee.

Abigail's mouth tightened. She wasn't sleeping with the scumbag. That was a given. The very thought made her stomach hurt . . . or maybe that was her hunger. Probably her hunger, Abigail decided. It had been growing since she'd woken up, and just seemed to worsen once she'd realized what it was. Her sense of smell had grown keener too. The hungrier she got, the more she seemed to be able to smell and much to Abigail's dismay, A-hole here was smelling delicious despite being a first-class scumbag. His scent made her think of bacon, or maybe she just associated him with it because he was a pig.

"He gets to live and you get to go out with a bang," Jake coaxed and laughed at his own play on words as the gun moved further up, pushing the hem of her sundress before it.

Abigail had never experienced a fury quite as pure as what roared through her then. It wasn't so much that he was daring to touch her even if only with the gun, although that pissed her off too. But that he could sit there and blackmail what he thought was a poor defenseless young woman with something like that? And then callously make a joke of it?

Trying to calm herself and figure out what to do, Abigail swallowed. However, she couldn't help thinking that while he'd said a lot trying to convince her that Mary was a monster because she'd been turned, he was the true monster.

"But you have to convince me you like it, or I'll kill your brother there after all, and torture him first, make him beg to die," Jake added as the gun barrel reached her upper thigh.

Abigail eased her eyes open to see that the barrel was straight down, pointing at the bed and was continuing upward toward the apex of her thighs. The attempt to grab and stop it was instinctive, and it was only as she felt the resistance of the rope that she remembered it and then the rope snapped. Abigail suspected her expression was probably as surprised as Jake's when her hands whipped around in front of her body, but she was committed now. Snapping her legs closed around the gun, trapping it, she covered Jake's hand on the gun and squeezed, crushing his fingers against the metal.

She heard a *crack crack crack*, but it took a heartbeat for Abigail to realize she was hearing the small bones in his hand breaking. Startled, she automatically eased her grip and Jake quickly snatched his hand back, leaving the gun between her legs.

He tried to back away then, but Abigail's right hand was already closing around his throat and squeezing. Grabbing the gun from between her legs, she lunged to her feet on the bed in one quick motion that startled even her. Whoa! She'd never been very athletic, more a bookworm, and this was practically Olympic gymnast medal-worthy, she thought in some part of her mind, and then was distracted by choking sounds from Jake. She'd lifted him off the floor as she stood, Abigail saw. The man's feet were dangling six inches above the floor and kicking weakly. His face was turning purple. She was killing him.

Cursing, Abigail flung him back away from her. Her thought was to toss him far enough that he had a hard landing and was left stunned so that she got the chance to shoot him with one of his precious darts as he'd shot Mary. It should put him out long enough for them to escape, she thought. But she was way stronger than she'd thought, and Jake had more than a hard landing. He flew all the way across the large room and crashed into the opposite wall with force.

Man, I'm Hercules in a sundress, Abigail thought almost hysterically as she watched him go limp and drop to the floor.

The jangle of chains caught her ear, knocking her out of her stunned state. Abigail glanced to Mary to see that the woman was trying to get turned around on the floor so she could see Jake. Jumping off the bed, Abigail rushed to the other woman.

"No," Mary said when Abigail stuck the dart gun in her mouth to free her hands and then lifted the blonde to her feet. "Just go. Get help."

Pulling the gun from her mouth, Abigail muttered, "I can't leave you and Jet," as she tried to find the start of the chain to begin unwinding her.

"Don't! Just take Jet and go," Mary insisted frantically.

"No, I—" Giving up on finding the start of the chain, Abigail stuck the dart gun back in her mouth and grasped a length of chain in both hands. She took a deep breath, and then jerked like she had done with the rope. There may have been a lot of chain, but the links weren't very large. It didn't snap apart like the rope had, but it did start to separate. Biting hard on the dart gun in her mouth, Abigail tugged again and this time it did break.

"Damn, Abigail," Mary muttered, sounding stunned. "You're Hercules in a sundress."

Startled at hearing her own thoughts aloud, Abigail glanced to Mary with surprise and then released a nervous laugh.

"I think we're going to be good friends, Mary," she said, dropping the two ends of the chain.

Abigail started to reach for another length of chain, only to pause and stare in amazement as the whole thing began to unravel and drop to the floor around Mary like bad knitting. Apparently, the amount of chain used hadn't been overkill after all, but their kidnappers really should have tried a more complicated wrap or something, Abigail thought as she removed the dart gun from her mouth. She'd just let it drop to her side when Mary cried out in alarm.

Jerking her eyes to Mary's face, Abigail noted that the other woman was looking past her shoulder, and immediately whirled. Her eyes widened when she saw Sully in the now open door, a gun aimed at her chest.

Abigail saw him pull the trigger. It was kind of weird actually and seemed almost slow motion. His finger moved, pressing on the trigger, there was a small explosion, and the gun jumped. Even as something shot out of the barrel, Sully was pulling the trigger again.

Abigail knew Sully's weapon wasn't a dart gun before the first bullet hit her in the chest. By the time the third bullet ripped into her, she'd raised the dart gun she held and was pulling the trigger.

The dart hit Sully midchest. The man jerked, peered down, and then fell backward, his head hitting the ground hard.

"Abs?"

Recognizing Jet's concerned voice, Abigail turned toward him. That's when the pain hit. The slow-motion sensation she'd been experiencing ended and the pain roared in. Abigail was unconscious before she hit the floor.

"GENTLEMEN."

Tomasso and Dante paused at that quietly growled word from Lucian. Both then glanced reluctantly back as the man approached the slight incline they had just rushed up.

"Think," he ordered once he reached them. "You cannot just go charging in there."

"They have Abigail and Mary," Tomasso growled, keeping his voice low as Lucian had, in an effort to avoid being overheard by the men in the villa before them.

"They also have those damned drug darts," Lucian countered and then added, "So unless you want to find yourself naked in a cage again, this time with your women naked in cages next to you, I suggest we come up with a plan."

Tomasso went cold at the thought of Abigail naked and afraid in a cage. And then he was struck by the realization that she might already be in that predicament. The possibility almost brought him to his knees. Tomasso had vowed to himself that he would protect her, and had already failed miserably at the task. That knowledge was a hard pill to swallow.

Abigail deserved better. She was . . . everything. Tomasso had met many women over the years, some he had liked, some he had admired, some he had found attractive, but Abigail was the first woman he'd met who embodied all of those things for him. She was wicked smart, picking up on things others would have needed explained to them. Her nervous chatter when she was uncomfortable was adorable and made him smile. Her kindness and caring though, and her concern and loyalty to her friend, those were characteristics that really made her shine in his mind.

Tomasso knew Abigail felt guilty about not worrying enough about Jet during their misadventures. The woman wore her emotions plainly on her face and he'd seen the guilt flicker there several times as they discussed her friend. But he thought it a wonder that she'd even considered the man with all that had been happening to them at the time.

And she was so strong, Tomasso thought with admiration. Another woman might have plopped down on the beach and waited either to be rescued, or for him to go get help. Or they would have wept and moaned or grown hysterical at their plight. Not his Abigail. She had stayed strong, ready to save herself and even him when he was laid low with his injury. She'd also remained upbeat throughout, usually smiling, often finding something to laugh at, but also prepared to do what needed doing.

In his eyes, Abigail was also the most gorgeous woman he'd ever encountered. Tomasso knew she hadn't believed he saw her that way before the turn, but he had and still did. The woman was a rare jewel, and he had lost her like a careless child misplacing a toy.

"You don't think this is the trap you thought they were setting, do you?" Justin asked suddenly, drawing Tomasso's attention back to the matter at hand. "Maybe they're in there waiting for us right now."

No one responded at first, Tomasso supposed because, like him, they were now considering that it very well could be a trap. Perhaps Jake and Sully had known about the cameras, and expected them to go look at them and then follow the trail here to the villa. Perhaps the two men were inside even now, watching them from behind curtains, waiting to shoot them with their darts when they approached.

Even as Tomasso had the thought several shots rang out from the villa. He wasn't the only one to flinch and half duck as he glanced around to see where the shots were coming from. But Tomasso was the first to realize the sounds came from a proper gun, not a dart gun. He also noted that they had been slightly muffled, as if they'd come from inside rather than from an open window.

Cursing, Tomasso turned on his heel and charged for the villa, Abigail his main concern. He knew she wasn't likely to die from a gunshot wound, but she could be hurt, and Jet *could* die. Tomasso knew without a doubt that Abigail would somehow blame herself for Jet's death if that happened.

The sliding doors into what would have been the living room/ dining room in their own villa were open, Tomasso saw as he leapt over the tall flowered bushes and landed on the terrace. Picking up speed, he headed for them and rushed inside to see that this villa was the same as their own and he was indeed in a living/ dining area that replicated theirs. His gaze shot around the space and—spotting feet sticking out of the door that should lead to the master bedroom—Tomasso headed that way even as Dante rushed through the doors behind him. Recognizing by the size of the feet that they didn't belong to Abigail or Mary, Tomasso's next concern was for Jet, so when he reached the door, he was very relieved to see that the feet belonged to Sully.

Still, that fact startled him, and Tomasso paused briefly to stare at the man, before the sound of rattling chains drew his gaze into the room.

Mary, he saw, stood with a circle of chains around her and she was struggling to get still more chain off of her hands, alarm on her face as she peered toward the floor. It was only then Tomasso saw Abigail and Jet. The man was trussed up like a hog and squirming like a worm, trying to inch his way toward Abigail who lay a few feet away.

"Dante!" Mary cried with relief, and the sound of her voice was enough to knock Tomasso out of his momentary shock. He started forward just in time to avoid being trampled by his twin as Dante rushed to his life mate.

Tomasso's gaze slid over Abigail as he hurried toward her, noting the pretty blue sundress with hundreds of white polka dots . . . and, he realized with horror, three bloodred ones blossoming on her chest.

"He shot her!" Jet cried anxiously as Tomasso knelt next to Abigail. "Is she alive?"

"Yes," Tomasso answered as he scooped her up in his arms and pressed her close. He started to turn, but paused as he spotted the bodies through the open bathroom door.

"Take the women back to the villa," Lucian growled, moving past Tomasso to begin untying Jet as Dante finished freeing Mary from the chains and scooped her up as well. "Justin and I will take care of things here."

"The villa?" Jet cried with alarm. "Abigail needs a hospital. She's been shot, for Christ's sake."

Tomasso didn't wait to see how Lucian would handle the man, but simply turned and carried Abigail out of the villa. He was aware that Dante was on his heels as he stepped outside, so wasn't surprised when he heard Mary's voice directly behind his right ear, asking, "Abigail's going to be all right, isn't she? He shot her three times. I'm sure he hit her heart, but she's immortal now, so will recover. Won't she?"

"Sì, bella. She will be fine," Dante assured her and then asked, "Why was she not chained up like you?"

That caught Tomasso's interest and he unconsciously slowed to hear the answer. It allowed Dante to move up beside him.

"They didn't know Abigail was a vampire," Mary explained. "She had the sunglasses on that Jet bought her, and they heard the doctor talking about her having dengue fever and thought she was still mortal like Jet so they only tied her wrists to the bed."

"Ah," Dante murmured.

They walked in silence for a moment and then Mary said with awe, "She was so strong, Dante."

Tomasso glanced over to see the blonde peering at Abigail with concern. "She snapped her ropes like they were spaghetti, and then just tossed that man in the white T-shirt across the room like he was a dishrag when he tried to—"

Tomasso glanced at Mary sharply when she suddenly cut herself off. Eyes narrowing, he growled, "When he tried to what?"

Mary hesitated, but in the end admitted, "He was trying to blackmail her into letting him rape her in exchange for Jet's life."

"*Let* him rape her?" Dante asked with disbelief. "Is that not a contradiction in terms?"

"He wanted her to pretend to enjoy it," Mary explained. "If she didn't convince him she enjoyed it, he threatened to kill Jet painfully, or make him beg to die. Something like that," she muttered, and then added angrily, "And the whole time he was telling her what he wanted, he was pushing the dart gun up under her skirt. I'm surprised he didn't shoot her in the groin when she broke her ropes."

Tomasso felt rage roll over him. That Abigail had been forced to suffer through such . . .

Swallowing the bile crawling up his throat, Tomasso picked up his pace, leaving the other couple behind as he hurried the rest of the way to their villa.

EIGHTEEN

Abigail opened her eyes to a rose-colored room with colonial fur-
nishings and quickly closed her eyes, then opened them again.
When she was still in a rose-colored room with colonial furnish-
ings, she immediately checked to see that she wasn't chained down
or otherwise restricted. Much to her relief, Abigail was unfettered
except for an IV leading to a nearly empty bag of blood that hung
from a stand next to the bed.

The sight of the IV reminded her of being shot, and Abigail
quickly lifted the duvet and sheets covering her to check her chest,
but there wasn't much to see. She was all healed. All that remained
to even show she'd been shot were three puckered scars. Abigail
suspected those would soon be gone too.

Sighing, she closed her eyes again and shook her head wryly.
She seemed to be forever waking up in different places. Even in
her dreams she—Oh, hey! Was this another dream? Abigail wondered and opened her eyes again, but wasn't sure how she would
tell. There should be signs in dreams to give you the heads-up,
she thought. A poster board on the wall that said something like,
"This is a dream. Enjoy!" would be good.

The bedroom door opening drew her attention, and Abigail
felt a smile claim her lips as she watched Tomasso enter carrying

a tray with various items on it. He eased the door closed with his foot, and then took the tray to a small table with two chairs that sat by the window. Balancing the tray on one hand, he carefully set out the items on the tray: two covered plates, two cups, a pot of something steaming, and two glasses of what looked like water. Silverware followed and finally a single rose in a bud vase. Once the last item was off the tray, Tomasso stepped back and eyed the table as if considering the quality of his presentation.

"It's lovely," Abigail said and Tomasso jerked around in surprise.

"You are awake," he murmured, setting the tray on the end of the bed as he walked over to peer down at her.

"Yes." She smiled wryly. "And once again I'm waking up in a new place."

Tomasso frowned. "There was only the villa and now here."

"No," Abigail assured him with a faint smile. "Since meeting you I've woken up on the floor of a cargo plane, on a beach, in a shower, in the bedroom in the villa, and now here."

"In a shower?" he asked uncertainly.

"It was a dream," she explained. "It started in the shower."

"Ah. Yes, I remember now," Tomasso murmured and when Abigail peered at him with confusion, explained, "We shared that dream."

"We did?" she asked blankly. Was that even possible?

"Shared dreams are another symptom of life mates," he explained.

"Really?" Abigail asked with amazement.

"Sì."

"Oh."

Abigail was trying to decide how she felt about that when Tomasso asked, "Are you hungry? I thought you might wake soon so . . ." He turned to wave to the table he'd so carefully arranged.

"Yes, I think I am," Abigail admitted and sat up, only to pause as she remembered that she was naked under the sheets and duvet covering her.

"A robe," Tomasso murmured and moved to a closet to quickly

retrieve a silky white robe. Carrying it back, he held it up expectantly.

Abigail hesitated, but then decided it was foolish to be shy after everything they'd done together. Besides, he'd probably been the one to strip her. Taking a deep breath, she quickly tossed the sheets and duvet aside and scrambled out of bed to slip her arms into the robe. Abigail couldn't prevent the blush that covered her from head to toe as she did though.

Tomasso helped her on with the robe, sliding it up her arms and even reaching around to close it and tie the sash in front. Abigail half expected him to take the opportunity to kiss her neck and slide his hands over her body as he usually did, but that didn't happen. In fact, he was surprisingly businesslike about the matter, as chaste as if he were dressing a child.

A little surprised, Abigail moved to the table when he urged her that way and settled in the chair he held for her. She eyed him a little uncertainly, though, as he removed the silver warming covers on the plates and set them aside, and then moved to claim the chair opposite hers.

"Where are we?" she asked finally when Tomasso didn't even glance her way, but picked up the water by his plate and took a sip.

Tomasso swallowed as he set the glass back and said, "Toronto."

"As in Canada?" she asked slowly.

He nodded and picked up his fork, his gaze on his plate of food. Abigail glanced down to see what captivated his attention so fully and saw that he had spaghetti and meatballs, a Caesar salad, and garlic bread piled high on his plate. Her gaze then dropped to her own plate to see that it held a bowl with some kind of soup in it. An invalid's meal, but she didn't feel like an invalid. She felt pretty normal actually and would have preferred some real food, the kind you had to chew. For instance, the contents of his plate were looking tasty, she thought, but returned her attention to Tomasso again and asked, "Why?"

"Why what?" he asked uncertainly.

"Why are we in Canada?" she elaborated.

"Oh." His gaze dropped to his plate again. "Because—" Tomasso stopped and frowned at his spaghetti.

"Because?" Abigail urged.

Sighing, he set his fork back on the table and stared at his plate as he admitted, "Because I feared you would not wish to wake up in the villa when it so closely resembled where you had been . . . taken."

Abigail's eyes narrowed. His hesitation before using the word *taken* was very odd, as was the fact that he had seemed reluctant to even explain. And why wouldn't he look at her? She frowned briefly and then her eyes widened.

"He didn't rape me, Tomasso," she said quickly.

"Perhaps not, but he sexually assaulted you," Tomasso responded soberly.

"No. He didn't," Abigail assured him. "He never touched me."

"He used his dart gun," he argued and she blew a raspberry.

"He ran his dart gun up my leg a bit is all," Abigail said with exasperation, and then admitted, "It wasn't pleasant, but it was far and away from rape. I didn't feel violated so much as pissed off. Now if it had been his hand . . ." She shuddered at the very thought of that creep touching her that way, and then shook her head. "But he didn't. I'm fine. Really. There was no need to leave the resort." Abigail paused and scowled before adding, "And I wish you'd look at me. Your refusal to do so makes me feel like you now see me as dirty somehow."

"No. Never," Tomasso said firmly, finally looking at her. "You are an angel. It would not have mattered if Jake had raped you, you would still be an angel in my eyes. I was trying not to look at you because . . ." He paused, hesitated, and then cursed and stood up. He then just stood there waiting as if the action should explain everything. When Abigail just peered at him in confusion, not comprehending, he gestured to his groin with both hands, arrowing them toward the spot as he bent his knees. "Because this is what you do to me."

Abigail lowered her gaze to the area he was framing and felt her eyebrows crawl up her forehead. The man's pants were bulging out as if his penis was trying to erect a tent in them.

"And I feared," Tomasso continued, "that after what happened you may not be ready to—You might need some time to—" He paused helplessly, and Abigail stood quickly and moved around the table to throw her arms around him.

"You are the most wonderful man," she breathed, squeezing him tightly.

Tomasso stilled, and then let his arms close carefully around her, almost as if he feared she would break. Voice uncertain, he asked, "I am?"

"Yes," Abigail said, pulling back to meet his gaze, her expression solemn. "Few men would be so thoughtful and sweet. And few men are as smart and handsome and brave. I like you, Tomasso. I find you incredibly attractive in all ways and I respect you."

Tomasso smiled slowly, and then, voice soft, said, "I love you too, Abigail."

"I didn't—" Abigail began with alarm, her face flushing, and then cut off the denial, because what else was love except that powerhouse combination of like, respect and attraction? After a moment, she nodded. "Okay, I love you." Raising her head she added sadly, "But I don't know how you can love me."

"No?" He smiled crookedly. "Perhaps because I like, respect and find you most desirable too," Tomasso said gently. "Because you're beautiful, intelligent, brave, strong—"

"But that's just it," Abigail interrupted on a cry of despair. "I'm not strong. Not at all. My mother tried to raise me to be strong like her, but on the beach and then when I was sick at the villa I—" She paused, shamefaced, and then admitted, "I liked it when you took care of me. I felt safe and coddled and I *liked* it," she admitted, sure that was probably feeble and shameful.

"Abigail," Tomasso said with disbelief. "Do you really think you are weak because when you were ill you appreciated my taking care of you?" He didn't let her answer, but pointed out, "You took care of your mother when she was ill, yet do not see her as weak."

"Yes, but she was *dying*," Abigail argued.

"So were *you*," he countered firmly, and reminded her, "It is why I turned you."

"Okay, but I *liked* it when you took care of me on the beach too. Bandaging my wound, catching fish and cooking it, bringing me coconuts so that I could drink the coconut water."

"*Bella*," Tomasso said with exasperation, "who tended my *pene* when it was all swollen and sore? Hmm? Who speared a fish and burnt—I mean cooked it for supper? And who brought me coconuts to drink from?" He shook his head and said gently, "I may have taken care of you when you were unconscious and then ill, but you did the same for me." Grabbing her hands, he squeezed lightly and said, "That is a team, a healthy relationship. We work together. Sometimes I will be stronger. Sometimes you will. But together, we can get through anything."

Abigail nodded slowly, acknowledging that he might be right, but then she shook her head and admitted, "But Tomasso, the whole time Jake and Sully had us I was wishing you'd come bursting in and rescue us. Or were even there with us, because I was sure you'd know what to do, that fear wouldn't have held you back like it did me. I even had chances to make an escape attempt earlier, but I was afraid Jet would get hurt and didn't have the balls to—"

"You do have balls," Tomasso interrupted insistently, and then frowned as he realized what he'd said. "Well, not literally, thank God, but you do have them metaphorically speaking, and big hairy ones too," he assured her. "You may have wished I would burst in and rescue you, but when I did not get there in time, *you saved yourself*. As well as Mary and Jet." Taking her face in his hands, he said softly, "Abigail, you are the strongest woman I know. The strongest, and the kindest and most beautiful . . ." He shook his head. "I wish I could make you see yourself through my eyes, because to me you are everything."

"A life mate," she whispered, recalling his response to her question of what a life mate was.

"Sì." Tomasso nodded. "A life mate is everything. She is the one person an immortal cannot read or control. She is the one person he can relax and be around without fear of his own thoughts being read or his actions controlled. She is the one who suits him in all things. She is the one whose presence beats back the loneliness of a life otherwise lived alone. She is everything. She is you, Abigail. You are my life mate. You are my everything."

"Oh." Abigail blinked back the tears now glazing her eyes. "I do so love you, Tomasso Notte."

Slipping his arms around her, Tomasso replied, "And I love you, Abigail Forsythe soon-to-be Notte."

Her eyes widened slightly and then she chuckled. "You could at least propose or something. Most girls would be annoyed if a guy just presumed she'd marry him."

His eyebrows rose with concern, but he said, "You do not seem annoyed."

"I'm not most girls," she countered wryly.

Tomasso nodded solemnly. "I do know that."

His mouth came down to claim hers and Abigail rose up on her tiptoes to kiss him back, her arms sliding around his neck. She felt him tug the sash of her robe loose, and moaned into his mouth, her body shivering with pleasure as his hands moved possessively over her naked flesh. When he suddenly broke their kiss and picked her up by the waist, Abigail wrapped her legs around his hips, and then glanced over his shoulder and noted the food waiting on the table as he moved away from it.

"What about the food?" she asked with a frown.

Tomasso paused and glanced to her with uncertainty. "Are you hungry?"

"A bit," Abigail admitted, and then added shyly, "But I think I can wait a little while to eat."

Tomasso smiled and continued toward the bed and Abigail glanced past him again, this time her gaze finding the window. Noting the snowy landscape outside, she wrinkled her nose and thought it was probably sunny and warm in Punta Cana right now. Caracas too, which made her wonder—"Why aren't we in Caracas? That's where the other kidnapped immortals are, isn't it? Shouldn't we be there helping to find them?"

"No. You should not be there," he said firmly, and then added, "Because it is dangerous."

When she began to look angry, he quickly added, "And not just for you and Mary. The pair of you need to learn to recognize your hunger before it becomes a problem. You also need to learn what you can and cannot do now physically, how to read and control minds and how to bring on your fangs to feed. You could be a danger to mortals otherwise."

Abigail scowled over that, but could hardly argue the point. If she and Mary had been able to read and control minds they could have easily got themselves out of the clutches of the disgusting Jake and Sully. Or, she could have, she supposed, since Mary had been knocked out by the dart pretty quickly. She supposed they hadn't used it on her right away because they'd suspected she wouldn't yet have those skills, which suggested Jake and Sully knew a lot about immortals and how quickly they gained such skills. That thought made her wonder what would be done with the pair, but first she wanted to know—"Why Canada?"

Tomasso paused again, this time frowning with concern. "Are you feeling all right?"

Her eyebrows rose. "Yes. Why?"

"I already explained that I thought it best you not wake in the villa and—"

"Yes, I know, but I just wondered why Canada and not Texas or Italy or . . . ?" She shrugged. "Why Canada specifically?"

"Ah," he said and smiled wryly. "Lucian arranged the flight. Jet had to come here for his training, and I have family here so it seemed the best choice at the time."

"Oh," she murmured and then asked, "Where will we live?"

Tomasso hesitated and then carried her the rest of the way to the bed and sat down on the side of it to settle her in his lap. He then said, "We can live wherever you wish. My home is in Italy, but I have been thinking of buying a condo in California and one here in Toronto to stay in when I visit family."

"I notice you didn't mention Texas," Abigail pointed out.

Tomasso grimaced. "Texas could be a problem. Only because you have friends and acquaintances there who might pick up on subtle differences in you now that you have turned. The silver in your eyes, for instance," he added, and then said, "However, we could live in Texas. Just perhaps not where you grew up. It is better to avoid that area."

She nodded in understanding and was considering that when he said, "Of course, we can live somewhere else too if your schooling calls for it."

Stiffening, Abigail raised her gaze to his again. "Schooling?"

"You should finish medical school, Abigail," he said quietly. "From the way you bossed me around when I was injured, I know you would make a good doctor."

She laughed softly at the words and shook her head. "Once I get a job and can afford to, I'll return to school. Until then, we can live wherever you want."

"You do not need a job. We have a lot of money," he assured her. "Enough you need never work again if you do not wish."

Abigail frowned at this news. He could say *we* all he wanted, but the fact was she had nothing, not even the two-hundred-plus dollars she'd started out with when they met. She had no idea where that was. Abigail had lost her jeans along the way and the money with them. So, Tomasso was saying *he* had a lot of money that he was willing to share with her.

That was pretty interesting. Not that he was willing to share it with her, but that he had a lot of money. She'd never even considered that he might. Perhaps because he hadn't even had clothes when she'd met him. The man had been naked as a jaybird and Abigail had just assumed he was a regular type guy who happened to be a gorgeous, sexy beefcake.

Clearing her throat, she said, "Thank you. But I'd rather pay my own way. So we can live wherever you want, at least until I have the money to go to school."

"Hmm." Tomasso scowled at her and then relaxed. "It is still winter. We have months until the fall when I presume medical school would start. That is plenty of time for me to convince you to attend. In the meantime, we will stay in Toronto for a bit so that you can meet my family here, and then we will go to California so you can meet my family there, and then we will return to Italy so I may show you our home, and where I grew up and introduce you to my parents and brothers and sisters and cousins and nieces and nephews and great nieces and—"

Abigail kissed him to shut him up, mostly because Tomasso was scaring the heck out of her with his list of all the people she had to meet and be inspected by. The thought of all of them looking her over and judging her as a possible mate for Tomasso was a bit alarming.

He didn't seem to mind the silencing tactic. Tomasso kissed her back, his hands pushing her open robe over her shoulders so that his hands could find and caress her breasts until she moaned and arched in his lap. Then he let one hand drop down to slide up her leg and, despite herself, the action reminded Abigail of Jake and his damned dart gun. It didn't upset her so much as raise questions in her mind that she wanted answered.

Catching his hand to stop him, Abigail broke their kiss and pulled back to look at him.

"Are you all right?" Tomasso asked with concern. "It is too soon after all?"

"No," Abigail assured him. "I just—what will happen to Jake and Sully?"

"Happen?" he asked uncertainly.

"Yes. I mean, I know you probably can't take them to the police. They might start squawking about vampires and stuff, so what will be done? Do you guys have a prison of your own you put them in, or . . ." She shrugged slightly, having no other idea of what could be done with the men. "I presume they won't just be let go to kidnap some other poor immortals or murder more mortals."

"No. They will not be released," Tomasso said slowly, and then cleared his throat and said, "In the normal course of events they would have had their minds wiped permanently and then would probably have been placed in a mental facility. The kind of wiping I speak of can do permanent damage," Tomasso explained. "However, if it did not do permanent damage, they would have been released into the population as a blank slate to start over. However, they would have been watched until it was ascertained that they would not be trouble again."

That sounded kinder than what they deserved, Abigail thought, but asked, "You said *would have been*? So that didn't happen this time?"

Tomasso shook his head, his expression troubled.

"Then what happened?" she asked.

"They are dead, *cara*," he said gently.

"What?" Abigail's eyes went wide. "Did Lucian have them killed?"

"No, *bella*. They were dead when we got to you," Tomasso said, his concern growing. "Do you not remember what happened?"

"Yes, of course, but who killed them?" she asked and frowned when he stared at her silently. Abigail started to shake her head as understanding struck. "No. Jake hit the wall a little harder than I expected. Actually, I didn't think I could throw him that far, but surely—"

"His neck snapped either when he hit the wall or when he fell to the floor," Tomasso said solemnly.

"It did?" Abigail asked faintly, her stomach turning over as she realized she'd killed someone. Pushing that thought away, she asked, "But what about Sully? I *know* I didn't kill him. All I did was shoot him with one of the drugged darts. That wouldn't kill—" She paused when she saw that Tomasso was nodding and asked uncertainly, "It did?"

"Normal tranquilizers do not work on immortals. The nanos clean them out of our system too quickly," Tomasso explained. "The drugs in those darts, and the amount needed to affect an immortal, even for a short time, are deadly to a mortal." Tomasso shrugged apologetically. "Sully overdosed. His heart probably stopped before he hit the floor."

Abigail just stared at him.

"Are you all right?" he asked with a frown.

Abigail nodded, and then shook her head. She'd killed two men. They'd been cruel animals, murderers and worse, but she'd still taken two lives. Their blood was on her hands.

Tomasso pressed her head to his chest and rubbed her back soothingly. "It was an accident. You were trying to save Jet and Mary and yourself. Jake and Sully would have done worse to you. But you are going to insist on feeling guilty about this, are you not?"

"I'm afraid so," she said on a sigh.

"Then I suppose I will just have to do my best to distract you every time you think of them," Tomasso announced, his tone businesslike.

Abigail lifted her head in question. "How—?"

His mouth covered hers, answering the question before she could fully ask it. At first, Abigail went still, but as he began to stir the passion in her that always rose to meet his, she relaxed and began to kiss him back. That was when Abigail realized that Tomasso hadn't been at all sure his method would work, because he relaxed then and his kiss deepened.

When her hand drifted down to touch the pup tent in his pants, Tomasso growled into her mouth as a shaft of excitement raced through both their bodies. Their kiss quickly became more violent, and Abigail reached down eagerly with her other hand to unsnap his pants and lower his zipper. She then gasped when Tomasso suddenly stood up, taking her with him. Much to her confusion, he sat down again in the next moment. But when he then lifted and turned her so that she was facing him with her legs on either side of his, she understood what that exercise had been about. His pants were around his ankles, she saw before he settled her to straddle his lap so that his erection was trapped between them.

"Oh," Abigail moaned as he eased her more firmly against his erection, his hands roaming her body. Arching forward, she covered his hands with hers and tipped her head back as he began to palm and fondle her breasts. She gasped as he tweaked both nipples at once, and then laughed breathlessly and said, "You're very good at distracting."

"It is my pleasure," Tomasso responded, his voice a deep growl, his eyes lifting to her face. He stilled briefly, and then suddenly released one breast and reached to the side.

Abigail turned her head curiously, to see what was now distracting him, her eyes widening slightly as he opened the front of the bedside table to reveal the mini refrigerator inside. Opening that, Tomasso pulled out four bags of blood one after the other, and then pushed the door closed.

"What——?" she began with a frown, but paused as she nicked her tongue on one of her fangs. They'd descended and she hadn't even noticed.

"You are still healing," Tomasso said gently, and then hefting one bag in his hand, he smiled crookedly and asked, "Do you think we can last through all four bags before fainting?"

"I don't know," she admitted and then grinned and pointed out, "But you did say together we could get through anything."

"*Sì*, I did," he agreed solemnly, and then, his expression wry, admitted, "But this may be the exception to the rule."

Abigail grinned, for some reason delighted at that, and then shrugged and suggested, "Why don't we find out?"

When she opened her mouth then, Tomasso hesitated only a heartbeat before popping the bag to her fangs. He then immediately let his hand drift back down to her breast, but he only let it brush gently over the sensitive, erect nipple before allowing it to continue on its journey. When his fingers slid between her legs to work their magic, Abigail rose up slightly on a gasp and clutched at his shoulders, thinking that he was probably right. While together they could do anything, this may just be one of the very few exceptions to the rule . . . but she would very much enjoy every minute they spent trying.

EPILOGUE

"Dr. Dressler?"

"Hmm?" Ian Dressler didn't bother to glance up at his assistant's voice. His attention remained fixed on the unconscious subject on the metal table before him as he carefully and almost painfully slowly eased a needle into the man's arm.

"Ramirez called. He said it was urgent I pass along his message at once."

Dressler stiffened, then withdrew the needle from the subject's arm and straightened to peer at his assistant expectantly for a moment before barking, "Well, spit it out then, Asherah. What was the message?"

"He said you told him to watch for anyone flying into either airport with the name Argeneau?"

"Yes, yes, and?" he asked impatiently.

"Three planes owned by Argeneau Enterprises have landed in the last twenty-four hours. All of them carrying at least four people, and there are two more flights scheduled, one today and one tomorrow."

"Twelve or more already?" he said with wonder. "And more coming?"

"No, sir, three," Asherah corrected gently. "Three planes have landed."

Dressler shook his head with disgust. "I was speaking of how many immortals have arrived. Four or more on each of the three planes makes at least twelve," he pointed out dryly.

"Oh, yes, of course," she muttered, looking chagrined.

They were both silent for a minute and then Dressler nodded. "Call Ramirez back and tell him to update me as these other planes arrive and let us know how many each contains. And then send men to the mainland and find out where all of these arrivals are staying. They'll need a villa, I'm sure, or several of them. I want them watched. I want to know every single move they make. But tell the men to keep their distance and be very, very careful they aren't seen."

"Yes, sir." Head bobbing, Asherah backed quickly out of the room.

Dressler watched the door close, but didn't really see it. His mind was racing with all that had to be done and how little time he might have to accomplish it. He was still standing there several moments later when a moan from the man on the table caught his ear. The subject was waking up.

Turning, he took a shot off the stainless steel tray, held it needle up and tapped the side to ensure any bubbles in the liquid floated upward before he ejected them out through the needle. It was more out of habit than anything. It wasn't really necessary with these immortals. While air bubbles would stop a mortal heart, it took a hell of a lot more than that to kill an immortal. He knew that for a certainty. He'd made it his business to learn everything he could about these creatures. And he was quite sure he'd discovered almost everything there was to know, except for the one thing he wanted most to learn.

Frowning, Dressler peered at the man on his table and pursed his lips. These immortals were stubborn bastards. Not one had given up how they turned mortals. He knew for certain that it could be done now, he just had no idea how and he needed to know. Quickly. Because while there was a possibility things would go his way and he'd soon have dozens of immortals to question and experiment on, and all the time in the world to do so, there was also the possibility things would not go his way. If that was the case, he was running out of time.

Another moan drew his gaze down to see that his subject's eyes were blinking open and closed, his expression a combination of confusion and pain.

"Relax, my friend," Dr. Dressler said soothingly as he bent to give him the shot he'd prepared. "The game is about to begin."

Can't get enough of Lynsay Sands?
Keep reading for a sneak peek
of her upcoming Scottish historical romance

FALLING FOR THE HIGHLANDER

Available February 2017 from Avon Books

"They're here!"

Murine glanced up sharply from the message she was writing as her maid entered the room. She waited until Beth closed the bedchamber door before asking, "Did ye find out who they are?"

"Nay." The brunette looked vexed. "None o' the maids or the lasses in the kitchen seem to ken, or if they do they're no' telling me."

"Oh," Murine said with disappointment, then shook her head and returned her gaze to the message she'd been writing. Mouth tightening, she signed her name to the bottom. "It matters not. They're Scots. Surely their trip home will take them past the Buchanans or the Drummonds and they will deliver this for me." Biting her lip, she began to wave the parchment about to dry it and added, "I ha'e a couple coins left I can give them fer their trouble."

"Most like they'll pocket the coins, say they'll deliver it and toss it away as soon as they've left Danvries," Beth said unhappily. "I do no' ken why ye just do no' send one o' yer brother's men with the message."

"I have sent three that way and got no response," Murine reminded her grimly. Mouth flattening with displeasure, she admitted, "I begin to suspect Montrose is not sending them at all."

"But why would he do that?"

"'Tis hard to say with my brother," Murine muttered unhappily. "He's a . . . difficult man."

Beth snorted. "He's a selfish, greedy cur, hell-bent on wagering his life away and yours with it. But I see no reason for him no' to send yer messages to yer friends."

"Neither do I," Murine admitted unhappily. "But if he did send them, then . . ." She bit her lip, unwilling to give voice to her biggest fear. If Montrose had sent her messages, then Saidh, Jo and Edith just weren't bothering to answer.

That thought was a troubling one and made her worry that she had said or done something when last they were together to upset them all. Murine had wracked her brain trying to sort out what that might be, but could think of nothing. She'd then switched to wondering if perhaps her brother wasn't sending them as he assured her he would. She couldn't imagine why, but was actually beginning to hope that was the case. It was certainly preferable to thinking her three best friends had turned their backs on her for some reason.

"It should be dry enough now," she muttered and quickly rolled, then sealed the parchment.

"How are ye going to get it to the Scots without yer brother seeing?" Beth asked worriedly as she stood up.

"I heard Montrose ordering Cook to be sure he has lots of food and drink on hand when the Scots get here," Murine explained as she slid the parchment up her sleeve and checked to be sure that it was concealed and wasn't being crushed. "I shall slip the message to one of the men when Montrose is distracted with eating."

"Yer brother is offering food and drink to someone?" Beth asked dryly. "I never thought to see the like. The bastard's so cheap I'd think he'd choke on the offer."

"I expect he's hoping to fill them with ale or whiskey to make them more amenable to accepting credit rather than demanding payment for the horses he wants," Murine said, satisfied that the parchment would be fine up her sleeve.

"Aye, well, Lord knows he has no' the coin to actually buy

them. He's already gambled away all of his own money, and your dower to boot," Beth said bitterly.

"Aye," Murine agreed wearily. It was not a subject she cared to contemplate. She'd been horrified when she'd learned that bit of news. She'd thought her situation dire enough when she'd had a dower but no betrothed, but without dower, it would be impossible to find anyone willing to marry her. It now looked like she would live out her days here at Danvries as an old maid, dependent on her selfish brother, and that was only if he didn't tire of her presence and send her off to the Abbey to become a nun.

Pushing that depressing thought from her mind, she brushed the wrinkles out of her gown, straightened her shoulders and headed for the door. "Come. We will sit by the fire in the great hall until they come in. Then once the food arrives, we will use that as an excuse to join the table and slip my message to one of the men."

"I'D BEEN TOLD your animals were superior and they certainly are that."

Dougall waited patiently as Montrose Danvries ran a hand down the mare's side and then circled the horse, examining every inch of her.

Lord Danvries next moved on to the stallion and gave him the same attention, examining his withers and legs, sides and head just as thoroughly. His expression was a combination of wonder and appreciation when he paused at the beast's head. Rubbing one hand down the stallion's nose, he murmured, "Exactly what I was hoping for."

"If they meet yer expectations, perhaps we should discuss payment," Dougall suggested.

Danvries stiffened, several expressions flickering across his face. Settling on a wide, fake smile, the man turned away toward the keep. "Come. Let us go inside for beverages."

"I told ye," Conran muttered, stepping up beside Dougall. "The bastard has no' the coin. He lost it all in that last wager with his king."

Dougall sighed at his brother's words, recognizing satisfaction amidst the irritation in the younger man's tone. Conran had always liked saying *I told ye so*.

"Come along, gentlemen," Danvries said without looking back. "There is much to discuss."

Mouth tightening, Dougall glared at the man's retreating back. Danvries should have tossed him a bag of coins, and bid him on his way. The only time the buyer wanted to "discuss" matters was when he didn't have the coin, or wanted to talk down the price. Dougall was not one to be talked down. Despite knowing this was a great waste of time, though, he waved away his brother's further mutterings and trailed the Englishman out of the stables and toward the keep. He didn't need to look around to know that Conran, Geordie and Alick were following. It had been a long journey here and they were all thirsty. The least Danvries could do was see them fed and watered before they took their beasts and headed home to Scotland.

"He'll try to cheat ye," Conran warned, on Dougall's heels. "Bloody English bastards. Most o' them'd sell their mother for a coin."

"Nah," their younger brother, Geordie, put in behind them. "It's their daughters they sell. The old women wouldn't be worth a coin. They're too bitter from years living with the English bastards to be worth anything. The daughters, though, are usually sweet and pretty and have not yet grown bitter. Get 'em away young enough and they're almost as good as a Scottish lass. Almost," he repeated, stressing the point.

"Lord Danvries has neither a mother nor a daughter, so I'm sure that's no' a worry," Dougall muttered impatiently.

"He has a sister though," Conran pointed out. When Dougall glanced to him with surprise, he nodded. "An old maid left to whither on the vine thanks to Lord Danvries wagering away her dower."

"He wagered away her dower?" Geordie asked with surprise when Dougall didn't comment.

"Is that even allowed?" Alick added with a frown.

"From what I heard, he was named her guardian in the father's will so had control over it," Conran said with a shrug.

Dougall shook his head and they all fell silent as they trailed Danvries into the great hall and noted the people milling about.

There were soldiers at the table enjoying their noon repast, servants bustling about cleaning, and a lady seated by the fire. Dougall's gaze slid over the woman in passing, and then almost immediately moved back to her. She was young. Not in the first blush of youth, but perhaps twenty or so and still retaining some of its dew. Dougall guessed she must be Danvries's bride. If so, he was a damned lucky man, for she seemed to glow as brightly as the fire in that dim great hall. Her gown was a pale rose color with white trim on a shapely figure, and her hair was a halo of golden tresses that poured over her shoulders and down her back. She was peering down at some needlework she was stitching, but when Danvries called for ale, she glanced over briefly and Dougall's attention turned to her face. Heart-shaped lips, large doe eyes and a straight little nose all worked together in an oval face to make her one of the most striking women he'd ever seen. Danvries was definitely a lucky man.

"Come sit."

Dougall dragged his eyes from the vision by the fire, suddenly aware that he'd stopped walking and the Englishman was now at the great hall table while he was still just inside the door with his brothers at his back. Danvries was eyeing him with a tinge of amusement that suggested he was used to men ogling his wife.

Forcing himself to move again, Dougall led the men to the table and settled on the bench where Danvries indicated, noting that it left him with a clear view of the woman by the fire. Women, he corrected himself, for a dark-haired maid accompanied the blonde, working diligently over her own stitching. But the lady's beauty seemed to cast the maid into shadow; he'd hardly noticed her ere this.

"My sister," Danvries said quietly.

Sister? The word echoed in Dougall's mind, and he felt a sense of relief he didn't really understand. She definitely wasn't the withered old maid Conran had described, but what did it matter to him if she was Danvries's wife or sister? It didn't, he assured himself, and turned determinedly to his host, pausing as he noted that the man was eyeing the woman with something like speculation in his eyes. He frowned over that and then said, "About payment fer the horses . . . ?"

"Ah, yes," Danvries offered a somewhat tight smile and said, "Your horses are, of course, every bit the quality animals I'd been led to expect. Lord Hainsworth did not oversell them when he told me about your abilities at breeding quality mares and stallions."

Dougall nodded, waiting for the *but*.

"Howbeit," Danvries began and Dougall just restrained himself from rolling his eyes. *But, howbeit . . .* However the man chose to phrase it, it was a *but*.

"Howbeit?" Dougall prodded when Danvries hesitated.

"Well, I had the money here ready for you, but a bit of bad luck came my way."

The wager with the king, Dougall thought dryly. That hadn't been bad luck, it had been stupidity. The English king always won at wagers, and had backed La Bête at jousting, a smart move. Danvries betting against La Bête when the warrior had never ever lost . . . well, that was sheer stupidity. It wasn't Dougall's problem, though, except that it meant he'd made this trip for naught.

Sighing, he stood with a nod. "So ye do no' want the horses now."

"Nay, nay, I want them," Danvries said quickly, catching his arm as the men rose to stand as well. When Dougall turned his eyes to the hand on his arm, Danvries immediately released him. "Sorry. Sit, sit. I do want the horses. Of course, I do."

"Ye just can no' pay fer them," Dougall suggested dryly, still standing.

"Nay. I mean, aye. Aye, I can," Danvries corrected himself quickly. "Of course I can."

When Dougall remained standing and merely waited, Danvries muttered a bit irritably, "Do sit down so we can discuss this. I am getting a crick in my neck looking up at you."

Dougall didn't think there was much to discuss. Either he could pay for the horses or he couldn't. However, a young maid had arrived with the ale, so he settled back on the bench. His brothers were quick to drop back in their seats as well. It had been a long dusty ride here. He'd give Danvries until he'd finished his ale, but unless the man could come up with the coin, he was leaving . . . and taking his horses with him.

Nodding his thanks to the young maid, Dougall took a drink of his ale, his eyes wandering back to the blonde by the fire. She and her maid were chattering quietly now and casting glances toward the table.

"I'm sure it will only take me a couple of weeks to get your coin," Danvries announced, drawing his attention again.

The man's words were abrupt and overloud, a sign of anxiety, Dougall thought and wasn't surprised. He nodded slowly. "I can hold them fer ye fer a couple weeks. Ye can come collect them when ye have the coin. But if the month ends and ye have no' arrived, I can no' promise—"

"Nay, nay, nay," Danvries interrupted. "You do not understand. I need them now. I cannot be without a horse. I—"

"What happened to yer horse?" Dougall interrupted.

Danvries dropped his gaze and looked away, a frown curving his lips. It was Conran who leaned close to Dougall and murmured, "Part o' the wager."

Dougall sighed. The man was gambling his life away. Shaking his head, he said, "Ye will no' be without a horse. I saw a good thirty in the stables, and—"

"They belong to my men, not me," Danvries said stiffly, and then added, "I need a horse. A lord without a horse is like a king without a country."

"A sale without payment is no' a sale at all," Dougall countered with little sympathy. It was hard to feel sorry for someone who had willfully and foolishly gambled away his horse and his wealth. Danvries had been one of the wealthiest estates in England under this man's grandfather, and then he had died and Danvries had inherited. Dougall had heard rumors the man was running through his inheritance with poor spending and worse bets, but had paid it little heed. His brother had apparently paid more attention.

"There will be payment. It will just take me a little bit of time to get the coin together," Danvries said pleadingly. "Surely you can extend me credit for a bit of time?"

Dougall eyed the man, and then glanced to his sister. She was staring down at her stitching, but unmoving. He suspected she was listening and briefly considered extending Danvries the credit he requested for her sake. The man wasn't just buying a stallion for himself. Dougall suspected the mare was for the sister. Obviously Danvries had also lost her horse in the wager and it seemed a shame that she would suffer for his bad habits. But in the end, Dougall shook his head. He never extended credit. He insisted on payment ere handing over any horseflesh and didn't like the idea of changing that now. Especially not with a man who had gambled himself so deep that Dougall suspected he wouldn't be able to pull himself back out.

"I do no' extend credit," he said calmly and stood.

"Wait." Danvries grabbed his arm again, desperation on his face. He then glanced wildly around, obviously seeking something to trade or to convince Dougall to give him credit. Dougall's stomach rolled over when the man's eyes landed on his sister and stayed there. Surely he wouldn't—

"My sister."

Dougall's eyes narrowed.

"Leave the horses and take her with you," Danvries said.

"I'm no' in the market fer a wife at the moment," Dougall said dryly.

"I did not say you had to marry her," Danvries countered at once.

Dougall glowered at the man and then deliberately misunderstood his offer in the hopes that he would rethink and recant it. "Are ye suggesting I keep her as a marker? A hostage until ye pay fer the horses?"

Danvries hesitated, his eyes on his sister, and then he turned back, determination on his face. "Or you could keep her in place of payment. Until you think you have got your value for the horses. Of course, you would have to return her eventually."

Dougall's gaze shifted to the women by the fire as a gasp slipped from the blonde. She had been looking over her shoulder toward them with horror, but quickly jerked her face away now. If he'd been tempted by Danvries's offer, and if Dougall was honest with himself, the idea of having this woman in his bed was a tempting one, the woman's reaction was enough to make him forget it. He had never forced a woman into his bed and didn't intend to start now.

He shifted his gaze back to Danvries, dislike rolling through him. The man cared so little for the lass that he'd sell her as a sexual slave in exchange for horses. It made it hard to believe that he was actually buying one of them for her. Now Dougall suspected it was for another woman, his betrothed perhaps, if he had one. All of which mattered little, he thought and said coldly, "Ye shame yer sister, yerself, and me with the offer." Turning to his brothers, he added, "Our business here is done."

He needn't have bothered; Conran, Geordie, and Alick were already getting to their feet.

WHEN THE SCOTS all stood to leave, Murine released a little shudder of relief, and then drew in a deep breath. It was only then she realized that she'd been holding her breath ever since her brother had offered her to the Scot in exchange for horses. Her mind was still reeling from that event. She couldn't believe he'd done it. She and Montrose had not grown up together and, in fact, had spent very little time in each other's company until her father's death had left her in his care, so there was little in the way of affection between them. Still, he was her *brother* and she was his sister and charge, and the idea that he would offer her out like some light-skirt . . .

Murine swallowed and got stiffly to her feet, eager to escape the great hall and the possibility of having to deal with her brother after his monstrous action. She glanced to Beth to see that the other woman was already on her feet and ready to follow. Re-lieved, Murine hurried toward the stairs. They'd managed to mount the first few steps when she heard Montrose cry, "Nay. Please wait! If you will not—I can get you the coin."

Murine didn't slow, but she did glance around to see the leader of the Scots shake his head in disgust as he reached the great hall doors.

"By tonight!" Montrose added, sounding desperate. "Ye can enjoy a nice meal and a rest and I'll ha'e the coin by tonight."

Murine noted that the Scot stopped at the door and turned to eye Montrose as if he were a bug scuttling out from under a rock. When his gaze then slid to where she and Beth had been seated, she hurried up the last few steps in case he glanced around in search of her. Murine didn't look again until she'd reached the safety of the shadowy upper landing, then she slowed and turned to have a good look at the men below. It was something she hadn't really been able to do until now. While seated by the fire in the great hall, she'd only dared cast quick, furtive glances at the visi-tors. Now, however, she examined each of the Scots in turn.

They were all tall and strong with dark hair, but Murine found her eye returning to the one who appeared to be their leader. She couldn't have said why. They were all good-looking men, but for some reason she found him the most compelling. He was obvi-ously angry and disgusted by her brother's proposition, but then all of the men appeared to be. However, when he'd looked toward the fire for her just now, there had been something else in his eyes. Not pity, but simple concern and perhaps sympathy.

"I can get you the coin by tonight. Tomorrow morn at the latest," Montrose repeated, drawing Murine's reluctant gaze away from the leader of the Scots and back to her brother as he added, "My neighbor and friend, Muller, has always had an eye for my sister. He'll give me the coin for the chance to spend time with her."

Murine actually had to cover her mouth to stifle the cry that wanted to slip out. Offering her up to these men for horses was bad enough, but offering her to Muller for coin? Her stomach turned over violently at the suggestion. The Scot had been kind and chivalrous enough to refuse the offer. Muller would not. He would jump at the chance and would not care whether she was even willing. She would be no better than a—

"I'll no' be a party to yer turning yer *lady* sister into a whore."

Murine winced as he said the word she was thinking.

"Coin or no coin, the horses are no longer fer sale to ye," the Scot added coldly.

When he then turned on his heel and walked out of the keep with his men hard on his heels, Murine almost wished she could give chase and go with them. Instead, she whirled and caught Beth's arm to rush her down the hall to her room. She had to get out of there, and quickly. Montrose would waste no time setting his plan into action and she needed to be far away from here when Muller arrived to claim his prize.

Once in her room, Murine paused and glanced around wildly before turning to Beth and ordering, "Fetch me an empty sack from the kitchens, please. But do no' let anyone see ye take it."

Beth nodded and was gone almost before the last word was spoken. Murine immediately hurried to the chests against the bedchamber wall to begin sorting through her belongings, trying to decide what she should take and what she could not. Traveling light seemed the smartest option. A spare gown, a spare shift, coins . . .

Her mouth tightened at that thought. All she had were the few coins she'd intended to give to the Scots for taking her message. She would be delivering that message herself now, and would need those coins.

By the time Beth returned, Murine had chosen the few things

she would take with her. She'd even rolled her gown and shift in preparation of packing them away.

The maid handed over the sack she'd gone to fetch. Her gaze then slid over the few belongings on the bed and she frowned. "Ye're fleeing?"

"Aye," Murine said grimly.

Beth hesitated and then asked worriedly, "Are ye sure this is the right thing to do, m'lady?"

Murine's lips tightened and she merely nodded as she stuffed the rolled-up gown into the sack the woman had pinched from the kitchens.

"But 'tis dangerous to travel at the best o' times, e'en with a large party. A woman alone . . ." Beth shook her head at the very thought. "Could we no' send a message to Lady Joan, or Lady Saidh instead? I'm sure one o' them would send an escort fer ye."

"Montrose is probably down there writing up his offer to Muller as we speak," Murine said bitterly. "If I do no' leave now, I shall no doubt be ruined by nightfall."

"But, m'lady," Beth said, tears in her eyes. "Ye can no' travel alone. Ye could be killed by bandits . . . or worse."

Murine stilled briefly at the words, thinking of her brothers Colin and Peter who had been killed on a trip two years earlier, but then shook her head and shoved a linen shift into the bag. "There are some things worse than death, Beth. And staying here where I will be sold off by me own brother . . ." She shook her head bitterly. "Thank ye, I think I'll take me chances on the road."

Beth was silent for a moment, her expression conflicted, and then raised her shoulders and said stolidly, "Then I'll come with ye."

Murine hesitated, briefly tempted by the offer, but shook her head on a sigh. "Nay, ye'll not. Ye'll stay here."

"But—"

"I need ye to stay here and help hide the fact I've left," Murine interrupted quickly.

Beth closed her mouth on her unfinished protest and asked uncertainly, "How am I to do that?"

"Stay here in me room. If Montrose comes looking for me, claim I am sleeping and send him away," Murine said as she finished packing and closed the bag. She didn't really think that ruse would work. Mostly she was using it as an excuse to keep from taking the maid with her. Murine had little hope of actually managing this escape attempt. She suspected she'd be hunted down and brought back ere the first night ended, but if she did manage to get away . . . well, as Beth had said, the road was dangerous. It was one thing to risk her own life to try to preserve her honor. It was another thing entirely to risk Beth's life as well.

"Where will ye go?" Beth asked worriedly, following her to the door.

"I'll slip down the back stairs to the kitchens and then sneak around to get Henry and—"

"Nay, I mean, where will ye go once ye leave Danvries?" Beth interrupted.

"Oh." Murine breathed and then shrugged helplessly. "To Saidh. Buchanan is closest, I think, and she did say if I ever needed assistance to not hesitate to call on her. I am in definite need of assistance now."

"Aye, ye are," Beth agreed solemnly, and then reached out quickly to hug her. "Be careful m'lady, and pray stay safe."

"I will," Murine whispered, then pulled back and forced a smile. "I'll send fer ye . . . if I can."

"Oh, do no' worry about me. I'll be fine. Ye just take good care o' yerself," she said bravely, dashing away a tear.

Murine squeezed her arm gently, then opened her bedchamber door and peered cautiously out. Finding the hall empty, she slid out and rushed for the stairs.

"I CAN'T BELIEVE the bastard tried to sell his sister fer a couple horses."

Dougall grimaced and glanced at his brother Conran at those bewildered words. After the debacle at Danvries, they had ridden

to the village inn for a meal ere starting the long trek home. The
conversation there had been focused on who they might sell the
mare and stallion to now, and to wonder how they would find
things at home. Not wanting to shame the sister in her own village, no one had even got near the topic of Danvries and his
offer . . . until now as they left Danvries's land.

"Aye," Dougall acknowledged.

"Ye do no' seem surprised."

"People rarely surprise me anymore," Dougall said, and then
added in a lighter tone, "The only thing that surprises me is that
ye were kind enough no' to discuss it in the village and waited so
long to bring up the subject."

"'Twas no' kindness," Conran denied quickly. "I just did no'
want to ruin me meal. Was like to give me indigestion."

"Oh, aye, o' course it was," Dougall agreed with amusement.
He knew that wasn't true. Conran just didn't like to appear soft.
Although, Dougall thought, talking about it now was making his
own lunch roll in his stomach.

"Ye ken that now the idea's occurred to him, he's going to sell
her off to his friend fer coin," Conran said heavily.

"Aye. He'll use her to make what money he can to make up fer
his gambling," Dougall said with distaste, recalling the glowing
woman.

"If she allows it," Conran said with a shrug. "Mayhap she'll
refuse."

"Hmm." Dougall muttered, but thought she might not be
given the choice. Danvries was obviously her guardian, although
she was of marriageable age. "Why is she still unwed?"

Conran shrugged. "As I said, talk is he gambled away her
dower."

"Aye, but how? It should have been protected," Dougall said
with a frown. "And she should ha'e been betrothed as a child and
collected long ere this."

"Mayhap her betrothed died," Conran suggested, and then
added, "And I'm sure the king would have stepped in and no' al-

lowed Danvries gambling away her dower . . . had he no' been the one who won the wager."

"So she'll ne'er marry," Dougall said thoughtfully.

"And be at the mercy of her brother all her days," Conran commented, shaking his own head.

"Dear God," Dougall breathed and almost felt bad that he'd turned down the man's offer. At least he would have been kind to her, and mayhap had things worked out . . . Well, he had grown quite wealthy through his horse breeding. The only reason he hadn't already purchased himself an estate was that their older brother, Aulay, had needed his aid raising their younger brothers and sister when their parents had died. A dower wasn't an absolute necessity in a wife for him. On the other hand, he didn't know the woman. She was pretty enough, but her brother was a weak man with a few bad habits, drinking and gambling among them. He also apparently had little in the way of moral fiber to him. For all Dougall knew, the same was true of her. But that gasp from her when her brother had offered her . . .

Dougall pushed away the memory. He had nothing to feel guilty about. He didn't even know the lass.

"'Tis a shame," Conran said. "She's a lovely lass."

Dougall merely nodded. She was indeed lovely.

"She looked sweet and demure," Geordie commented from his other side when he remained silent.

"Aye, she did," Dougall said on a sigh. "Mayhap me refusal to sell him horses no matter whether he has the coin or no' will stop his plans."

"For now, maybe," Conran said dubiously. "Though I suspect he'll go ahead with it in hopes ye'll change yer mind when he presents the payment. On the other hand, he could buy horses elsewhere . . . were he to get the coin."

Not wanting to encourage this line of conversation, Dougall didn't comment. He had no desire to think the woman would still be sold off like a cheap lightskirt. Besides, he could see something on the path ahead and was distracted by trying to sort out what it was.

Noting his sudden stillness in the saddle, Conran glanced ahead and squinted. "It looks like someone on horseback, but . . ."

"But 'tis a very strange horse," Dougall murmured. It looked short and wide, a squat creature that moved with a somewhat awkward gait.

"Is that a cow he's riding?" Conran asked with amazement as they drew closer.

"A bull," Dougall corrected as the rider shifted and he spotted a horn poking up into view. "And if I'm no' mistaken, he is a she. That looks like a gown to me."

"Hmm," Alick murmured behind them. "A rose gown. Lady Danvries was wearing a rose gown."

"Aye, she was," Dougall agreed, and urged his horse to move more quickly.

"DAMN," MURINE BREATHED when she heard the approaching horse. She'd spotted the men on horseback behind her just moments ago and had recognized them as the Scots Montrose had been trying to buy horses from. It could have been worse. Montrose could have discovered that she'd fled and come after her, but this was bad enough. These were the men her brother had tried to sell her to and the embarrassment and shame of what he'd done was overwhelming. She'd really rather not have to face them again.

"M'lady."

Murine kept her gaze straight ahead, hoping that if she pretended not to hear him, the man might just leave her be and travel on.

"Lady Danvries," he said, a little more loudly and when she again didn't respond, commented, "Yer brother did no' bother to mention ye were deaf when he offered ye to me. I should ha'e guessed as much, though. He's obviously a cheat and a louse, so o' course he'd try to pass off a defective lass in exchange fer me high-quality beasts."

Gasping in outrage, Murine gave up her pretense and turned

to glare at the man as she snapped, "I'm no' defective! And ye'd
ha'e been lucky to ha'e me, I'm worth a hundred o' yer horses."

When his mouth quirked up on one side and one eyebrow
rose high on his forehead, she realized what she'd said and quickly
added, "Not that I'd ha'e agreed to such a shameful bargain."
Turning forward again, she muttered, "Me brother has obviously
lost his mind to sink so low."

"And so ye're running away before he offers ye to someone
who is no' as honorable as meself and might accept?"

Murine's mouth flattened with displeasure. That was exactly
what she was doing . . . or trying to do. But now she was fretting
over the possibility that this man might somehow interfere and
prevent her escape.

"Dougall."

Murine glanced around at that shout, her eyes widening when
she saw that his men, who had been keeping back apace, were
suddenly urging their mounts to catch them up.

"What is it, Conran?" Dougall asked with a frown.

"Riders," the man explained, glancing worriedly toward
Murine. "And I'm thinking it's Danvries' men after the lady here,
to take her back."

Cursing under her breath, Murine started to turn her bull
toward the trees, intent on hiding, but found her way blocked by
horses as the other men caught up and surrounded them.

"No time fer that, m'lady," Conran said sympathetically.
"They're moving fast; ye would no' make cover."

"Then we shall have to be her cover," Dougall said grimly.
"Surround her, and cover her hair and dress. I'll meet the riders."

Murine opened her mouth to protest, but then let out a startled
gasp when a cap landed on her head.

"Tuck yer hair up, lass," someone said.

"And here, put this round ye to hide yer pretty gown," someone else said, dropping a plaid around her shoulders.

Murine didn't argue, but clumsily shoved her hair up in the
cap, then clutched the plaid around herself and glanced about at

the Scots and their horses. Her bull sat perhaps a hand lower than their mounts, which helped hide what the plaid didn't cover of her skirts, but there were only three of them now and the two riderless horses they'd hoped to sell to her brother.

"Mayhap we should . . ." Rather than finish the suggestion, someone suddenly tossed another plaid over her, this one covering her head as well. She then felt pressure on the back of her neck as someone silently urged her to press herself flat to the bull's back. Hoping it was enough, Murine ignored the fact that she found it difficult to breathe in this position with the heavy cloth over her, closed her eyes and began to pray.

DOUGALL MANAGED TO get about twenty feet back up the path before the oncoming English riders reached him. He hoped it was far enough away from the woman his men were trying to provide cover for, but there was little he could do if it wasn't. The choice then would be whether or not to fight for the lass. Dougall hadn't yet made up his mind on the matter. It wasn't the fact that there were twenty of them. He and his brothers were skilled fighters. They could easily beat twenty lazy, poorly trained English soldiers. But he wasn't sure if Lady Danvries was worth fighting, and killing, over. If she was anything like her brother, she definitely wasn't . . . and really, this was none of his business. He supposed he'd have to play it by ear.

"Did Danvries find coin fer the horses, after all?" he asked lightly by way of greeting once the riders had stopped.

"Nay." The man in the lead glanced past him to his brothers and then back. "We are looking for Lord Danvries' sister. She went out for a ride and has not yet returned. Her brother grows concerned."

"A ride ye say?" Dougall asked, feigning surprise. "Are ye sure? I understood she was without a mount. 'Sides, she was sitting in the hall when we arrived and 'tis sure I am that she went above stairs ere we left."

"Aye." The man frowned and glanced back the way he'd come. "I gather she left after you and your men, and we did not pass her ere encountering you. She must have gone another way."

"That would make sense," Dougall agreed and he supposed it did make sense if you didn't know that he and his brothers had stopped for a meal ere leaving Danvries land.

The man nodded, and spun his horse back the way he'd come with a brusque "Good journey to ye."

"And to ye," Dougall said cheerfully and grinned as he watched the English soldier lead his men away. He hadn't even had to lie. Gad, the English were stupid. Of course, now he had to deal with the woman, he acknowledged, his smile fading.

Ah well. Dougall shook his head and turned to ride back to his own men.

"Lookin' fer the lass, were they?" Conran asked as the men eased aside to allow Dougall to move his horse up beside the woman's bull.

"Aye." Dougall glanced toward Lady Danvries, expecting her to thank him for his aid. But she proved she was English by refusing to even acknowledge his presence. The woman was still huddled low on her cow, the plaid covering her like she was a sack of wheat.

Scowling, he tugged the plaid off her, and then leaned quickly to the side to catch the woman when she started to tumble from the back of her beast.

"Well," Conran breathed with disgust when Dougall pulled her unconscious body across his horse to peer at her. "It looks like she's gone and died on us. That could cause trouble with the English."

"Nah, 'tis a faint," Dougall said, but then had to tear his gaze from her pale face to her chest just to make sure she was breathing. She was, but shallowly.

"It can no' be a faint," Alick protested at once, standing in the saddle and craning his head to try to get a look at the woman. "If the lass is brave enough to run away on her own, she's hardly the type to faint o'er a little scare like this."

"Unless it was no' courage that had her running away," Conran pointed out.

"What else would it be?" Alick asked with a scowl.

"She could be lacking the sense God gives most," Geordie suggested.

"Or she could be a few men short o' an army," Alick added reluctantly.

"This lass is no' daft," Conran snapped. "Nor is she witless. The two o' ye ought to be ashamed to suggest it."

"Well, why do ye think she's fainted then?"

Conran eyed her briefly and then said, "Well, now, mayhap she's ailing. 'Tis obvious her brother cares little for her well-being. Mayhap she's taken ill."

"And mayhap," Dougall said, shifting the woman to a more comfortable position on his lap, "Ye should stop acting like a bunch o' old women so we can continue on with our journey."

Conran raised his eyebrows. "Are we takin' her with us then?"

"Well, we can hardly leave her here by the side o' the road in her state, can we?" he pointed out with exasperation. "We'll carry her with us until she wakes."

"And then what?" Conran asked, eyes narrowed.

"And then we'll ask where she's heading and if 'tis on our way, we shall escort her there," he decided with a small frown. The woman was turning out to be a bit of trouble and he wasn't happy about that.

"And if where she is going is no' on our way?" Conran asked. "Or what if we've carried her right past where she was headed?"

"Then we'll deal with that at the time," Dougall said with forced patience, and then added irritably, "Right now, I'd jest be well pleased if ye'd get yer arses in gear and yer horses moving."

"All right, no need to holler," Conran said soothingly. "'Tis obvious the lass has set ye aback." He glanced around and then asked, "What about her cow?"

Grimacing, Dougall glanced at the beast and shrugged. "Leave it behind. It'll most like return to the keep. Then mayhap they'll think she took a tumble and'll waste days searching Danvries' woods fer her."

"But then she'll have naught to ride when she regains her wits," Conran pointed out.

"Then she'll have to ride with me, will she no'?" he asked dryly.

"Aye, but what if her travels lead her away from us. She can hardly follow her own plans with no beast to ride."

"'Tis a cow, Conran," he pointed out with disgust. "No one with all their faculties would ride a cow anyway." Sighing impatiently, he shook his head. "I shall supply her with a horse. We've two spare with us right now anyway."

"Two fine beasts worth a pretty coin or two," Conran pointed out sharply. "Ye can no' be thinking—"

"I'm thinkin' I'm tired o' listening to ye bend me ear and am eager to be off," Dougall snapped. "Do what ye like with the cow, but we are continuing on now."

He put his heels to his mount, sending it into a gallop that had Lady Danvries bouncing around in his lap like a sack of wheat. Muttering under his breath, Dougall slowed the beast and rearranged her before setting out again. But he found himself glancing down repeatedly at the woman in his arms, wondering what she would have done had he agreed to the trade with her brother. Had she been offered and used thusly before? That thought hadn't occurred to him ere this and now that it had, it angered him for some reason. He grimly turned his attention to the path ahead and urged his mount to move faster. But he also tightened his hold on the woman to ensure she wasn't bounced out of his lap in the process.